17/7/2018

To Bridget,
with love,
Alilacy Conor

W0009112
1999596900

Prologue

An anthology where writers bring to bear all their hidden and known experiel wrote this book for three reasons. The first, was to do my part in giving voice to the precious babies left sleeping and silenced in mass, secret graves. My prayer is that this book helps in some way to align them in God's everlasting peaceful embrace.

The second, was to do my part and contribute to a wave of change. My hope in writing this book is that it goes towards helping to acknowledge and heal the depths of pain, anger and grief suffered in the hearts and minds of those effected by Ireland's social history. Those whose actions caused the pain may be long gone, or at least remain unaffected by the detriment of their actions, yet the sadness resides in the hearts of the innocent. They say that holding on to anger is like eating poison and expecting another to become sick. To those effected, with all my heart I sincerely hope this book shows you a way forward through your silent hell, so as you can evolve, be free and celebrate yourself. You deserve to.

The third reason I wrote this book is perhaps a more selfish reason. Writing this book was my own personal way forward out of the abyss of devastation and deep sadness upon hearing of the Tuam babies. Born in a Mother and Baby Home in 1974, the thoughts of 'it could have been me' haunted my mind and filled me with grief, guilt and utter devastation. My empathy and sadness for the little ones left sleeping, along with my own survivor's guilt was the unshakable force that caused me to do my part. I found that beginning to write this book was the medicinal effect that helped me to climb out of my own devastation and move forward through the heart break.

Each of the characters you are about to meet in this book depict the different facets within Irish society, whose consciousness had the effect that created our social history. Some were in charge, some were afraid, some judged and some were completely innocent and saw only love. I believe we are where we are today, (although not completely out of the woods) because of the voice of innocence that saw only love, chose love and acted from same, which led to a way forward.

It is my belief that, If we are to evolve as a nation it is necessary to see both ourselves and each other through the eyes of love. I also believe that it is the only way forward. We need to unite with both each other and with a higher power and communicate from there, in support and encouragement of our own and one another's brilliance, intelligence and resources. Perhaps it is a non-contemporary belief, but it is the only one which I feel will be effective in fast tracking this nation into evolution, healing and peace.

One of the most important things I wish to point out, is that this book is not about me. Although, like Saoirse, I was born in a Mother and Baby Home and I too am psychic and live life from a spiritual perspective. The fundamental difference between me and the beautiful Saoirse Corcoran is our parents and siblings. Thanks be to God my parents were not like Lil and Joe. At all times I felt unconditionally loved and accepted for who I am (with the ability to see dead people included!). Thanks to mum, dad and my inspirational sister Claire, due to their ever-present guiding light, I am who I am today. In some cases, I drew from my own psychic experiences throughout the story and I wish to assure all readers that my parents response to same experiences were worlds away from Lil and Joe's response.

This story, albeit fictional, aims to address our social history, show the pain caused, address that pain and embrace it with the power of self-love and move forward to evolution.

Acknowledgements

First and forever my greatest gratitude is to the Source of all things, whom I fundamentally know I would never have written this book without his guidance. Second, with tears in my eyes, thank you to all of the countless babies left sleeping, I know you were with me the whole way through this process. May God bless you and keep you always.

I wish to thank my birth mother. Thank you for your strength, your courage and thank you for enduring a punishment for no sin. From the depths of my heart thank you for giving me life.

I thank my parents, Marie, Lar and sister Claire. Thank you for the love, the laughter and the clarity. Thank you for everything.

I wish to extend eternal thanks to Catherine Coreless. You are one of life's living legends, your strength, courage, commitment and compassion holds no bounds. I know I am on no island when I say I celebrate you in my heart with an explosion of gratitude every day. Thank you, Catherine.

One of my greatest teachers is a lady whom I have never met, yet whose teachings I have taken into my heart and have contributed to profound and deep transformation within my soul. Marianne Williamson thank you for your wisdom and life-long commitment to being a guiding light to humanity.

Suzanne Power, you are an editor by profession, but I am so grateful that my experience working with you went far deeper. Thank you for being one of those people who can see right into the depths of one's soul and remind them who they are. This book would never have been what it is without your unwavering support, insight, encouragement and eye for truth. It is my belief that, along the way on this journey called life we meet our soul friends, I am deeply happy to have found one of mine in you. Thank you for believing in me. Thanks for being you. Eternal gratitude and much love always Suzanne.

Diane Kelly, you show me every day what true strength is. I am blessed to know you, thanks for the proverbial kicks up the backside, your invaluable feedback on the first draft and most of all your friendship. I am blessed.

Mandy Walsh and Grainne Cahill, I could write a list of my thanks to you both, but I don't have eternity in a lifetime, so thank you both for everything.

To all my friends whom I am blessed to know, thank you for your never-ending support and encouragement. Your guidance and direction holds priceless value within my heart, thank you.

I wish to extend thanks to all my clients. Your strength inspires me every day. Thank you for the encouragement and support.

Last and always, thank you to the greatest loves of my life and the people that cause me to wake each day and smile right from my heart. God gave me four eternal blessings, they are, my absolute rock of a husband Brian and my three beautiful daughters, Brianna, Sophia & Gabriella. Thank you for your unwavering support, encouragement and thank you for being my inspiration. Without your smiles and the joy that beams from your hearts each day, the process of writing this book would have been a much darker journey. Thank you for your love and thank you all for believing in me.

*'Out beyond ideas of wrong doing and right doing there is a field,
I'll meet you there.'*

Rumi

"Our deepest fear is not that we are inadequate. Our deepest fear is that we are powerful beyond measure. It is our light, not our darkness that most frightens us. We ask ourselves, Who am I to be brilliant, gorgeous, talented, fabulous? Actually, who are you not to be? You are a child of God. Your playing small does not serve the world. There is nothing enlightened about shrinking so that other people won't feel insecure around you. We are all meant to shine, as children do. We were born to make manifest the glory of God that is within us. It's not just in some of us; it's in everyone. And as we let our own light shine, we unconsciously give other people permission to do the same. As we are liberated from our own fear, our presence automatically liberates others."

Marianne Williamson, A return to Love

Chapter 1

An Infant is Born

I am a mother standing over your crib. Beautiful baby girl, you are just one month old, and you already radiate the embodiment of perfection that you are.

I cannot stay long but may the words I am about to share with you whisper in your heart forever and always.

Always know that you are stronger than your pain.

Always know that you are stronger than any depths of sadness and tears you may cry.

Some will understand you and many will not. Either way, you have a courageous heart. You are a force of Love.

You are perfection, you are always enough.

Remember my words, my beautiful child. May they take resonance in your heart and always remind you of the Strength that is you.

Before I go, there is one more thing I want you to hold in the precious wisdom of your heart. When you feel you are trapped and lost in your darkest moments, when the confusion and sadness weigh deep in your heart: know that the pain you experience will never leave you blind to your truth.

The love that is you will fill all of your being. It will empower you in your darkest moments and guide you back to who you are. And so it is.

I have to go now, but we will meet again. Until then my wish for you is that you may always hear that still strong voice down deep in your heart, as it whispers the reminder of the strength and love that is you.

My beautiful child, listen to the force within that reminds you, that you are strong, you are loved, and you are always enough.

Chapter 2

It's cold, and I'm hungry.

Maisie was here every day, but now I miss her. I lie in this crib all day. I can hear the other babies cry.

A few times a day, women come to us and feed us. They are deeply sad. Their hearts are in so much pain, but they can't talk about it. They are not allowed. Because there are other women here, they are called the Sisters and they are in charge. All the ladies are afraid of the Sisters. and that's why they don't talk about how sad they are. The Sisters won't let them.

If they do, their body will hurt as well as their heart, because of the Sisters.

This place is even more sad without Maisie. She really loved me, I could feel it. She held me and cuddled me and gave me kisses. I loved her smell. She was very sad here too, but when she picked me up, joy and happiness flowed from her heart. That made the sadness bearable, for those few moments. I liked that I could be the one who did that for her in this horrible, miserable place.

But now she's gone. And I know that when the other ladies feed me their minds are off elsewhere, in some place of deep sorrow and sadness.

I don't ever feel any love from the Sisters. I feel their anger, fear, rage, hate, guilt and regret. But I know that all they are willing to acknowledge is the anger, and they take it out on the ladies and blame the ladies. But it's not the ladies' fault.

The ladies are afraid too, but I can see that they are innocent and beautiful. The Sisters treat them like they are bad people. I don't know why, but that seems to be just the way it is.

I'm only very small, and I can't talk yet, but if I could, I would tell them not to feel bad or guilty, just because the Sisters tell you to. I would say that I don't know what you did to get you into so much trouble and cause the Sisters to be so nasty towards you, punish you and take their anger out on you. But, don't forget whatever it was, just like my Maisie, you did something awesome.

You created a beautiful little baby, and you gave birth to a whole new life. That is awesome! You are awesome! I celebrate you. I applaud you. And I think, that what this world needs are more people like you.

You are strong, loving, life-giving mothers. You have immeasurable love.

That love flows from your hearts so naturally, even in the depths of pain and sadness such as places like this. So, whatever you did that was so wrong, you got this so right, and that's what matters. Thank you. That is what I would say.

I can hear another baby crying. He has been crying a lot. I wish I could help him. He has been crying for a long time. He sounds like he is in a lot of pain. He is trying to catch his breath between his cries.

Maybe his tummy hurts like mine. I wonder why nobody helps him. I know I would if I could.

Only the Sisters can help him. The ladies are not allowed, but I can sense that they want to. Maybe he's hungry, or maybe he's cold. It's cold in here, and I am hungry all the time. I wonder if all the other babies in this room wish they could help him too.

His cries are getting weaker now. Maybe he is going to sleep, but I don't feel that he is. I can tell when the babies here are crying themselves to sleep and he sounds different. It's like he is in too much pain to cry anymore. He is barely making any sounds now. He is gone silent.

Here is one of the Sisters coming into the room. She is going over to him. I wonder why because he has gone silent now. Earlier he was crying so hard I could feel his panic. She is picking him up from his crib. I wish she was gentler. His body looks different now, it looks lifeless.

She is carrying him out of the room. I don't know where she is taking him, but I really hope he is going to be ok.

It's quiet now. The other babies are sleeping, and it's cold. Maybe Maisie will be back tomorrow. I hope so. I really miss her and her love. It's not the same without her. I feel sad and lonely. The Sisters are always angry, and I'm scared.

I can feel myself drifting now. I am falling asleep, and it feels nice. I can drift back to that peaceful place that I came from before I was here. Everything is easy there. There is only love in that place, no sadness or fear or fight. I'm there.

Chapter 3

"Mammy, what did Daddy say? Did you ask him?"

Maisie had been anticipating her Daddy's answer since yesterday afternoon when her Mammy left and promised to have a word with Daddy about her wishes. They walked side by side down the empty corridor of St. Patricks Mother and Baby Home.

"Ah I don't know Maisie, Daddy's not having any of it. Like he said, he just wants you to do what you have to do, and we can go back home to Bunratty and put all of this behind us. It's for the best."

Maisie could hear the good intent in her mother's voice, but she was set on changing her father's mind. She was determined to keep the new love of her life, her bundle of joy that she loved so unconditionally. It was a love that she had never known before, and she was adamant to fight to keep her baby girl:

"Oh but Mammy once he sees her he will fall in love with her just like I did, just like you did. He won't be able to resist, and I will look after her myself, you know. Sure I'm well able. I'm seventeen now, and God knows I've had to grow up a lot over these last few months"

Maisie glanced out the large window, into the grounds of St Patricks Mother and Baby Home.

Images of the nightmare she had lived here flashed before her mind's eye once again. The horror and cruelty she had witnessed wore heavy in her heart and had taken its toll on her young, vibrant personality.

The plain dark grey uniform she wore reflected how she felt inside. The A line dress falling mid-calf, buttoned down the front, with white socks and heavy black shoes. Her dark shoulder length hair was tied neatly at the nape of her neck.

She hated this place and Mary was the one and only thing that gave her the resilience to withstand her time here.

She looked straight ahead and held her head high. She linked her mother's arm firmly:

"Anyway Mammy, I can feel it in me bones. I'm sure I can convince Daddy to let me keep her. I can't let her go, not now. It will surely break my heart

I know they are taking her from me tomorrow, but I have a whole nine months before I have to sign the final forms. I'm sure I can convince Daddy in that time."

Maisie's mother placed her hand over her daughters:

"Let's just wait and see Maisie, but don't be going getting your hopes up love.

Now get your coat, and we'll go into town, I think there's a bus in quarter of an hour. We'll head up to Thomas Street and pick up something nice for Mary to wear for tomorrow....

A beautiful outfit for a beautiful angel..."

Ellen's face filled with her warm reassuring smile. She felt the sting of tears well up in her eyes as that all familiar lump took residence in her throat.

"go on now Maisie, get your coat" She nodded down the corridor and turned away from her daughter.

Maisie's eyes looked to the floor and she began to walk away:

"Mammy" she paused and turned back to her mammy "they said she was going to a well to do family. Do you think it's a doctor or something?" the quiver in Maisie's soft tone deafened out all other sounds.

"Maybe Love, who knows?"

The women left St. Patrick's Mother and baby home on the Navan Road and off they went into Dublin City Centre to shop for an outfit for Mary to wear tomorrow. Maisie wanted her baby girl to look so beautiful for her new parents.

She stared out the window on that bus journey into Dublin town. Dublin city was hopping with the hustle and bustle of the usual Saturday morning business, but Maisie did not notice a thing.

It was a mild, fresh March morning in 1965. The market stalls from the traders filled the streets. The smells of the bakeries and coffee shops wafted through the air. Maisie and her mother browsed the shops on this unique, heart-breaking and somewhat surreal shopping trip.

Maisie pushed the door of the boutique and stepped inside. The shop owner looked up from behind the counter:

"Grand morning out there now ladies?"

"It is thank God, we're just in to have a look if that's ok?" Ellen smiled at the friendly shop lady and nodded to the crochet piece she was working on. But Maisie was already smitten:

"Mammy, look, isn't it beautiful" Maisie beamed at her mother, marvelling at a pink baby dress and matching cardigan. The dress was faux satin with white lace on the collar, cuffs and two pretty lace frills finished the end of the loosely pleated skirt. The pink cardigan was crochet with a satin ribbon through the cuffs and neckline. There was even enough ribbon to tie a pretty bow over the top button on the cardigan.

Maisie held the outfit before her, stroking the skirt of the dress. Her fingertips fell in love with the feel of the soft satin. Its smooth perfection caressed her senses and she carefully examined the flawless stitching. She gently massaged the cardigan sleeves, her breath shallow holding the piece of natural perfection, she didn't want to let it go.

She looked at her mother, eye wide, her smile beamed from ear to ear.

"Beautiful love, it's truly beautiful. But Maisie look at the price tag. It's far too much money love"

"Ah but Mammy, would you look at it? It's beautiful. Please can we get it, please? I can just see Mary wearing it."

Ellen took a deep breath, looked at the outfit and gave a long sigh. Then she paused.

"I'll tell you what, how about we look around and see if we see anything else okay? Sure this is only the first shop, we might see something else down the road?"

"I don't think so..." Maisie reluctantly hung the dress back on the rail. With her eyes fixed upon the beauty, she gave it one last caress and a backward glance before leaving the shop.

They shopped Thomas Street and Meath Street, in and out of the shops, keeping an eye on the clothes stalls that lined the streets along the way. But nothing came close to how beautiful the pink outfit was. It was special, and Maisie's mind kept going back to it, no matter what else she saw.

Ellen showed Maisie another potential outfit for Mary. Maisie responded with another disinterested glance and shrug of her shoulders.

Ellen turned her eyes to heaven, in eventual surrender to her daughter:

"You're not going to settle for anything less are you?"

"Oh but Mammy, there's something about it, and I honestly haven't seen anything as nice. Can we go back and get it, please? It will be surely gorgeous on her, I know it."

"Maisie, I am warning you, not a word to your father about the price, do you hear me? Not now, not ever" Ellen wagged her finger sternly at her daughter.

"Now come on, we best hurry before the shop closes for lunch"

"I won't say a word Mammy, I promise. Mammy, thank you. You really are the best." Maisie linked her mother tight with the return of her beaming smile.

Side by side they walked back to the boutique with the pretty pink outfit for Mary.

Maisie could tell despite her mother's strict outer expression she was equally as thrilled as she. It was the twinkle in her eye and the glimmer of a smile that gave away her sweet satisfaction to return to that boutique, with the beautiful outfit for a beautiful angel.

Time was getting on, and Mammy suggested that they go for a cup of tea and a bit of lunch before heading back to St Patrick's to feed Mary. Maisie knew that her mother wanted to spend some time with her granddaughter before she left for her new family. For the last month her mother travelled by train from Bunratty to Dublin and stayed in her brother's house with his family two nights a week, not too far from St. Patricks Mother & Baby Home. She spent as much time as she could with Maisie and Mary.

Maisie knew she would have been lost without her and she knew her Mammy loved Mary. It was the way she held her close at feeding time and cuddled her for just that little bit longer every chance she got. Mammy was only forty-four, but Maisie knew she had aged ten years in the last few months. She also knew that Mammy was going to miss Mary just as much as she was. They were both completely smitten by her and the thoughts of giving her away was becoming more and more a reality now as the window of hope was closing in, albeit somewhat still there.

They went into a small coffee shop off Thomas Street. As she sat over her ham sandwich and pot of tea, Maisie's mind wandered back to Mary and the future that awaited her. With all her heart, she remained hopeful that Daddy would agree to let her bring Mary home to Bunratty. She didn't care what the neighbours would say, so what about them. She didn't care about Catholic Ireland and what the priest would say or think either.

The moment she gave birth to her little girl she knew that all anyone would have to do is meet Mary, and they would feel the same. She was beautiful, and there was something so special about her that she couldn't put her finger on. Because of this, she knew that she had to rear Mary herself, not someone else. Even if people judged her for being 'a fallen woman' she knew that she had enough love for Mary and being with her would make it all worthwhile.

Her thoughts then wandered to the possibility that someone else would rear Mary.

What if they don't see how special she is? What if they don't see what she sees? What if they can't give her the love that she is going to need to nurture that something special? Then again what if they see how special she is, but it's not important enough to them?

She feared that they wouldn't understand her like she did.

Ellen sat across from her daughter. She sensed that Maisie's mind was wandering into a helpless place and could feel her pain. Her heart was breaking also. If it was up to Ellen her beautiful grandchild would be coming straight home to Bunratty, no question. Whatever about money, the priest and the judging eyes of the community. This was Mary we were talking about and no amount of discriminate looks or lack of a few pound could change the depths of love she held in her heart for that baby girl.

They were not the richest of families, but she knew that together they could all find a way. If it meant that her precious gift of a grandchild was coming home, nothing else mattered.

For the last six months Ellen had held it together for everyone. The shock of her sixteen-year-old daughter arriving home pregnant shook the whole family.

She had two older children and two younger than Maisie. Her husband John was incredibly disappointed. Maisie had always been the apple of his eye. She was the oldest daughter and a typical daddy's girl.

Not knowing what else to do they went to the local parish priest and did the done thing. Arrangements were made by Fr. Doyle and Mary arrived in St. Patrick's Mother & Baby home in early November 1964.

Ellen felt everyone's turmoil and tried to protect everyone from same. She tried to protect her husband from his disappointment in his daughter, along with his consequential guilt. She tried to protect the rest of her children from the shame that went with their sister being a 'fallen woman'. She tried to protect the secret that an act had been done that was outside of the rules of the Roman Catholic Church.

At the same time, she tried to protect her daughter from going through the single most heart-breaking, destructive experience of her life, the judgement, the shame, the guilt, the loneliness, the rejection and the loss of the most precious gift God could ever bestow to a woman.

The fact was, Ellen felt that no matter how hard she tried she wasn't protecting anyone. And now, not only was she facing the possible heart break of losing her grandchild for good, she was also watching her daughter go through the pain of losing her baby girl. Apart from death, she had never experienced a greater pain.

"Come on now love, eat up your sandwich and get that tea into you, it's getting chilly out there. We best get back." Ellen paused and leaned over to look straight in her daughter's eyes,

"Maisie, I hope Daddy changes his mind I really do. I love Mary too, she is beautiful and is a real bundle of joy. But let's just see what happens and stay hopeful. Say a prayer and light a candle to St Anthony...I love you Maisie, and your daddy loves you too. We just want what's best for you and Mary that's all."

The young girl drank her tea with a heavy heart and headed back to be with her baby in the Mother and Baby Home.

That night Maisie cradled Mary during feeding time. She hugged and cuddled her one-month-old infant, taking in every tiniest detail, her smell, her head of dark hair, sallow skin and rosy cheeks, her long eye lashes, the shape of her face and her tiny button nose. She listened to every sound Mary made and felt her soft, tiny fingers wrapped around hers. All the while hoping the reality of this moment would sink deep into her memory and last a lifetime. In the dead of the dark night she rocked Mary in her arms and she whispered to her baby girl:

"I can't tell you how much I love you Mary, because there are no words to describe how much I do. I don't know what the future will bring but I promise you that no matter what happens I will always remember you and treasure the time we had together. The happiest moment of my life was the moment I held you in my arms for the very first time. I will never forget your tiny little face looking up to mine. Your new born eyes squinting to the light, and you gasping for your breath as that horrible Sister handed you to me. From that moment my life changed forever. I changed forever, because of you and I will always love you for that.

You are perfect, and I wish you love, I wish you happiness and I wish you peace. I pray to God above that I will see you again. But no matter what happens always know that no matter how far away we become, I will always carry you in my heart.

I promise you I will be thinking of you every day and hold you in my heart for the rest of my life.

You're so special, never forget that, ever"

Maisie sat cradling her child for as long as she could. With a broken heart she continued to take in every detail about Mary through her senses and hoped by the grace of God she would remember them for as long as she needed to until she saw her baby again.

She laid her down in her crib for the last time and made her way back to her dorm.

The tsunami of hope and fear consumed and overwhelmed Maisie in the silence of the night. Hope that mercy would be delivered, enabling her to share Mary's life. At the same time consumed with the fear that the deepest, loneliest grief was already here.

She got ready for bed in her dorm, surrounded by the other ladies. No one spoke a word.

That last night she spent the endless hours reflecting on the last five months.

She hated it here in Saint Patricks. The Sisters were horrible, cruel excuses for individuals. They treated the young girls worse than animals. They called it 'penance for your sins' because they had made love without a wedding ring on their finger. They called the young girls the devil's spawn.

Over the last four months, Maisie had kept her head down and had seen more cruelty, bullying and violence to last her a lifetime. Saint Patrick's Mother and Baby Home was a place of deep loneliness and terror. Her days were spent washing floors until her back ached.

Every morning was an early start at 6.30am. It was always cold.

Maisie and the girls went down for a bland breakfast. From there each girl made her way to do her chores. Each day, Maisie scrubbed and washed the marble floors of that miserable building. She washed hundreds of square feet with an aching back and during most of that time, with a baby in utero. She was quite often in severe pain and hungry, feeling light-headed with dizzy spells blocking her vision became a normal part of her day. She just kept going, she had no choice because the ramifications of anything otherwise would be a lot worse than what a night's rest would soothe.

On more than one occasion the Sister arrived at the corridor that Maisie had spent hours scrubbing. It was always just as she was finishing up and about to go down for dinner. She was tired, weak and every bone and muscle in her body was in crippling pain. The Sister patrolled the area, inspecting Maisie's work. Maisie was sure she was only looking until she found a spot of dirt or dust. Eventually, the Sister would stop and say:

"Well, it looks like you are not using the gift of competence the Lord himself gave you girl. How dare you abuse your duty? Start over and do it properly this time, I will be back to inspect these fine floors before bedtime." The middle-aged Sister turned on her heel and walked back down the corridor without a backward glance, leaving Maisie on her knees behind her.

One morning she woke to the usual routine. The bell rang loud over a tannoy, deafening all other sound throughout the dorms. Each of the girls had to stand beside her bed while the Sister walked around the dorm, inspecting the girls' bed linen. She was making sure the sheets were still clean. This morning, she stopped at the bed next to Maisie's bed. The girl who slept in that bed had given birth to her baby boy two days previous. The Sister stared sternly at the new mother. Her name was Alice, and she was eighteen years old. Maisie could see on Alice's face that she was petrified, her sheets were slightly unclean. Rage filled the Sister's face. She grabbed Alice's arm.

"It's only the devil's spawn that would do such a deed. You are an evil excuse for a person."

Alice pleaded apology. Her cries filled the dorm and echoed down the hall, begging for the Sister's forgiveness, but the Sister was furious and took no mercy. Alice was dragged out of the dorm and taken elsewhere. She was not to be seen again until the following night. She returned to the dorm when all were sleeping.

Maisie lay awake in the bed in the dead of night.

She heard Alice arrive back and turned to watch her.

Alice slowly made her way over to her bed, carrying clean sheets and began to dress her bed in the still silence of the dorm.

Maisie wanted to ask her if she was ok, but she was terrified a Sister would hear her and she would be next. She could tell by the way Alice was moving that her body was tender and in pain. Maisie desperately wanted to reach out to help bring comfort to the young mother, but fear gripped her and paralyzed her from doing so.

The following morning, Maisie turned to Alice to give her a subtle, supportive glance. Alice's beautiful long auburn hair had been cut off right to the scalp. Her hands were red and blistered, Maisie knew by the marks it was from boiling water. Alice took off her nightgown. She moved slowly, her back was covered in bruises and cuts from strikes of a stick.

Alice's hell was not the only one Maisie had witnessed, and the girls lived in constant fear that next time it could be them. The pain went deep, on all levels. Physical, mental, emotional and spiritual torture, all because they made love to a fella they loved and conceived a baby without paying a Catholic priest to marry them first.

Other girls were in here not because they got pregnant from an innocent courtship. In some cases, it was a lot more sinister. Rape and incest saw some of the girls in this division of hell. Stripped of their innocence and then made to pay for no sin.

Regardless of how these young girls ended up in this hell, most of them had no choice. Most were sent there by their family, under the recommendation of the local parish priest. One way or the other it was a certainty, that these girls fell victim to a grave punishment for no crime. It was a punishment that would continue to haunt them deep in their psyche for the rest of their lives.

Some would find answers only to lead to more questions. Others would never find the answers and would go to their grave still questioning. Some never asked questions, for fear of being judged by others.

The root of this judgement lay deep in the dark, disempowering belief system, lived throughout Irish society and taught by the clergy. The simple, cruel belief was that a woman who conceived a baby out of wedlock had sinned and she must pay. This belief filtered down into a suppressed society. The effect left these girls carrying pointless guilt, shame and disempowerment for decades.

Every single one of the girls got on with it. They had to. Persecuted every day, the only saving grace they had was the very reason they were here, their little bundles of joy. Despite the cruelty, the hell and the persecution, each one of these girls responded to their baby in the very way Mother Nature had intended. They each took one look and fell deeply in love. This love was to last forever, every single day, no matter what was to come.

They say there is a God and Maisie believed there was. But she also believed that the God she knew was not the same force that these Sisters claimed to represent.

The God Maisie knew was a very different force. He was a force of love and strength. Her God was the very same source that created the love for the little bundles of joy that made this place bearable.

Ironic as it was, when she thought of her Mary and reflected on the love she felt for her, she observed that God could not control the beliefs of society, only society could do that. Nor could he control his so-called representatives, men and women of the cloth living up to their responsibilities, only they could do that.

But when he was going to create something truly beautiful, powerful and perfect, he was going to see it through, despite the pain and persecution to be endured along the way.

During that time of deep sadness, it was the God that Maisie believed in, who created something that served as the vessel, to be the reminder of hope and peace that came only from Him.

It came in the form of the deep love and joy a mother felt when she held God's creation in her arms. For Maisie, that was the source of her strength, and the vessel of that strength was Mary.

She lay in bed that night, wide awake as always, and she thought about the way the Sisters called the girls the devil's spawn.

Maisie couldn't disagree more, these mothers were heaven's angels, strong enough to endure the harshest darkness and still find love in their hearts for innocence. As far as Maisie was concerned, these girls were angels and the Sisters were the devil's spawn.

Within the darkness of the Mother and Baby home, God and truth were nowhere to be found, except in the purity and the innocence of these beautiful children and the vessels of strength that carried them.

In the depths of this darkest night, she prayed to her God in the hope of an answered prayer. She prayed that her daddy would come around and agree to allow her to keep her baby girl.

Mary was the only thing right in this hell, and her love for her was the purest source of happiness she had ever known. All was perfect when she held her. She loved Mary's touch, her smell, her breath and the little sounds she made. She was her daughter, and the worst thing in the world she could think of right now was the thought of having to hand her over to someone else. It made her feel like she was dying inside.

The fear of same haunted her mind to a state of paralysis. This was going to be her last night in the Mother and Baby home, and no matter what, she knew that tomorrow Mary's new adoptive parents were coming to collect her and take her away.

The Sister said that her new parents would be here in the evening time. At least she had the best part of the day with Mary.

She reflected once again on the last eighteen months. Her mind wandered back to Jim, her first love. Jim was an up and coming rock star, in Maisie's eyes. He had a band and everything. Maisie worked all week at the local factory, where most of her town were employed. On the weekends she looked forward to heading out to the next town, to unwind. That was where she met Jim.

His band was the regular entertainment, hired by the owners of the biggest bar in the small country town. Jim was the lead singer. He sang all the top numbers that dominated the 1960's charts. He never failed to do fantastic covers of The Beatles, Louis Armstrong, The Beach Boys and the Drifters, and there was always the odd Buddy Holly number thrown in there too. He even prided himself and boasted that he wrote his own songs too.

Maisie caught his eye. He made it his business to get her attention and ask her out. He was mad about her. She was cheeky, quick-witted and well able for Jim's boyish over-confidence. He could afford to be confident, he was a good-looking guy and could have his pick of the ladies, but he chose Maisie.

After not long they were going steady. They went on dates to the cinema on Saturday evenings. They met again on Sunday afternoons and went for ice-cream.

She was mad about him, and he was mad about her. They were both young, and neither took themselves or the relationship too seriously. But after a few months of courtship, Maisie realised something was not right. She knew she had fallen pregnant and she also knew she had to tell Jim first.

"Jim, I've something to tell you."

The young couple sat side by side swaying on the swings in the park beside the bus stop. That was where Jim always met Maisie. She travelled the short twenty-minute journey from Bunratty to the picturesque historical town of Adare.

She took a deep breath and prepared to break the news to Jim that everything had changed forever.

"Don't tell me, your daddy has finally come to his senses and realises I am the best thing that ever happened to you after all?" Jim jumped off his swing, his arms out-stretched in animated presentation of himself. His cheeky grin stretched from one ear to the other.

"No Jim, I'm serious. This is serious. There's no easy way to tell you this, so I'm just going to come straight out with it. We're going to have a baby. I'm at least three months gone."

Jim went quiet, but in those moments of silence, she could feel something leaving Jim. He sat back down on the swing, placed his hands in his pockets and stared at the ground. He stayed silent for a few moments and Maisie insisted he say something.

"My sister lives in England," he eventually said with an air of solution. It was the first time Maisie had ever seen Jim serious and right now, his ever-present smile was absent from his eyes. It was replaced by a combination of controlled fear, dominated by the immaturity of his young years and an aloof detachment.

"No one will know. We'll just get the boat over to England and tell everyone we are going on a romantic weekend and see my sister or something. We'll get the deed done, and no one will have to know, sorted."

Maisie was not surprised at Jim's unthinkable excuse for a solution. She rejected the suggestion with a fierce intolerable tone in her voice.

"Absolutely not Jim Kavanagh. This is our baby, and I am not doing away with it. You can come down to Bunratty with me and tell my father you are going to marry me and that's the end of it. "

That day was the last day he spoke to her. She saw him in town once or twice, but each time, he crossed over to the other side of the road.

It wasn't long before she felt very alone in an unfamiliar place. Her father insisted she go to St Patrick's on the Navan Road before she began to show. The plan was to stay there until she had the baby and give the baby up for adoption. Then she can come home, and everyone can forget all about it. In the meantime, her father had a word with Maisie's boss, explaining that his sister was expecting a baby in Galway and Maisie was going up to help her aunt until after her baby was born.

The matter of fact, solution-based plan was executed. Arrangements were made with the local parish priest and off Maisie went to St. Patricks on Dublin's Navan Road.

During that time, she experienced what she always remembered as hell on earth for the rest of her life. She employed a tactic of keeping her head down and getting through the time she had to spend there. It was a tactic that helped her to cope and stay out of the target realm of the nuns. But she was fully aware that some of the other girls were not so fortunate. If that was the right word.

Maisie had a tough time in the delivery ward. She went full term, and labour accelerated fast. She could not believe the level of pain she felt. She remembered thinking that she was going to die because she was in such pain.

She lay on the bed, in a cold room, alone, for most of the labour stage. No one held her hand. No one told her she was going to be ok. There was no comfort and no love, only the immeasurable pain in a cold and lonely room. From time to time the Sister came in. Maisie asked for pain relief. The Sister refused and told her that this pain was her punishment and penance and she had to pay. Her only company in that room was four blank walls and a small picture of the Virgin Mary hanging on the wall. She pleaded in silence to the loving eyes of the Virgin Mary to help her get through her agony.

The young girl felt like she was facing death and she did her very best to hold it together. She told herself that she was the vessel, the woman, who gives birth to the miracle of life. She wanted to crumble, at times the pain was so great she wanted to die.

In the latter stages, the Sister was in the room. Maisie was pushing and pushing, under the orders of the Sister. She pushed for two solid hours. The baby was not coming. Her young body was so tired. She had no more to give and could not withstand any more pain. The Sister fixed her stern and cold eyes on Maisie's.

'You're going to have your baby now.'

She produced the forceps. The nun abruptly delivered Maisie's child. Maisie screamed deafening cries, in the throes of pain and panic. Her pride and dignity battered, as well as her body.

She gave birth to a baby girl, at 11:10am on the 22nd February 1965.

Her baby girl was 7lb 2oz, and she was beautiful. The Sister swaddled the baby in blankets and handed her to Maisie. The Sister's demeanour was still cold and unemotional, but now, Maisie didn't care.

The whole world of outside mother and daughter disappeared completely or was at least irrelevant at that moment in time. This tiny bundle and her panicky little face, not knowing what the heck just happened looked up to Maisie as if to say just that.

Maisie smiled from the depths of her soul at her beautiful baby girl. She held her in her arms, close to her bosom while the rest of the world disappeared, and she was in awe. She fell in love in those moments. This tiny perfect little person, totally dependent on her mother, Maisie knew it and so did Mary.

This moment was a perfect moment in time, where the story of time changed forever. Maisie could have stayed right there forever, embracing the perfection that she had given life to. It was, without doubt, the happiest moment of her life, so far.

The sun was beginning to rise and bring light into the dorm. Maisie smiled to herself as she relived that sunny February morning in her mind. It was always the same. Every time she recalled, the harsh, cruel darkness of this forsaken place slipped away.

No matter what happened, she will forever treasure, deep within her heart, the memory of the moments she held the new life she gave birth to and the depths of love she felt at that time.

Just like every morning, she couldn't wait to get breakfast out of the way and the chores she had to do. It was only a few hours away, and she prayed to God to help her to slip into a light sleep state, before her early rise.

Her mind filled with the image of the tiny little dependent person in her crib, she was always so placid. When Maisie picked her up and held her, she felt only peace and joy. Mary was the only thing that made her smile right now. She treasured the time she had to feed her, taking in every little detail about her beautiful bundle of perfection.

But the time she got to spend with Mary was never long enough. The Sisters allowed a ten-minute break in between chores to feed the babies and then back to work she went.

This was her last night. The previous day the Sister called Maisie aside:

"A well to do family is coming to collect your child tomorrow evening. I believe your mother is coming today to visit. Tell her to bring money and go into town. Buy decent clothes for the baby. Make sure you dress her in the morning ready to go."

The nun turned on her heel and walked away. Maisie stood tall, outwardly remaining strong. But she was falling apart inside. This was it; tomorrow was going to be the day, her last day with her perfect child. The reality was exploding in Maisie's heart. They were going to take her baby away, for the foreseeable future, if not forever.

Maisie had been awake all night, and her body felt heavy and tired. Her mind was haunted by the thoughts and fears of what might be. She felt scared. She searched her mind, wondering how she was going to find the strength to cope. The fear crippled her with silent despair. The darkness of loss had crept in, blinding her to the hope that might yet remain.

Chapter 4

The following morning, Maisie woke from a light lucid sleep. For the shortest time, she drifted to someplace else. It was a beautiful, peaceful place that she recalled very little about upon waking. When she woke she fell back down into the dorm, and the dark, strangling limitation of hopelessness and the reality she was living hit her hard.

This was her last day with Mary. It was like as if there was no light, no life and no hope beyond this day. All control was in everyone else's hands but hers, the Sisters, her parents and what society thought. And the result left her feeling completely empty. To slip into numbness was the only way she could cope.

'At least I will get more time with Mary today.' The bittersweet consolation, a knife twisting in her heart.

The Sisters always gave the girls time to prepare their babies for their new parents on the day they were being adopted. Maisie knew she would have the morning with her. She hoped she would be able to spend the afternoon with her too. She thought she would ask Mammy to ask the Sister to allow her to. Today was going to go down as one of the hardest days of Maisie's life. She was determined to take it one step at a time. Through it all she remained hopeful that Daddy would give in. Life might become a dream come true. She held it together looking forward to her last few hours with Mary.

"Hello my precious sweetness," Maisie's heart was sinking and leaping for joy at the same time. She leaned down to pick up baby Mary in her arms, just like she had done every morning for the last month, but this time her heart ache raged heaviest of all days. Mary was wide awake, looking around her and responding to all the nearby sounds. "How are you today? Oh you look very pretty, I think you are getting prettier by the day, do you know that?"

She carried Mary down to the room allocated to the mothers and babies on their last day. She continued to chat with Mary about anything and everything except what today would bring.

As much as she held it together, she could sense that Mary was picking up on her sadness. Mary was a lot more upset than usual. She was always a placid baby who rarely cried, even when she was hungry. The only times Mary got upset was when Maisie was placing her back in her crib after feeding and changing her. It was like as if she didn't want Maisie to go. But today was different, Mary was unsettled and wanted Maisie to hold her close to her chest all the time.

"Do you know what my beautiful baby girl? You are more precious and beautiful than you will ever realise. And I will always, always, always love you, from the depths of my heart." She fought back the tears every moment. "From your head to your little twinkle toes you are loved now and always will be." The young mother stood in the corridor cradling her daughter in her arms and rocking her gently." I hope you always know that, no matter what."
Eventually, Mary settled.
"God put me on this planet to do the best job I could while I am here, in this life. But I think that the greatest gift he could ever have given me is you, and I thank God for that."
Mary drifted off to sleep.

The midday sun was shining in the window and Maisie thought to herself she was halfway through her last day with her baby girl. She turned and looked over her shoulder. She saw the Sister thundering down the corridor towards her.
"I'm taking your baby now."
"No. You can't. Not yet." Maisie pleaded with the large middle-aged nun. Every emotion flowed sharp and deep into her heart, disbelief, despair, panic. She thought that she had more time. The other Sister had said evening time.
The Sister completely ignored Maisie's pleas and snatched Mary from her. Without a backward glance, she turned and walked away with her child.
Maisie fell to her knees, watching the Sister walk briskly away down the corridor. She could hear Mary cry louder and harder than she had ever cried before. The echoes of her cries filled the corridor as the distance between her and her child became greater and greater.
She lay on her knees reaching hopelessly out for her child, her heart, her womb, her life, wrenched from her in one tug. So fast, so easily, as she bore the impossible.

She cried so loud, but no sound came out, the pain was too deep. She lay on the floor desperately reaching out for her baby, knowing her efforts were hopeless, there was nothing she could do, she was completely powerless.

She cried so hard watching the Sister disappear out of sight with her daughter, her life ripped away, and the grief was beyond the greatest pain imaginable. She had nothing, no hope, no light, and no one was there to tell her everything was going to be alright. The young girl lay on the floor, broken.

A short time later, she stood to look out the large window at the front of the building. The window gave view to the front drive of St Patricks. There was a black car parked outside the front door. A man and woman walked out holding a baby and got into the car. The Sister accompanied them to the car to see them off.

Maisie banged on the window screaming deafening cries as she watched the car drive away. But no one heard her, and no one cared.

Maisie returned home to Bunratty that same day. Her heart was broken, and she could not speak. The Sisters left her with one word of advice, spoken through a cold smile before she left the Mother and Baby home.

"Put all of this behind you now and get on with your life"

She stared out the window of the bus with her mother by her side. Her only living hope was that her father agreed to her pleas to keep Mary and raise her child herself. Right now, that was the only hope that kept her standing.

There was not a word mentioned upon her return. No-one spoke about the last few months, except for Maisie. Every day she begged her father's mercy. Her daddy was a good man, a quiet man. He worked hard and did his very best to provide for his family. He did his duty as a father and raised his children as best he could. He kept his loved ones close and went along with the norm in life. Maisie had always been a daddy's girl, and he often gave in to her, but not this time.

After some months her daddy's denial of Maisie's sadness and refusal to give in began to take its toll. He became distant and depressed.

One evening after dinner Maisie's mother called her to one side:

"Maisie leave them dishes and sit down for a second, I want to talk to you" Ellen sat down too, she put her tea-towel on the table and rested her hand over her mouth.

Maisie knew that when her mother gave that pose there was something serious coming. It was usually the cue to a talk about something that had been weighing on her mother's mind. Maisie put the pile of plates down on the draining board and sat with her mother at the kitchen table, in front of her uneaten dinner.

"Maisie, you have to let this go love"

"I can't Mammy, I keep seeing her in my mind. My body just wants to know where she is, what she's doing, how she is. I can't let it go Mammy, it's all I can think about"

"Maisie love, she is with what's best for her. Your father has to keep working and living. It's hard enough he lost you for four months, now you're gone from him altogether"

"No I'm not, I'm here aren't I?"

"Maisie come on now love, don't be cheeky"

"Jeez Mammy, I'm not a child" The words snapped out of Maisie's mouth without her thinking. The realisation of what she just said heralded the experience of what created the woman she is now flashing before her mind's eye.

"Maisie, when was the last time you and your daddy had a proper conversation? We used to never be able to get a word in between the pair of you. Please love, it's best for everyone. I'm not saying to forget about Mary and get back to normal. No-one can ever expect you to do that, but you have to let her go so as you can move on with your life. So as everyone can move on.

Maisie, I will always love that baby girl and you will too. But she is gone, and we are here. As I said Daddy misses you and I know you miss him"

Maisie saw his uneaten dinner. Her father had a great appetite up to this, especially for corned beef. It had been a family favourite before St. Patricks.

Now food just did not taste of anything. She ate only to keep standing. In the home she ate very little. A lot of the girls didn't even show their pregnancies. A lot stopped being pregnant after a while. But she and Mary had survived, got through scrubbing and starvation together. Got through that labour. She and Mary.

Once she had been a child. Her father's child. She was a woman now and Mary was some other woman's child.

Her father had other children to support, as she would have had to support Mary. Suddenly, she saw how helpless he was. How he would suffer at work, how her mother would suffer in the community, not to mention the toll it's already taking on her mother to hold it together for everyone else, and then there was always the judgement at mass of a Sunday.

Suddenly, she knew that the advice the Sister had given through her cold smile was correct. For the world they lived in was the world of those Sisters, not the world of ordinary people, making ordinary mistakes and willing to live with them.

In this world those mistakes were taken away and people behaved as if they never happened.

Chapter 5

It's a long time since Maisie was here. When she was here, I couldn't open my eyes that much. Now I can, and I can see really clearly too. I think I have been here longer than most of the other babies. I wonder where they go when they leave. I wonder what else there is here, in this life.

Some of the babies here cry really hard, for a really long time. Some cry until they can't cry anymore, and their cries turn to whimpers until they go silent. When they do the Sisters come and take them away and they don't come back.

The first time that happened I remember the same baby's mother didn't come in for two days. When she did, she was told to feed another baby because her own baby was no longer here. The sister came in the night before and took him away. His mother had really beautiful long red hair, but when she came in after two days, all her beautiful hair was gone. I thought she looked so much prettier with long hair. I think his mammy's name was Alice. I remember because it was a few nights before Maisie left.

I know I came into this place for a reason. I had heard it was going to be hard at times, but a very exciting experience. I can't seem to find the exciting part. Where I come from they call this 'life'. They say it has up and downs, happy times and sad times and at times it can feel like a roller coaster, whatever that is. But so far, I don't get it.

I just lie in this little body, in this crib all day, in this room, with the other babies. Some leave, some stay, and more babies are coming in almost every day.

The ladies come in and feed us a few times a day, and the sisters are still cruel. Every day it is the same routine. Nothing new ever happens. I am still always cold and always hungry.

This place called life is boring. Maybe it will get better. But it's very sad here. I can't think why I came. There is no adventure, only sadness.

July 3rd, 1965

"Hello."

"Hello, could I speak to Mrs Corcoran please?"

"Yes, just hold on, and I'll get her for you now."

Tommy Dempsey carefully laid the telephone receiver on the small mahogany table in the hall and opened the front door. He hopped over the dividing railings to his neighbour's house and knocked.

Lil answered her door wearing her pink slippers, a blue A-line skirt and pink knitted top. She was glad that she had just removed her rollers from her short blonde hair and looked half decent. Tommy knocked while she was getting ahead, peeling the spuds for tomorrows dinner. Lil was a natural home-maker. She ran an organised, clever and clean home, ensuring it was filled with a sense of harmony and function.

"How'ya Lil, there's someone on the phone looking for you." The teenage neighbour gestured with his thumb towards his hall door.

"Thanks, Tommy," Lil knew that whoever was on the phone it was important. Lil and Joe didn't have a home telephone. The only time anyone rang the Dempsey's house looking for Lil or Joe was if someone was sick, dying or it was someone important. A million thoughts ran through her head walking down her garden path and into the Dempsey's, hoping nothing was wrong.

"Hello," Lil said in her posh voice.

"Hello. Is that Mrs Corcoran?"

"This is she."

"Mrs Corcoran. This is Eileen Rose. I'm the social worker calling you from St Ultan's Adoption Agency. How are you?"

Lil's heart skipped a beat and began to race. She and Joe had applied to adopt the previous year and were waiting to hear word at any time. It had been months since they were approved, and the agency said they would contact them once a baby came available.

"All is well. I'm good Ms Rose. How are you?"

"Fine thank you, Mrs Corcoran. I wonder if you would be

available to come to St Patricks Mother and Baby home on the Navan Road tomorrow? The Sisters called this evening, and they have a baby for you. It is a baby girl like you requested, and she is four and a half months old."

Lil caught a glance of herself in the mirror hanging in the hall. The thirty-year-old woman noticed her eyes had filled up with tears and her face was completely flush. Her hand was on her forehead allowing her fingertips to cool her brow. She searched for words to respond to the voice at the other end of the line, but nothing came out.

"Mrs Corcoran?" The voice on the other end sounded mature.

"Sorry, I'm just, it's been so long…erm…. this is fantastic news Mrs Rose, thank you. Eh…what do we need to bring? Do you have anything else to tell me? How old is the baby? Oh I do apologize I can't even think here…" Lil couldn't really control her mouth or her mind with the feelings, the images, coming up, another baby, another Ruth, another chance.

"That is the only information I have for the moment," the woman laughed. She must have been used to giving news that made people not able to think straight. "Oh, sorry, of course, there is her name. Her name is Mary, but of course, you can change your baby's name if you wish."

"Your baby. She had said your baby." Lil thought to herself, her hands were shaking like a leaf trying and her mind struggled to envisage the reality.

"Thank you, Eileen, or I mean Mrs Rose…. We'll be there, myself and my husband. Thank you"

"Oh and Mrs. Corcoran, could you bring clothes for your baby. The Sisters requested that you bring clothes for her to wear home"

"Clothes, got it. I will." Lil's mind's eye raced through her knitting bag. She hoped she had a forgotten ball of wool lying in the bottom of the bag to knit a dress for 'her baby'. She glanced at her watch, it was just after 4, there was no time to get to the wool shop now. "Thank, thank you Eileen, or I mean Mrs…erm…yes, thank you. See you tomorrow"

"You are very welcome Mrs. Corcoran" The social worker gave an understanding laugh again. "It would suit to come at twelve noon if that's ok?"

"Yes, twelve noon is perfect. We'll see you then. Thanks, thanks, thank you"

Lil placed the phone receiver on the hook and stood in shock in the Dempsey's hall. A million thoughts and images flowed through her mind absorbing how that single phone call had changed their lives forever. Her mind failed miserably to take it all in. Just like that, after months of waiting, months of hoping and one Saturday evening, out of the blue, whilst she was peeling the spuds for tomorrows' dinner, it happened. They got the call.

She rushed back in to tell Joe the news through the smile that she could not wipe from her face.

"Joe.... Joe?" Lil closed her front door behind her. "Joe, they called, that was the social worker. Where are you?" Lil searched aimlessly through the rooms of their new semi-detached home. She ran in and out of the hall, searching the kitchen, the living room, dining room and calling up the stairs. Even if Joe was in any of those rooms Lil would not have seen him.

"the grass Lil, he's out cutting the grass" She remembered.

"Joe.... can you come in for a second?" She hung out the back door and shouted at her husband over the sound of the push lawn mower.

"There has to be an easier way to cut that grass" Joe stepped into the kitchen and wiped his grassy boots on the door mat, his tall frame was almost tipping the head of the back door. "That mower needs new blades again. What's wrong?" Joe asked placing his garden gloves down on the small utility counter by the back door.

"Joe, sit down, they called!" Lil stood in the middle of the kitchen, her hands over each cheek, cupping her face.

"Who called?" Joe asked rubbing a bar of soap between his hands under the warm running water in the kitchen sink scrubbing the grass stains from his hands.

"The adoption agency Joe.... oh I can't believe it...they have a baby, tomorrow, we have to go tomorrow....I have to get a dress.... knit a dress.... she's four months, and Eileen or I mean Mrs. Rose rang the Dempsey's… she's a girl…I thought I might get up to Dun Laoghaire to buy a ball of wool, but I'll never have time, maybe Mammy has some wool…. can you imagine, just like that Joe…?"

"Lil…. Lil slow down. Who rang?" Lil had her husband's full attention.

"The adoption agency…. oh Joe just like that, they have a baby. I mean I was only peeling the spuds there now for the dinner tomorrow and……"

"Lil, will you hold on and start at the beginning" Joe sat down at the kitchen table after pulling out a chair for his wife too.

"Ok" Lil took a deep breath and sat down. "Mrs Rose, from St. Ultan's adoption agency just rang into the Dempsey's" Lil deliberately placed her hands out flat on the kitchen table and directed every bit of energy she had into focusing on explaining to Joe what just happened, step by step.

"Right, go on" Joe encouraged.

"She said that they have a baby for us. Her name is Mary, but we can change the name if we wish and we have to go to St Patricks Home on the Navan Road tomorrow, I think she said twelve of clock? Yes, actually she did. Twelve of clock tomorrow to collect her….and bring clothes. Joe, she even said 'your baby', I can't believe it!"

"Right" Joe whispered. He glanced around the kitchen table, "Jeepers, just like that….and it's a baby girl?" His eyes grew wide and face filled with a smile "Ah Lil that's fantastic news. She's four months old?" Joe slowly allowed the details to register taking his hanker chief from his pocket. He wiped his eyes and blew his nose.

"I know Joe, it's happening. I can't believe it's really happening." Lil looked at her husband and sat back in her chair, her voice had turned soft and quiet now, allowing herself to finally take in the news.

"Me neither love, as you say, just like that" Joe's folded his arms on the table, his broad build accommodated the width of the table's end.

"Ruth is up in Mammy's, we'll have a cup tea and I'll go up and tell Mammy the news then" Lil stood up and began to fill the kettle.

"Another little baby Lil, a little sister for Ruth, it's great, it's fantastic news" Joe stood up, the large smile on his face and eyes filled with tears exposed the big softie behind the 6ft 2" broad built man.

Lil noticed his eyes welling up with tears again. She threw her arms around her husband and the couple embraced what was to become the next chapter of their lives.

Lil and Joe were both thirty this year. For almost a third of their lives they had been trying for children. Ruth came in the middle of that trying. Then three years with nothing Joe said to Lil:

'I think that's enough Lil.'

She cried for the last time with another disappointment and another broken heart and agreed with Joe to try another way.

They breezed through the adoption process. Joe owned a well-known third generation drapery shop in Dun Laoghaire, just down the road from their home in Glenageary, a south county Dublin suburb.

Corcoran" was a familiar name across all of Dublin. Joe took over the business from his father, who had taken over from his. Well-established with a loyal customer base, Joe was now putting his own mark on the family business. For two years solid he researched expanding into a women and children's clothing range. In 1962 Corcoran's Menswear was rebranded and became Corcoran's. The expansion was well received among their customers and the business was going from strength to strength.

The business man and his young family were enjoying a prosperous start in life. His hard work paid off and Joe, Lil and Ruth moved into their new home in 1964. They both grew up in Dun Laoghaire, Co Dublin. Once new developments began to sprout up around the area of Glenageary, they jumped at the chance of owning one of the large, two storey homes. Both sets of their parents lived just down the road, they both loved the area and Joe did not plan on changing his job any time soon, so it made perfect sense to jump on the property ladder without hesitation. The business man's mortgage application was immediately approved and so began the new life for the young family.

The adoption agency immediately recognised their application as a promising one and they received immediate approval. In November 1964 the agency assured them that they would be in touch with news of a baby once one became available. On Saturday 3rd July 1965 that news came.

They put their daughter Ruth to bed that night and tucked her in. Ruth was almost four years old, she lay in bed hugging her brown teddy, listening to her Daddy sat on her bed reading the ritual bedtime story. That night it was 'Goldilocks and the Three Bears'.

"Five more minutes guys ok?" Lil popped her head in the bedroom door, ushering the curfew for lights out.

"Mammy, why do I have to wear these rollers in my hair and why are my Easter Clothes hanging on the wardrobe door? Where are we going tomorrow" Ruth hated wearing rollers to bed. She squirmed her tired head on the pillow, every strand of her blonde hair was meticulously weaved into curlers. Lil always felt that the curlers gave her naturally fine hair volume and saved the curlers for special occasions. Tomorrow definitely qualified as one of the best of them.

"Ruth, you need to get a good night's sleep tonight," Lil kneeled beside Ruth's bed "we have a very special day tomorrow", her heart leapt with the fortune of the moment, feeling blessed to be sharing such news with her daughter.

"Why?"

"We are going to bring you to collect your baby sister and bring her home." Lil's smile said more than she could ever say in words.

"What's her name? Can she sleep in my room? Can I bring her a present?" Ruth sat up in the bed, still hugging teddy but leaving her sleepiness behind "Can she have one of my teddies? Mammy, you better knit her some clothes. She might not have anything to wear."

"You read my mind, Ruth. I'm going downstairs now to get my knitting needles out and knit her a new dress because the lady on the phone said she had no clothes."

"OK," said a satisfied Ruth, proud of herself for her wise suggestion. She lay her head back down on the pillow in trust that her mother will take care of the finer details.

"Now straight to sleep Ruth, as mammy said tomorrow is a big day" Joe tucked her in and they each kissed her goodnight. She snuggled back down into her bed and closed her eyes.

She drifted to sleep filled with pictures in her mind of what tomorrow would bring and who her new baby sister would be.

That Saturday night Lil and Joe sat side by side in the living room couch watching a film on TV. Lil was delighted that she found a big ball of yellow wool in the bottom of her knitting bag. It was enough to knit a dress for her new baby. She had no idea how big or small to make the dress, so she thought it best to go large, just in case.

Lil had always knitted. She flew through those stitches and rows like Wonder Woman. Within a few hours, she created the most beautiful dress, cardigan or jumper, without even looking at what she was doing for most of the time.

They sat watching TV. There were a thousand things running around in Lil's head. She thought of what to call the baby. Then, she figured she would have a better idea when she met her.

One of the characters in the movie they were watching was called Saoirse, pronounced, Sir-sha.

"Joe, what does that name mean, Saoirse?" Lil observed the character on the TV screen with a curious frown, continuing to wrap strands of wool around her needles and weave those stiches without taking her eyes off the TV.

"Freedom. Saoirse is the Irish for freedom."

Joe's general knowledge seemed to hold no bounds. There was never a day went by that he did not read the newspaper from cover to cover and complete the crosswords too. His father saw him through a good education and he reciprocated with hard work and commitment. He always went beyond the expected when it came to accomplishment and enjoyed the respect it earned him from his peers. Lil figured he was somewhat of an encyclopaedia when it came to information. Thus far, his thirst for knowledge had served him well and in his eyes, he was only beginning.

Lil thought of tomorrows date: 4th of July, Independence Day typically celebrated in America. She quietly wondered to herself if there was some symbolic meaning in the coincidence. She opted not to share her thoughts with her husband for fear of him thinking she was mad. But banked her observation until tomorrow and see if the name suited her daughter.

"We better leave early in the morning Joe. You know, just in case there is anything on across town"

"I didn't read anything in the newspaper but you're right. We'll give it plenty of time nonetheless. Is your mother coming over tomorrow?

"Is she coming? She's up there now baking a half dozen apple tarts and queen Victoria sponges! She was almost making dinner for half the town too only I told her I had a stew and shepherd's pie on already."

"Do you think there will be many popping in tomorrow?" Joe folded his arms lounging back on the couch. He was not one for crowds in his home.

Lil loved the company and could host for as many people who came. She got it from her mother, having grown up in a home where the hall door was always open and no matter what, there always seemed to be plenty of food so no man, woman nor child ever went hungry.

"I'm not sure Joe, but I met Dolores and her sister on the way home from Mammy's this evening and told them. I told the Dempsey's too of course and I popped into Mrs. Cross there just before I sat down tonight to tell her.

"Dolores and The Dempsey's know? I shall expect a full house tomorrow so" Dolores was Lil's best friend. She had a younger sister who knew everyone in the community. It was a given that If a baby was born, an engagement announced or a death in the area, one was most likely to hear it first from Dolores' sister, Nora.

The Dempsey's next door had six children ranging from a young baby to aged twelve. They had a lot of friends and there was no doubt that by the end of Sunday Mass tomorrow morning, word will have spread like breaking news.

Joe loved his privacy when it came to his personal life. Behind the counter in his shop he spoke about drapery and fashion trends to anyone who listened, but at home he was a private man who kept himself to himself. Lil on the other hand recognised the value in friendship and enjoyed the sense of unity within the young community in which they lived. She knew most of the other mums in her estate from childhood. Over the last few years she witnessed one family after another have more and more children. Meanwhile her heart ached with disappointment one month after the other. This time it was her chance, her turn once again and for the very last time too.

For the last four years Ruth was her whole life, and everything revolved around her. Now there was going to be a new addition to the Corcoran family, to create and give more love to. The thoughts of what these new beginnings will bring filled Lil's heart with immeasurable joy. She felt more alive this evening than she had felt in a long, long time.

"There. What do you think Joe?" Lil held up the beautiful hand knit yellow dress, examining it with her self-trained eye for flaws or discrepancies, there were none.

"Ah, that's lovely Lil, it's flawless. Lovely" Joe sat back on the couch, and admired another remarkable creation, knitted by his wife in a matter of hours.

Chapter 6

"Lil, are you ready?" Joe called up the stairs with insistence

"Yeah, I'm ready, just hold on."

Joe impatiently rolled his eyes to heaven. He paced the hall again and looked at his watch. He had been ready to leave for the last twenty minutes. Lil was running a brush briskly through her hair in front of the full-length mirror in their bedroom. She was pressed for time because she left herself until last and tended to Joe, Ruth, breakfast and the tidying up first.

"I'm ready now," Lil grabbed her handbag and threw on her coat while running downstairs.

Joe opened the hall door with impatience. Lil followed him holding Ruth's hand.

Ruth felt very pretty today in her 'good frock'. She hadn't had a chance to wear it since Easter. She could feel her new curls bouncing with each step she took, gently tickling the side of her face and nap of her neck. She wore a pretty pink bow holding her hair back from her forehead and she admired her black patented leather shoes walking down the front path.

In her hand, she held a little gift bag for her new baby sister. She had packed a dolly and a teddy and couldn't wait to give them to her. She really hoped she was going to like them.

Joe drove across Dublin town with his eyes fixed on the road. His strong sense of responsibility was applied to his driving skills as well as his time keeping. A bomb could go off and he would still use the Highway Code.

"Have you got the clothes?" His white knuckles gripped the steering wheel like a raft at sea.

"I have the clothes, Joe." Lil always calmed him down but today she felt numb and tense. She hadn't had a chance to iron her blouse and hoped the creases were falling out.

"Have you got the forms they told us to bring?" Joe continued to scan both his mind and the road for anything that could hinder a successful arrival.

"They have the forms, Joe." Lil's mind flashed back to the hours the pair spent debating answers to those forms all those months ago.

"Right....have you got the ID? How is Ruth in the back there is she ok?" He daren't glance through the rear-view mirror, his eyes remained firm on Dublin's roads.

Ruth was sitting in the backseat sitting very still. She usually would have asked the: 'When are we going to be there?' question by now, but even her young mind knew that now was not the time. Her mind was full of questions: 'When can I meet my baby sister? What is her name? Is it far away? What does she look like? Do you think she will like my dress and my present?" But not right now.

"Jeez Joe, I have the clothes. They have the forms. We don't need ID and Ruth is happy out there in the back. Will you stop worrying. It'll be fine." Lil's tolerance ran out. "Now please, this is supposed to be a happy day, can you stop fussing and lend a bit of trust that every-thing is under control?"

Joe didn't respond.

"Mammy, are we nearly there yet?" Ruth chanced.

"There it is sweat-heart, right in front on us." Joe turned the steer-ing wheel into the large grounds of St. Patrick's Mother and Baby home.

They pulled up outside the building that they had been instructed to go to. The big red brick building was old and dreary looking, stand-ing four storeys tall, with a big red hall door.

Joe knocked on the door and stood to wait with Lil and Ruth on the doorstep.

"I'm so nervous Joe" Lil's hands both clutched the strap on her bag which hung on her shoulder

"It'll be fine love" Joe reassured. He put his arm around his wife's back. "Everything will be fine."

A young Sister opened the large door.

"Good morning, Mr. & Mrs. Corcoran" Joe introduced "Ms Eileen Rose called us yesterday evening. We have a 12-o clock appointment"

"You are all very welcome. If you would like to come with me I can show you to the Head Sister's Office" She smiled, welcoming them into the old building.

"Thank you" said Lil and followed the Sister. She walked ahead of the family through the reception area and down the hall. "Beautiful weather we're having isn't it?" the young Sister was quiet spoken.

"Yes, we've been very lucky this Summer, thank God" Lil welcomed the small talk.

"Here we are. If you would like to take a seat the Head Sister will be with you shortly" she stood in the doorway of a small room. There was a bureau type desk at the opposite wall, behind it was a large window overlooking the well-manicured grounds and each wall was lined with pale grey filing cabinets. A large picture of The Sacred Heart hung above the large window.. The old desk was filled with filing trays stacked with a sea of documents and paperwork.

Lil and Joe sat down on the two chairs in front of the desk and Ruth sat up on her mammy's knee. Lil welcomed the refreshing breeze flowing in through the open shutter window.

"Good afternoon" A large heavy-set Sister briskly entered the room and shut the door behind her. "Pleased to meet you" she extended her hand and gave both Lil and Joe a firm hand-shake "I am Sr. Benedict" Her large presence and effortless etiquette dominated all space in the small office. "Beautiful weather we're having isn't it? Are you too warm, I have the window open to allow the air to flow through, it can get very stuffy in here" She walked around the desk and took her seat on the opposite the Corcoran's.

"Yes, thank you, one would need it this weather" Joe engaged.

"Now, now now, where are we?" She scanned her files. "Oh yes, Mary. Let me just ask you a few routine questions and then I will share the information I have for you about the baby" The Sister began to take a few details.

Lil and Joe confirmed the easy questions about their names, age, address and so forth.

"Mammy, where is the baby?" Ruth whispered in her mother's ear. She had been patient thus far in the strange place, but the heat and the boredom were taking its toll.

"Sshhh Ruth love, the baby will be here shortly" Lil assured rocking her and kissing her head.

"Now, as you are probably aware, your baby was born here on the 22nd of February 1965 and has been in our care since." The Sister referred to the details in the file. "Her birth name was Mary which you are free to change and finally her mother was too young to keep her resulting in her family requesting us to take care of her adoption proceedings." She looked up from the file with an empty glance. "Do you have any questions?".

"No Sister, I don't think so" Joe looked at Lil with confidence that she agreed, which Lil nodded with her husband.

"Well in that case, Ruth, is that your name? You have lovely curls I must say" Ruth hugged into her mammy feeling shy. "Would you like to meet your new baby sister now?" All three smiled like a weight had been lifted from their shoulders.

The sister stood up "I won't be long, and I will be back with your baby" With a reassuring nod she closed the door behind her.

Lil grabbed Joe's hand with a tight squeeze, her eyes widened.

.

"Jeez Lil, I'm sweating here and it's not from the heat" Joe took out his hanker chief and wiped his forehead. "I know she was just doing her job, but I felt like I was back at school there"

"Joe, I am pinching myself here, is this really happening?" Lil's blue eyes beamed. "Oh I think I am going to cry, my heart is leaping in my chest, look…." She held out her hand to show her fingers shaking like a leaf.

"Mammy, is the baby coming now?" Ruth was still holding onto the gift bag for her sister. She had not let it go since leaving the house.

"Yes, Sweetheart, any moment now" Lil fixed Ruth's hair in place. "The nun will be back in a few moments with our new baby. Are you excited?" Ruth nodded, her eyes were in a daze.

The office door opened. "Here we are" Sr. Benedict entered the room holding a baby.

Lil, Joe and Ruth looked at the bundle wrapped in a white cotton blanket in the nun's arms. All Lil could see was her head of dark hair and the outline of her face.

The lump in Lil's chest gave way, her tears immediately began to flow and out came her sobs through her smile.

Joe's heart leapt in his chest. Being so tall he had the best view, he held Ruth's hand and did his very best to take in as much detail about his new baby daughter as he could. Her big brown eyes were wide open. She was looking around taking everything in and compared to Ruth she was so tiny. The probability of her having her sallow complexion was something that had not entered Joe's mind until now.

Lil took one step closer to the Sister and the nun held her baby out for her to hold. She took her daughter in her arms for the first time. Her eyes streamed with tears, holding her baby close, taking in every detail of her little face.

"She's beautiful" Lil tried her very best to speak "You are beautiful, aren't you? Yes, you are" She rocked her little bundle in her arms embracing this new beginning.

The baby was fully alert, responding to all the new sounds and new faces.

Lil bent down onto her hunkers to Ruth. "Ruth lovey, this is your new baby sister, isn't she lovely?"

"Ruth was feeling shy and a little overwhelmed. She was still holding the gift bag waiting to give it to her new baby sister.

The little wide-eyed baby reached out to Ruth and gently tugged her hair. The adults laughed at the initial bonding between the two siblings.

Ruth wasn't too sure to begin with, but in her own little mind saw that the baby was just curious and was quick to forgive. She took the teddy out of the bag and gave it to her new baby sister. Straight into her mouth it went as soon as she grabbed it with both hands.

After a few brief moments, the Sister showed them to the door, and they left St Patricks to begin their new life as a family of four.

There was huge excitement in the car on the way home. The baby 'ooohhed' and 'aaahhhed' and each time they all reacted with 'aaawwww'. The baby seemed to love this because she responded every time with a great big smile.

"Lil, I just thought of something?" Joe said with an air of urgency in his tone.

"What are we going to call her? Have you any ideas?"

Lil looked down at the beautiful child upon her lap and smiled knowingly.

"Saoirse, her name is Saoirse."

Lil could not take her eyes off her new baby girl. Saoirse was happy, placid and full of smiles. Unconditional love for her baby girl filled her heart. A new beginning had begun. She looked forward to the lifelong journey of joy that waited, with her new bundle of joy and becoming a family of four.

When they arrived home, Lil gave Saoirse the tour of their four-bed semi-detached home. She carried her baby girl in her arms introducing her to every room and explained what happens in each one.

That afternoon, Saoirse's new granny and grandad called to see their new granddaughter.

Lil's best friend Dolores also called along with her mother and her sister, Nora.

The table in the sitting room was covered with plates filled with fairy cakes, custard creams, bourbon creams and swiss rolls. Large pressure cookers sat on the hob, simmering with Lil's Irish stew. The kitchen counter was lined with apple tarts made by Lil's mother and the Victoria sponge cake was offered on side plates to anyone who walked in the door, along with a cup of tea. The kettle was constantly on, facilitating the continuous flow of neighbours from the road, who politely popped in to see the new baby. Everyone brought gifts from boxes of Maltesers and Irish Roses in the local shop to flowers, more homemade cakes and even more pots of Irish stew. They brought new frocks and even bags of hand me down girls' baby clothes.

There were two things everyone agreed on and was usually the first thing everyone said in one form or other when they met Saoirse. One was how beautiful she was, and the other was that she was surely an old soul. Lil and Joe both found this to be a strange thing to say at first, but after the fifth or sixth time, they figured that their well-wishing guests must be right.

After tea, the house went quiet. All the guests in the close-knit community who came to share the celebrations and pass on their congratulations had gone home, and the house emptied out. Lil's mum and best friend Dolores stayed behind to help clean up.

Lil thought of one neighbour who had not stopped by. It was the elderly lady who lived next door, Ms Cross. Lil and Joe always looked out for Ms Cross. Everyday Lil made her dinner, and on Saturdays, Joe brought her spuds and vegetables home from the vegetable market in Dun Laoghaire. They brought her The Evening Press newspaper each evening. Ms Cross exchanged the paper for The Evening Herald. Over the past year she had become part of Lil and Joe's life, and she idolised Ruth.

It was only when Lil saw the newspaper on the sitting room table that she thought of Ms Cross and wondered why she had not called to see Saoirse. She thought to herself that she would pop in and introduce Saoirse tomorrow morning and gave it no more thought.

Chapter 7

There are no other babies here. I am the only one.

So this is what they must have been talking about when they said that life is exciting. I don't ever remember being so tired, and I don't remember feeling this happy before. This crib is so cosy, but the new people call it 'your cot'. I am not in the place with the Sisters or the ladies anymore. I am in a new place. There is only one cot in my room and a big huge bed and only two windows, a big window and a small one too.

Earlier today, the Sister came and took me out of the room away from all the other babies. She carried me much differently to Maisie. I used to feel Maisie's gentleness. I felt her love. I didn't feel that from the Sister, she was empty and cold like she didn't care about me. It didn't hurt, but it was very different, and I wished Maisie was back.

It is a long time since I saw her. I really miss her.

The sister brought me into a room I had never been in before. It was far away from where the other babies were. It even had different smells and everything.

There were other people in that room too. I had never seen them before, but they looked really happy. The Sister held me differently in front of the happy people. It was like as if she cared. I knew it looked that way, but I did not feel that she cared, I don't know why.

She handed me to the lady. When she took me into her arms, it felt so good. In that moment I could feel her love. She was so happy. I could feel the love in her heart. It flowed more and more every moment. I looked at her face, and her eyes were filled with joy. She was so warm. Her voice was full of love.

Then she showed me to the small person and called her Ruth. She had lots of hair and I tried to say hello and tell her I liked her hair, and they all made this big loud sound that I have never heard before. It sounded really joyful. I don't know what it was or why they all made that sound at the same time. Just then, happiness filled up in my chest, and my mouth went wide. The lady said:

"Look at the big smile."

I don't know what that is but every time my mouth went wide, and I felt happy in my heart she said, look at that big smile.

I like this place. It's warm, and I don't feel hungry anymore. The lady who they call Lil gives me food, a lot. She tried to give me white stuff in a bottle, but I don't like it. When I taste it, I think of the Sisters and how nasty they were. I think of the ladies too and how heartbroken they were and how sad the room with all the babies was.

This new place is so happy and so different that I want to forget about the room with all the babies and I really want to forget about the Sisters too.

Instead of the white stuff, Lil gave me yellow food and called it custard. It was yummy, I really liked it and drank it all up, so she gave me more until my tummy was full.

There are a lot of people here too. They are all happy, and everyone says 'congratulations' to Lil and Joe, a lot. That is a big word, and I never heard it before today, I wonder what it means.

Everyone was looking at me with happy faces, and there was a lot of joy in everyone's eyes. I have never felt so much joy from so many people in my life.

I hope I can stay here. They say 'aaawwwwwe' a lot too.

Especially when I feel excited and happy, which has happened many times today.

Lil is looking after me most of the time. She gives me lots of clothes and food. She talks to me a lot. She is always asking questions and then answering them herself, followed by another question. She asks me am I hungry and then says:

'yes you are, aren't you?'

And then she asks me if she will change my bum?

'Have you a dirty nappy?' And then she says: 'yes you do, don't you?'

Then she gives me new clothes, and I feel so comfortable and warm.

I feel tired now. A lot of new things happened today, and it was all really nice. I feel so different, so happy. This is a happy place, full of love.

Chapter 8

Lil woke to the sound of traffic outside.

The sun had risen high in the summer sky.

She immediately knew they had all slept in.

She gasped with a million thoughts running through her head all in the one moment.

She thought of the baby, Saoirse, why didn't she cry, was she ok? A million thoughts of terror flew through her mind.

She turned to the cot to check Saoirse, terrified at what she might find. Saoirse was lying on her back, arms up either side of her head, her head was held slightly to the side, and the covers were in the very same position Lil had tucked them in last night. She had not budged, all night. Lil reached down to stroke her little face. Her rosy cheeks were warm and soft.

'Thanks be to God, my heart' Lil paused in gratitude.

Saoirse slowly opened her eyes and looked up at Lil. A big smile filled her face. The little bundle went into another big stretch, coming alive and wakening her body up, all the while continuing to smile.

Lil could hardly believe she had slept for so long. She had expected to be woken by Saoirse's cries for breakfast at around 6am. But Saoirse slept right through and so did everyone else.

"Oh hello my sweetie, you had a big day yesterday didn't you?" Lil lifted Saoirse out of the cot. "You must have been exhausted from all the excitement."

She sat Saoirse on her knee and wrapped a blanket around her back to keep the heat in. She glanced at the clock on the bedside table, 9:10am. Joe always leaves for work at 7:20am, but he was lying beside her fast asleep.

"Joe, it's ten past nine." She was careful to keep her voice calm and neutral, so as not to startle Saoirse.

Joe didn't budge in the bed. Only his lips moved when he responded

"I rang Graham on Saturday evening and told him I was taking the day off. He's opening up"

'Thank God for that' Lil thought aloud.

"The last time your daddy took a spontaneous day off was the day your sister was born" She held Saoirse on her lap and explained the history. "He never takes time off unexpected, no he doesn't" Saoirse smiled and aaahhhed at her mothers' story telling. "But are we complaining? No we're not!"

"And speaking of your big sister, I think I can hear her now" Lil's eyes widened glancing towards the bedroom door. Ruth was always up by now, usually because Joe popped in to give her a kiss goodbye just before he left for work.

"Mammy I'm hungry?"
A sleepy Ruth walked into Lil and Joe's bedroom, rubbing her eyes.
"I think we're all hungry Ruth and I think we all needed that rest too. It was such a big day yesterday, wasn't it?" Ruth climbed up into her mammy and daddy's bed and lay down beside Joe.
"Yeah" she pulled the covers over her, still half asleep.

Lil brought her two children downstairs and prepared breakfast for her new family. Ruth had porridge oats and toast with jam and a bottle of custard for Saoirse it was.
Lil thought she would clean up after breakfast, dress the kids and bring the new arrival next door to meet Ms Cross. Ms Cross was so fond of Ruth and was like a second grandmother to her. Lil was so excited to introduce her to Saoirse.

"Helloooooo?..... Ms Cross?"
Lil made her way in the back door to Ms Cross' kitchen after stepping through the gap in the railings adjoining their back gardens. Her back door was always open for Lil, Joe or Ruth to make their way in during the day. They also had a key to her house, in the event that they might need it.
Ruth ran ahead of her mother, through the house and into the front room where she knew she would find Ms Cross, usually reading the newspaper and watching the day go by from her front window.
"Aaahhhh hello my little Ruth....don't you look very pretty today? Ms Cross was an elderly woman, originally from Wicklow. A spin-

ster lady with long silver hair, always tied up in a bun at the nape of her neck. "And look at your new shoes, they are very smart." Ruth modelled her new shoes to Ms Cross feeling very proud. Then remembered:

"Ms Cross, I have a new baby sister! Her name is Saoirse"

Lil was standing at the door of the front living room, holding the future in her arms. But Ms Cross did not come to her. She was a well-rounded lady and was slow on her feet. Lil put it down to this and followed Ruth in. But her daughter was already in full flight and Ms Cross didn't turn to greet her.

"Well now isn't that a big surprise," Ms Cross' blue eyes widened, humouring the young child.

Ruth explained yesterday with detailed animation.

Lil stepped forward, toward Ms Cross, who was seated in her usual chair by the fireside.

There was only one armchair in the room and a small wooden chair that Ruth usually sat on during her long chats with the old lady about anything and everything. Otherwise, the room was sparsely furnished with an old heavy mahogany sideboard and a tall glass cabinet, filled with antiques and bone china, which she had already promised to Ruth when she goes. Although Ruth had no idea what she meant or where she was going.

"Hello Ms Cross" Lil took advantage of the pause in conversation between Ruth and Mrs. Cross, proudly holding Saoirse in her arms "this is Saoirse, our new daughter."

Ms Cross looked at the baby, over her spectacles, which sat on the bridge of her nose and nodded. She was holding a newspaper on her lap. Her hands had gone back to holding either side of the newspaper after hugging Ruth when she arrived. She glanced at the baby and turned her head down to the newspaper.

"You must be delighted with yourselves."

Lil ignored the tone of dismissal from Ms Cross.

She was far too happy and proud to entertain anything non-congruent with the magic of this time. Right now, she was flying high, and she was well familiar with the pain and grief that comes with the longing for a baby. She was going to embrace every moment. Nothing was going to stop her treasuring the deepest happiness and beautiful sense of joy that filled the air so tangibly right now.

She felt like this world had suddenly become a wonderful place. There was an atmosphere that surrounded her, and although it was something unseen, it was palpable. She could almost touch that love in the air over the last twenty-four hours. This was one of the good times. Those times where you feel God and his angels are that little bit closer and present with you, watching with loving satisfaction, as you enjoy the happiness you deserve.

This was one of those times in Lil's life, and nothing was going to bring her down off this natural high. It was an answered prayer, sent from God above.

To deflect, she asked Ruth to tell Ms Cross all about yesterday and the way she got to show her new baby sister off to everyone who came to see her. Ruth continued with excitement and related all the details about yesterday and included that she had lots of biscuits and cake.

Saoirse remained quiet initially, taking in her surroundings.

After a few moments, for the very first time in the last twenty-four hours, she began to cry. It was an uneasy cry at first, more of a whimper, and Lil rocked her with love to settle her. But in a very short time her cry gradually got worse until she seemed very upset and no amount of consoling and reassuring words from Lil would settle her.

Saoirse just wasn't hearing her.

Lil cuddled Saoirse close, and Ruth stroked her head in a caring effort to soothe her cries. Ms Cross gave no reaction and continued to read her newspaper, unmoved by Saoirse's upset.

Lil thought she might be hungry and explained to Ms Cross that she would take the children inside and feed Saoirse.

"Bye bye Ruth, come and see me later-on, won't you?" Ms Cross raised her voice louder than the baby's cries. She opened her arms to give Ruth her goodbye hug.

"I will Ms. Cross. I'll bring the papers in to you after my dinner" Ruth was delighted with the invite and yelled above Saoirse's upset. She hugged Ms. Cross goodbye before skipping out behind her mother and baby sister.

Lil sat at the kitchen table back home. She cuddled and rocked Saoirse. She had no idea why she was so upset and could only think that she might be hungry. Saoirse eventually settled somewhat but tears were still flowing down her little red cheeks. Her cries turned to a whimper and after a few moments she began to be show signs of her happy, placid self again. She looked at Lil who was smiling down at her and sharing consoling chatter.

Through the wet eyes and cheeks, dotted with a few residual tears, Saoirse gave Lil a big smile and snuggled her head into Lil's chest. A lot more settled now, she began to goo and gaa and make screechy little sounds. She was happy again.

Chapter 9

Over the next few weeks, the new family settled into their new routine with ease. Saoirse had a big appetite and was growing fast. She seemed to always be happy and bonded well with Lil. She always had lots of smiles for everyone who doted on her.

She was particularly fond of Lil's best friend Dolores, who lived around the corner. Lil and Dolores had been the best of friends since childhood. People often said that once you see one, you knew the other was not too far behind. Dolores had the most beautiful head of dark brown hair which she wore in a flawless beehive every day, and it was envied by many. A lady who knew her fashion, she had a gifted eye for colour and coordination and was always on trend with the latest styles. So much so that Joe hired her part time in the shop to dress the mannequins. A widow for the last six years after her husband died in a fatal road traffic accident, she was a friendly, chatty lady who was glad of the social interaction and the few pound.

Lil popped in each morning on her way home from the local shop for the bread, milk and sliced ham. Dolores always gave Saoirse lots of attention. She sat Saoirse on her knee and engaged in full blown conversation with the baby. Saoirse's responded full of smiles, giggles and awe. She was fascinated by Dolores' hair. Lil was always nervous that one of these days she was going to succeed in pulling that perfect beehive apart while sitting on Dolores' knee, but Dolores never seemed to mind, she was smitten with Saoirse and gave her all the time in the world.

Lil's mother, known to everyone but Lil as Granny, had her own mind and her own spot on the family sofa, called in most days to see Ruth and now her second grandchild. She was a tiny lady with a big heart that Lil had inherited. She and Lil's dad, a tall, quiet man who usually left all the talking to his wife had six children, four sons and two daughters. Lil's sister, Bernie lived in England with her husband and four children. Lil was the youngest and her mother was a big part of her life. She often wondered how she would cope without her.

Granny babysat the children when Lil and Joe went for a social drink in the local pub at the weekends.

She was strict but kind. She never let the girls away with anything, and the same rules went for all the grandchildren. She was firm but fair, and if she got angry, it never lasted long.

Saoirse grew up in a housing estate called Ashlawn in Glenageary, a suburban area of Southside Dublin

Prior to the 1960's the area was a landscape of fields adjacent to the thriving portal town of Dun Laoghaire. In the early 1960's Dublin's population was growing fast, and land was sold for residential development to accommodate the next generation of families across Dublin town.

Lil and Joe were living in Lil's parent's house since they were married in 1955. When the properties went for sale Lil and Joe applied immediately to purchase one. They couldn't believe their luck feeling like the opportunity could not have come at a better time.

The new houses were large three and four bed semi-detached. There was a garage to the side and Lil foresaw many a happy summers day, enjoying her children playing in the large back garden.

They were just down the road from both sets of parents and the family business, plus it meant that they could settle into their new life among all of their lifelong friends.

In summer 1964 they moved into their new home. For the first few weeks after moving in Joe often came home to find Lil daydreaming out the kitchen window. Each time she turned to him and shared how blessed she felt that they got so lucky. She loved her new home and ran a tight ship right from the start. Through her gratitude to God she had one more prayer: that he would bestow one more child for them to love and complete their family.

Every time she looked at Saoirse she reminded herself of that prayer back in the early days and silently thanked God for the deliverance.

During the first few years of Saoirse's life Ashlawn grew into a well desired affluent area, on the outskirts of Dublin. It was a close, friendly community where everyone knew everyone by their first name. Neighbours looked out for one another. Help and support was always a door knock away, and a friendly hello and chat among neighbours at the garden gate was a familiar scene.

Saoirse was finding her feet too. Summer mornings were spent playing with her soft teddies and plastic tea set in the front garden. She had her own blue and white check blanket that Lil laid down on the grass and there she occupied herself for hours.

Sometimes Ruth joined in, but she was six now and allowed to go as far as the end of the block on her bike, once she stayed on the footpath, so Ruth was enjoying her new sense of freedom outside the garden gate.

The cooler months were spent inside, Ruth and Saoirse loved playing hide and seek, but it never lasted long. Saoirse was still too young to get the concept of having to hide while Ruth counted. Instead she stood wearing a giddy smile in the middle of the sitting room floor while Ruth covered her eyes on the couch and counted. Ruth's patients never lasted long.

One Tuesday night in Spring, when the evenings were beginning to take their daylight stretch Lil came home from bingo with a doll. She decided to give her prize to Saoirse. It was a few days after Saoirse's second birthday, and Lil thought it would be a nice additional birthday gift.

Granny had just got the girls ready for bed when Lil arrived home. Saoirse's was sitting on the couch in her new nighty, dressing gown and slippers that she got for her birthday.

"Mammy!" A sleepy little girl smiled welcoming her mother home.

"Are you not in bed yet, you little monkey?" Lil tickled her belly and kissed her forehead "Well I am glad because I have a present for you sweetheart" Lil reached into the white paper bag and took out the doll. She held it in front of Saoirse, with an anticipating smile.

Saoirse eyes fixed on the doll. Her face lit up with her eyes wide. She took the doll and held it in front of her taking in every detail. Her little fingertips stroked the dolls thick shoulder length brown hair, it was just like Saoirse's hair. She had big brown eyes and the longest eyelashes she had ever seen, and she wore a beautiful knitted pink dress and hand knit pink cardigan. She had little pink hand knit boots that tied with a bow. Saoirse did not make a sound, she continued to stare at the doll. The doll smiled warmly back at her.

Saoirse took the doll to her chest, closed her eyes and cuddled her new toy. Her young face filled with a smile of fulfilment and content-ment. She fell in love with her new doll immediately.

"What will we call her?" asked Lil, delighted with Saoirse's obvi-ous approval.

"Maymie," Saoirse quietly replied, cradling the doll in her arms.

"Mammy?" Lil asked.

"Maymie," stressed Saoirse.

From that day on, Maymie went everywhere with Saoirse. She al-ways made sure Maymie was within arm's length. She brought her for walks around the house in Maymie's small pram. Maymie sat be-side her when she ate her meals. She slept in Saoirse's bed every night without fail. She even accompanied Saoirse to the sleepovers in Granny and Granddad's, because Lil and Joe were heading to their annual Dinner Dance.

As the months went by and Saoirse's speech developed and be-came more fluent, Maymie's name transitioned to 'Maisie' and Maisie never left the child's side.

Chapter 10

One of Saoirse's favourite games was to play with her colourful toy pots in the front garden. Lil closed the front garden gate and Saoirse entertained herself and 'Mr & Mrs Pots' along with the little pots, also known as 'the children' for hours. Lil left the hall door open allowing Saoirse to be within earshot and Saoirse could come in and out when she needed to. There were four pots in total, one green, one yellow, one blue and a red one. Each plastic pot was a different size, and they all had big smiley faces on the front.

They all had their own individual personalities too, hours passed while her imagination ran wild, creating a life for the toy pots.

Every day Mr Ryan, an elderly man from down the road, passed by on his way to the local shops. No matter what the season Mr Ryan always wore a knee length tweed coat and tweed cap. He never failed to stop and to have a chat with Saoirse on his way to run his errands. He was a gentle friendly man who always took time to inquire about the latest news in The Pot family. Saoirse loved his genuine interest and explained the updates in great detail.

He was a kind and sincere gentleman and always had time for Saoirse and her news. He was married to Mrs Ryan, a quiet, soft-spoken lady, with a graceful demeanour. Saoirse always felt that she was such a kind lady. She felt the strength in her gentleness and often thought to herself that, when she was old, like Mrs. Ryan, she wanted to be just like her.

Chapter 11

"What? You mean I can actually go to Aunty Una's and Uncle Richards for a sleepover?" Ruth sat on the couch in the living room, Lil and Joe sat either side. She was about to burst. She had been begging Lil and Joe to allow her a sleepover in Joe's sisters house for as long as she could remember.

"Well you're ten now Ruth and me and daddy were talking and decided to take the chance" Lil explained. They were biding their time until she got a little older. Both Lil and Joe agreed that the fear of landing their in laws with a young girl crying to go home at three in the morning was not a chance worth taking. But lately they figured she was ready.

"Oh Mammy and Daddy, you are the best. Thank you" Ruth threw her arms around her parents, and repeatedly kissed both their cheeks. She was mad about her aunt and uncle and often joked that they were her favourite aunt and uncle on her daddy's side of the family. Una was Joe's only sibling.

So that Saturday night off she went with her overnight bag to stay in their home across town in Terenure for her first ever sleep-over in anyone else's house apart from Granny and Grandad.

As always, that time of evening came to bring the newspapers into Ms Cross. It was the first time Ruth was not around to bring in the newspapers. Usually, the routine was that both girls went into Ms Cross together. They both hopped over the back-garden railings. Ruth went first, and Saoirse followed. Ms Cross always made the biggest fuss, doting on the children.

Due to Ruth's absence this particular evening, Lil asked Saoirse if she wanted to bring the evening newspapers into Mrs Cross on her own. Saoirse agreed and happily made her way in to Ms Cross' home.

On her way, the six-year-old child anticipated the conversation she was going to have with Ms Cross. Ruth was always around to initiate conversation and usually answer on Saoirse's behalf too. But this time it was only Saoirse and Ms Cross. Thoughts played in her mind the possible subject of conversation. She practiced the conversation in her mind, explaining that Ruth had gone for her first ever sleepover and talk about her Aunt and Uncle and that Mammy and Daddy said that she could go on a sleepover too when she was older, but Ruth was ten now and she was only six, so she had to wait until she was a little bit older, like Ruth. The conversation played out in her mind and her little heart raced thinking of the debut one to one with the old lady.

She made her way through the empty kitchen and the adjoining dining room which led into the dim-lit hall. The front parlour was on the right, where she trusted to find Ms Cross.

As she walked through the house on this particular evening she noticed the silence for the first time. Every night for the last few years she had ran through Ms. Cross' house right behind Ruth and never noticed how quiet it was, until now. She assumed it was because Ruth was not with her this time and dismissed the persistent uneasy feeling in her belly.

The short walk seemed to take forever, and time even seemed to slow down. For a brief moment, she thought that Ms Cross might be asleep, hence the quietness. No sooner had the thought entered her mind, she was standing in the doorway in the front parlour, to find Ms, Cross with her head down engrossed in a book. She noticed the Evening Herald on the table just inside the door. Saoirse figured Ms Cross must have been expecting her and left it there for her to bring into her parents.

"Hi, Ms Cross, here are your newspapers," she said cheerfully because she knew what was coming next - Ms Cross' big fuss.

She always gave Ruth a big hug every evening when she arrived and now it was her turn. She took a deep breath and braced herself.

"Thank you." There was a cold tone in Ms Cross' response. Her eyes never left the book she was reading, and she never lifted her head.

She remained in the same position, in her chair by the fireside of that dim lit room and the cold words of shallow gratitude were as far as she went to acknowledge the six-year-old girl in her front room.

Saoirse could feel each thump of her heart in her chest. She wondered where the fuss had gone. The young child stood in the silence, waiting for the familiar bravado that was part of the evening routine.

Ms. Cross continued to read her book.

She thought for a moment that Ms Cross forgot to make the fuss. Her eyes scanned the room. Her body wanted to run back home, but her feet stayed frozen on the floor. She didn't want to be rude and just run home and figured that maybe any moment now Ms Cross will remember, and everything would fall back into place.

Those long few moments, standing in the doorway, in the silence, with no reaction from Ms Cross, helped her realise that there was not going to be any fuss made this evening. She gradually realised, over the following moments that she was standing in the company of an old woman, who was choosing to ignore her.

Saoirse thought that maybe the book she was reading must be very interesting but deep down she knew, the old woman was acting as if Saoirse wasn't even there.

The doorway to Ms Cross' living room had become the state in between the normal and the now, between the expectancy of hugs with a ritual welcome fuss and the realisation that Ms Cross' was not going to make a warm fuss this evening.

She stood there for endless moments, until she felt too awkward to stay there any longer. Filled with a sense of just wanting to return back home, to belonging, she stepped back into the hallway and ran back home.

Saoirse climbed through the railings into her backyard, feeling a very strange and different feeling.

She wondered why Ms Cross behaved the way she did. At the same time, she knew it was because Ruth had not accompanied her this time. Yet she was aware of the isolating sense that nagged her mind. It was a sense that told her it was personal. The strange feeling told her that there was something far greater going on. She had not noticed or felt it prior to this evening and she began to realise that she was not ever going to be Ms Cross favourite person.

"Well, how did you get on lovey? What did Ms Cross say?" Lil asked with a big expectant smile.

"Fine." replied the child making her way through the kitchen. Lil was at the sink doing the dishes from dinner. She sat down on the couch beside her daddy, who was watching the evening news. He put his arm around her, and she snuggled up to him, feeling the security of home and belonging. She watched the TV with an absent gaze, allowing the news of world events go over her head.

The following evening Ruth was going into Ms Cross with the newspapers. Lil asked Saoirse if she wanted to go, but Saoirse declined, and Ruth went on ahead.

"Ah go on in and say hello to Ms Cross, love. She loves seeing you two coming in and keeping her company," Lil attempted to persuade her daughter to keep the daily routine.

"I'll go in tomorrow Mammy. I'm just doing Maisie's hair."

"Ah love, go on in, just for a minute, bring Maisie in with you and show her to Ms Cross."

The child reluctantly obeyed her mother.

She had put last night's incident to the back of her mind, and the last thing she wanted to do was go into Ms Cross to be ignored again. She was now aware that it was always Ruth that was fussed over. Saoirse had always been present but ignored.

She had always known that Ruth was Ms Cross' favourite but had never felt ignored. Yesterday's experience enabled her to see that the volume of attention shed on Ruth, was what blinded her from seeing the real dynamic.

Appeasing her mother, she made her way into the old lady's house. She walked through the hallway, feeling a little nervous and unwelcome.

She could hear Ms Cross talking in a serious tone to Ruth. It was a tone in which she had never heard her speak to Ruth before.

"Why do you always say that Ms Cross. She is my little sister?" Ruth asked in a curious tone.

"I'm telling you, Ruth, she's a nothing, a nobody, don't ever have anything to do with her Ruth, I'm telling you."

"But why is she a nobody?"

"Because she's adopted and adopted people are nobodies. She's a nothing. Take my advice, Ruth. I've been telling you for years. Have nothing to do with her. You are better than that. You always were, you know that. An illegitimate child is what she is; she's nothing." Saoirse could hear the hate and disgust in Ms. Cross' tone. She knew Ms Cross meant every word she snapped at Ruth. She stood in the hallway her heart began to race and her blood ran cold.

"But Mammy and Daddy love Saoirse?" Ruth pleaded for Ms. Cross' understanding.

"I'm warning you, Ruth. If you have anything to do with her, no one will want to know you in life. She is nothing. Ignore her and have nothing to do with her."

The conviction in the old woman's tone left the innocent child feeling alone and isolated in the hallway. She searched her mind to understand why Ms Cross was saying such horrid things about her to her big sister. Why? And what did she do wrong?

But in those moments she felt something fall away and leave her. In its place was an ugly, hallow, emptiness.

She felt less important than she felt moments before. She felt less than good enough. Less worthy than everyone else and less entitled to love.

An unfamiliar sense of guilt flowed into her heart, and she began to feel very different and very sad.

Ms Cross was Saoirse's first introduction to vessels of judgement. The judgement stemmed from unnecessary, untrue, suppressing belief systems. The systemic beliefs were posed in the false representation of religion. This was cast through society, one generation after the other. It was an on-going poison that spewed into the minds of society. Those acting in the name of God maintained authority and control of society through the infliction of fear. It was a fear of a god, and a threat of punishment imposed on those who did not buy into their lies.

It destroyed the beauty and power of innocence. Ms Cross was an angry and bitter woman who bought into the systemic lie and allowed it to blind her view of truth. She had done so for so long, that both truth and hope disappeared from her perspective completely. All that remained was an empty shell of a woman, filled with anger, judgement and resentment. Bitter and negative to the core, she had become a vessel for the systemic poison, and it was only the truly strong who held the antidote to her poisonous words.

Joe and Lil had always explained to Saoirse that she was adopted and did so in a compassionate and loving way.

They explained that her mammy was very young, and she had a lot of pains. Therefore, she had to give Saoirse to a new mammy and daddy who would love her, just like she would have wanted. And then mammy and daddy came along with Ruth. They told her how they went into the nun's place where Saoirse was with all the other babies.

They explained that Ruth got to choose which baby they brought home and out of all the babies in the room, Ruth chose Saoirse. They then brought her home and loved her from the moment they met her. She never felt rejected by her birth mother. She was fully aware that her birth mother acted with Saoirse's best interests at heart and she certainly didn't feel that there was anything wrong with being adopted or adopted people. Lil and Joe had made sure of that, until now.

Overhearing Ms Cross insisting the deeply cruel message to Ruth hurt her deep inside and part of her knew that something inside her died. She had lost something precious, and she knew she would never get it back. The innocent six-year-old turned on her heel, feeling sad, confused and numb and ran back home once again.

She asked her mammy why Ms Cross would say such horrible things to Ruth. Her mother assured her that Ms Cross was old and old people are like that. It didn't cut it for Saoirse. Her mother's words did nothing to ease the pain in her heart. There was a sense of emptiness in her mind, other than the confusion and sense of loss and sadness that filled her head.

She went to bed that night and hugged Maisie close. She felt loved by her parents, and that was a consolation, but Ms Cross' words haunted her mind. She couldn't understand why she would communicate such a cruel message to Ruth, and she wondered why Ms Cross thought that way and was it true? Was she 'a nobody' and a nothing? She wondered if this was something that everyone knew, and no-one had told her. She feared that the poisonous, destructive lie was the truth and it left her feeling that she was less important than everyone else and her beautiful innocent mind wondered why. She wondered what she had done wrong and fell asleep searching for the answers to that same question.

The next morning, she made one of the first conscious decisions of her life. She decided that she wasn't going to go to Ms Cross' house anymore.

Chapter 12

As Saoirse grew, her childhood was spent playing with the other kids from the surrounding housing estates. The large green adjacent to her road, where all the children from the three surrounding housing estates gathered during bright Spring evenings and long Summer days. Football, Rounders, and Bulldogs Charge were common play in the field.

Closer to home, outside their house, it was relay racing from the wall to the first lamppost. There were often rows and strops over who won and who cheated. But the children's sulks never lasted long. There was no doubt one guaranteed voice of reason among the crowd to come up with a solution or sort the problem. Plus, there was too much fun to be had to allow any hostility to prevail.

Joe's strict curfew was set in stone for the girls. They had to come inside once the street lights came on. The instruction was never usually obeyed, because they were often in the middle of a game when that happened, resulting in Joe standing on the doorstep and whistling. That was their signal to make their way home fast, or else!

Despite Saoirse catching Ms Cross's silhouette behind the curtain whilst playing outside with her friends, her days were spent happily learning everything from team work to leadership, winning and losing, cooperation and standing ground, all through the laughter that came with the play.

However, the ghostly sense of being different always murmured deep down.

She had a strong bond with Lil. There was an ever-present, deep fear anytime Lil and Joe left the house. The persistent worry that they might not return. Despite her fear never being validated, it never dissolved to make room for the trust that all was safe and well. However, she kept her anxieties hidden and to herself.

Every Sunday night Lil and Joe went up to the local pub to meet with friends over a few social drinks. Like clockwork they returned home around eleven thirty. Each Sunday night Granny stuck to the same routine, it was storey time and then bedtime, just before the nine-o clock news.

Saoirse was to be found awake, far past bedtime, sitting in darkness in her parents' bedroom. She sat on the little stool under the window, peering as far up the road as she could see, until she saw her parents coming home. The more minutes that passed on the alarm clock on Joe's bedside table, the more worried Saoirse became. She eventually caught sight of Lil linking Joe's arm, walking down the road upon their return. Saoirse immediately ran into bed so as not to be caught up so late and lay down to sleep with peace of mind, feeling safe in the relief of her uncontrollable, irrational fear.

As time passed her relationship with Ruth became typical with sibling squabbles. Both children were deeply loved by Lil and Joe and playing referee to the two girls became a daily occurrence.

There was also another dimension to Saoirse's childhood, these were experiences that she kept to herself.

She had a fantastic imagination and was well able to entertain herself in play. Her routine was to sit in the middle of the living room floor, with Maisie sat by her side she played with her toys and time disappeared. Her other dolls and teddies were welcome in the typical game of the day. They all shared the same wardrobe and quite often her brown teddy with a permanent dickie bow was dressed in a bright pink dress, laced with frills and matching hat. The game varied from 'house' to 'doctors' to 'mammies and daddies'. Each teddy or doll adopted his or her very own personality and Saoirse guided their roles line by line. She could play for hours in an imaginary dimension.

She sat on the living room floor, her toys laid out in front of her knowing that she was not alone:

"Why do girls wear dresses and boys wear trousers?" she asked her team of magnificent loving teachers surrounding her, ever ready to help and guide the child.

"Because that's just what they do in your world Saoirse" The grand loving being explained the ways of the world to Saoirse. "They say that girls are supposed to be pretty and sweet and boys are brave and strong" He was her main teacher from realms beyond the physical. The loving spirit being knelt by her side radiating the most beautiful golden light. His long brown hair was bone straight to his shoulders and the chest of his white robe was the resting place for the abundant ruby and gold jewels around his neck.

The rest of her spirit helpers radiated in the back ground, each one ready to assist where needs be.

"But I can be brave and strong, and my mammy says I am pretty too?" She held her dolly in one hand and teddy in the other, glancing back and forth to each.

"Yes, you are Saoirse. Both girls and boys are strong and brave. But in your world, they need to understand them to be different" His communication always opened Saoirse's understanding of the three-dimensional world and helped her remember what she already knew. "But why?" She looked up to her wise teacher and searched the wisdom in his eyes for conclusion. Even though he was kneeling on the floor beside her, his presence towered over her and was three times her width.

"Because humans think they are doing the right thing" His gentle tone explained the introduction to the reality in which she lived.

"But who tells them it's the right thing to do?"

"They tell each other" His wise, knowing smile shone down on Saoirse. The confidence in his eyes reminded her not to forget the knowing that came with remembering the bigger picture.

"Well that's silly. I am going to be brave and strong too and I'm not a boy" She concluded.

"You already are brave and strong Saoirse"

"The other day John Reilly was crying in school because he fell in the yard and hurt his knee. It was bleeding and everything, but Miss Kelly kept telling him that big boys don't cry. But why did she say that? His leg was really hurting, and he had to cry, he couldn't help it"

"You see, you already understand. Just because the grown-ups say something it doesn't always make it right. Always listen to that little voice in your heart Saoirse"

"You mean the one that I can't hear but I do hear?" She smiled, recalling the teaching from a previous lesson.

"That's the one."

She knew her friends were invisible in the eyes of anyone else, but she could see them as clear as day. They were beings, teachers from another place. The beings took on a human shape, but they were a lot taller and broader in stature and were of a different time than the 1960s/70s Ireland. Saoirse knew there were always two to three beings surrounding her. Another aspect that made them different to a typical human being was the beautiful light they radiated. The colour of the light changed and varied frequently from golden to purple to white, but it was always there and always reminded her of who she was and where she came from.

From time to time there was also a lovely lady present, more similar to human beings in stature and proportion. She had the kindest eyes and just like the beings from another place, she too emanated pure love. Although her presence was occasional, the magnificent masculine beings were always there.

Their presence was warm and familiar, and they tended to her with a strong sense of pure unconditional love. She asked them questions, and they answered in a way that she came to an understanding of her query, how the world in which she lived functioned and a remembrance of who she was. They had endless patients too, regardless of the volume of questions the curious child had.

Even though she knew that no-one else could see them, she never questioned why. Nor did she question why they disappeared from her view when Lil, Joe or Ruth walked into the room.

Saoirse just knew and accepted that that was the way it was in her world. But some-how she completely understood that just because she couldn't see them anymore, she knew they had not gone away.

She also knew that these loving beings came from the same place that she came from and everyone else comes from. They came from Heaven, and it was not until years later in adulthood, she would come to realise that these beautiful, loving teachers were in fact known as her Spirit Guides. For now, they were her teachers that gave her trusted guidance with the purest, deepest unconditional love.

The nature of the questions she asked was usually to do with the game she was playing at the time. Their responses to her aired on the side of insight.

Each time she spoke with her loving teachers she felt restored with clarity, strength and the courage to continue to hold the balance between the magical, mystical world of the unseen and the grounded structure of the three-dimensional world that was dictated by human beings.

Saoirse took on board their wise and loving counsel every-time. As a result, she was a kind, caring and empathic child. She was sensitive to others and had an intuitive nature to bring happiness and peace to wherever, or whomever it waned. Her nature was one of love and compassion, seated in the depths of her heart, regardless of who was able to recognise her strength and who failed to.

One dark winter's evening Joe arrived home from work. Saoirse could not wait for her daddy to come home this particular evening because Lil had bought her a new dress and she was looking forward to showing it off to her daddy. It was pale blue cotton with short sleeves and when she did a twirl the dress spun out further than any other dress she had. She admired herself in Lil's full-length bedroom mirror, twirling around until her head spun.

She heard Joe's car pull up outside and the car lights shone in the bedroom window. She ran down the stairs to greet her daddy arriving in the door.

"Lil, we have a new girl in the house! Who's that lovely girl?" Joe called, humouring Saoirse modelling her new dress in the hall.

She couldn't help to notice despite her daddy's cheerful demeanour, he was worried. She saw the worry on his face behind his smile. Her daddy was a giant in her eyes, even when he was sitting down. She thought he could do anything. But tonight, he looked sad and she wondered why.

"Are you ok Daddy?" She accompanied Joe at the kitchen table when he was having his dinner.

"Sure I am. Don't you worry your little head about me" He reassured tucking into his cabbage, mashed potato and bacon.

Saoirse didn't believe him. The look in his eyes told a different story to the words from his mouth. Lil told her to go inside and watch some TV before bed time.

"I don't know Lil, it's getting worse. Two cheques bounced today, and sales are lower than they have been since I took over the shop" Joe's uncharacteristic disempowerment was more worrying to Lil than the shop not doing well.

"Joe, look it. It will be fine, it's a quiet time of year, everyone is smashed after the kids going back to school and keeping the few pound they have for Christmas"

The weariness Saoirse noticed on her Daddy's face was something she had seen in other adults too. She often wondered why everyone was so stressed and why they were so worried over nothing.

She recognised that the adults had problems and concerns but what are they so worried about when we are, who we are?

She saw people as visitors from another place, a powerful place and the same infinite power that comes from that place was always part of us.

Saoirse didn't see the human race in the same way as the rest of her world. She did not see individuals, limited in time and space. She knew that who we truly are went far beyond the limitation of the physical body we inhabit.

She saw this place called earth as a temporary home.

She also understood that we are never alone and there is infinite help from this same source available to us whenever we need it. For her, that help came in the form of her teachers, that accompanied her during playtime.

She knew that everyone is always connected to this infinite Source and to each other.

She knew that this same Source is what created us. Its Power lived and flowed through everyone. It was pure love.

She knew that there was always a way, no matter what. Because we are who we are, and with the powerful help that's available to us there is no obstacle that cannot be overcome or problem that cannot be solved.

Her mammy and daddy came into the living room after dinner and Joe turned on the RTE evening news and stood in front of the fire to warm up.

Saoirse was tired and chilling on the couch. She observed the anguish in his face, although he tried to keep it well hidden. Beyond his anguish she saw his truth. It was visible to her as was Lil's and Ruth's. She watched the light in the room surround, fill and emanate through the whole of Joe's body and stretch beyond, out into the room. Joe's light connected with Lil's light, Ruth's and her own. She knew they were all part of the same oneness. She knew they all came from somewhere beyond this physical realm and there was so much more to each of them that went beyond the physical body. She also knew, that they had forgotten. Hence their worry. They had forgotten their power.

In that power she knew there was no need for fear, sadness, worry, pain, judgment, resentment or hurt. All these feelings came from the real nothing, as opposed to the type of 'nothing' Ms Cross had labelled her with.

But the young child was beginning to realise that there were not many like her and what she knew naturally was not common knowledge. She put it down to everyone being different, and this was one of the ways in which she was different.

Just like she never spoke of her spirit beings and their help, she never spoke of what she knew to be true, that all humans are really powerful beings from another place and that we hold much more ability within us than we realise. The truth that the humans she had met in her young life had forgotten.

When Saoirse was eight years old, she had a lucid dream.

"I have to go now Saoirse. I came to say goodbye..." the friendly voice awakened Saoirse in her dream.

She looked at the man standing in front of her. She felt herself rushing to wake up and focus on what was happening. Even in her lucid sleep state, she knew that this encounter was important and would not last long. She also knew that it was the dead of night and everyone was fast asleep in her home.

Standing before her was Mr Ryan from down the road. She was always fond of Mr Ryan. He never failed to express an interest in Saoirse's childhood game with Mr and Mrs Pots.

She looked at the man, aware that she was still dreaming. He stood before her, with warmth in his eyes and a peaceful smile. She knew he was at the beginning of a new journey, one that was not for this three-dimensional earth plane.

He was surrounded by a beautiful white light, which seemed to continue forever behind him until she couldn't see it anymore. Surrounding the exterior of the white light was just darkness, nothing, it was completely black.

Mr Ryan appeared to be floating at the mouth of the white light, and Saoirse felt grateful for his thoughtfulness not to pass her by. Mr Ryan was true to his nature in life right to the end. This was the last chat they would ever have together, in both of their lifetimes.

"Ah, you're awake now love…" The mild-mannered man smiled, surrounded in the most beautiful peaceful light. Saoirse could not make out his feet due to the glow of bright light surrounding them "I have to leave Saoirse, you won't be seeing me anymore…"

Saoirse knew their conversation would not last long, In the same way as she knew the light that surrounded him was waiting for him to take him to someplace else.

"Ok Mr Ryan, thank you for coming to say Goodbye" Saoirse waved and whispered softly filled with a combination of gratitude and sadness to the neighbour who had become her friend. "I'll miss you and our chats"

"Look after yourself love, and thanks for the chats" His eyes were filled with a deep sense of unspoken peace.

"It looks like you are going to a really lovely place" She whispered with a smile.

"It feels that way love, it's my time. Take care Saoirse and God Bless" With a warm smile, he went out of sight, into the tunnel of radiance, and he was gone.

The following morning was an overcast Saturday morning in Dublin. Saoirse woke with the replay of her dream in her mind. She could still hear Mr Ryan and see him floating in the brilliant light in her mind's eye. She felt sadness that he had left this world and that she would never see him again, although she found a deep sense of peace and honour that he came to her to say goodbye. His visitation to the child upon leaving said that the beautiful man really had a genuine fondness for her.

Walking downstairs she could hear the TV and then she saw her father was sitting in the living room, reading the newspaper. Lil was in the kitchen peeling the vegetables for the traditional Saturday coddle.

She joined her mother in the kitchen and took a cereal bowl out of the cupboard and prepared her own breakfast. Saturday was the only morning that she helped herself to breakfast. Lil was always one step ahead on weekday mornings ensuring the morning went like clockwork and the girls arrived in good time for school.

Saoirse stood beside her at the kitchen sink:

"Mammy, I feel a bit sad, Mr Ryan died last night" still contemplating his visit in her mind while filling her cereal bowl. "But he's ok. He's happy, he's gone to Holy God in heaven" Her mammy only knew Mr Ryan to say hello to, so she knew it wouldn't upset her too much.

Her mother stopped what she was doing. She put the half-peeled vegetables on the kitchen sink and turned to the child with hostility and almost anger. She snapped at her daughter:

"How do you know that?" Lil looked stiff and shocked. Her hand was on her hip and she had that look that usually meant if Saoirse gave the wrong answer she would be sent to her room for sure.

Saoirse chose the honest response:

"He came to me in a dream last night and said goodbye."

Her mother did not respond. Nor did she ask for any further detail. Saoirse had a sense that her mother didn't believe her. She wondered why, and she also wondered why the conversation ended so abruptly.

"Joe, I'm going up to get bread and milk, I'll be back shortly." Lil had her coat on, and her purse clutched in her hand.

Saoirse looked at the half-prepped vegetables on the draining board and wondered why her mother had abandoned her task so quickly.

Lil never left a mess, or a job half done.

Saoirse worried that she had said something wrong. She analysed the conversation she had with her mother moments before and could only find honesty in what she had said.

About an hour later her mother returned. She hung up her coat in the hall and went into Joe who was just finishing up the crossword in the newspaper:

"Hiya love, what's up?" Joe's eyes stayed on the crossword, marking his clues off.

Saoirse was watching the end of her favourite show The Wombles of Wimbledon. Her mother looked slightly paler than her usual rosy completion.

"Mr Ryan died last night Joe" She sat beside Joe on the edge of the couch "He passed away in his sleep. Mrs Ryan is beside herself with shock"

"My God that's terrible" Joe empathised "Poor Mrs Ryan"

"He was only sixty-six Joe, a massive stroke is what their saying. It's terrible sad, such a lovely man. Everyone's shocked by the news, they were all talking about it in Doyle's grocers this morning" Lil stared at the floor recounting the morning to her husband "Nora was in first thing and told Mrs Doyle."

Saoirse remained quiet and thought against questioning why Lil accepted the news from the neighbours at the local shop and gave no reference to her visitation from Mr Ryan in her dream. She intuitively knew not to say anything. However, she failed to understand why.

"Suppose when your number's up and all that Lil. Only two things we're sure of in this life, death and taxes" Joe folded his newspaper and left it on the coffee table for Ms Cross later that evening.

"Ah for God's sake Joe, the man's not even cold, would you stop" Lil dismissed. "Anyway, I may go and finish the vegetables. No doubt he's gone to a better place for sure" She walked through the dining room into the kitchen passing Saoirse on the way.

Saoirse looked to her mother for eye contact, but Lil did not reciprocate.

Lil never mentioned Saoirse's dream to Saoirse or anyone again.

Every Saturday evening the Corcoran family visited Joe's childhood friend, Mr Bennett and his wife, Sally. They lived a short drive from Saoirse's home in Sandymount.

They had no children. Saoirse and Ruth loved visiting the Bennett house. Sally never failed to have a press full of goodies for Saoirse and Ruth. All the girls had to do was finish their tea, which was easy because every week it was sliced ham and corn-beef with a chunk of fresh Vienna roll. The table was also laid with lettuce, tomato, beetroot, pickles and other salad options, but the girls were exempt from having to eat that food.

From the time the family arrived the house was immediately full of chat. Lil and Sally made the tea and caught up on each-others week in the kitchen. Mr Bennett and Joe chatted about the week's news. Mr Bennett was a man who loved his rugby, football and GAA. Sport had never been something that grasped Joe's interest, but Mr Bennett was the only man that he conversed with about sport.

After tea, everyone followed the same routine. They all made their way into the living room to watch Saturday evening TV. Sally filled the coffee table in the centre of the room with more pots of tea, cakes and biscuits.

But Mr Bennett never joined them. He held back and stayed in the kitchen. The reason why, was because he wanted to catch the match on his little transistor radio. The reason everyone went into the living room was that he wasn't able to hear the match over all of the chat among everyone else.

One week, Saoirse went back into the kitchen to get herself a drink. She saw Mr Bennett sitting at the kitchen table on his own beside the radio. She felt it sad that he was here all on his own, thinking he most probably feels left out. Being the caring young girl she was, she thought she would keep him company and stay and chat with Mr Bennett. During all the visits to their home in the past, she had never really chatted with the man. Other than greeting each other upon arrival and saying goodbye when leaving, there had not been much conversation between the man and young girl in between.

Rather than fetch her drink and run back into the sitting room where all the goodies and chat were, something inside felt it right to sit with Mr Bennett and chat with him. She felt it wrong that he was left out and didn't think it was right to just leave the room and Mr Bennett on his own.

The young girl took initiative and popped herself down on the spare chair beside the kitchen door and began to make small talk with Mr Bennett. He was cutting himself a slice of Vienna roll, so she started there.

"That's really nice isn't it?" She piped up, swinging her legs and sitting on her hands.

Mr Bennett lowered his ear to the transistor radio and politely answered Saoirse

"It is, Love" Then the after-thought occurred to him that maybe it was a hint, a request from the perhaps hungry child. "Do you want some?"

She shook her head:

"No thank you. Is that your radio?" Saoirse attempted to keep the conversation going.

The radio commentator's voice was getting more and more intense. He was beginning to talk faster and louder. The crowd cheered and roared. His voice got faster and faster, and the sense of intensity grew and grew. Mr Bennett stuck his ear right up to the speaker, his hand cupped behind his ear, his mouth open, and his face tense. For a moment he was focused only on the radio nodding to the child.

"I have one of them too" Saoirse continued "Well, it's not really mine, its Daddy's. But he said I could have it in my room, so it's on my bedside table. It's really nice" Saoirse paused, "They're handy to have, aren't they? I have an alarm clock radio too actually, and I always set my alarm for the morning at 7.30 so as I'm up for school on time" She was on a roll, glancing around the room relating her routine to the man "That way Mammy won't be annoyed because I won't be late for school. I really like school. I'm in second class, and my teacher's name is Ms Murphy" Not even looking at him now she chatted her heart out finding this conversation quite easy. "My best friend is Lorraine O'Reilly, and sometimes she thinks she's the boss of me, but she isn't..."

The child went on and on, and Mr Bennett politely nodded and courteously smiled at her, desperately trying to catch what the match commentator was saying.

It was the All-Ireland Senior Hurling Championships, Limerick vs Kilkenny.

"I like your shoes" She continued looking at his black patent leather loafers and held her feet in front of her, clapping her own black patent leather, buckle strap shoes together. "They're like mine, I got mine in Guiney's in town. Mammy brought me in before Easter to get them. Mammy says I'm getting a great wear out of them all the same"

She looked at Mr Bennett for any other common ground to converse. The crowd screamed and roared, and the commentators voice got faster and faster, louder and louder.

"You have a really good head of hair Mr Bennett" She complimented him nodding to his thick head of dark wavy hair "My daddy used to have lots of hair but now he lets the top part grow longer to cover his head. I read in the encyclopaedia in school that it's down to your genes, but I don't really understand that part."

In between the intense moments when the commentator related the game in play to Mr Bennett, the man conversed politely with the eight-year-old girl sat in-front of him.

Half time arrived, and he sat back in his chair and lowered down the radio.

"Do you play hurling in school Saoirse? What position do you play?" He settled in his chair folding his arms.

"Well, erm, no. I don't really like sport…. It's raining really heavy today isn't it?" She quickly relieved the awkward silence finding common ground.

"It is, it hasn't let up all week. Some summer we're having eh?" He glanced out the window over the child's shoulder.

"Yeah, daddy says the grass grows like ninety this time of year. Does yours?"

"Oh sure I can't keep up with it" Mr Bennett laughed appreciating the child's efforts "Hopefully it will let up now for the summer holidays and you kids will get a decent summer on that green of yours, do you play much on the green?" Now Mr Bennet felt like he was finding his feet. He got up to put the kettle on.

"Yeah, all the time, well when it's not raining. Actually, we play rounders a lot, that's a sport isn't it" Her eyes widened, she was gaining momentum now that the conversation was running both ways. She hopped up off the chair to help Mr Bennett with the tea. She opened the press to get the mugs.

"It is indeed love, very like cricket I believe. We used to play that when we were kids too in fact, me and your da. Do you want a drink love?" He held the bottle of red lemonade over a tumbler glass for Saoirse.

"Yes please Mr Bennett. Anyways what were you listening to on the radio?"

"The Hurling, it's the All Ireland Final, it'll be back on in a couple of minutes"

"Oh ok, who's playing" She carefully poured her lemonade ensuring not to spill any on Mr Bennetts counter.

"Limerick V's Kilkenny" He smiled down at the child. Leaning on the kitchen counter with his arms folded he admired the child's interest.

"Who are you up for?" She looked up at him, both hands cupping her tumbler glass and taking a sip of lemonade. Her whole face shone with the cheekiest grin.

"Oh Limerick of course" He stated with pride, standing beside the kitchen counter waiting on the kettle to boil.

"Oh it's coming back on again, come on!" Saoirse recognised the commentators voice and took her seat back under the kitchen window.

Mr Bennett abandoned the tea and hired up the radio. The pair sat listening to the second half together. Mr Bennett explained the play of the game when appropriate, passes, points, wide and goals. Saoirse nodded appreciatively, keeping her eye on the little sound box beside Mr Bennett. Together they shared the intensity and punched the air with their fists, cheering their team on, at one with the cheering crowd. Their screams and roars filled the house, egging their team on to the win.

Limerick won the All Ireland Hurling Final that day. It was a wonderful day all round, where teamwork and comradery played a blinder by all.

Mr Bennett felt an appreciation for her friendliness and her company, although he had no idea why she was sat in the kitchen talking to him when everyone else was inside. He hadn't a notion that she was just trying to keep him company and help him feel included. Saoirse equally had no idea that he just wanted to be on his own, to listen to the match, in peace.

Saoirse felt she had created a bond with her dad's best friend, independent of her daddy. Not only that, she was also chuffed with the added bonus of learning a thing or two about hurling. She left the Bennett house that evening feeling proud of herself for being so thoughtful.

One of the closest relationships Saoirse had in her life was her relationship with God. She loved being inside the church. The sense of peace that she found there, naturally brought her back into that all familiar state of clarity. Being present inside a chapel echoed where she came from.

She was not a child who prayed because she was supposed to. Even though she went to a convent school and religion was a strong part of day to day life in 1970s Ireland. She lived in a society where God was feared, as was the clergy.

Saoirse saw past this fear, and she also saw past the authority of the clergy. She saw nuns and priests as people. She was aware that everyone else feared them and noticed how well everyone behaved around them. Saoirse never saw them as people who were any more important or special than anyone else. She had an equal respect for those of the cloth as she did for any other adult.

Her love for God was something much greater. God was someone or something, (she was always conflicted on which) who was ever-present and all loving. She understood that all good acts came from Him. Sometimes it was by a work of a miracle and other times through the work of people. But all goodness sourced from God and the absence of love and anything good was when people were looking away from God and distracted by something else.

She had a deep sense of knowing that God was always present. Her knowing went beyond what she was told by her teachers in religion at school, and it also went far beyond weekly Sunday Mass that she attended with her parents.

The differentiation within her young mind and what the representatives of religion communicated was that God judged and punished his people if we disobeyed. She knew that God did not judge or punish anyone. She knew that we judged and punished ourselves. This was not an opinion made through logic, rational or reason. It was a deep knowing within her soul.

She felt God. She knew God. He was the essence of strength, clarity, peace, courage and above all love. He was the source of energy that lifts us up to the life our soul came here to live. With God we can create far more than we could in any state otherwise. We can be all that we can possibly be. She knew that the possibility that came when working with God had a potential that was infinite and endless. She didn't know how she knew it, she just did. Nor did she ever wonder why she had no compulsion to tell anyone else, she just didn't.

She often observed the difference between how she saw it and how everyone else did. How everyone she knew walked through life day to day, entranced in the debilitating hypnosis that we are bad people and sinners and need to pray for God's love and forgiveness.

Everyone she knew lived in an unnatural state of fear. This foundation of fear had become normal, due to the masses of society who bought into the hypnotic trance, ever vibrating through society. As a result, the people forgot who they really were and lived their lives to the limitations of this belief.

She saw that everyone was trapped behind an invisible veil. The veil blinded us to the truth, and the depths of happiness available to all lay idle, but present. While the people believed in an illusion of fear and called it 'life'.

Saoirse considered this to be a great tragedy that killed the potential of who we are, and she hoped for the verbal articulation to communicate the same someday. But for now, she was only eight years old, and this was a madness that she would just have to tolerate.

But in the meantime, she made time for her God, the real God.

She never disliked the nuns or the priests. She knew that they believed the message they shared. Most of the nuns and priests she knew were nice people, good people.

She loved to sit quietly in the church and feel the still, powerful peacefulness. She effortlessly became one with the sense of peace. It felt like home. All she ever wanted to do was work for God.

Her only understanding at the time as to how she could do this was to become a nun. That way, she could marry God, how that would work was something her young mind couldn't figure out. But she had heard that marrying God was how a girl becomes a nun.

At the time, her natural calling to be close to God was called 're-ligious'. It wasn't until later years that she was to find out that the more appropriate defining word was 'spiritual'. Either way, she just wanted to spend each day of her life working for God. She wished to be embraced and centred in his peace and light each day, close to him.

All she ever wanted to do was share his message of who he was and how he can help people. She wished to be a vessel to carry the potential for peace and magnificence that came from him. So as that peace can grow from within and throughout everyone's lives. By doing so, she knew the pain in people's eyes would dissolve, upon the realisation of the truth and glory of who they truly were.

It was a message she longed to share in a world where the status quo dictated had suppressed that knowing within everyone.

But for now, she was only young. She knew she had little influence and preaching God's word was not something she planned on doing. Instead, she preferred to do her part through sharing the kindness in her heart and thoughtfulness in her mind.

There was a period during the early seventy's when a lot of her parents' family and friends seemed to be sick and end up in hospital. Joe and Lil's evenings were spent visiting sick friends and family in Elm Park. Saoirse always tended the hospital with them, and Ruth stayed home in Ms Cross's house.

Saoirse had no interest in going up to the ward to see the un-well friends of the family or even family members. She felt the hospital wards were boring and bordering on depressing.

She always looked forward to the trips to Elm Park, because it meant that she could go into the small oratory church on the ground floor of the hospital and sit in the space and talk to God. She could happily sit there for hours and the passage of time would just disappear, and she became one with the stillness of her surroundings.

She loved the smells of the incense, the silence that spoke such a deep, peaceful sound and the love that emanated from the faces of the artefacts in the small church.

When she was here, she felt like she was home.

Lil and Joe never spoke with her about her love of God, and they didn't pay much heed to her passion either. They were raising the girls Roman Catholic and did as expected. But Saoirse's love of God went far deeper than the level of a curricular expectancy; it was part of who she was. God was never far from Saoirse's thoughts and anything she did, was always with effortless intent to serve him.

One night, Saoirse had another dream, which would change her innocent life as she knew it.

She was in Mr and Mrs Bennett's house. For some reason she was on her own, standing at the bedroom window, looking out into the garden. She was watching neighbours, and family members arrive at the house, walking up the driveway. Everyone was very well dressed and looking very solemn and sad.

'I was only getting to know him....and now he's gone, and I'll never get to know him now.' Deep sadness filled her heart in the house full of strangers. Everyone was there to pay their respects to Mrs Bennett for the loss of a great man.

Saoirse lay in bed, fast asleep watching her dream unfold like an invisible bystander at the scene.

Mrs Bennett was woken early morning by a bang downstairs. It was still dark outside, and her husband was gone from the bed beside her.

"Alan, Alan…." She rushed downstairs, her heart racing in the still of the silence in the dark night, terrified at what she somehow knew she was going to find.

She found him lying on the kitchen floor, his heart medication on the kitchen counter. She threw herself down beside him calling his name. Mr Bennett was not moving. His tall body filling the ground of the kitchen floor, she thumped his chest and cried out so loud. Her whole world went black, the nothingness of despair screamed and deafened the silence in the house.

Medics rushed him to the hospital in efforts to redeem his heart but were too late. He passed away shortly after arriving at the hospital. He was thirty-nine years old.

Mr Bennett was her daddy's childhood friend, his best friend. And he was the man whom she had begun to make a deliberate effort to speak to, only a few weeks ago. She connected with him that day while they shared the thrills and excitement of the game. Now he was gone and future encounters and the chance to build and nurture that connection was taken too and lost forever.

She woke up the following morning and thought of the vivid dream and how sad it was, followed by the comforting relief thanking God that it was only a dream, despite how real it felt at the time. She allowed the dream to leave her mind and went about the rest of her day back to normal.

Saoirse spent that Saturday playing outside in the limited October sunshine with her friends. She didn't tell Lil about the dream either, not after her reaction the last time with Mr Ryan.

Plus, this time, she knew that Mr Bennett had not actually died.

Ding Dong....ding dong...knock knock knock.

The early morning alert to the Corcoran family's hall door was the type that they all intuitively knew something was very wrong that October morning.

The rain pelted off the window in Saoirse and Ruth's bedroom and the wind howled loud and uncontrollably. It was still dark outside, and the rooftop landscape over the houses behind theirs showed a skyline, beginning to brighten, as dusk began to fill the morning sky.

Joe went down the stairs to open the hall door. Saoirse could hear a man with a strong Dublin accent talking to Joe at the door. He attempted to keep his voice low over the sound of the pouring rain, lashing onto the doorstep.

Saoirse sleepily sat up in the bed, trying to listen to what was so urgent. By the tones of the two men talking she could tell that Joe knew the caller, but not very well. She knew that he had another man with him, who did less talking, and she knew that it was very serious.

The men left after a few moments, and there was quietness in the house.

Lil and Joe were downstairs in the sitting room. Lil came up the stairs after a few minutes:

"Girls, you have to get dressed. We're going to drop you to Granny and Granddads house" Saoirse could tell Lil had been crying and she looked distracted.

"What's wrong Mammy?" A sleepy Ruth slowly peeled herself out of her bed, rubbing her eyes.

"Mammy what's wrong?" Saoirse could feel her heart thumping in her chest, the words came out of her mouth, but she was afraid to ask and even more afraid to hear the answer.

"Girls, please, just do as I say" Lil pleaded seeming elsewhere and dismissing their query.

The girls knew to obey their mother. They had never heard that tone before and they knew by it something was very wrong.

Saoirse sat up in her bed after her mammy left the room, her knees were to her chest and the covers tucked under her chin.

"Come on Saoirse, Mammy said we have to get dressed! You're always holding everyone up" Ruth ordered, already up and busily organising her clothes on her bed.

That day the girls went up to their grandparent's house, and their parents were gone until late that evening.

Lil attempted to converse with the girls in the car on the way home, although Joe was very quiet. His usual chatty, witty demeanour was gone, and the girls had never seen him this absent before. Lost under a cloud of heaviness his face was like a shell of the man Saoirse knew as he father.

Lil came up to the bedroom that evening and sat on Ruth's bed.

"What's wrong, Mammy, what happened?" Ruth enquired.

"Girls, today was a very sad day," Lil began to explain. "Mr Bennett died earlier this morning." Lil swallowed and took a deep breath, trying with all her might to hold it together to explain to her children.

Saoirse watched her mother and felt an unfamiliar darkness fill the room. Suddenly her and Ruth's bedroom became an empty place only for the sadness that filled the air. Her mind went to her daddy and her heart sank into a sense of hopelessness.

"How did he die?" Ruth's lip quivered.

"He had a heart attack last night love. Mrs Bennett called the ambulance, and they tried to save him, they got him to the hospital, but it was too late, and he died at 4.30 this morning." Lil explained to Ruth, her eyes welled with tears.

The sadness filled the room with the grief of an ending in everyone's lives. It felt like all lights had gone out and in their hearts. They wished that it wasn't happening, and this could be just another normal night, but it wasn't. Mr Bennett was gone forever, and Joe had lost his best friend. No matter what came, Joe and everyone would have to live with the loss of a great man for the rest of their lives. Saoirse wished she could make it all ok, but she couldn't.

It was a solemn evening, and the girls lay down to sleep with the state of loss and sadness in their tummies for their Daddy's pain and knowing that they will never see Mr Bennett again. They didn't speak to each other, they just each went to sleep praying for their Daddy and that he would be ok.

On the following Monday, the girls were kept off school to go to Mr Bennett's funeral. It was another grey, and rainy day, Throughout the morning the clouds seemed to clear to reveal some blue sky and short spells of sunshine.

The large church began to fill with hundreds of people. They poured in and took their seats until there were no vacant seats left. Mr Bennett was a hugely popular man. He had the kindest nature and a quick wit. He was the type of man who had 'The Likeability Factor', and his genuineness and honesty were picked up by all who met him.

The church filled with people of young and old, men, women, families, elderly people and everyone in between. All dressed in black, the crowd filled the church until it was bursting at the seams and then overflowed past the church walls out into the grounds. It was a beautiful send off for a beautiful man, and it was apparent that he was a man who would be missed by countless people.

Later that afternoon, the Corcoran's went back to Sally's to help her with the visitors coming to pay their respects. They had gone to a nearby pub for sandwiches and tea, but some people were still popping by to pay their respects and pass on their condolences to Sally.

"Saoirse love..." Sally caught a quiet moment in the hall, at the bottom of the stairs with Saoirse, among all of the hustle and bustle of the busy house.

"Are you ok Mrs Bennett? Can I do anything for you?" Saoirse looked up at Ms Bennett, hoping Ms Bennett was about to ask for her help. She was feeling pretty absent and eager to help in any way she could.

"I'm ok love." There was a warmth in Sally's eyes that shone from her heart. She was holding herself together in the deepest sadness she would ever feel. "Will you go upstairs love, to our bedroom. On the bedside locker, the one over by the window you will find Alan's watch. I want you to have it, love. He was always very fond of you and always said that you are a lovely kid. 'There's something about you', is what he used to say." Her warm smile held back the tears relating her husband's words.

"I want you to have his watch because he joked over the last couple of weeks, saying that you have the most impeccable timing!" Her eyes lit up with a laugh and her tears escaped down her cheeks. "It's not an expensive watch Saoirse, but Alan said that even though you were well able to pick your moments, he loved chatting to you in recent weeks and that you have a way about you. I know he would love you to have something small of his. It's on the locker love, go on up and get it."

"Thank you Mrs Bennett, and I'm really sorry, I hope you will be ok, I really liked Mr Bennett too" Saoirse instinctively threw her arms around her, and in her embrace she knew that she couldn't take Mrs Bennetts grief away with one hug, so she tried to make her hug help as best it could.

Saoirse climbed the stairs. She was surprised at what Mr Bennett had said about her. She believed every word, and knew Sally was coming straight from the heart for love of her husband and deep respect for the child.

Until now, it was always Ruth that was doted on. People always made comments about Ruth's personality, looks and her character. Up until this point, Saoirse always blended into the background, unnoticed.

She ran up the stairs to fetch the watch and went into Mr and Mrs Bennett's bedroom. She walked past the end of the bed towards the window. She paused for a moment, looking out the window at all the people sadly and solemnly walking up the driveway. They were all well dressed, popping by after the funeral. Saoirse watched and thought to herself:

'I was only getting to know him....and now he's gone, and I'll never get to know him now.' The sadness in her heart gave way to a deep sense of regret and loss. Tears began to flow down her cheeks as she watched out the window. Mr Bennett was gone forever, and she had only begun to become his friend.

Suddenly, that moment became so familiar. She realised that she had seen this before, not in a way that was something similar, but she had seen this very scene before, in her mind. The scene played out before her eyes and she remembered her dream, as it mirrored what her physical eyes observed.

"Oh my gosh, my dream. I saw this before…" Her mind raced while the realisation downloaded from her memory along with the dream.

She watched a middle-aged man with a peak cap and three-quarter length tweed coat walking up the driveway and told herself that another lady about the same age will briskly walk up behind him in a few seconds so as they could walk in together.

"Blue coat…she was wearing a blue coat" She waited and a moment later her dream played itself out. A middle-aged lady in a blue coat quickly walked around the hedge and entered the driveway, trying to catch up with her husband.

"She calls him…. he's called John" she held her breath and waited.

"John! John wait for me!"

She stood in front of the window for a few moments. It was her very first time in Mr & Mrs Bennetts bedroom but suddenly, her surroundings were more familiar than moments ago. She recalled a few other callers who were about to leave and enter the Bennetts home and was right every time.

"I dreamt this. Why did I dream this?" She knew the answer was due to something very natural and normal to her. But for now, she dismissed her realisation out of respect for Mr Bennetts day and stayed present in the sadness, that a great man had left and the sorrow that was left behind. She didn't know the answer to the question she asked herself, but she knew that this was not the time to try and work that out either.

Just before she let it go she quickly searched her mind and traced back to when she had the dream. It was nine days ago.

She turned her attention back to the reason she was standing in the Bennetts bedroom. She sat on the side of the bed and looked at the watch on Mr Bennett's bedside locker. She took the digital watch in her hands. It had a silver strap and a black face. It was a strange feeling sitting on the bed looking down at a watch, given to her by a man who was no longer here. Yet he was the centre of focus in everyone's hearts right now. She watched and listened to the sounds that filled his home. Mr Bennett was gone, but his presence was so alive and ambient. It filtered through the distance between wherever he was now and the life that he loved so much.

Saoirse tried the on watch. It was way too big for her growing wrist. So, she carefully held it in her hands feeling a deep appreciation for the kindness and thoughtfulness of a good man she knew and would never see again.

She made her way downstairs to find her mother. Lil was in the living room sitting the couch. The room was full of people. Lil was chatting to a lady Saoirse had never seen before:

"Mammy, can you put this in your bag please?" She wanted to ensure the precious gift was in a safe place.

Lil paused her conversation and took the watch from Saoirse "Where did you get this?" she looked both puzzled and distracted.

"Mrs Bennett gave it to me. She said that Mr Bennett wanted me to have it." As Saoirse spoke, she was surprised to find her bottom lip and chin tighten, and she immediately fought back the lump in her throat and tears in her eyes. She hoped her mother would not ask her to explain further. Instead, Lil looked puzzled at Saoirse's claim. She didn't notice her daughter's upset.

She put the watch into her handbag and carried on conversing with the lady beside her without a second glance at her daughter.

A few days later, Saoirse was having her after school snack. Ruth was not due home for another hour or so and this was usually the time when she had her mother all to herself and shared any concerns that bothered her with her mum. Her dream had played on her mind since its realisation and she decided to tell her mother:

"Mammy" Lil was ironing the school uniforms. She always did her ironing at the same time on a Monday and Thursday.

"Yes love" Lil did not look up from the shirt she was pressing,

"You know the way Mr Bennett passed away? Well I had another dream" Saoirse stirred her soup "before he died, about two weeks ago…." Her voice became broken and a lump formed in her throat, she fought back the tears.

Lil placed the iron standing upright and looked at her daughter waiting on her to finish her sentence.

"Mammy, I dreamt that Mr Bennett died" she revealed just above a whisper, her tummy was in knots. She looked up at her mother and her big brown eyes were filled with tears.

Her mother listened and gave no reaction.

"Have you told your father" Lil said finally, using her strict tone. Saoirse firmly shook her head to indicate that she hadn't, and her mother did not respond. She picked up the iron and continued to press the school shirt.

"Right, you've told me now, no need to say any more about it ok." Her eyes were back on the ironing board.

Saoirse paused half afraid to ask her mammy why they can't talk about it but even more afraid to know why. She debated whether to ask her mammy for the reason or not.

"But mum, why not?" She asked, biting the bullet and her lip.

"Saoirse, because I said so that's why. Now that's the end of it" Her mother ordered.

That was the end of the conversation about the dream predicting Mr Bennett's death.

Lil and Joe were young, middle class people. Joe's drapery shop had come under strain in recent years and right now, reputation came before everything in the small city. They were doing their best to keep their heads above water and make the shop work in a growing competitive market.

To keep the best side out and appear to be thriving was important to Joe. He had learned from his father that that's what a man in his position does. He was a business man. People respected him, and he was recognised as someone who knew how to lead the way in the times they lived in.

They had a beautiful home in an affluent area of Dublin. They drove a car that most could not afford. The children were always dressed in the best of clothes. They attended mass every Sunday and on Holy Days. They even adopted a baby gave and gave her a great chance in life. She was lucky. Society looked up to the Corcoran's. They had worked hard for their reputation and were committed to hold on to it.

They also aimed to ensure the best chance that their children would continue to do the same as they did when they become the next adult generation in society. So far, their children were a credit to them.

The Corcoran's were admired by their friends, the girls' teachers and the local priest and nuns at the school thought the world of them.

Lil was not particularly religious although she tended church and did all of the right things. She knew enough to know that just like women who fell pregnant out of wedlock were frowned upon, so too were people who claimed to see beyond the physical veil. Anyone who claimed to have such ability was evil, in the eyes of the church, even little children.

Back when she was younger herself and Dolores often visited psychics, at the time Lil just wanted to hear the psychic predict that Joe was going to propose, and they would live happily ever after. Even though it was frowned upon by the church, Lil couldn't help giving some credence to it.

One time after another visit to a psychic Lil and Dolores had a long conversation on the way home, trying to understand why the nuns and the priests dismiss a persons' ability to see beyond, what's more call them evil. They talked about how it didn't add up and it didn't make sense. Given the prophets, prophesies and predictions made throughout the Bible, how could the Roman Catholic Church dismiss anyone who claimed to see past the three-dimensional world. But Lil and Dolores were just a couple of twenty years olds trying to relieve their guilt for visiting one at the time, they gave the contradictory message little thought since.

But today that judgement was sitting at her kitchen table. She knew Saoirse was far from evil, although she could not understand how she could see what she sees or know what she knows. Either way, the churches message went loud and deep. How could she stand up against that, who would believe her? Let alone support her? Added into the mix Saoirse was adopted, she was already born of a woman, frowned upon by the church. To say nothing was the best thing to do.

Chapter 13

The mid-seventies saw a succession of bereavements for the Corcoran's. Lil's mother, passed away after a short illness. A malignant tumour took reign over all her organs causing her to pass away within four months of diagnosis. 'Granny' was only sixty-eight and her passing devastated Lil.

Joe's brother in law, a builder passed after a fatal fall from scaffolding, he was only thirty-four with a young family. His wife, Joe's sister followed three months later from a terminal stroke, leaving behind two young children, Susie was three, and Natasha was only a year old. Ms Cross also passed away that same year. It was a very sad year for Lil and Joe. They did their best to come to terms with such great loss in such a short space of time. But it was hard.

Saoirse found that Joe spoke to her a lot less than he had done in the past and Lil had become increasingly snappy with her. She tried to share her jokes or tell interesting stories, but her jokes were no longer entertained, and her stories were not met with any level of engaging interest.

She couldn't help notice that Ruth was treated differently. Ruth was given more chores around the house and commended for her efforts. Her ability to bake and cook was also encouraged and supported, particularly in the company of extended family members and neighbours who called by to visit.

Saoirse's underlying feelings of not being good enough began to increase day by day. Her parents' behaviour left her feeling more and more separated and different from the family unit. It was as if the fact that she was adopted used to be something that once made no difference in the eyes of her parents. They loved their children equally, and Saoirse felt that. But now the pendulum had swung to the other side, and it had become the very thing that made all the difference.

The feeling of not being good enough and less important than everyone else was slowly becoming part of Saoirse's psyche. She was beginning to believe that it did matter that she was adopted and that she was different to everyone else.

The realization that she was different in the Corcoran household left her with a grieving feeling that she wished she could return to the innocence that used to be, not so long ago.

By now Ruth was allowed to stay up a little later than Saoirse to watch TV. Ruth was twelve now and insisted the unfairness of having to go to bed at the same time as her younger sister.

She had also become very distant from Saoirse. Their relationship was never one that saw them as siblings united, mainly due to daily conditioning by Ms Cross, that Saoirse was 'a nothing', 'a nobody'.

Ruth and Ms Cross had a bond that was very unique, and she took on board what the old lady said. By now, Ms Cross's words had sunk deeply into her psyche. Ms Cross's foreboding threat of condemnation and judgement should she love her sister, continued to echo deep in her mind. It had become what she understood to be the reality. As a result, she pulled back her love and rejected her sister, mainly in the act of ill-educated self-protection.

Ruth believed she was doing the right thing. She felt no guilt in doing so. The projection of her inherited belief onto Saoirse added another dimension to the loneliness and separation that Saoirse was increasingly feeling of late.

"Hi." Saoirse happily greeted Ruth as she walked into the bedroom to prepare for bed. Saoirse was sitting up in her bed playing with her favourite doll Maisie on her lap.

Ruth ignored Saoirse's greeting and looked at her with a look of disgust from head to toe and back again.

"What?" Saoirse widened her eyes as she threw her hands in the air. "What are you looking at?

"Oh, Nothing." The tone of Ruth's words added volume to the deliberate attempt to insult Saoirse.

"Here we go again, Ruth, you always say that to me, every time you walk into a room. You always look at me like that and then say you are looking at nothing. Yeah well, I know what you mean you know, and I'm going to tell Mammy on you."

The girls heard the sitting room door open downstairs abruptly. Ruth rushed on her nightdress as fast as she could and jumped into bed, forgetting to turn the lights off.

"What's going on in here?" asked Joe. His tone was one of intolerance.

"She told me I was a nothing," Saoirse stood up for herself. "Daddy she says that to me all the time and it's not fair"

"I'm telling you, if I hear another word from you, you are going to be sorry. Do you hear me?" Joe wagged his finger at Saoirse "Now I'm warning you, give it over"

"But Daddy I just said hi and"

"I'm telling you, I'm sick of you," Joe cut her short.

"Now give it over, I don't want to hear another word out of your mouth, do you hear me? Now go asleep the pair of you." Joe slapped off the bedroom light and made his way back downstairs.

Saoirse had nothing to say after Joe's statement. She lay down on the bed and curled up in the foetal position. She faced the wall, hugging Maisie in her arms, in the dark.

Joe's anger and intolerance was something she had become very familiar with in recent months. It was like as if something had gone. The love and affection that he used to have for her in the past had left. It was simply no longer there.

She went to sleep in her bed that night, in a space that used to feel comfortable and safe, in a home where she used to feel love and belonging. Her world was now a different place. The space now in which she lay, felt like an isolating bed of loneliness.

Chapter 14

"That's it there isn't it?" Joe asked Lil as they drove down a long suburban avenue in the leafy Dublin suburbs. Their appointment was for 10am. Joe took the morning off work and stopped by the house to pick Lil up on the way.

He was referring to an old large redbrick building. It stood centred among a large complex with tennis courts, a hockey pitch and basketball court to the left. To the right, a car park and the mature oak trees stood tall and wide. They filled the large green area that met the long driveway. Blooming flowers and shrubs fringed the edge of the green, painting the landscape with the brightest colours. Their uplifting scents wafted through the air, reminding the subconscious of natures' intelligence. The grounds were impeccably kept and very beautiful.

"That's it yeah," Lil looked out the windscreen. She had hardly said a word to her husband for the whole journey.

"What's the nun's name again?" Joe would have preferred not to speak at all. There was enough chat going through his mind as it was, none of which he wished to talk about. He and Lil had made their decision and it was final. He drove towards the car park at the end of the long drive to the old building.

"Sister Agnes" Lil looked out the passenger window and tried to take in the majestic surroundings, although nothing could distract her from the knot she felt in her stomach.

Joe parked the car in the closest parking spot to the main door. They walked up to the large front door at in the centre of the red-brick building. Apart from a couple of short comments about how fine the weather is, they did not speak another word to each other upon approaching the building.

Joe rang the doorbell, and a young nun answered after just a few moments.

"Hello, we have an appointment to see Sr Agnes please, 10 o clock?" Joe requested.

"Yes, come in. Sr Agnes is expecting you." The young nun replied.

She directed the couple to Sr Agnes' office, to the left of the main door.

"Sr. Agnes, Mr and Mrs Corcoran are here to see you" the nun tapped on the office door.

"Thank you Sister. Come in Mr and Mrs Corcoran, take a seat. Lovely Spring weather we're having isn't it?" The middle aged, heavy-set nun was dressed in grey. She signalled to the two chairs in front of her desk.

"Close the door on your way-out Sister. Now let's begin." She fixed a pile of paper work on the desk in front of her, joined her hands and leaned over the desk giving Lil and Joe her full attention.

The April sunshine danced in the breeze outside Saoirse's class-room window.

Her teacher, Miss Murphy was giving an English lesson to the class. Saoirse was looking out the window, miles away in another daydream.

The large panes of glass framed a fantastic view of Dublin's south side, supported by the backdrop of the Dublin Mountains. She loved that scene. It was as if the magnificent hills seemed so close and served as a protector of the capital city. They seemed to roll on for-ever, stretching further than the eye could see.

The scene always had a way of drawing her into a world far from the curriculum being taught in the classroom. The collage of yellow cornfields, accompanied by the green fields of farmland on a land-scape dotted with cattle, sheep and sparsely scattered country homes and farm sheds.

Saoirse always thought that when she was older, and all grown up she was definitely going to live in the countryside. Even though she was only young, she never felt like a city girl. She loved nature, wide open spaces and the sense of space around her.

She dreamed of owning a two-storey cottage. Her dream home also had a large front and back garden. She was definitely going to work for herself, although she had no idea what she was going to be, for now, serving God was the only thing she could think of when it came to her dream job.

The alternative was to be at home with her children, and her husband will be the breadwinner. Being rich when she was older was never top of the priority list for Saoirse. Her dream life was going to be centred around a happy home, filled with love.

She also knew that she would value a sense of freedom to do what she pleased and live as she chose. Being true to be who she is was also going to be top of the list.

"Saoirse? "

Ms Murphy was beside her, standing over her desk. Saoirse had not seen or heard her approaching. Ms Murphy was smiling a warm smile of encouragement. She held a copy in her hand. It was Saoirse's copy and was open on a particular page waiting for Saoirse to take it from her.

Saoirse was immediately thrown back into reality. She scrambled the pieces together in her head. She took the copy from Ms Murphy and stood up, knowing that was her cue to read out the poem she had written for last nights' homework to the class.

She read the poem from start to finish. Upon doing so the teacher began to clap, and the rest of the class followed. Saoirse never knew where to look when the class clapped applause for her. A sense of complete awkwardness came over her every time, clenching her teeth together and dancing her eyes around the desk front of her.

Writing in any form was something that came easy to Saoirse and English was her favourite subject in school by far.

"Right, that's it for today class," Ms Murphy announced. "Be careful going home and don't forget to leave in single file.'

Saoirse gathered her books and copies and packed her bag. Just like every day she said goodbye to her teacher, but this time Ms Murphy called her back.

"Saoirse, you have a real gift for writing do you know that?" Ms Murphy's sat in her teacher's chair, her soft brown hair loosely caught back into a ponytail at the nape of her neck. She was a kind and encouraging teacher. She could be cross too but never without good reason. There was something about her smile that told Saoirse she had more to tell her.

"Saoirse, you know the Berkeley Young Writer's competition is coming up shortly" She picked up the forms ready in front of her on her desk. "I strongly advise you enter. You have a very good chance of doing well. At the very least it will be a good opportunity for you to step outside of your comfort zones, dig deeper and see where your talents can take you." Her smile oozed confidence in Saoirse.

"My…my gosh, me Ms Murphy, really?" Saoirse wasn't expecting that.

"Really" Ms Murphy laughed, her eyes widened, she knew Saoirse was also modest. She handed her the forms.

"Oh but Ms Murphy I don't know if I'm good enough, like, it's a big competition and I don't know much about it" Saoirse took the forms in her hand.

"Saoirse sweetheart, I have been teaching third and fourth class for twenty years" She took hold of Saoirse's hands and made firm eye contact "I know talent when I see it, and I have not come across one as gifted as you. You've just got something and it's something that can't be taught by me or anyone. You must know that. I'm sure your mammy and daddy tell you the same all the time how gifted you are" Ms Murphy searched her eyes, she knew she was right.

"Erm, yeah," Saoirse turned her eyes to the floor and forced a smile. "thank you, Ms Murphy, I'll bring the forms home to mammy and daddy and show them to them tonight." She carefully rolled them into a scroll and popped them into the side of her bag.

"Good, I'm glad. You need to ask your parents to look through them. You have the choice to enter two competitions. You can enter one or the other, or both. One is a short story of 500 words and the other is a poem. Entries need to be in by the 25th of this month." Saoirse paid attention taking in everything her teacher was saying "Just bring back them to me, signed by mammy and daddy, and I will do the rest. How does that sound?"

"It sounds great Ms Murphy, thank you." Saoirse could not wipe the smile off her face. It went from ear to ear and came straight from her dancing heart.

She left school with a spring in her step and a feeling in her belly that told her she was worth something, that she had something to offer and what's more, somebody recognised it.

She skipped, hopped and ran home from school that day, sometimes her little legs couldn't carry her quick enough. That smile stayed there the whole way home.

She couldn't wait to tell her mammy and daddy what Ms Murphy had said. It was like her whole world had opened up, the sky seemed higher in the sky and the day seemed so much brighter. The world had expanded. There was freedom and a sense of liberation in the air, and she loved it.

When she arrived home, her daddy's car was parked outside. She thought it strange because he was never home at this time of the day. But all the better, that meant she could tell both her parents the good news together. She hoped they would be so proud.

"Mammy, Daddy?" Saoirse ran into the hallway of their home. "Mum....Dad?" She closed the hall door. Her hands were shaking and her heart beating so fast in her chest. She ran into the kitchen.

Lil and Joe were sitting at the kitchen table. There was a stranger sitting at the table with them. It was a nun, and Saoirse wondered why a nun had come to visit the Corcoran's.

She gave Saoirse a stern look. Not dissimilar to the same look Ruth often gave her, just before she called her 'a nothing' or 'a nobody'. Saoirse immediately didn't like the woman.

Her heart sank. She knew this was different. Something had changed, and it was about to change her life as she knew it.

Lil looked down at her hands resting on the table.

"Hiya love" Joe said and rested his eyes on the table too. The nun stared at her.

"What's going on Daddy?" the words that she dreaded the answer to fell from her mouth, her body suddenly felt numb, gripped tight by an invisible force.

"Saoirse," Joe finally said. "this is Sr Agnes. She's from the Sisters of Charity Boarding School for Girls. Myself and Lil have been talking, and you are going to stay with them for a while. Okay?"

".....What?....."

The excitement in the young girl's belly had gone, and it was replaced. with a sense of her world caving in and darkness falling onto her reality. Her mind filled with chaos and confusion, casting out all light and hope.

Denial grew in her mind. She didn't understand what her father meant or why. And why did he say Lil and not Mammy, he always referred to her as Mammy. Saoirse quickly realised something had been discussed, decisions had been made, and it was all about her.

"But Daddy what do you mean? Why? Why do I have to go and stay with her? for how long?" Her lip quivered, and her eyes welled up. She could feel her life as she knew it was coming to an end.

"That's enough now. These good people have been through enough. You are coming with me now." The cold nun stood up filling the room like a dark shadow and ended the conversation before Joe could answer. Although he didn't look like he was beginning to volunteer a response to the child.

Sr. Agnes, thanked Lil and Joe for their time and announced that they would be on their way. She caught Saoirse by the upper arm.

"Come on now child; my car is the red car outside." She gripped Saoirse's arm tight with her eyes on the hall door.

Saoirse was confused. She hoped and wished for a chance of denial of what was happening. The nun continued to make her way to the hall door.

"Daddy, please! Daddy why? She begged, and she cried, but Joe continued to look down at the table.

Lil turned to Saoirse and there the smallest bit of hope from the look in her eyes that she would say something to stop this. She hesitated, and she toyed with conflict of whether to do so or not. In the end, she chose not to give in to her empathy for the child's plea. Instead, she watched with noticeable pain in her eyes, as Saoirse was escorted out through the house to the car by the stranger.

Saoirse begged and pleaded to stay all the way to the car. Her heart broke when the car drove away from the home that she had loved and the life that she had.

Lil and Joe remained in the kitchen and failed to respond to their child's deafening cries for them.

"It's for the best Lil. We didn't know what we were taking on, and we couldn't have planned it would turn out this way. But I can't risk any more loss. I just can't." Joe attempted to convince both himself and Lil.

Lil had her hand over her mouth. She couldn't speak. Tears flowed from her eyes in silence. The lump in her throat choked and her heavy heart ached so hard it felt like it was going to break. She listened to her husband and took on his point of view. Trying to convince herself that in theory, this may be for the best.

Saoirse's schoolbag lay on the kitchen floor. The writing competition forms were rolled in a neat vertical tube shape, tucked carefully into the side of her school bag.

Chapter 15

The car drove on, and her home went out of sight.

In the confined space in the back of Sr Agnes's car, Saoirse felt like she was dying inside. Her face, soaked with tears as she attempted to call louder.

When her home went out of sight and the car drove out onto the Dublin streets she surrendered denial, confusion and powerlessness, she had no escape and was locked in a state of existence only to survive.

Her cries had gone from loud screams of despair, calling to her mammy and daddy as the car drove away, to silent sobs trying to catch her breath.

The emotionless nun drove the car with her eyes fixed firmly on the road.

All that could be heard was her pain silently calling from the deepest depths of her heart. A pleading opposed to this abandonment and the darkness she was to face, knowing her world was dissolving around her.

She surrendered her pleas to be in vain, met with no justice or compassion.

She tucked herself into the corner of the back seat. Her heart shattered into a million pieces. The helplessness suspended her in hopelessness and imprisoned her in darkness. She felt nothing. It was too painful to feel. There was only despair and pain with nothing of grace to hold onto.

Her eyes were swollen, and her face was burning from the heat of the tears, her breath was short, and her throat hurt. Her heart was heavy as she sat braced in the helplessness of the backseat of the car. A familiar coldness came over her. She could not identify its origin, and she couldn't be bothered trying.

The car approached the large redbrick building.
Teenage girls were playing a game of hockey on the pitch, and

others sat on the benches chatting in animated exclamation. Many of the girls strolled through the grounds in pairs. From what Saoirse could see, the girls ranged in age from her own age of about nine right up to young adults.

She noticed that it looked not too dissimilar to the secondary school that she used to pass on the way to Cornalscourt to do the weekly shop with her mammy. All the girls wore a grey uniform, a grey jumper and skirt with a white shirt, grey socks and black shoes. Saoirse looked out the back window, so far, this place looked quite normal and the girls looked normal too, just like any other school.

The car pulled up into a space right outside the front entrance to the redbrick building. Sr. Agnes pulled up the hand-break and stepped out of the car, onto the gravel drive. Saoirse followed, and Sr Agnes did not say a word as she made her way up steps to the main door, Saoirse followed her lead.

She led the way down a long hallway, around a few corners of the old, well maintained, spotless building. The white walls were filled with mahogany framed pictures of nothing that was interesting and the high ceilings in the main entrance became lower with every corner they turned.

They went down a flight of stairs into an area that reminded Saoirse of a typical hospital, without the hospital equipment. It was a long corridor with doors either side. All doors were closed, but through the small windows on each door Saoirse could see the beds lining the walls either side of each room.

Sr Agnes came to a pause at door No.11 and entered the dorm. There were ten beds in the well-lit room, five beds either-side and two large shutter windows on the opposite wall. There was a splendid view looking out into the gardens at the back of the building.

She led Saoirse to the last bed on the left, under the window and spoke to her for the first time since leaving Lil and Joe's house:

"This is yours. You will keep your area clean and tidy. You will make your bed every morning, and you are fully responsible for your area." There was an unsaid command in her tone that told Saoirse that she had better do as the nun said or she would be in big trouble. "There is your uniform. Get dressed." She pointed to a neatly folded uniform at the end of the bed.

Saoirse waited with a hesitance to be shown where she could get changed. The nun stood with her arms folded waiting for the child to follow her orders. Saoirse got changed, and in an attempt to please the nun she began to fold her old school uniform neatly on the bed.

"Leave that there, Child, you won't need that uniform anymore," the nun snapped.

She led Saoirse back down the corridors, through the building towards the entrance and went into a small office to the right, just before the entrance door and took a seat at her desk.

"These are your school books and everything else you will need."

She placed a pile of books and copies on the table all covered meticulously in the same brown paper that Lil had always used to cover their school books and copies at the start of each September.

The nun stood poker straight behind her desk and placed her hands on the table:

"Now, this is why you are here. You are an evil child. You were born an illegitimate child, and therefore, you are a child that is deemed to be of less importance in society" She eye-balled Saoirse, her tall shadow towered over her.

"Nobody wants you. So, we The Sisters of Charity have come to take care of you because no one else will or can" Her lips were the only part of her rigid body that moved. Her strict tone was devoid of emotion and fuelled with authority.

"Mr and Mrs Corcoran filled me in on the trouble you have brought upon them, and I can tell you now, this is a sacred building filled with God's love and your evil will have no power here. Am I making myself clear?" She spilled the words out of her mouth without taking a breath or blinking an eye.

Saoirse had no idea what the woman meant. It was as if she was talking about someone else. What trouble? What evil? What is an illegitimate child? What kind of things had Lil and Joe filled her with? What trouble were they talking about? And why did she feel she needed to say these things to Saoirse? Why was she warning her off?

It was as if she was talking about a stranger. She felt as if her identity and her nature were completely unrecognised or misunderstood. She could tell the nun placed full credence in what she had just said.

Saoirse felt as if her true self, her true identity was being stripped away. She listened to the nun speak at her. Her heart was breaking, and she felt that her true self was being covered with an ugly, disempowering mask, of untruth. It was a mask that left Saoirse alone and destitute in a horrible light.

Stripped bare of all recognition Saoirse knew that there was no point in responding to the nun or asking her what she meant and there was certainly no point in trying to convince her of the truth either, she knew she would be wasting her time.

"Class is completed for today. You will commence class tomorrow morning. That's all for now; you are dismissed."

Saoirse left her office lost in so many ways. Sr Agnes's words belted away in her head, and confusion and bewilderment took over. She walked down the corridor, not really knowing where to go. Her physical state of loss mirrored how she felt inside.

She made her way back to the dorm, hoping to remember the route along the way. She walked alone along the empty halls and corridors, she felt her steps quicken, the familiar lump came into her throat throbbed, and her eyes filled up with tears.

Alone and lost in so many ways she hurried back to the empty dorm and threw herself on the bed. Her whole body cried, as she lay curled in foetal position. The tears flowed endlessly from her eyes. They felt as if they sourced from every part of her cellular being.

Her whole world had entered into a state of proverbial death in the last couple of hours. Her body, mind and soul were falling apart. And she had no idea what she had done wrong.

She already hated this place, and she hated her life.

She cried so hard that she made no sound, only to inhale a breath. In the absence of hope and no point in searching, she was trapped, stuck, imprisoned in the result of decisions of authority and the loss as to why those decisions were derived.

She lay curled in the bed, still dressed in the uniform she already hated, and she cried. She had no idea what time it was or long she had been there.

"Saoirse, beautiful girl, don't cry."

A soft loving voice arrived at her side and took her hands in theirs.

The child looked up through her tears and immeasurable pain to see a lady kneeling beside the bed. It was the same lady that used to visit her from time to time when she could see her spirit guides. The lady's eyes were filled with warmth and comfort.

"I'm so sad; there is no hope, Why? Why do they hate me? What did I do?" Saoirse's innocence begged for answers.

"Beautiful child you didn't do anything wrong. No matter what they say or what they do, this is no reflection on you. That's not easy to understand right now, but it is the truth" She shone with the most beautiful light. Saoirse had forgotten how peaceful that light was.

"They are trapped in the hypnosis of illusion. Their words are not true, and they are not reflective of who you are. However, they are going to keep on saying these words. They are also going to keep on believing these words too.

But Saoirse, that's not what's important. What is important is that you know who you are: a beautiful child with a huge heart. You are caring, loving and clever." The peace in her eyes went so deep. She radiated the warmest motherly essence. The horror of the promise she faced was somewhat lifted, even if it was just for now.

"Your body is young, but your soul is old. Therefore, you are wise. Beautiful child, be in that wisdom now, know who you are and be true to you. Know that they are caught in a belief system that traps and enslaves. Many fall into the trap, but beautiful child, shining angel of strength, you know that it was never your destiny to do so. Not now, not ever" Her words, her tone and her essence emanated the deepest love. She radiated the strength that comes with peacefulness and re-minded Saoirse of the truth that had become silent in her heart.

"You came here, to this place called life, to help set them free. You know that deep down in your soul. And that dear child is exactly what you will do." She had no idea how she was going to set anyone free, but there was a knowing in the lady's presence and Saoirse believed her.

"But for now, you must stay here in this awful place. It's part of your journey. Saoirse, know that I am with you, every step of the way. You may not always see me but know that I am always there.

You are made of strong stuff dear child. You are courageous, beautiful and strong. You have a heart so pure that no wrong can destroy it. Be strong and know that I am here, always."

Saoirse smiled at the lady. Her heart filled with a sense of belonging. The lady spoke with deep love and recognition, that she inherently knew she could believe every word. It was like the lady knew her and she knew exactly how she felt. She said all the right things and every word resonated deeply with Saoirse.

There was no need to ask further questions, the lady had made herself clear, and Saoirse had the clarity to the degree that she needed it, for now.

In those moments, gentleness filled Saoirse's heart, which fed her great strength. She felt clarity fill her mind with the deepest sense of peace, knowing she was loved, unconditionally.

She looked up at the lady again to whisper "thank you".

But the lady had disappeared.

Just like before, Saoirse didn't question the lady's invisibility. She knew that her reason for her visit was fulfilled and Saoirse felt grateful for the priceless gesture of love and support. The brief visit from the lady bestowed the love and the hope needed to light the dark state of loss of moments ago. The love in the lady's essence and presence awakened her strength within to go on.

She looked out the window and night time was beginning to make its appearance. The last few hours had slipped by in a blink of an eye.

She could hear voices and footsteps approaching and excited sounds from the girls heading to their dorms to rest for the night. Saoirse didn't feel like making light conversation with strangers right now, not to mention being quizzed by curious dorm mates about who she was or why she was here. She pulled the covers over her and noticed that she was already in her nightgown. She didn't remember getting changed although neither did she remember much else about the last few hours only the sense of peace and clarity that she now wanted to stay centred in. She fell asleep in its strength.

Chapter 16

The following morning Saoirse woke with a loud bell ringing. It rang three times and paused. It rang three times again and repeated the same sequence a couple of minutes later.

The other girls were stirring. She looked around and counted five girls in total. Each of them slowly peeled themselves out of bed, and she noticed that they were all around her own age. No-one spoke in an attempt to put all of their energy into waking up their sleepy bodies. They made their way into the bathrooms, which adjoined the dorm.

One of the girls gave a friendly smile to the new girl as she passed by her bed. As did another girl. The third girl didn't even seem to notice Saoirse. She was too busy halfway between her body being awake and her head still half asleep. The last two girls walked closely together, one behind the other and stared curiously at the newcomer in a way that Saoirse felt like pointing out to them that she can actually see them too.

The girls got dressed and began to communicate with one another. Mainly groaning about how tired they were and not to talk to them yet. The conversation progressed into which subject was first on the timetable today followed by an outburst of more groans.

"Uuuuurrrgggghhhhh nnnnnooooooooo, we have Gleeson up first today. The most boring woman on planet earth." Complained the girl who had not even noticed Saoirse, she seemed to be in pain.

Saoirse stayed quiet and tensed up with shyness, feeling like a distinct outsider, the girls had clearly bonded and knew one another well. She continued to get ready one or two steps behind the girls, discreetly following their lead of protocol.

They gathered their things in preparation for breakfast and then class. Saoirse left immediately behind the girls trusting she was to go to the same place.

"Hi, I'm Maria" one of the girls slowed down her pace to walk with Saoirse. She had a friendly face and big blue eyes. Her hair was glossy dark brown to her shoulders.

"Gosh you have the longest eye lashes I have ever seen!" She admired, slightly leaning in to examine Saoirse's long eyelashes "and they're so thick too!

Are you boarding full time or part-time?" she asked.

"Full time, I think" replied Saoirse, taking a wild guess, given yesterday's events.

"Me too, most of the girls go home for weekends and holidays, but my parents live in Co. Donegal, so it's too far to travel up and down every weekend." Maria explained.

"You don't have a Donegal accent?"

"I'm from Dublin, but my parents opened a seafood restaurant in Donegal. They wanted me to continue my education in Dublin, so here I am." She explained with a smile.

"What about you? We heard rumour only yesterday that there was going to be a new girl coming but didn't think you would be here so soon. What brings you here?"

Maria's blue eyes looked at Saoirse, waiting on an answer to her innocent question. Saoirse felt completely unprepared to offer an answer. This first encounter with her new friend had been going so well for the last thirty seconds, to ruin it now with the reasons Sr. Agnes had given yesterday would be quite a lame way to end what could have become a beautiful friendship.

"Yeah I know, it was very sudden in fact. My dad took ill quite suddenly, and both my parents figured it best that I come and board here, while he's recovering" Saoirse could hardly believe what was coming out of her own mouth. She remembered the hypnosis and the illusion that the lady had talked about last night and figured to herself that it wasn't all a lie, not really.

"Oh I'm sorry, I hope your dad is going to be ok," Maria frowned a look of genuine concern.

The girls walked down to the breakfast hall with Maria explaining the general routine of the day ahead. She filled Saoirse in on who is who and what to expect. Saoirse listened intently to her new bubbly friend.

She was surprised at how articulate Maria was. In fact, all the girls seemed to be well able to hold a conversation in such a way that was so much more mature than the girls back in her national school. There seemed to be a sense of independence here in The Sisters of Charity that was far more advanced than any other nine or ten years old she knew.

Saoirse attended class and got through her first day following the lead of her classmates. Maria introduced her to most of the other girls in her class at lunchtime and breaktime. Saoirse was met with an overall friendliness in her new surroundings. She felt less isolated, and although she would not go so far as to say that she liked it here, at least she didn't feel that it was going to be as bad as she thought it would be yesterday.

After school was homework time, and the girls had the choice to go to the study or the library. Saoirse stuck with her new friend and went to the library with Maria. Maria explained to her that she was relatively new here too. She had only started in September, but even though it's not like home where she would prefer to be, she has made the most of it and grown to like it there, stating that it could be a lot worse.

"The only warning I will give you Saoirse is that Sr Agnes has her favourites and if you are not one of them, keep your head down. She is not nice that woman." Maria's face seemed to change colour when she spoke about Sr Agnes.

Saoirse didn't have to spend much time wondering if she was going to make the favourite list or not.

The girls sat side by side in the library. Their books and copies laid out on the table not getting much attention from the chatty pair.

"The girls in our dorm Maria, what they like?" Saoirse was cautious to keep her voice down not to disturb the other girls with their heads in the books.

"They're ok. There's Freda. She's the eldest. She's twelve, going on twenty-two! She can be a bit moody and sometimes rude, but she doesn't mean it. She has our backs at all times, and she can't stand anyone getting a hard time unfairly. Don't bother her when she is waking up in the morning or going to sleep at night time. Otherwise, she is good fun, wysiwyg." Maria concluded, resting her elbow on the desk and hand under her chin.

"Wysiwyg?" Saoirse frowned.

"What You See Is What You Get.....duh!!" Maria laughed.

"Then there's Alvagh" Maria smiled and sat back in her chair "She's lovely. She's a very strong personality, and some of the girls get jealous because she's so confident but she doesn't care what anyone thinks. She is her own person and does her own thing. Oh, and she sings, a lot!!" Maria's definitive nod said it all. "There's lots of music in her family, her aunt is a well-known singer on the Irish music scene"

Saoirse listened to Maria chat away about her friends and who is who here in this place. Maria was completely wysiwyg: Kind, warm, fun- loving and caring. Her eyes danced around the room explaining the way of the land, talking with her hands in animated expression.

"Alvagh is so funny and friendly. She really made me feel at home when I came here, and she is the one that I'm closest to here. I really like her and glad she's around.

Then there is Jennifer and Jacqueline" Maria rolled her eyes and slumped in her chair. "Once you see one the other is never too far behind. They are ok, but sometimes I think that they share the same brain" She twirled her pencil between her fingers, staring into nowhere "If Jennifer thinks one thing, well so will Jaqueline. They tend to get quite jealous of Alvagh and make fun of her, but it's so obvious that it's their problem and not Alvagh's. They're ok but take them with a pinch of salt and don't let them get to you, they are the same with everyone. I think it's a sad power trip, to be honest. Oh, and if you have three pairs of shoes, they have ten. If you have £5, they have £50 if you get me."

The funny thing was that even though Saoirse only saw the girls for a brief time this morning, she knew exactly who Maria was talking about as she described each of the girls' characters with honesty and diplomacy.

She was so glad she met Maria. She felt like she had made a very good, genuine friend. There was trust and honesty in Maria's eyes. She clearly had a sense of humour and was good fun to be around. Thanks to her new Godsend, Saoirse's first day into the new routine was kind of ok.

It was Friday night, and that meant that the girls could stay up until 10pm, as opposed to the usual bedtime lights out rule of 8pm. They had all retired to the dorm just after dark at nine o clock, which was quite unusual for the girls, but they each wanted to get to know their new room-mate.

Freda sat on the large window sill overlooking the gardens. Like the rest of the girls she was already in her pyjamas and dressing gown, she rested her legs out stretched on the deep window sill, with big fluffy pink slippers finishing her look. She smiled at Saoirse and asked how her first day was.

"At least you survived it Saoirse," she said with a friendly smile. Freda had a natural air of leadership in her presence.

Perhaps because she was older, there was a sense about her that she had learned to conform. She did so to the degree that was necessary to keep her out of trouble for the length of time that she was here. It was as if she was tolerating this place for as long as she had to, knowing that it won't be forever.

"It was ok, thanks, not as bad as it could have been" Saoirse replied, shyly.

"Well thanks very much!" joked Maria.

"Ah, you'll get used to it. Sometimes it feels like a glorified prison sentence and other days it's just like school. But one thing to make you feel better is that we are all in the same boat so don't hesitate to shout if you need anything," Freda assured.

Again, Saoirse was surprised at the maturity of the girls.

"Oh get out your disposable girls and take a photo, it will last longer!" Freda rolled her eyes and directed her comment at Jennifer and Jacqueline across the room. They were sitting side by side on Jennifer's bed, staring at Saoirse.

Jennifer and Jacqueline awkwardly shuffled and fidgeted not quite knowing what to say. Saoirse thought to herself that those maturity levels were limited to most, but not all.

Alvagh finished her nightly routine in the bathroom, brushing her teeth and washing her face with Simple soap, moisturising with Nivea cream and tying up her long blonde hair into a well-groomed pony tail at the top of her head. She was only eleven years old but had already begun the daily ritual of looking after herself with religious morning and night-time skincare routines.

"So, Saoirse, what music do you like?" She bounced onto the end of Saoirse's bed, tucking one leg in under the other, ready to engage in conversation with her new friend.

"Oh, I like all sorts of music. I love music in fact. I like The Beatles, of course, Queen, David Bowie...."

"Right that's it, girls, you're all blown out I have a new best friend for life here" Alvagh announced, throwing her arms in the air and flinging her head back. Then she began to belt out Killer Queen by Queen, strumming on her invisible air guitar like no-one was watching.

Saoirse laughed, not quite ready to join in but knowing it was only going to be a matter of time until she got over her initial shyness among her new friends.

"That's one thing I really miss in here. You just can't pop on your tapes when you want to and no radio" Alvagh slumped, her legs crossed in lotus position "oh gosh it's so hard. My whole family are music mad and as you can see it rubbed off on me. Are your family into music Saoirse, is that where you get it from?" Alvagh continued, resting her elbows on her knees and palms under her chin.

"No, I don't think I get it from my family. I'm not sure where I get it from, to be honest. I've always had a love for music though, so I hear what you are saying."

And for the first time in her life, Saoirse wondered where did she get her love of music from?

"See what I mean Saoirse?" Maria nodded to Saoirse with reference to her earlier heads-up on the girls.

The girls chatted until lights out curfew at 10pm, at which time they each obediently settled down in their beds and drifted off to sleep.

Chapter 17

Given the circumstances Saoirse felt quite lucky to have met such lovely people in this awful place. There was a sense of unity and camaraderie here amid the four walls of this dormitory. Aside from Jennifer and Jacqueline of course, but the other three girls were so nice their hostility didn't count. Saoirse felt empathy for the girls, knowing that they were ultimately coming from a place of their own insecurity deep down.

She raised a prayer of thanks to God from her heart, as she settled off into a deep sleep.

Saoirse settled in well to boarding school. Her teachers were nice normal people in her opinion, and she made sure to stay out of Sr Agnes's way as much as humanly possible.

She listened to Maria who continued to give her advance warning where necessary. She found her way around the premises pretty quickly, and she made new friends easily.

The girls here were from all sorts of backgrounds, but for the most part, they came from either rich families or, like Maria, families where their parents had moved away for work but wanted their children to be educated in Dublin.

Saoirse even signed up for the after-school hockey team. Even though she resigned to the fact that sport was never going to her thing but being on the school hockey team meant more 'away' matches. For now, that was the only way she could get to go off the grounds, even if it was only for a couple of hours at a time.

Friday arrived and Saoirse's first week in the Boarding School was coming to an end. Most of the girls were packing to go home for the weekend. The grounds and school were filled with the usual Friday evening hype in the air. It was amplified even more at this time of year, now that the evenings had that stretch.

The girls could be heard shouting to each other down the halls. Their excited voices bellowed from dorm to dorm, each packing their things for the weekend. They filled each-other in on their plans while home with their families. Even those who stayed on campus for the weekend felt a sense of excitement, knowing that in a few hours the premises would have emptied out. One by one each girl would be collected and gone home to her weekend life.

Saoirse held the smallest bit of hope in her heart that maybe Joe and Lil might come and collect her. All that day, in the back of her mind she wondered if they would show up, whilst minding herself at the same time so as her hopes would not rise to convince her.

That evening after tea, she went outside and sat on the bench outside the front door of the grand boarding school building.

By nine pm that Friday night, everyone who was going to go home had already left and gone. The grounds had emptied out, and the sounds of the girls' laughter and hype had left with each car door closing and driving away.

Saoirse sat on the front bench, waiting outside the main building. Darkness was falling, and a chill was beginning to fill the air. Even the sound of the birds chirping in the trees had become silent. She noticed the chill that came with the darker skies. She stood up to make her way back to the dorm, trying to convince herself not to feel disappointed. She knew that Joe and Lil were not going to come and collect her anyway.

For the first month in the Sisters of Charity Boarding School, Saoirse repeated the very same expectation, every Friday evening, followed by the same pattern of events each time.

She became used to the pain and heaviness in her heart. She learned over time to balance the act of getting on with it, to make the best of what she had and feeling like something was dying inside. She felt rejected and guilty all the time, and she never knew what she had done wrong or why everyone thought she was such a bad and nasty person.

Evil was the word used by Sr. Agnes. She knew she wasn't evil. She believed the beautiful lady by her bedside on that first night. There was an authenticity in her voice and in her eyes. Saoirse knew that the lady was speaking from a place of deep love and love does not lie.

If she knew anything, she intuitively knew that love is the only truth there is. It is the only thing that is truly real. She held on to the lady's message. But she found it more and more difficult to do so, living each day faced with the conditional messages in every-day life and the unknown source of guilt in her heart. Even though she had no idea why she felt guilty, it was a feeling that was always there.

One Friday evening, after waiting on Lil and Joe for the last time she was walking down the last corridor towards her dorm she could hear Jennifer and Jacqueline talking in the room to someone else. She knew that Maria was still studying in the library trying to catch up on homework she had completely forgotten to do during the week. Freda had gone home this weekend. Then she remembered Alvagh's voice coaching lessons had been cancelled due to her voice coach having the flu.

"Oh hi Saoirse, we're playing scrabble, wanna join us?" Alvagh sat with her legs in lotus position. Jennifer and Jacqueline lay on their bellies around the board in the middle of the floor.

'OK sure. How's it going?' Saoirse asked kneeling to join the girls.

'Jenny is hammering us' Jaqueline laughed.

The girls continued to play and joke together. As always, there was the noticeable clique with Jenny and Jackie, but it was bearable. Jenny and Jackie's jokes gradually became more personal and Alvagh became more and more hostile and quiet. Saoirse noticed this, and she also noticed Jenny and Jackie continued to administer smart comments and innuendos, each one cutting a little deeper than the last. Some of the comments referred to singing, others were directed at famous people in the music industry and others referred to girls who look after their appearance, Jenny and Jackie called this vanity. Each remark was as degrading and mocking as the last. One girl made a comment, and the other would giggle down into her chest. It went beyond humour to uncomfortable. Saoirse looked at Alvagh knowing the girl's comments were all directed at her. Alvagh was staring at the two girls. By now her face wore a distinct look of intolerance.

'Do you know that every comment you have just made in the last fifteen minutes has been a direct insult not only to me but my family too?' Alvagh asked.

The girls, unashamed and equally unapologetic looked at one-another and laughed again.

"Is that what you need to do to feel good about yourselves? Run other people down?" She continued.

Saoirse had not said anything yet but observed the change in tone. She felt for Alvagh and felt mighty proud of her friend for standing up to the girls, and with such confidence too.

"Yeah well Alvagh, if you can't stand the heat, get out of the kitchen," Jenny said and looked to Jackie again for the support of her mockery.

"Oh for God's sake, how pathetic," Saoirse snapped "is that the best you can come up with? Would you two ever grow up, the pair of you?" She couldn't help but put the two girls in their place.

"Were we talking to you Saoirse? No, we weren't. So stay out of it, you nobody," Jackie's words grabbed and clenched Saoirse, the shock pierced her heart like a dagger.

"Yeah yeah we know all about you, little miss nobody, no one wanted you, so you ended up here. So stay out of it, it's nothing to do with you" added Jackie.

Saoirse could feel the blood rush straight up her neck and her face go red hot with humiliation and embarrassment.

"Saoirse's right, you two are beyond pathetic. I would call you bullies, but bullies have power over their victims. You two don't know what that is. You wouldn't know power if it jumped up and bit you in the face" Alvagh put the girls in their place with that tone of confident certainty. Every part of her body language reciprocated the words she said. She was clearly giving her honest opinion of Jenny and Jackie's behaviour.

The two girls were no match for Alvagh's conviction and had nothing to say. Each of them searched for a come-back. One looking to the other for words of redemption. Both failed, miserably.

Alvagh broke the silence and asked Saoirse if she wanted to go for a walk outside, to look for shooting stars. Saoirse welcomed the break from the tension. They got their coats and left the dorm.

"What pathetic excuses for human beings," Alvagh said once they were out of earshot. "thanks for having my back in there, you're a real pal." She linked Saoirse and smiled with a look of deep appreciation as they walked along the long corridor.

'the nobody'. Who told them? How did they know? Saoirse's mind was filled with questions.

Alvagh picked up on Saoirse's silence.

"Oh Saoirse, honestly, don't let them get to you" Just for that split moment Alvagh's arm tugging around Saoirse's shoulders was a shining light, melting the isolation in her heart. "They give me a hard time all of the time just because my aunt is a well-known singer and all of my family have a crazy passion for the music industry. I don't let it get to me and nor should you. They are idiots with nothing else better to do."

Saoirse appreciated Alvagh's attempt to console, but the pain still lingered. Within moments her mind rationalized that at least Alvagh was being slagged off because of a talent, because she had something to offer. She couldn't help feeling that there was underhanded gossip going around in her name and she wondered who else knew what the girls knew.

"Thanks, Alvagh but why did they say that? Who told them?" Saoirse bit her lip fighting back the tears.

Alvagh laughed.

"Told them what? That you're a nobody?" Alvagh's eyes widened below her frowning forehead at the ridiculous notion.

Saoirse realised by the look on Alvagh face that it was the first she had heard of it. In those moments her thoughts raced. Perhaps the girls got lucky in their attempt to insult her and happened to hit the nail on the head. Maybe there was a chance that nobody had said anything after all, although her gut told her otherwise. It was far too accurate for them just to get lucky, besides they didn't strike her as clever folk, not to mention intuitive or even perceptive. This also meant that whoever confided in the girls had not confided in Alvagh and maybe that meant that they had not confided in anyone else either, she hoped.

Alvagh was still looking at her, innocently waiting for a response. At that moment Saoirse surmised in her mind that it was her turn to confide:

"Oh Alvagh, you don't want to know all of the ins and outs. It's a very long story, but yes, that's what Sr Agnes calls me, 'a nobody'. It's because I'm adopted, and my adopted family didn't want me anymore." Saoirse had to pause, she felt her lip quiver and her throat was about to explode. She took a deep breath and continued to explain "I don't know why, I wish I did, but hence why I'm here. That's it really. Sorry to bore you with the detail." She shrugged her shoulders and awkwardly fidgeted with her hair, twirling the ends around her fingers.

Alvagh's face had dropped. She stood in the corridor with her mouth open trying to understand what Saoirse had just said. While at the same time deep compassion exploded from her heart for Saoirse and what she must have gone through.

"Oh Saoirse, that's awful, how could they? I had no idea. I thought your father was ill. That's what Maria said. What a disgusting thing to say. How mean and cruel and you are so lovely too" Alvagh spilled out the words trying understand and digest everything she had just heard.

Saoirse smiled at Alvagh's kindness. Her friend's warmth and compassion filled her heart with love and acceptance.

Alvagh only knew her as Saoirse.

She had never known her as the one that was adopted or the one who was less important. In fact, Alvagh and Maria were the only two friends she had become close to in her life so far, who did not identify her with the adoption label.

"Thanks, Alvagh, that means a lot," Alvagh's warmth and compassion blasted the heaviness in Saoirse's heart for the second time, she searched her pocket for her tissue and wiped her eyes.

"Oh, and don't worry I won't say a word to anyone, I'm really good at keeping secrets, hey I have a famous family, say no more. I can never open my mouth about anything personal in-case the newspapers get a hold of it and twist everything around. So I am used to keeping my mouth shut about confidential stuff. But it ends there I'm afraid. Otherwise, I never shut up," Alvagh assured.

"Have you heard from your family since you came here?" Alvagh was afraid of the answer and immediately regretted asking the question.

Saoirse shuck her head and looked down at the floor.
Alvagh was absent of words to say, she could see the depth of sad-

ness in her friend's eyes. She gave her the most heartfelt hug, holding Saoirse as tight as she could, for as long as she could without suffocating her. Saoirse released her tears.

"And by the way, I really mean it about sticking up for me with those two" Alvagh's big blue eyes were fixed on Saoirse's "you didn't have to, and it was very kind of you and brave. I'm not used to people sticking up for me. Most people think that I deserve it because I have a famous family and they don't."

"Ok that makes no sense at all Alvagh, it's not your fault your family are famous. Besides, why give you a hard time because you do? Anyway, being famous for something you are good at is something to be proud of. I admire your family, even though I have no idea who they are. People are just jealous that's all. Anyway, I think you are lovely, and great fun too, famous or not famous." Saoirse nodded decisively. "Now come on, show me where all those shooting stars are. I heard that you can wish upon a shooting star while it's falling, and your wish will come true."

"So it seems, let's go," Alvagh replied.

The two girls pushed open the heavy exit door at the end of the corridor. They lay down on a large green lawn, side by side. The following hours passed in the blink of an eye. The girls gazed up to the cool night skies in search of shooting stars.

Alvagh explained to Saoirse all about the galaxy, the planets and constellations of stars, pointing out The Saucepan and Orion. Saoirse listened, and Alvagh shared her knowledge of the galaxy with her friend. Saoirse was fascinated.

The following months saw Saoirse, Maria and Alvagh become the best of friends. Most of their time outside class was spent laughing, joking and sharing their ideas and perceptions. Each was fascinated by the other's personality and what their character had to offer.

Alvagh's enthusiasm for life and bold outlook would light up any grey day. Maria's kind and social nature warmed the cold air in the convent school just by her very presence. She was self-less with endless compliments and observations about another's talents.

Saoirse felt like she could completely relax and just be herself. There was no judgement, no ridicule and she knew she was always enough in her friends' eyes.

Alvagh's dream to grow to her potential in the music industry complimented Saoirse's passion for music. One evening Alvagh decided that Saoirse could write her songs and she can create the melody. Saoirse thought it was the best idea and enjoyed every minute putting pen to paper, allowing her creative juices to flow on behalf of her friend's dream.

Most of the boarders went home for Summer breaks. The three girls stayed on in school. Alvagh's family were on a UK tour. Her aunt's new album was doing very well on the UK charts. Her mother was her aunts' manager, which meant she toured with her.

Summer times heralded the busy tourist season for Maria's family at the restaurant. They assured Maria that she would be bored at home with long days spent on her own. She was still too young to help out at the restaurant, but she was happy enough to stay put with Saoirse and Alvagh.

The girls had to help out on the grounds and do chores during the summer days. Their free time reflected the same timetable as a typical school day. They spent from seven a.m. to five pm doing chores, meals etc. and free time was five pm until lights out at ten.

When Saoirse lay in bed late at night, she often thought about who she was. Sr Agnes' words on that first day echoed in her mind, as did wondering why Lil and Joe sent her to the convent.

No matter how much she thought about it, she could never figure out the answer. Even so, she felt a deep sense of guilt and blame inside, never knowing why. She felt like a back-seat passenger in the vehicle of her life. In the driving seat was a big black cloud that vibrated the beliefs of the adults and their influence. It's negativity driving her through deep pain inside.

No matter how hard she tried to understand, she could never figure out why they thought the way they do. Her thoughts then turned to what the lady who visited her on her first night had said:

"You are made of strong stuff dear child. You are courageous and beautiful and strong. You have a heart so pure no wrong can destroy it. Be strong and know that I am here, always."

Not once did Saoirse ever question who that lady was and how she just disappeared. The faint memory of when she could see those spirit beings as clear as day was still alive in her mind, and she assumed that this lady was simply from the same place. The energy and unconditional pure loving presence of the lady were what she recognised as one that comes from spirit, from God.

She thought about the great conflict in the two messages and wondered why the adults in her life saw something different. Her need for them to see her in her true light and their failure to do so left her with a sense of lack. She subconsciously integrated this sense as her own lack of not being good enough. The subconscious belief began to take hold, deep down inside.

Every Autumn welcomed the driveway to the convent become gradually busier with students arriving back from summer break. The quiet air faded and was replaced by the growing momentum of excited voices.

The students began to fill the corridors and grounds. The girls wheeled their luggage through the building. The refreshed boarders arrived back on campus and connected again. Their welcome buzz filled the air. The girls caught up with their friends, sharing and swapping stories of their summer breaks. Every year was the same, the girls seemed to have grown so much taller and their absence in the short time magnified the rapid changes of the adolescent life.

The seasonal cycle was clearly visible amidst the changing land-scape and sounds of mother nature. The leaves on the mighty oak trees began to turn copper brown. Before long, they shed their crisp leaves, filling the lawns with blankets of autumn shades. The scenes were reminiscent of the shadow of what was, as the golden blankets lay under the breast of the scantily clad trees.

The evening melody that filled the air on long summer nights grew quieter too. The sweet song of the swallows grew absent. They had long left for the seasonal journey to their temporary home far away. Autumn was surely progressing, and the air filled with the chill of darker, cooler nights.

The girls settled back into the daily routine of class, study and rest-time. The hockey teams began to practice again in preparation for their weekly matches on Saturday mornings. Saoirse would have liked to think that she was improving throughout the years, but the wise child knew it was best to be honest with herself. The only reason she was on the hockey team was that it allowed her to visit elsewhere. It was the only way she could leave the grounds that had become her world.

The following years were spent committed to the routine life the convent demanded. Saoirse remained steadfast in focusing on what brought her happiness as much as she could. She allowed herself to hope for the future. For now, hope was where she found optimism. In her wisdom, she knew that this state of circumstance was temporary. Time would move on and someday she would no longer be here. The knowledge that this current state would not be forever helped her to look forward to a time when she would be free.

She planned to create a life of happiness and meaning with that freedom. She nurtured her dreams for happiness and finding indepen-dence someday deep in her heart. For now, she held on to that hope and made the very best of the heart in this place. She found that heart in the friends she had made, Maria and Alvagh. She cherished those bonds and felt blessed by God each day for their presence in her life.

She continued to visit the oratory chapel on the grounds too. The teen-age girl sat in peace for as long as time allowed, talking to God. She never questioned if he could hear her. She always knew he could. Her knowing went far beyond trust. There was no need for trust in Saoirse's eyes. As far as she was concerned God just is and what is simply, is.

She loved just to sit, present in His peace. The feeling of wholeness reminded her of where she came from, and all that really mattered. She felt restored, connected back to who she really was. The feeling of peace that filled every part of her mind and her body was all she needed to restore the natural strength that flowed from her heart.

She never rekindled her relationship with Jacqueline and Jennifer. They hurt her that evening over the game of scrabble. They broke her trust that night, and she never had any time for them again.

At times they tried to press her buttons and wind her up, but she had completely detached from them, and nothing they said could ever hurt her, at least not deeply.

One day she found out who told them that she was 'a nobody' and the real reason she was sent here. It turned out that Sr. Agnes warned them about her and 'encouraged' them to keep an eye on her the week she arrived.

She only found out because they got frustrated that she was unfazed by their consistent remarks. Jenny let it all out one night in another attempt to upset her. It was the last straw. Both girls had let themselves down miserably. Freda, Alvagh and Maria let the girls have it. All respect for them was gone, and no one held prejudice against Saoirse.

Chapter 18

Lil fastened up her rain mac and reached for her umbrella in the press under the stairs. She had checked the bus timetable the night before, and a No 17 bus was due at 9:30.

The No 17 bus and the No 86 were the most unreliable buses that passed through Ashlawn. Lil checked her watch. It was just before nine in the morning.

She pulled the hall door behind her and entered the cold, blustery October morning. The wind and the rain came unapologetically from all directions. She walked up the road, her frame being hit from all angles by the elements. She held her umbrella steady, shielding herself from the heavy rain, hoping the bus would be on time, this morning of all mornings.

Lil came out onto the main road and looked behind her. It was only five minutes past nine, but sure enough, there was the unreliable No.17 approaching the bus stop. She hurried her step and pressed the button on the pedestrian lights. The bus stopped at the red light and Lil made use of the pause to briskly cross the road to the bus stop, some 30 meters from the pedestrian lights.

She boarded the bus, greeted the bus driver and paid her fair. Her umbrella was drenched, and the raindrops flowed from her rain mac. She placed her umbrella on the floor at her feet and sat back on the warm bus.

She looked out the window through the sheet of rain. It belted furiously with the force of the wind behind it, immediately breaking into little drops and each one trickled down the glass. This time, she was feeling glad that the unreliable No.17 was early this morning, relieving her from standing in the cold, blustery elements.

As well as the No 17 bus being early for once, Mother Nature sent another work of a little miracle that morning. Just as the bus approached the coast nearing the end of its journey, the clouds broke to reveal blue skies. The sun began to shine, and the dark, cold morning dissolved into a beautiful bright day. The rain cleared, and a large rainbow arched over the horizon of the Blackrock coastline.

Lil stepped off the bus, relieved with the quick change in the weather to her favour. She had a twenty-minute walk to her destination, and her appointment was for 10.30. She checked her watch, and it was only half past nine. She decided to take advantage of the time to spare and popped into a coffee shop for a pot of tea and a fruit scone to warm up.

"Saoirse would you get the ball!!!! Saoirse get the ball!!! Saoirse!!!!"

Mary O'Rourke was the highly competitive right back on the hockey team. Saoirse, the not so competitive left-back was running as fast as she possibly could towards the hockey ball. Her legs had gone numb at this stage, not due to the cold, rather due to the screams of Mary O'Rourke to run faster and the pressure to keep up with her demand. She moved those little legs with all her might and Mary continued to scream. The opposing team players were also fast approaching the ball, but Saoirse got there first. The ball was rapidly rolling towards the line, and if it went out of play, it meant a free to the opposing team. Saoirse reached out with her hockey stick and stopped the ball dead in its tracks. Now all she had to do was hit it far up the pitch, out of danger. She raised her hockey stick, focused her eye on the ball. The other team were right beside her by now. She swung hard focusing with all her might and she missed. The ball remained right there on the pitch, exactly where she had stopped it. The centre-forward of the other team took full advantage of the opportunity, gained control of the ball and went on to score another goal.

Saoirse once again watched the familiar sight of Mary O'Rourke jumping up and down, lifting her knees as high as she could and stomping her feet into the ground, repeating the word 'No' as loud as she could.

For the last five years Saoirse could never understand why or how Mary took the game so seriously. As always, the reason for Mary's little outcry went completely over her head, and she made her way back to her starting position, again.

Off the pitch, Mary was always kind, funny and nice. Saoirse considered the idea of an alter ego, who came alive only during hockey games. It didn't matter whether it was practice or tournament matches, Mary was extremely competitive and Saoirse, well Saoirse just enjoyed the game.

The girls got changed in the hockey pavilion. The usual dynamic was in play. There were the stronger, louder personalities ruling the conversation. Shouting banter back and forth. The quieter ones got changed in groups of two's and three's and chatted among themselves. Hockey practice always finished just before lunch for the second years and the girls were in a hurry to get down to the canteen to fill their hungry bellies.

Saoirse was one of the first to be ready. She sat waiting for Maria, so as they could walk together back to the canteen.

"Ok girls come on, don't delay. If you're finished getting changed make your way on to the canteen." The PE teacher ordered the girls.

"Aw, I'll catch up with you Saoirse, keep me a seat, will you?" asked Maria.

"Sure, see you in a bit," Saoirse threw her bag over her shoulder making sure to sweep her long ponytail out of the way, and headed back to the main building.

The birds were chirping, and the rain had almost dried up. The wind had also calmed to a mild breeze. Lil walked up the long avenue towards the red brick building and thoughts of what she was going to say during her forthcoming meeting ran through her mind. She was mostly worried about being challenged on what she had to say. She knew she was going to be dealing with a force to be reckoned with and Lil was a non-confrontational lady by nature. She insisted to herself to remain assertive in tone, word and deed.

That's all she had to do, stick to her guns and don't be bullied. Then all will be ok.

She walked through the large gates onto the gravel drive. The large trees either side swayed gently in the light breeze. She looked ahead to the main door and saw a group of students coming from the hockey pitch making their way into the building. She observed to herself that they seem to be happy and just like any other school children. There again this was 1978 after all. The days of residential convent institutions being run somewhat like prisons or detention centres for children were long gone. As were the children who were grey in complexion, lacking in nutrition and walking in a dual file like humans who had lost their spirits.

Of course, the girls looked normal and happy.

She approached the steps in front of the door. Most of the girls had already gone through by the time Lil arrived at the door, except one. A happy go lucky girl with brown, shoulder length hair ran towards the door just ahead of Lil.

"Oh sorry.....me and my manners, here you go" the girl smiled at the stranger and stopped herself cutting past Lil to rush to lunch. "I'm always Paddy last and rushing. She stood back and politely held the door for the lady.

"Thankyou. It's taken up lovely now hasn't it?" Lil glanced to the sky, accepting the girl's invite to go first.

"Yes it has, I hope you weren't caught in that shower this morning. Even our hockey practice was almost cancelled and everything."

"I was unfortunately" Lil looked the girl up and down "Are you a second-year love?"

"Yes. My name's Maria, pleased to meet you" Maria extended her hand to shake Lil's.

"Thank you, Maria. That will be all," Sr. Agnes said standing in the hall outside her office door.

Maria smiled at the lady and briskly walked down the hall towards the canteen.

"Good morning Mrs Corcoran. In perfect time, I see," Sr Agnes greeted her with a shallow smile.

"This way," she prompted Lil into her office and closed the door behind her.

Saoirse spotted Alvagh in the busy canteen sitting at their usual table. Alvagh's thick, wavy blonde hair and long body stood out a mile, even when she was sitting down. She always sat tall with her back straight, chin up, shoulders back and great posture. She oozed a natural confidence and self-assurance, and it was growing day by day.

Even though she was now fifteen, her skin had not one blemish, just a naturally soft, dewy complexion that glowed in all the right places. Saoirse filled her tray with her lunch and made her way over to join her friend.

"Oh, there you are, listen I was thinking" Alvagh said reaching for her napkin and wiping the crumbs away. Saoirse sat down beside her and unwrapped her lunch. "My voice coaching lessons are not starting back until after Christmas. Tomorrow night why don't we hook up in the music room and go over that song you wrote again, the one about the seasons changing? I asked Ms Byrne if it would be ok to use the music room after hours and she said it was no problem. I have been telling her about your song writing Saoirse, and I have been working on putting the melodies to them myself. She is in full support of the idea, thinks it's great. Would you be on?"

Alvagh's big blue eyes anticipated Saoirse response. Saoirse could almost see a million different possibilities of where this might take them dance around in Alvagh's mind. Alvagh was always supportive of Saoirse's gift to put together a few lyrics so easily.

"She just had it," is what Alvagh would say.

Saoirse never really figured out what 'it' was. As far as she was concerned, she just wrote down how she felt about whatever she was writing about, and it came together easily. Saoirse thought that anyone could do it.

The truth was that Saoirse did have a gift for writing. She naturally reached deep into the soul of whatever topic she was writing about. The reason she found it so easy was because she had learned to live from her soul. For her, it was the only place that there was peace. It was the kind of peace that opened the flow of remembrance, unity and harmony, in a world that seemed to live in illusion, denial, chaos and conflict.

She had not consciously chosen to live from her soul. It was more of a survival mechanism. Staying anchored in that sense of peace was the main thing that fuelled her strength. At thirteen she had learned that her fundamental source of love and happiness had to come from within her own heart. She had learned not to depend on external sources for love and acceptance. It certainly wasn't always easy, but she had learned that it was the only resource of happiness that she could depend upon.

By now, however, a conflict had evolved. Deep within her heart was a stillness of never-ending peace, love and strength. It fuelled her sense of who she knew herself to be and it made perfect sense. Its harmony reminded her of her perfection, the perfection in all things and the perfection of everyone else. Yet she was growing up in a world that denied any recognition of this perfection, not only in her but in everything and everyone else too. She had learned that the ignorance of this denial was deemed normal. Everyone denied it because everyone else did. As a result, everyone forgot that this perfection even existed. It was like everyone had resigned to live in a world that suppressed the power and potential available within us all, if we just unite together, support each other and connect with a Higher Power.

The reason Alvagh thought that she simply 'had it', a gift for writing, was simply because her writing reminded everyone of who we are. That powerful part of us, who resides deep down in that still peaceful place and knew that we are here for a reason.

Saoirse believed that the challenges we face were given to us for the very same reason: to remind us of who we are. And one is pointless without the other. It was like light and dark, or up and down. The still peacefulness within, helped her know herself through the challenges. It was her strength. Without it, the pain of the challenges, the rejection and abandonment she experienced would have surely destroyed her.

By tapping into her soul, she saved herself and only for the challenges she would never have gone so deep. In the crazy world that she lived in, where conflict and confusion seemed to rule in a world filled with unanswered questions, it was the only thing that remained truly real to her.

Her heart skipped a beat in response to Alvagh's invitation.

"That would be brilliant Alvagh, great idea; I'll have another look at those lyrics in the meantime, always room for improvement and all that" Saoirse smiled with gratitude and excitement to be doing what she loved, it was made even better alongside Alvagh's passion and enthusiasm.

"Cool, we could even make it a regular Friday night thing. Who knows what we could come up with by the end of term next year," Alvagh shared her enthusiasm once more.

"Heads up girls, looks like someone's going home early" Maria shared her insight with the girls. "I can't believe there was still some lasagne left!"

"Who's going home? How do you know?" Alvagh sat forward in her chair. She scanned the room for who it might be.

"I have no idea but whoever she is, she's in our year. I met a lady on the way in, nearly knocked the woman over. She had an appointment with Agnes and asked me was I in second year." Maria tucked into her lasagne "Oh good Lord no wonder there was still some left, that's rotten"

"What did the woman look like Maria?" Saoirse's heart was beating faster in the last few moments.

"Pretty lady, clearly well to do. Blonde curly hair, I would say mid-forties, maybe," Maria looked at Saoirse's face "Oh no Saoirse,"

Saoirse nervously bit her thumbnail, she didn't need to say anything, her face said it all.

"Saoirse, let's just wait and see" Alvagh assured. "I mean how many blonde, well to do mammy's have daughters here? It could be anyone".

Chapter 19

"Mrs Corcoran, I cannot stand in the way of your decision, but I hope you have considered and evaluated it thoroughly?" Sr. Agnes said strictly. The subtle tone of threat and authority spoke louder that her words.

"You are dealing with an extremely complicated issue here. One in which most do not understand. I trust Mr Corcoran is united with you in your decision?" she added.

"I need to do what feels right in my heart," Lil responded. She kept her eyes fixed on the desk that stood between herself and Sr. Agnes "And yes, I can assure you I have discussed the matter with Mr Corcoran," she concluded, choosing her words carefully.

"All I am saying is that you have to think of what is right for you and your family. Life is difficult enough these days without adding extra burdens on oneself if you understand me?," Lil heard what the Sister was saying but she had considered the bigger picture more than enough of late to know what was right "I may inform you that the child has shown no signs of disruption while under the rule of our institution. I can only conclude that our approach and influence seem to be effective," Sr Agnes maintained her strict tone, this time with an air of persuasion.

Lil kept her eyes fixed on the desk, with her hands firmly clasping her handbag resting on her lap.

"Very well," Sr. Agnes resigned "I will update the files during the week and tend to all other business relating to the matter. We will see you on Friday."

Just before class ended for the weekend, Sr Agnes knocked on the door of one of the classrooms. Upon entering all the girls rose to their feet:

"Dia duit, Sr Agnes," the class of girls, sang in unison.

"Dia agus Muire daoibh," Sr. Agnes replied. She glanced around the classroom.

"Saoirse Corcoran, where is Saoirse?"

Saoirse raised her hand and felt a sharp pain of butterflies in her tummy.

"Come with me please," she exited the classroom and Saoirse followed.

She walked behind Sr Agnes all the way to her office.

"Shut the door behind you," ordered the nun, taking residence behind her desk.

"Mrs Corcoran arranged an appointment earlier this week. She and Mr Corcoran have revised their long-term plan. You are no longer going to be a full-time boarder here. From now on you will be going home on weekends and normal school holidays." Saoirse's whole world shifted, a million thoughts ran through her mind. A surge of confusion filled every part of her being. For a brief moment, she even had to think of who Mrs Corcoran was. She had not forgotten about Lil or Joe; she was not used to hearing her mother being called Mrs Corcoran. Then she thought of Lil. She had come back for her. Five years later. She must love her after all. Part of her couldn't help feel gratitude to Lil for being strong enough to claim that love and come for her. While the rest of her couldn't let go of how she had abandoned her that day she came home from school. A lot had changed since then, including Saoirse. But that little girl still cried out for her mammy inside and was grateful that she came back after all.

"Mrs Corcoran advised that she will collect you this evening at 7pm. Go to your dormitory and prepare to be outside in good time. That will be all, shut the door on your way out,"

Saoirse stood before the nun. The last place she wanted to be right now was standing in that nun's office, but she did not want to move at the same time because that would mean change, more change. She was frozen between the resistance to that change and the little girl who wanted to finally return home to what was. This was clearly something wonderful. She got to go home on weekends. She also got to be part of her family again. She could see Ruth, her daddy and family life. She could regain a sense of feeling normal. Live a normal life, almost. She got to go home to her own bed. Home to a place where day to day routine meant being within the world outside, where she could see her friends on the street, play kick the can, relay racing and bulldogs charge.

But right now. the prevailing image of Lil and Joe's faces sitting at the kitchen table, that day they let her go was all she could see in her mind. She heard her screams and cries for her mammy and daddy play like a movie and watched their faces sitting in ignorance and denial of her pleas.

"I said that will be all" Sr Agnes glared over her glasses on the bridge of her nose "Shut the door behind you,"

Saoirse walked back to her dorm in a daze. Her heart was beating fast, and her knees felt shaky. Her blood rushed through her veins and she felt completely out of alignment.

In the blink of an eye, every thought possible ran through Saoirse's mind, playing out the possibility that had brought about the decisions of the last week. She imagined the discussions, the meetings and the thoughts behind them.

Her world had once again been abruptly turned upside down due to the decisions of adults. This is something she had accepted. She was a child and children are at the mercy of adults until such a time that they are old enough to make their own decisions. Part of her felt excited and hopeful, part of her felt confused, part of her felt disappointed at the level of energy she had put into tolerating this place and finding peace amidst the cloud of dread that constantly filled the air in this place. Part of her felt, for God's sake here we go again, would they ever make their minds up. Like she was being thrown from pillar to post depending on what the adults felt at the time. And she continued to wonder why, why now? Why was Lil changing her mind now?

She went into the dorm to find Alvagh sitting on the bed, wide-eyed with a beaming smile, all ready and waiting to begin their new venture in the music room. She looked at Alvagh, and her heart sank.

"Oh, Alvagh....." Saoirse couldn't help it, she welled up, perhaps the realization that she was letting her friend down was the trigger, or maybe it was the love in Alvagh's presence that helped her release the emotion that was building up inside. She burst into tears and stood in the dorm with her hands over her face.

"I'm so sorry; I won't be able to go to the music room with you today." She forced herself to speak through the tears, feeling more and more upset as she spoke. "Sr Agnes just called me into the office. My mum has decided to take me home on weekends."

Alvagh immediately ran to her friend and hugged her tight, consoling her with all her might, trying to take her pain away.

"Hey that's ok, come sit down," she wrapped her arm around Saoirse and walked her over to the bed and sat down beside her. "But isn't that a good thing?" Alvagh's intuition saw past the reason for Saoirse's sadness being a music session.

"Yeah, I suppose it is. Yes, it is. I'm just sick of it you know," she snuffled, and composed herself with deep breaths, "I'm glad, kind of, but I'm sick of it at this stage. Of course I would rather go home on weekends and holidays, but I just wish they would make their minds up. I want to go home more than I want to be here but at the same time I won't go so far as to say that I like it here, but I wish I had a say, you know?......I can't stand Sr. Agnes, like she just spat it out, no feeling, no emotion; she's so cold. 'Mrs. Corcoran arranged an appointment earlier this week. You are no longer going to be a full-time boarder here' she talks to you like you are a thing." Saoirse wiped her tears with the cuff of her sleeve.

"Oh don't talk to me, that woman hates me....in fact, I think she hates everyone. Sometimes I think she has lost her soul, the oul bag. But listen, don't worry about her, you get to go home. You get to go home!!" Alvagh's eyes widened, pointing out the positives to Saoirse trying to take her mind off what she could not control and help her focus on her good fortune.

"I know, I have to be outside before seven," Saoirse forced a smile and looked around to assess what she needed to pack.

"OK I'll help," Alvagh ran into the bathroom and returned in seconds. She opened Saoirse's drawer and placed all the items on the bed.

"There you go, toothbrush, hairbrush, two pairs of clean knickers, two pairs of clean socks and Maisie, do you have a bag?" She stood tall over the pile and folded her arms.

The girls both stood over the bed looking at the small pile of Saoirse's belongings. They looked at each other, and both burst into uncontrollable laughter.

Saoirse bag was packed with hours to spare.

"Oh Alvagh, I shouldn't be laughing. I'm blinking furious to be honest"

"I don't blame you. I honestly don't get your parents. Clearly hence why you're adopted...." Alvagh shocked herself at the words that just popped out of her mouth "oh Saoirse I...I'm so sorry that was incredibly insensitive of me. I didn't mean..."

"Alvagh I know what you mean and no need to apologize. I don't get them either"

Alvagh looked at Saoirse, her eyes still red and her face was still puffy. She glanced outside to the fresh autumnal afternoon:

"Saoirse, I don't know about you but how do you feel about taking a rain check on the music room for today. I can reschedule with Ms Byrne for a weekday, I'm sure it won't be a problem. What do you say we take a long walk around the grounds instead?"

"Music to my ears Alvagh"

They wrapped up and went outside. Alvagh linked her friend's arm, and they chatted about anything and everything, light and shade, walking through the large gardens of the convent grounds. Together the girls entered their own little world during those few hours. It was just them, no one else's thoughts or influence mattered.

They discussed their different perspectives based on their experiences of life so far. They each shared their insecurities and what gave them strength. They swapped ideas about who they were, and they shared their hopes for the future. It was one of the most beautiful afternoons each girl had spent in her life to date.

Both wished they could have stayed in that world for longer, but both knew that it had to come to an end and felt fortunate to have experienced something so special together.

"Right young lady it's time to go, come on, I'll walk you down," Alvagh said to Saoirse in an almost 'mammy' like tone.

Saoirse put her bag on her shoulder and prepared for another transition.

"Thanks, Alvagh" Saoirse said, pausing before walking out of the dorm. Alvagh knew her extension of gratitude went deeper than just the offer to chaperone.

"Come on, hop to...Aggie will be keeping an eye out," Alvagh chopped her hands together.

Giddiness came over the girls during their walk down to the main entrance. Born out of nothing more than each sharing the nervousness of the change that awaited. They giggled about the most stupid things and the more stupid it was, the funnier it became.

As they approached the main door, Sr Agnes stepped out of her office. She stood and looked at the girls as they walked past doing their very best to compose themselves.

"And you are going where Alvagh Cahill?" Sr. Agnes asked.

"Oh Sister, I'm just walking Saoirse to the door to say goodbye," Alvagh knew she was doing nothing wrong.

Sr Agnes gave no response and walked back into her office.

"Told ya," Alvagh leaned into Saoirse. The pair burst, releasing the giddy giggles into the October air.

They sat on the outside bench waiting for Lil. It was ten minutes to seven.

"What does your dad drive?" Alvagh asked, looking down the long gravel drive towards the entrance gate.

"It was an Audi 100 the last time I saw, silver with," Saoirse attention was distracted by a lady walking up the drive. She recognised the lady's frame. Her walk brought back the image in her mind of when she was a little girl, and she used to sit under her parents' bedroom window looking out into the night as far as she could see, praying to God that they returned home safely.

But this time Lil was not linking Joe like she always did all those years ago. This time she was on her own.

Saoirse knew something had changed.

She had assumed that Lil and Joe would be collecting her. Where was Joe and why was he not with her? She thought quickly and remembered that Sr Agnes definitely said that Mr and Mrs Corcoran had revised their long-term plan for you, which meant he must be still alive, so that put her worst fear at ease.

So where was he?

'Maybe he had to work late, or something', but her instinct told her otherwise.

Lil walked straight up to the bench where the girls sat.

"Hello Saoirse, how are you?" she said, holding her handbag over her shoulder with both hands clasping the strap. "Are you ready, we can get the next bus if we go now, it's due in half an hour?" Lil checked her watch and waited for Saoirse to pick up her bag.

She could hardly believe the difference in her daughter. She had grown in so many ways. She was much taller; she had filled out. Her baby face was almost gone. Even though she still looked like Saoirse, her big brown eyes, long eye lashes and sallow complexion had matured to that of a very pretty teenager. Even her long, dark hair was weaving down her back. Lil had never allowed Saoirse to grow her hair long, she figured shorter hair was clean and tidy. She was almost looking at a complete stranger. Saoirse was confident and high spirited, she had a self-certainty about her presence that Lil was not expecting to be met with at all.

Saoirse was so surprised at how cool Lil was. She had not seen her in almost five years. She was only a child when she saw her last. Even back in the old days when Lil met her coming in from school she showed a heck of a lot more enthusiasm to see her.

Saoirse noticed her mammy had changed too. She still had impeccable dress sense. She was still a well-groomed lady. Her bag and shoes matched, her coat looked expensive and her nails were of course manicured. But her face held the story that told of pain, she had aged. She looked tired and more than just five years older.

The awkward silence was palpable. Saoirse obliged and picked up her bag. Alvagh looked at Saoirse, and the look on her face expressed the confusion that Saoirse was also feeling. Maybe open arms and a hug were going to be a bit too much to expect, but at least she asked me how I am, Saoirse thought, but Lil's body language expressed a different message.

Alvagh stood up and hugged her friend.

"See you Monday, take care," she said into Saoirse's ear.

"I will. I love you girl. Tell Maria I said same and see you guys on Monday ok"

They walked down the long drive heading out of the convent grounds. It was the first time Saoirse had ever walked that path all the way to the other side of the gate. It felt strange, as if she was heading into forbidden territory. It was ironic to think that Lil walking by her side did not do anything to ease the feeling of guilt and the underlying feeling that she was doing something that was out of bounds. She had always felt safe as a little girl when entering unfamiliar territory once her mammy was by her side, but this time that feeling wasn't there.

Saoirse decided to break the silence.

"So, how are you? How are Dad and Ruth? I'm really looking forward to seeing them again." She smiled at Lil, aware of her superficial attempt to make a conversation. She immediately thought to herself that she might as well have talked about the weather.

Back there on the bench, it was like as if the rug had been pulled from under her feet. All afternoon she had not had time to think of what it was going to be like seeing Lil again, but she just assumed the re-encounter would be warmer than this.

"Aw, grand, we're fine. It's gone cool now isn't it?" Lil replied.

Chapter 20

Lil was completely out of her territory. There had been a feeling of emptiness in her heart since the day Saoirse left. As a mother, she felt guilty for giving her little girl away. Saoirse was nine years old. She was in her care. Every decision made about Saoirse's life was in the hands of her and Joe. She was completely at their mercy and Lil knew it.

She also knew that when they decided to adopt her that they were taking on a whole new life, a person, with a character and personality all of her own. An individual who would grow to have her own thoughts and feelings about the world around her, but at the time she was only a harmless, helpless little baby.

From the moment Lil held her in her arms that first day in the mother and baby home she loved her. Saoirse was precious, and she knew she would love that baby unconditionally for the rest of time.

The years naturally passed, and that little baby grew. She began to develop a personality of her own, as all children do. It was then and only then that the divide and difference between a birth child and the adopted child became apparent. Saoirse was not displaying the same characteristics inherent in her family. She was worlds apart from Ruth and even her cousins. She was nothing like Lil or Joe in any way. She was different.

It wasn't so much what Saoirse didn't do or couldn't do. It was more so what she could do that her parents could not understand. She could see beyond the veil of this three-dimensional world. In the eyes of the Catholic Church that was wrong.

Lil and Joe could not understand it so how could they defend or support what they do not understand? Where would they find the courage to defend something that the whole of society believes to be wrong? And if they don't understand how Saoirse can see worlds beyond our own, this begs the question of what other 'powers' does she have? What else can she do that they don't understand? Fear took over. They didn't know what they were dealing with and they were afraid.

They were afraid of a little girl who was asking to be loved and looked to them and only them for their love. She was herself. She was unconditionally embracing her nature and trusted that they would too. But their courage to do so failed them. They failed to seek to understand, and they failed to listen to the same voice that Saoirse's natural intelligence always listened to, without question. That voice inside their hearts that said:

'This little girl is the personification of pure love, and she is asking for your love. You promised to give it to her, and now you are afraid of what you do not understand. Your fear is casting you into darkness, where you can't see the truth, where you can't see understanding, where you can't see the light.'

Lil and Joe tried to rationalize and intellectualise what was going on. But you cannot rationalize mystery. They cut off the inner voice of wisdom and listened only to their fear. As a result, suffering took reign.

Lil was a woman who regarded her husband Joe as the more intelligent one in their relationship. She listened to him and trusted his opinion. The final word was always based on what Joe said.

Joe lived simply under the mantra of work hard, be a good person and do your best. He lived from his head. He had done so all his life, and up to now, this approach had served him well. He was rational, intelligent and pragmatic. Yet this time his predominant left-brain approach was trying to make sense of something that did not make any sense in the limitations of the three-dimensional world. This left him in a situation where he felt he had no control. He did not know what to do and that frightened him.

He was afraid that he was dealing with something far greater than what he could understand. He became lost in the fear that inhabited his mind and Saoirse was to blame.

The fear of a fatal consequence and loss that he believed Saoirse might be the cause drowned out the still voice of trust that was forever residing in his heart.

His lost his brother-in-law tragically, followed shortly afterwards by his only sibling. His best friend suddenly passed away and Lil's mother passed too, all in a very short space of time.

Meanwhile he was learning that his little girl can see beyond the veils of the physical dimension. In his heart he knew there was no connection. It was just life. But his fear of what might be true blocked all trust of that knowing.

The fear was chaotic, terrifying and made a lot more noise. Joe chose to listen to it and became paralysed in its grasp. From this dysfunctional place, his love for Saoirse was out of reach.

At the time, the complex dilemma of right and wrong took over the Corcoran's home. Lil was faced with the dilemma of supporting her husband or supporting Saoirse. Her silent battle was antagonising. To give away the baby girl that needed her or to see her husband in the paralysis of fear that she knew would grow to hate.

She watched Joe withdraw from being the daddy that Saoirse needed. He also withdrew from being his chatty, humorous self. She saw the heaviness in his eyes every-day when he returned from work and heard it in his voice which spoke so much less than before.

"Joe, we can't blame Saoirse. We don't know if she's the cause of this. Maybe everything just happened?" Lil tried reasoning with her husband many times. But his only response was to stand up from the dinner table leaving a half-eaten meal or walk out of the sitting room, abandoning the newspaper on the coffee table.

Tension took reign in their home and the solution was to rid the cause.

Lil's option to support her daughter or support her husband became an unbearable reality that suffocated happiness every single day.

The third option was one that was never explored: The option to see the bigger picture, to look outside the box and recognise this beautiful little girl, who had a gift. Her gift was centred in love, joy and peace. The third option was to recognise that she simply had not lost her conscious connection with the worlds we hear about at Sunday mass. The worlds we were told to trust and believe exist. We were told to have faith that God existed, heaven existed, and everlasting life existed. Saoirse was simply reporting her encounters with same.

But the third option, to see this for what it is was drowned out by the very people who told us what to trust at mass on Sundays. The bellowed beliefs of the Catholic Church drowned out the voice of trust in Lil and Joe's hearts. The belief that the ordinary man, woman or child who can see worlds beyond our own are bad, or wrong, or evil was a rumour spread so widely by the clergy and was also a vast contradiction in the churches sacramental messages.

It was a gross misinterpretation and manipulation of religious text. The suppressive influence of this institution imprisoned a whole family in an illusion of fear, guilt, confusion and pain. A pain whose reality only existed in their minds, yet its effects brought unnecessary torture to every living day of Lil, Joe, Ruth and Saoirse's lives.

They heard the church's message and believed it to come from God. Consequently, fear, judgement, despair, rejection and denial took over. None of which exist in the reality of God's love. This was living hell, for all.

Lil had lived in that hell for the past five years. The solution to end the fear was to send Saoirse away. The consequence of this decision added guilt into the equation. At the time, she believed that she was going to feel guilty no matter what. Be it as a mother or as a wife. At least there was somewhere else for Saoirse to go. She told herself that Saoirse would have the hope of a private education, a safe upbringing in a disciplined environment. To keep her at home meant an environment of hostility and rejection.

As a wife, she felt a moral duty to stand by her husband and support him in his belief and his decisions. In her mind, she concluded that she was doing the right thing by everyone. It was the only way she could make sense of it all. And even though she knew that she wasn't being true to her own heart or true to her promise to Saoirse, she could not find the strength or the courage to battle for what her heart was telling her to do, until now.

Lil knew Saoirse was going look somewhat different to the girl who left their home that afternoon, but she was surprised at how Saoirse was different.

She seemed confident and comfortable in her own skin. She seemed happy. This surprised Lil, and she didn't know where to place those observations in her mind. She had always felt a sense of pity for Saoirse. She had been adopted after all, and it can't be easy what with how society felt about adopted children. So she always felt a need to protect her, knowing that she was always going to be the underdog and because of society and its judgement, Saoirse would never be as strong as everyone else either.

But the girl on the bench that walked tall beside her now did not seem weak. She was almost carefree. There was harmless mischie-

vousness in her eyes too. It was also something that she ha*
before now.

"So, is the bus-stop far?" Saoirse dragged up the small talk, this
walk was painfully surreal. Saoirse's mind was filled with the noise
of the last day she saw them. She could still hear her cries for her
mammy to save her. She didn't know why her mother was here now,
and part of her felt angry for uprooting her again. But that little girl
inside was so happy that the mammy her heart had yearned for had
come back.

"No, it's just up here." Lil deflected the small talk invitation and
focused her eyes on the road ahead to the bus stop. She dreaded Saoirse asking questions. She had no idea how she was going to answer.
The guilt pulled at her heart. Humiliation for what she had done
pulsed through her veins as she walked beside this beautiful, strong,
articulate young woman.

"Right," Saoirse said.

"It's gone cool now isn't it?" Lil observed, tugging her coat around
her chest.

"Oh Mammy what's going on? Saoirse's tolerance for nonsensical
talk ran out and she stopped her paces dead on the footpath. "Honestly, don't you think this is all a bit strange? Like, you don't see me for
years. We'll talk about the reasons why later, but meanwhile you are
supposed to be my mother, and after all this time, you come along, out
of the blue, and all you can talk about is the weather? Where is Dad,
is he ok, honestly now. Tell me the truth." Saoirse called it with Lil.

Lil took a deep breath, and she appeared nervous anticipating her
own response. She looked at the ground and replied.

"Joe is fine Saoirse. This was my decision to come and take you
home." Lil mustered all the strength she had to confess her words to
Saoirse and saying them out loud sounded even stranger.

Even when she was nine Saoirse was old enough to recognise that
her mother never made any decisions without her father's go-ahead
and she always went with whatever he said, until now.

Lil took another deep breath and tried to find words to continue her matter of fact explanation to Saoirse's questions. Instead, her mind went blank, and her heart took over.

".... I missed you so much and....."

Lil failed to hold back her tears. The release of emotion suddenly took over, and she broke down.

Saoirse had never seen her mother cry. She stood before her watching the uncontrollable, vulnerable emotion flow from her mother's eyes. Her first instinct was to hug her, forgive her and tell her it's ok. She wanted her to be ok and help lift her mother's pain.

But as her mother's words sank in, anger rose to the surface and took reign:

"You missed me so much?" Even when she said it aloud herself it sounded even more selfish and pathetic.

"How in the name of God to you think I felt?" She looked at her mother for a response but just kept going instead. "Jesus Christ mum, you pack me off here to that Godforsaken place. I don't hear a word from you, dad or Ruth for almost five years and now you tell me that you came back because you missed me so much? " Saoirse couldn't stop, something took over and it was flowing.

"How the heck do you think I felt? Wrenched from all I knew, a little kid mam. Nine years old. Up and gone and never a word since"

"Saoirse keep your voice down," Lil looked up and down the road.

"No mam I won't. I haven't had a say until now and I am going to talk. Have you any idea how many nights I cried myself to sleep in that hell hole? Because I don't. I have no idea," her eyes welled up in fury. "have you any idea how many times I watched out the window hoping to God that maybe, just maybe there was the tiniest chance you had a change of heart? Or the hours, days, months in fact years I spent in my head trying to figure out why you sent me away? Because I don't know the answer to that either. I lost count a long time ago Mam. Speaking of which, why? Why?" She paused for an answer. Her heart was beating so fast, the adrenalin pumped and her whole body was shaking. But her mouth could not stop and wait for Lil's answer.

"Every summer mam, I watched the whole place empty out. Girls heading off on holidays with their families. Happy mammy and daddies coming to collect their beloved daughters, full of hugs, kisses, delighted to see them. Did you bring Ruth on holiday mam? Where did you go?

In fact, do you know, my first Christmas in there I cried and prayed all night that Santa would actually know to bring my gifts to the end of my bed and not to your house?" Saoirse had to stop talking, choked with the block of emotion at the back of her throat, her lip was shaking was and chin was tight.

"For the record mam, he never came."

She stepped out of the conversation holding her head in her hands. She had to take a couple of steps back from the circle of home truth between her and her mother. Facing the road, she pressed her fingertips over her mouth to stop herself saying anymore. She took a deep breath, the truth that she just spilled to both herself and her mother pounded through her whole body.

"Saoirse I don't know what to say.... I.... I'm sorry, were sorry" Lil meant every word. She had not budged an inch since she began to cry, frozen with both hands still clasping her handbag. Lil had never felt so small in all her life. She searched her mind for a defensive ground to stand on. There was none. She knew Saoirse was right.

"Look, let's go home. We can talk about it later and see where we go from here, things will be different from now on, I promise" She reached out to Saoirse.

"I'm done talking today mam" Saoirse looked at the road ahead and joined her mother's side towards the bus stop.

Neither spoke a word all the way home. Lil didn't know what to say and Saoirse had said it all.

The heat in the house hit Saoirse as soon as the hall door of the home she was reared in opened. It was a crisp cold October evening. The bite of winter had well and truly crept in.

Those familiar smells of home brought Saoirse right back in an instant. Memories of her things, her bedroom, routine, the laughter, the loneliness and that sense of safety that she had felt for her first nine years of life flooded her mind and her senses.

The house was silent, all for the sound of the TV in the living room. Lil opened the living room door, and Joe was sitting in his chair. He was reading the newspaper. He had the newspaper fully open, shielding the upper half of his body from view. He continued to read and gave no reaction to Lil and Saoirse's arrival.

Saoirse immediately felt the palpable tension in the air. The sudden sense of isolation kept her from speaking a word. She knew she was unwanted and unwelcome. She knew her presence was disapproved of. She stood in the doorway feeling awkward and frozen in the cold, silent reception.

Lil took off her coat and hung it in the hall.

"Do you want a cup of tea?" she asked Joe.

"No."

"Are you hungry Saoirse, will I make you something to eat?"

"No thanks I'm fine, can I go to my room?" Saoirse asked craving release from the tension.

"Yes, of course."

Saoirse left quickly and ran up the stairs, feeling as if she could breathe again. She threw her bag down on the bed and looked around. The room had changed completely. The royal blue wall paper was new, and the matching yellow curtains and bed linen. The bedroom wall was lined with fitted wardrobes and there was a dressing table in the corner filled with Ruth's make-up and a multitude of cosmetics.

"Eh, that's my bed now. Mum and Dad bought me a new bed when you left," Ruth walked into the bedroom. She looked so different. She was thirteen the last time Saoirse saw her, not much younger than Saoirse is now. She was so much taller now and her fresh young face was completely different. Ruth had become a woman. She was wearing eye shadow and even lip stick. She had a figure to die for and her clothes were impeccably matched with dark blue flared denim jeans and V-neck fitted top, with navy and white stripes. Her tight blonde curls were gone, and her hair was teased into big curls that tumbled around her shoulders.

"Can you please remove your stuff from my bed?" Her tone was as hostile and cold as her request.

Saoirse put her bag on the other bed and began to unpack. She took Maisie out of the bag first and lay her on the pillow. She continued to get on with unpacking her things. Her heart was sinking in the silence, and a sense of emptiness filled her whole body. She became aware that Ruth was staring at her.

"What? What are you looking at?"

Ruth was lying on her bed reading a magazine, she looked Saoirse up and down and up and down again before she answered.

"Oh, nothing, I am looking at nothing" Ruth's smile laughed with mockery and satisfaction. Saoirse had taken the bait.

Saoirse wasn't surprised. Maybe the room had dramatically changed as did Ruth's physical appearance, but evolution and maturity had not touched Ruth herself. She unpacked the small bag, feeling the absence of hospitality and a warm welcome home.

A heavy sense of loss flowed from her heart and filled every cell of her being. It was the strangest feeling that came with the realisation that her sadness was over the loss of something that was never there in the first place. In those moments her loss turned into a dark emptiness.

She couldn't help feeling that she was present in a reality that was grossly out of tune with the way things could be if people had made different choices.

For a split instant her mind dared escape to imagine Joe standing at the hall door, smiling a warm smile, welcoming her home complete with tears of joy and long warm embraces. She imagined Lil smiling proud and fussing around her at the kitchen table. Even a quiet fuss, with cake or some mark of gratitude and appreciation for the gifts that come with familial unity based in love. She couldn't help feel the absence of a parallel reality where everyone communicated with an open heart, unity and acceptance of one-another.

She stood with her back to Ruth, she was less than three feet away, but the two girls were already worlds apart. They were on completely different pages of the same volume.

The room was silent all for the frequent sound of Ruth flicking the pages of her magazine and clearing her throat every time she turned a page.

The irony that these two girls had so much in common but were polar-opposites for those very reasons. They were both parts of the same family, Saoirse longed to fit in and be the same, knowing she was always going to be so different. Ruth needed to be different; in her eyes, this was a need that had to be met for her sense of importance to be validated. The tragedy was that it was all based on an illusion.

It was an illusion based on fear, weaved through society instilling an illusionary hierarchy, made manifest by belief in its existence. The beliefs were the framework which enabled the pain to thrive in the hearts and minds of all involved.

Right now, the girls, Joe and Lil were all blinded by the illusion of fear, and each one of them was suffering silently and tremendously as a result.

There was a familiar tune coming from the TV downstairs: The tune heralded the end of an episode of Coronation Street. Saoirse had not heard that theme tune in years, and it too threw her right back to not so long ago, but forever away from the world she lived in now.

She was tired. She just wanted to go to bed. Her heart was heavy now, weighed down by the hostility from Joe and Ruth. She became aware of the sense of guilt she felt standing in front of the hot press on the upstairs landing. She fought back the tears, feeling empty inside, looking blankly at the neat piles of freshly ironed clothes for a fresh pair of pyjamas. She felt a paradox pull at her heart. that she was helping herself to nightclothes in her home, but it was now another family's home. She didn't belong here, but she did belong at the same time. Both conclusions tore her apart.

She climbed into bed and faced the wall. Silently she lay in the bed curled up into a tiny ball and felt like her heart was screaming wide open. An immeasurable sense of imprisonment filled her with frustration which turned to anger. She had no idea what to do with the anger, but she felt like she wanted to explode, break free and get out and at the very same time, she felt like she wanted to crumble and cave.

The mix of sorrow, pain and fury turned to loneliness. She searched her mind for where to turn. She found nothing, no-one, no-where. She was alone, and nobody knew. She was curled up in the comfortable bed, in the warm bedroom, in the home that Lil had gone to take her home to, yet she felt like she was in complete isolation.

Her thoughts wandered to a familiar place that only ever existed in her mind. That place where she belonged. She thought of her birth mother. No matter what, she knew she could always belong with her birth mother within her mind. She wondered who she really was and what she was like. Does she have brown hair like Saoirse's? Does she get her big brown eyes and long eye lashes from her too? She imagined her birth mother to be very pretty, with a lovely laugh. As always, she pictured a beautiful lady with a kind open heart, a pretty face and a big warm smile that made her whole presence shine with gentleness. She imagined what her voice sounded like as she expressed that kindness, it sounded soft and her eyes always danced filled with wonder and a ready sense of humour.

In her mind, her birth mother was a lady. She was strong willed and stood up for what she loved. She stood up for Saoirse and put Saoirse first, no matter what.

She imagined what it would be like if her mother could see her pain now, what would she say? She knew she would say the very words and do the very thing that would make everything whole again.

She knew that her birth mother would tend to her every emotional need. She had no doubt that she was the type of person who would think of Saoirse first and place her priority over everyone else.

Saoirse wondered if her birth mother ever thought of her. If so, she wondered what does she imagine Saoirse to be like? Saoirse just wanted to tell her that she was just like her, not like her adopted family. She was just like her.

She could feel the comfort in the escapism now and hugged Maisie close in the bed. She wondered what her mother's name is. From the time when she was a little girl, and especially when she was in big trouble with Lil or Joe and sent to her room, she used to try an exercise to remember her mother's name. During the exercise she went back in time in her mind to when she was a baby and imagined she could hear her birth mother's voice and someone call her name and try with all her might to be right there and hear her name being said.

This time, she closed her eyes, leaving her warm bed and hostile room and went into that place within her imagination: the place where all moments are present at the very same time. She stepped into one of those moments. She was a tiny baby again, suspended in her natural helplessness and complete dependence. Her limited vision could see only brightness and shade. She watched the blurred images recognising walls, ceilings, cribs and doors. Then, she felt her presence, she felt her love: the love of her mother.

She watched her mother's slow movements, the blurry bright presence reaching down to pick her up. The gentle echoes of her soft voice filled the room and her beautiful smile filled her whole face. Saoirse was home, cradled in the gentle sway within her mother's arms, wrapped in the embrace of her mother's love. She was safe, she was loved, and she belonged.

She remembered why she was here and listened for someone to call her mother's name: 'Maisie, Maisie' a voice called within her mind.

It was the very same name every time. All she ever heard was 'Maisie' and every time she dismissed it because she was always hugging her beloved doll Maisie tight every time. With a kiss on Maisie's head, she hugged her doll close to her chest and came back into the hostile room, leaving the magical place within her mind, where all moments are present at the very same time.

Saoirse wondered if she had younger brothers and sisters. She wondered if she looked like them too and what they were like.

In the sadness and pain that the new reality today brought, she found comfort in the escape to hope. Hope that there was somewhere out in the world where she belonged, where she was accepted, important, celebrated and loved unconditionally. This hope was always Saoirse's escape, and it was the anchor that kept her centred in her truth.

Chapter 21

During the following two years Saoirse surrendered into her life of dictation. She knew it was only temporary in the grand scheme of things and someday she would be free.

Her escape from judgement and dismissal were her friends, Maria and Alvagh. At school most classes were spent passing notes between the girls. They each paid attention enough to grasp the lesson but then boredom moved in and they each relieved one another with the slip of a note when the teacher wasn't looking, only to start a conversation back and forth to last as long as the class did. Sometimes they were caught, but most times they mastered the art of discretion.

One class she never found herself bored in was English class. She loved the pros and poetry. She particularly loved the analysis of the characters in the Shakespearian plays. She found herself lucky to have a young English teacher, who was down to earth and incredibly quick witted. Saoirse wished she could keep up with her teacher's effortless, one-liners, but she never could. Ms Black was just too good. Refreshing sarcasm rolled off her tongue as easy as her breath.

Ms Black did not take herself too seriously and her constructive criticism was communicated to the girls in a way that was relative to the cause. Plus, she was never shy about offering it out either, weather they liked it or not.

Saoirse often thought Ms Black looked like a fairy. Her bone straight black hair was cut just at the start of her jaw line, below her earlobes. Her pale complexion was dotted with freckles around her nose and her cheeks. In her flat shoes and A-line skirt she danced wispily around the classroom in and out of those rows of desks. Her face full of animated expression bringing characters to life, taking the girls back hundreds of years to the times on the pages between book covers.

One evening during Saoirse's Intermediate Certificate year, she gave the girls an essay to complete for homework. Saoirse took her essay writing very seriously. She had never forgotten her fourth-class teacher Ms Murphy in her old national school, encouraging her to enter the writing competition …I have not come across one as gifted as you. You've got something that can't be taught…..'and the look of authenticity on Ms Murphy's face embedded her message deep into Saoirse's psyche. Alvagh constantly raved about Saoirse's gift to write lyrics Saoirse I'm telling you, you did it again, you'll be famous for this song writing one day!. She always took Alvagh's prediction with a pinch of salt, given Alvagh being the most enthusiastic, positive person she knew. Either way, the idea of sitting down and creating a world, giving animation to characters and stories with words was a task she embraced with passion and perfectionism every time.

She had to complete the assignment over the weekend and hand it in on Monday morning.

On this particular weekend, her cousins had come to stay. They were Lil's nephews, Ronan and Mathew. Lil adored them, and they often stayed over. It was a home away from home. Saoirse got on well with them most of the time apart from the odd disagreement, which was often soon forgotten. Although Ronan and Mathew were Saoirse's cousins they brought life to the sense of having a functional sibling relationship to her home, one that she rarely experienced with Ruth. The four-year age gap had also brought the girls further apart. They were in different places in their lives now, Ruth was a second-year student in Trinity College studying a degree in Business and Law. Saoirse was fifteen years old, months away from sitting the Inter Cert.

She went to her room early in the evening to start her essay. Ronan and Mathew were in the adjoining bedroom, and the boys were giddy and restless. They were having a pillow fight, from bed to bed and the room was filled with laughter.

Saoirse sat down on the floor between the bed and the wardrobe. She had an A4 writing pad on her lap and began to search her mind to begin her essay. Her concentration was interrupted, and she found herself distracted by the noise from the boys in the next room.

She asked them to keep it down that she was doing her homework. They got louder. She asked them again, they continued. Saoirse found herself repeating the act of focusing, concentrating and starting her homework with the ideas and images flowing into her mind and being distracted by an outburst of laughter from the boys. The continuous interruptions to her trail of thought landed her in frustration. Eventually, she shouted at them:

"For God's sake will you's ever shut up, I'm trying to do my homework."

Downstairs the sitting room door opened abruptly. Lil and Joe stormed up the stairs and came into Saoirse.

"What's all this shouting for?" Joe burst open the bedroom door. At first Saoirse was surprised Joe was shouting at her, not her cousins. Then when she looked at him in the doorway she could almost see his heart thumping, the tension in his face said he was ready for attack. He never spoke to Saoirse, only when he wanted to scold or punish her.

"I'm trying to do my homework, and they keep messing," Saoirse stood up for herself.

"Do your homework? What for? You're thick, you're stupid, that's what you are" Joe's words spewed out and Saoirse watched her father look different than ever before. This time he wasn't speaking to her father to daughter, this time it was person to person, shamelessly divulging what he thought of her. He leaned forward and continued. "There's no point in you doing your homework; you're a failure. Do you hear me?, a good for nothing failure, you're thick, that's all you are," His raised voice gave volume to all of the thoughts and feeling behind his silence over the last few years. Every time he ignored her in the hallway, the kitchen, the stairs. When his newspaper became a shield every time she walked into the room. The innuendo sarcastic comments that bounced between him and Ruth was not Saoirse's imagination, Joe was now letting her know she was right. She felt the release of his pent-up anger roll of his tongue like poison and hit her hard.

Saoirse could feel the heat of the tears well up in her eyes and begin to flow. He continued to shout at her. The fury of receiving both his words and the injustice welled up in her chest and filled her whole body.

"You're a good for nothing, you're thick" followed by Lil, repeating Joe's message.

This time she fought back. She knew she was in the right and surely her homework was more important than a stupid pillow fight.

"I'm trying to do my homework, and they keep messing, and you are shouting at me?" She exploded, standing up she shouted back "Surely if it was the other way 'round it would be my fault too, no doubt. It's always my fault, no matter what the scenario, you always blame me." Saoirse was also leaning forward now, the rage in her heart was now the fire that kept that flow of emotion channelled through her heart break.

She tried to continue through the tears, she couldn't believe she was shouting at Joe, but she also couldn't believe his confession. But he interrupted her.

"Shut up, shut up, shut up, shut up...." he looked her in the eye, Saoirse knew by the look in his eyes, that that was all he wanted to do: shut her up.

She continued to fight back.

He continued to deliberately repeat the two debilitating words until Saoirse couldn't talk through the tears anymore.

"You're thick, you're stupid, and you're nothing, do you hear me? And you're grounded too; you're not going out for a month," he gave one last glance having taken the last word.

Lil repeated his words as if once wasn't more than enough.

They left the room, and there wasn't another word from Ronan and Mathew.

"I'm already stupid grounded!!" Saoirse shouted back in a fury at the bedroom door that just slammed shut. She shouted so loud that the words cut into the back of her throat and it hurt.

Saoirse collapsed into the foetal position in the small space between the wardrobe and the bed. Her face felt like it was out like a balloon. Her eyes throbbed and felt like they were swollen five times their size. She cried and cried in the sense of hopelessness.

This time she felt like she will never be able to stop crying. The loud echo of Joe and Lil's cruel words filled the room. They were so angry at her, and she knew it had nothing to do with shouting at Ronan and Mathew. She was falling apart with nothing to hold on to. She began to think thoughts that she had never thought before:

Maybe it's true what they say. Maybe I am a nothing. Maybe I am thick, stupid. Maybe it's true that I have nothing to give. And this time, for the very first time, she began to believe it.

Up until now, there was always something inside that told her otherwise. Despite what her parents said or Sr Agnes, Ms Cross, or anyone else that judged her, it didn't matter because inside she always felt a sense that told her otherwise. It was intangible, but it was always there. But right now, for the very first time, the echo of her parents' words drowned out all sense of that knowing.

She seriously considered the truth of the illusion and right now she had no strength to convince herself otherwise. She was surrendering into nothingness, and her pain was killing her strength.

Something was beginning to leave her now, taking the light of hope with it, leaving her suspended in a human shell of nothing.

"Saoirse, where there is a will there is a way.
Where there is a will there is a way."

She did not know where that voice came from, or who or what said it, but it was loud and clear. It was outside her mind, and the powerful unconditional love in the words flowed in through the back of her head and down into her heart with goose bumps first and then with love and only love. Its clarity filled every part of her being and shone light on all that she was.

For the rest of her days she will never find out who or what that voice was, but it was there. It was real.

She listened.

She heard, and the sense of strength and peace that came over her validated its presence. The feeling in the room had completely changed, and the dense echo of Joe and Lil's words had dissolved into a quiet meaningless hush that did not matter anymore.

The voice was greater than them, greater than her.

Saoirse slowly looked around the room. Everything was just as before yet so different now. With her mind's eye she watched and with all her senses she felt the presence of what was greater than her shine bright. She basked in its radiance, becoming one with its luminous. The silence of the room was filled with the most beautiful celestial sound, it seemed distant but so close, so invigorating she integrated the silent sound with her breath as its vibration filled every part of her being. Somewhere deep inside she recognised it, deep down she knew who and what it was, but right now, she had no interest in searching for a conscious understanding. Instead she sat centred in the unshakable strength, the kind of strength that centred her in peacefulness, and filled her mind with clarity and courage and the most beautiful quiet confidence.

"I'm not alone, I'm never alone, they are still with me" she whispered, sat still in the small space between the bed and the wardrobe.

She slowly stood up, consciously remaining centred in its strength. The pain and paralysis of surrender that consumed her only a few moments ago were somewhere else right now.

She carefully walked around the bed, filled with peace and knowing she was in the proverbial hands of something truly great.

"...where there's a will there's a way...'

She sat up on the bed and with the energy and the love of the voice surrounding her, she wrote her essay.

In those moments and for the rest of the weekend, it didn't matter what Joe or Lil had said. Nor did it matter what they thought. The pain of their words did not hurt her right now; she knew that they should, but they didn't. This feeling was too beautiful to dwell on what does not really matter.

It took her the whole weekend to write her story. It was a sad story about a young boy who died in a mountain climbing accident and the impact it had on all of his friends. It was a story of grief, loss and sadness.

As she wrote the essay, she was aware of Ms Black's wit and her constructive criticism. She thought the story might be too long, so she wrote in small writing. She read and re-read her sentences carefully hoping to capture the essence and bring her story to life to the reader. She hoped she was doing it right, but all weekend she reminded herself of the message the voice delivered:

"Where there is a will there is a way."

And she felt its love.

The following Monday she handed in her story to Ms Black with the rest of her classmates. It was Thursday before Ms Black returned them.

She distributed the graded essays around the class one by one. Saoirse waited for hers. She did not receive it.

Her first thought was along the lines of what she had done wrong this time. But she knew she had written something good. Ms Black did not give out compliments, so she began to become a little afraid and worried that her teacher may humiliate her story.

After all Ms Black was one of her favourite teachers, but she didn't seem to be the sensitive type. Saoirse watched Ms Black closely, reading her every move. She tried to see if her essay was on her desk and at this point, she had become so worried that she hoped Ms Black forgot her essay. That option was a lot better than the humiliation of her essay being slagged off to the class.

"Listen up people. I am about to read you an essay. I want each and every one of you to listen very carefully and learn from this writing. This is the way an essay should be written." Ms Black glanced around the class, composed herself and began to read.

Losing a Friend, by Saoirse Corcoran

The class listened.

The odd shuffle and fidgeting were soon replaced by silence, only for Ms Black's narration of the words on the page. Each student listened intently. By the end of the story, the class was silent, including the teacher. Each of the thirty girls in the class sobbed tears of sadness for the characters in the story and the message within.

Saoirse sat with her head down. She was mortified. She dared not make eye contact with anyone and did not know how to handle the unusual situation she found herself in.

The silence was broken by one girl down the back of the class who began to clap, and the rest of the class joined in. None of the girls could talk at the time, most of them were lost for words, as was Ms Black, which was a first.

Ms Black walked down to Saoirse's desk and placed her graded essay before her. Saoirse looked down at her grade in the top right-hand corner of the page. Her constructively critical teacher had issued a first for her, and it was also a first for Saoirse. Neither teacher nor student had ever given or received the A+ grade in all of their years in education, until now.

Chapter 22

"Good evening, Corcoran's, Saoirse speaking, how can I help you?" Saoirse answered the phone in her Dad's drapery shop. The shop took a substantial dip in sales during the recession and three of Joe's staff emigrated to England and Boston. Sales were down as well as staff, but Joe believed he needed one to create the other, but the bank balance was influencing his reluctance to hire more staff.

The shop was becoming more and more quiet week after week. People were being laid off from their jobs every day and money was tight. Larger chain stores were also opening their doors selling clothing that was easier on the wallet and Joe's store was feeling the effect. The worry of the health of the third-generation family business was taking its toll on Joe and Lil.

Ruth was in second year in Trinity College and Saoirse was still in school, which meant they were both free at weekends. Saoirse suggested to Lil that herself and Ruth could do a few hours at the shop on Friday evenings and weekends, except for the days when she had a hockey match. Joe thought it was a great idea, although he never shared his enthusiasm with Saoirse but arranged for the girls to start at the shop the following week.

Saoirse took to her new role like a duck to water. She particularly enjoyed the interaction with the customers and had a real gift for knowing what works and what doesn't. After only a couple of weeks people were arriving into the shop asking for Saoirse in particular.

Corcoran's was renowned for First Holy Communion and Confirmation outfits and Saoirse's assistance was particularly required by mums and dads to help choose the perfect outfit for their little darlings. Saoirse obliged and loved every minute of offering a helping hand.

After the first month, sales were already up and the buzz had arrived back in Corcoran's once again.

"Hi Saoirse, it's me, Maria, listen would you be able to make it for 7 this evening, we are meeting outside the church in Blackrock and going for a game of bowling. The lane is booked for 7.15? Please say you can come?" Maria's cheerful voice sang down the phone like a breath of fresh air.

Saoirse checked the time, she had almost an hour to get there. She was helping Dolores finish up the receipts for the day.

"Go on Saoirse, I'll finish up here, it's pretty much done anyway" Dolores whispered with a reassuring wink. Her broad smile beamed appreciation at Dolores, she had always been like a second mammy to Saoirse from the time she was a baby.

She knew there was a bus due at 6:30. She was cutting it fine but could possibly make it.

"See you there," she assured Maria.

"Ok cool, just follow us over to the bowling alley if you get delayed ok."

Saoirse hung up the phone and thought to herself that she would chance to ask Joe for a lift to Blackrock.

'He always drops Ruth wherever she's meeting her friends, anyway what have I got to lose, all he can say is no.' the thought raced through her head.

Usually Saoirse avoided asking him for lifts because on the rare occasion she did, she got the same response every time. Joe refusing eye contact and without batting an eyelid, the answer was a very loud, clear and short: "No."

But this evening, she thought she would chance it. After all, she was already prepared for the predictable worst outcome.

Joe was in the small back office cashing up with Ruth and locking the day's takings in the safe. Saoirse was never asked to do the important work of cashing up and placing the takings in the safe. She got the job of vacuuming the shop floor which she always finished promptly and helped Dolores sort the day's receipts. It meant Dolores could get out a little earlier too.

"Dad, would you drop me into Blackrock please, I am meeting the girls at 7?"

"No," cue the prediction. Joe never lifted his head from the neat piles of notes in front of him and Ruth.

"Tut, Saoirse we're trying to concentrate here" Ruth snapped. Each week Ruth marched down to the back office with her dad in tow, her head held high carrying the trays full of cash from the cash registers. .That was everyone's cue to leave them alone to do their important work, and so they did.

Annoyed with herself for giving them both the satisfaction she rushed back out to Dolores at the front desk.

"Are you sure you don't mind D?" She asked grabbing her coat and bag from under the shop counter.

"Go on love, enjoy yourself. See you next week and thanks for your help today, you played a blinder as always" Dolores folded the receipts and filed them away. Apart from her beehive hair-do cut into shoulder length layers, she had not changed a day in the last sixteen years, she was just as stylish and beautiful as always. She blew Saoirse a kiss and waved an encouraging goodbye.

Saoirse pulled the heavy shop door and rushed out into the pouring rain. Her legs were walking as fast as she could move them, breaking into sprints towards the bus stop just around the corner. Checking her watch, she hoped to God she hadn't missed the bus. She arrived at the corner and kicked herself again, watching her bus at the bus stop with the right-hand indicator on, pulling away.

She slowed her pace in disappointment and gave optimism to the hope that another bus might arrive shortly.

Standing as close to the wall as she could to shelter from the pouring rain, she watched in a daze as the cars drove by one by one. She hoped to God that someone she knew would drive around the corner, maybe another punter from the street her dad's shop was on would be on their way home, spot her at the bus stop and take mercy. It was a long shot, but you never know.

She spotted one car pulling out from her dad's street with its indicator on to turn left. Squinting her eyes. she peered through the showers to focus on the car, hoping it was someone she knew. It was a silver Mercedes. In fact, it was Joe's silver Mercedes, with Ruth in the passenger seat.

Saoirse then remembered Ruth saying earlier that she had plans to meet her friends in Stillorgan. Blackrock was on the way to Stillorgan. In fact, to get to Stillorgan, it was almost impossible to avoid passing through Blackrock.

Saoirse stood in the rain and watched her dad and sister drive by the shallow path, where the bus stop stood. The pair had their eyes fixed straight ahead, stone-faced.

Saoirse found herself throwing her eyes up to heaven, and she thought of every choice word she could think of for Joe and Ruth too. She was even more annoyed at herself for giving Joe the opportunity to refuse her request for a lift. She stared down the road, waiting for the bus that was already gone and continued to hope that another would miraculously come along soon.

She considered walking to Blackrock and thought of Murphy's Law, knowing she would typically be between bus stops and the bus would drive straight past, most likely drowning her with the spray of a big puddle in the process. She waited and waited and waited, and the rain was not letting up.

She checked her watch, and it was 7:15pm, the moment of surrender. She was now officially late and feeling bad for letting her friends down. Her anxiety grew in her heart, and she hoped that they had decided to go ahead without her, trusting she would catch up. Feeling her helplessness, she glanced to her left, and once again she spotted the silver Mercedes Benz, on his way back from Stillorgan to lock up the shop.

She vowed to herself that was going to be the very last time she ever asked Joe for anything. It was a promise to herself that she kept for the rest of her days.

The following morning Saoirse woke and enjoyed the first couple of moments of the day with a sense of happiness and contentment before remembering the way things were.

Her heart immediately filled with heaviness and she thought to herself that this was before she even got out of bed. She searched her mind for the plan for the day and remembered that she had a hockey match against St. Brigit's. It was a home game, and she had plenty of time to get ready. She took advantage of the extra few minutes in bed.

"Mum, can I talk to you for a second please?" Saoirse arrived downstairs to Lil, who was ironing the school uniforms. Saoirse decided to bite the bullet.

"Have you got your gym bag ready, and your purse? Oh and a change of clothes? Make sure you pack a pair of tracksuit bottoms for coming home" Lil always double-checked Saoirse's competence. She glanced at the clock above the kitchen door "The match starts in an hour, and it's going to take half an hour to get there. You know what you're like, always late for everything. Have you got change for the bus?" Lil continued running the iron over Saoirse's school shirt.

"Mum, our hockey match starts at 10 o clock. It's a home game, and I'm meeting the girls in half an hour. Mary O'Rourke's dad is giving us a lift to the school. I have everything sorted.

Mum, why does Dad hate me so much?" she sat forward on the couch.

"He doesn't hate you. He cares for you a lot." Lil ran the iron over the school shirt, the wrinkles and creases dissolving on contact with the steam.

"Mum, the man can't stand the sight of me. He never talks to me. He blames me for everything, even when it's not my fault.

Take the other night for example. I was in the bathroom, and Ruth needed to go. Ruth banged down the door, shouting at me to hurry up and get out of the bathroom. He tore up the stairs and shouted at me for causing trouble. I never said a word! She was the one having the hissy fit.

It's always the same. Ruth gets full interest and conversation with him. He always gives her lifts anywhere she wants to go. She even gets pocket money. He never even gives me the time of day. What did I do?" Saoirse let everything out.

"Well you should be more considerate Saoirse, we only have one bathroom in the house and in fairness you do spend a lot of time in there," Lil went on and Saoirse rolled her eyes to heaven "God knows what you're doing. Oh, and that reminds me, will you please wash your foundation marks off the hand basin in the bathroom? You're getting it everywhere. Every day I have to clean it down after yourself" Lil folded the school shirts neatly into a pile.

"Mum, you're changing the subject" Saoirse glared at her mother, unmoved by her scolding.

"He does care for you. That's why he is so strict with you because he loves you.

Now, come on you need to get up the road to meet your friends".

"I've plenty of time Mum, and I'm not convinced at all. The man can't stand the sight of me, and I don't know what I did wrong."

Saoirse resigned the hope of receiving a relevant explanation with any level of depth or substance from her mother. She reluctantly stood up and picked up her gym bag and hockey stick, consoling herself that at least she had made her feelings known.

"I'll see you later Mam. I'll be home around 1 o'clock."

Throwing her gym bag over her shoulder, she checked her appearance in the full-length mirror in the hall. She could not help disliking what she saw looking back at her. She felt frustrated and agitated by her reflection.

"What's wrong?" Lil asked.

"Nothing, I just wish I was taller, thinner, prettier. I wish my hair was straighter and I had a whole new face, but other than that, nothing at all. Oh well, and it would be nice if my Dad loved me too. But I think that's it for now. See you later Mum." She pulled the hall door behind her causing it to slam. The overwhelming feeling of not being good enough was, by now, present every day. It strangled her heart, she was trapped, limited and frustrated.

The adults called it hormones, but Saoirse knew it was deeper than some generic chemical imbalance.

Some days were worse than others. This was one of the bad days.

"Oh hello beautiful," Alvagh greeted her friend into the hockey pavilion. She was already changed and almost ready to go out onto the pitch but decided to hang back and wait for Saoirse. "What's with the long face?"

"Nothing, I'm just not in the mood for Mary O'Rourke screaming at me for an hour and a half today on that hockey pitch" Saoirse answered with intolerance and deflation.

Alvagh took a moment to observe Saoirse reluctantly unpack her gym bag.

"Nope, sorry, but I'm not buying that one Missus. Mary has screamed at you on that hockey pitch for over seven years, and you have never as much as flinched," Alvagh's big blue eyes searched

Saoirse's face for more information. "Ok, Miss Corcoran, after we smash this game, we are off to Stillorgan for hot chocolate, marshmallows and some serious time out, and don't even think about giving me an answer because that wasn't a question," Alvagh asserted, tying her long blonde locks up in a high ponytail.

"Aw Alvagh, I told Mum I would be home around 1 o'clock. I can't I'm afraid." Saoirse regretted.

"You know, there are these mad new inventions out these days!" Alvagh looked up at the ceiling, searching her mind for the correct terminology. "Not sure if you have heard of them. Some bloke called Alexander came up with the idea. What are they called? Gosh, hold on, it's coming to me...." She snapped her fingers while she was thinking so hard. "They've got numbers, and they ring, and you can talk to people through them, even long distance." She raised her perfectly arched eyebrows and explained to Saoirse demonstrating the appropriate gestures with her hands. "Oh, it's on the tip of my tongue now...."

Alvagh's loving sarcasm brought a reluctant smile to Saoirse's face.

"OK, I'll ring home and tell Mum, smart ass," Saoirse's smile turned into a warm grin. She tied the laces in her trainers into a double knot and placed her gym bag under the wooden bench that lined the internal circumference of the pavilion.

Chapter 23

The pressure cooker went off filling the kitchen with steam. Lil switched off the hob and ran the pressure cooker under cold water. She opened the small window above the sink, relieving the condensation that fogged the glass.

"Hiya, perfect timing, your dinner is just ready," She greeted Joe home from work. In recent years he took on a half day on Saturdays and returned to help Ruth close-up in the evening time. While the children were little he limited working to Monday to Friday. He placed his keys in their usual spot in the drawer in the hall unit and put the newspaper on the coffee table in the sitting room. "Was it busy this morning Love?" Lil mashed the lumps out of the spuds and mixed in the butter.

"Ah, it was busier than I thought it would be, thanks be to God. Mostly communion and confirmations. Everyone's getting sorted early paying deposits and that, but yeah it was busy" Joe said washing his hands.

Lil dished out his cabbage, potatoes and pork chops. The phone rang behind Joe on the wall beside the kitchen door.

"I'll get that Lil," Joe offered.

"Hello."

"Hi Dad, it's me Saoirse. Can you tell Mam I won't be home until around 5? I'm going to Stillorgan with Alvagh for........"

"Right, bye," Joe hung up the phone.

"Who was that?" Lil wondered how such a short conversation could take place and with whom.

"Saoirse is going to Stillorgan, she'll be home later," Joe related the message and brought his dinner over to the kitchen table.

Lil quietly took a deep breath and looked to heaven in a short moment of prayer for patience and diplomacy. She followed her husband to the kitchen table and sat down. She always sat with Joe when he was having his dinner. She took the time to fill him in on what happened during the day. This particular Saturday the news went a lot deeper than the usual superficial type.

"Joe, Saoirse asked me this morning why you hate her so much."

She folded her arms onto the table. "Joe....did you hear me?" She pressed for a response from her husband, eating his dinner in ignorance of the statement just made. "She said that you always blame her for everything and she wishes you loved her."

"Joe, will you answer me?" Lil raised her voice, seeking eye contact with Joe.

"What? I don't hate her" he said finally. His tone was absent from emotion.

"Joe she's sixteen. She's just a normal regular teenager. I know you still think that she had something to do with bringing bad luck, or whatever, but maybe that was just a coincidence. Nothing bad has happened since she came back home. I know she used to say that she can see people who have passed away when she was younger, but she doesn't say any of that stuff anymore. Maybe she has grown out of it. What do you think?" Lil tried to reason with her husband.

"Lil look. It was your decision to take her back home here." Joe refused eye contact, and paused briefly from eating his dinner, but kept his eyes on the plate "I told you already I don't understand any of that stuff, that's all."

"But Joe, you can't just keep ignoring Saoirse because you don't understand her. Like she said herself, she didn't do anything wrong. We are her parents, Ok, she is adopted, but we promised to take on that role 16 years ago when we signed those adoption papers with the nuns" Lil paused to take a breath, "We don't know anything about her background, but we knew that was the case when we adopted Saoirse. It's not right for us to reject her just because she has turned out the way she has. She didn't ask for any of this."

"Lil, like I said before, I will put a roof over her head and provide for her for as long as I have to. She will want for nothing. That's what parents do. But don't ask me to understand something that I don't understand."

"Joe she needs you to love her too."

"Look Lil, maybe it is because she's adopted, maybe it a genetic thing or something. But I don't understand it, and I have yet to meet anyone who does. Even that nun agreed there was something wrong" He sliced through his pork chop knowing his reasons were valid.

"The priests and the nuns don't agree with her mother falling pregnant out of wedlock either Joe, but that doesn't mean there's something wrong with her. Just because the church says there was something wrong with her because she could see all that stuff doesn't mean there's something wrong with her either" All of a sudden Lil could feel her heart beginning to race. She deliberately stopped herself from going too far from the spoken tongue. She composed herself and brought her communication back to speaking Joe's language.

"We are her parents Joe and I feel it too, there is a difference with Ruth and Saoirse. I can see the likeness with Ruth. Sometimes she's like your side and sometimes she's every bar of my aunt Rita the way she orders everyone around. I don't see those resemblances with Saoirse and we don't know what kind of background she comes from, but you can't hold that against her, it's not her fault." Lil sat back in the kitchen chair and stared blankly at the kitchen table, her mind pondering the words she just said.

"But at the same time, I agree with you," she continued to stare at the kitchen table "we didn't know what we were taking on or what kind of background she comes from. I mean God knows what kind of psychological problems there are in her blood line. So how can we understand?" Lil shrugged her shoulders "We just have to do our best that's all"

"Lil" Joe looked up from his plate. "That's exactly what I have been trying to tell you" He continued to eat his dinner.

Chapter 24

"BUS!!!!!!" cried Alvagh and took to a sprint to the bus stop.

Saoirse glanced over her shoulder and saw the No 75 two hundred metres away and ran behind Alvagh. There was nobody waiting at the bus stop, but the bus driver turned on the indicator, pulled in and waited on the girls running as fast as they could.

"Thank you," gasping for breath, Saoirse gave a smile of appreciation to the bus driver climbing on board.

"No bother love, with lungs like that, you should really consider a career as a loudspeaker," He joked with Alvagh.

The girls noticed the windows of the bus were wide open to allow the warm breeze in and the heat out. They considered that is how he must have heard her. She couldn't have been that loud.

"25p each, girls, you're going as far as Stillorgan yeah?"

"That's right, thank you, Jim," Alvagh said to the bus driver.

They plonked themselves down on a double seat halfway down the bus and began to chat.

"That was a great game; you played brilliantly Saoirse. Gave that Mary O'Rourke one a run for her money anyway, never mind hammering St Brigit's. I think that is the very first time we ever won a match against that school."

"Anyway, where are we going in Stillorgan? You seem to know the place better than me" Saoirse changed the subject. "And how are you on first name terms with the bus driver too?"

"Wait and see, it's a surprise, and when we get there, I want you to tell me all about that long face this morning. As for Jim, I'm a regular at the place where we are going, and he is the regular Saturday lunchtime driver on the number 75"

Alvagh led the way through Stillorgan. It was a sunny Saturday lunchtime. The leafy shopping suburb was hopping with all types of people. From families with young children going from one activity to another, to older people out to get their bits and pieces and twenty-somethings, fetching what they needed for their social weekend ahead.

The girls turned into a gap between the three storey 1930s buildings, leading to a gem of a secret in the busy southside suburb. They walked through an old archway, up a small laneway which opened into a cobblestone courtyard.

It was quite like stepping back in time. There was an antique shop where the window was filled with old furniture, paintings and memorabilia of times gone by. The second-hand bookshop had tables lined outside its shop window, filled with the wisdom of words and imaginary tales. Saoirse was drawn to the second-hand clothes shop with eclectic outfits on the mannequins in the window. There were tables outside filled with jewellery holding gemstones from all around the globe.

Saoirse gazed at the crystals and pendulums, afraid to touch anything for fear of being scolded.

"Ah Alvagh love, how are ya?" A middle-aged lady appeared from inside the shop. She was a short, well-rounded lady. Saoirse noticed a depth of warmth in her demeanour, and she felt like she was looking at a familiar soul as soon as she saw her. It was as if she had met her before but knew that she never had.

"Hi Mary, this is my friend, Saoirse."

"Hello, Saoirse love. Freedom, isn't that right?" The lady's eyes met Saoirse's with a knowing smile. "Your name, it means freedom?"

"Erm yes, apparently so" Saoirse replied.

Mary laughed.

"Oh sweetheart, it doesn't feel like so now, but wait until you're older, you'll see." In that moment something moved deep within Saoirse, she knew Mary's warmth saw deep into her soul and the most natural, expansive sense of comfort reached from Mary's eyes and throughout all of Saoirse's being.

"Mary is really psychic Saoirse, but she doesn't like me to say that about her," Alvagh knew she was being bold, but Mary deserved the recognition.

Saoirse felt a pang of butterflies in her tummy.

"Don't be paying any heed to that one. There's nothing special about me. We all have something. It's just a matter of listening to it, that's all. You like the stones I see?" Mary smiled her effortless warmth to Saoirse. Saoirse had never felt as close to home in her motherly presence.

"I've never seen them before, what are they for?" Saoirse gazed down at the large selection of crystals and gemstones on the table. Her eyes scanned the whole table ensuring not to miss any of them.

"Pick one, which one are you most drawn to?" Mary offered.

Saoirse's gaze was drawn to the large purple stone and became aware of the most natural sense of what felt like the most comforting infinite light, flow through the top of her head right down to her heart.

"The purple one" she responded to her physiological response. "Definitely the purple one."

"Ah, the stone of the Pisces, also the birthstone for February. That one is amethyst. It is for clear communication with God, believe it or not, among many other wonderful things." Mary smiled and reached for the amethyst Saoirse had pointed to.

"Really? Wow! I'm Pisces and my birthday is in February." She took the stone into her hands, her heart leapt, Her fingertips felt the hard stone, brushing over its many dimensions, her hands vibrating at one with its solid energy.

"Well, there you go. I'm not surprised in the least. You have that way about you, love." Mary assured, her gentle eyes smiled at Saoirse.

Saoirse looked at Mary. There was a part of her that understood exactly what Mary meant, but at the same time, she had no idea what the stranger was talking about.

"Oh, you have no idea, Mary. Remember I was telling you about my friend who writes the songs? That's Saoirse," Alvagh explained.

"Ah I see, I have heard lots about you Saoirse. You are a talented young girl with a beautiful imagination. A wise old soul for your young years" Mary shared, with her hand over her forehead, shielding the sun from her eyes. Her compliments to Saoirse were filled with authenticity.

Saoirse felt very much at home standing on the cobblestones of this almost secret courtyard and the world within it. She felt that Mary's generosity with words was of kindness that she had not yet experienced, until now. She wished that everyone else had the same sense of selflessness. If so, her world would be a much brighter place to live in.

"Right, Saoirse it's hot chocolate time. Mary, later," Alvagh gave Mary a warm hug. Saoirse knew that Mary was no relation to Alvagh, although she picked up on a deep bond between the two and knew that Alvagh shared a similar bond with all the other traders in this quiet, easy going courtyard.

There was a sense of genuine openness and acceptance for one and all here. It was off grid, and everyone was here because there was something very special about the place. Each one of them felt it, including the newcomer, Saoirse.

Alvagh skipped across the courtyard towards a tiny little coffee shop tucked away in the corner. It looked quaint and shabby from the outside, and Saoirse thought it added to its charm.

"Hello May, it's only me," Alvagh said cheerfully. The sound of the little bell dinged as she closed the door behind her. The aromas of coffee and cake filled the small, pretty patisserie. The tables were covered with red and white gingham table clothes and arranged to accommodate all interests. The small space accommodated everyone from a group of four or six meeting for lunch to small tables for one, tucked in the corner by the window. Those tables for one were reminiscent of an inviting portal, to become lost in the world of a good book, with nothing but a long coffee and a fruit scone for company.

Canvas prints of French art lined the walls, alongside framed black and white photos, telling stories of Stillorgan in the bygone days. The subtle hum of the fridges and coffee machines filled the small cafe in a way that only the subconscious mind notices.

"Well hello dear, how are things with you?" May was arranging the freshly made cupcakes on the cake stand. May was no more than thirty years old. Her shoulder length black hair was tucked up in a ponytail. She was very pretty with a perfect complexion and typical Irish pale skin tone. There was a quiet confidence about her, and her pink apron encouraged a sense of humour with a large white print that said:
KEEP CALM EAT CAKE

"I'm good thanks. This is my friend Saoirse. May is new here Saoirse. She did her degree in food science. Then she worked in some swanky patisserie in France for eight years. She came home and opened the bakery. Now she's living the dream here in Stillorgan, isn't that right May?" Alvagh stood tall, beaming the biggest smile at May.

"Living the dream is right," she smiled wiping the butter icing off her hands on the paper towel. "Hello Saoirse, it's lovely to meet you. What can I get you, girls?"

The array of her freshly baked cakes under the counter had Saoirse thinking she must have been baking night and day. Either that or she is super-efficient and organised. Ninety minutes to make a Madeira sponge cake in home economics ranked into the impossible for Saoirse, and that was working with a partner.

"Two hot chocolate with marshmallows please?" Alvagh asked.

The girls took a seat next to the window.

"Coming up," May reached for two side plates and two large mugs.

The scream of the steam from the coffee machine soon filled the room as May began to make the hot chocolates for the girls.

"Alvagh, its lovely here," Saoirse removed her hooded fleece from around her waist and placed it on the back of her chair.

"I knew you'd like it. I come here most Saturdays. All of the people here are really lovely. Anything goes, and there's no pressure to be anyone other than yourself. It's therapy for the soul really." Alvagh eyes were anchored in peace, sitting back in the wooden chair settling herself for a long chat in the haven she clearly loved.

Saoirse had never considered Alvagh to be someone who got stressed or allowed the outside world to get to her in a way that she needed to come to a place like this, but there was a different look in her eyes now. It was like as if she was more herself than ever before.

"Gosh Alvagh, I always thought you were very comfortable in your own skin, you are so confident," Saoirse commented.

"I am, I suppose, but you know, sometimes you just need to feel the love." Alvagh appeared more relaxed by the moment.

"Here you go girls," May arrived with a tray of the biggest, fanciest hot chocolate and marshmallows Saoirse had ever seen. Two tall glasses with tiny handles on the side. The hot chocolate was topped with whipped fresh cream, covered in pink and white marshmallows and sprinkled with chocolate flakes. There was a plate to the side with the biggest slice of chocolate fudge cake, drizzled with strawberry sauce and a generous dollop of homemade ice cream, with two forks.

"Oh wow," Saoirse said wide-eyed

"Saoirse, did I tell you that I know the best baker known to man, she's standing right there! Thank you May, you are the best." Alvagh never failed to give May the very same smile of gratitude every week.

"It's no bother girls, enjoy." May modestly placed the works of art in front of each of the girls.

"Anyway, down to business. I am worried about you Saoirse. What's going on?" Alvagh sliced her fork through the chocolate fudge, making sure to get the warm chocolate, strawberry sauce and ice cream onto the fork.

"Ah Alvagh, you'll be bored to tears listening to me. It's nothing really." Saoirse dismissed.

"Tut tut, I told you already, I'm not buying that, what's up?"

Saoirse stirred her marshmallows into her hot chocolate.

"Ah, it's just life, my dad, home, everything. Basically, my dad hates me. I can't do anything right. As far as he is concerned, I am thick, stupid and a good for nothing. I will never amount to anything. My sister is the golden girl who can do no wrong. It's getting worse by the day, and I have already had enough." Saoirse paused in an attempt to conclude. She looked out the window into the courtyard. And then she forgot the concluding part and went on. "The thing is, I am afraid that part of me is starting to believe it. Sure even the teachers in school think I'm a loser. No matter what I do. It's like as if I am labelled a failure by some default." Saoirse spilt, saying a lot more than she had intended to ever divulge for fear of judgement.

"I thought as much. Saoirse honestly, I mean this right from the heart when I say this. You are far from a loser. Just look at what Mary said to you, she only just met you and saw there was something really special about you." Alvagh leaned towards her friend, her forearms resting on the table "Plus, I have been meaning to tell you to tell you, I was home over Easter break and showing my Mum and aunts photos of me, you and Maria. Every single one of them said that you were stunning. They commented on those eye lashes and eye brows, saying what they would give to have them" Alvagh giggled. "They thought you were turning into a 'really stunning young woman'. Of course, I agreed because it's true. By now it's like as if they all know you from me talking about you and think you are a real gentle, loving soul because you are.

You are kind, caring and one of the best friends anyone could ever wish for. And might I add, as for being clever? Who is the one who gets the A+'s in English all of the time? I go to you all the time for help with maths, and you're fantastic at geography too. It's just a shame that excuse for a teacher has her favourites.

The point is, I think you are really clever. I see it every day."

"Right you can stop now; I am mortified" Saoirse laughed through her embarrassment. "But thanks, Alvagh. That means a lot. It's lovely to hear although hard to believe it myself. I just wish I could do something right. I feel like there is this big black cloud over me and everything I do, that no matter what, it's never going to be good enough because it's me."

"Saoirse that's far from the truth, believe me. I hear what you're saying, and I get it. No matter what anyone else says, everyone needs the 'T.L.C' to start at the roots. If you don't get it at home, it's so much harder to believe in yourself. My aunt calls it 'core beliefs'. She went to a therapist for years to help her to cope with the false world of fame and the therapist told her that it doesn't matter what everyone else thinks of you, whatever message you receive as a child will always override that, unless you do lots of work on yourself and put your own beliefs in there.

But please believe me when I say this, I believe in you, and I am so glad you are my friend.

Now Saoirse, you know me, and I don't do soppy often, but I am telling you this now because I mean it, heart and soul. I think you are really beautiful in every way and I know that anyone else who knows you thinks the same thing." Alvagh's big blue eyes were locked on Saoirse's. She knew her friend needed to hear the truth from someone.

"Thanks, Alvagh, likewise and it really means a lot,"

"Do you think being adopted has anything to do with it?" Alvagh kept the conversation going.

"Oh yes, I think it has everything to do with it," Saoirse was certain.

"Do you ever think about your birth mum?"

"Yeah I do, a lot more often than just now and again" Saoirse sat back in her chair. Her dreamy glance was shared between Alvagh and the view of strangers passing through the courtyard.

"I think when you don't fit in you look for the reasons why and that leads me to think about my birth mum. Especially when I'm sad and when I am looking to understand the reasons I am the way I am.

Then, before I know it I have created this big fantasy in my mind about who she is, what she is like and how we would get on. It's all a bit mad really. But yeah, I do think about her, it's something that's always there, even when I'm not thinking about it I suppose." Saoirse replied gazing out the window of the coffee shop watching the world outside, without observation.

"Do you think you will look for her someday?" Alvagh asked sitting back in the chair listening inventively to the story of her friends' world.

"Oh gosh no Alvagh, I couldn't. I would hurt mam and dad too much. They have done everything for me. They are my parents. Even though I understand it wasn't her decision to give me away, they still took on the role of my parents. I couldn't do that to them," Saoirse poised herself upright in the chair and snapped out of the dreamy state she had been in moments before.

"Well I think you are so strong, I don't know how you do it. I couldn't imagine life or who I would be without the love and support of my family," Alvagh complimented.

"How did you get to always be so old for your years Alvagh? From the first time I met you, you were years ahead of anyone our age; I love that about you."

"I dunno, I grew up with a down to earth family in the music industry. Being streetwise and staying grounded in what's important is something that they have always drummed into me. Guess it's paying off now eh?" Alvagh dared speak pride like only Alvagh could.

"What keeps you going Saoirse?" she asked curiously seeking insight into Saoirse's strength.

Saoirse thought for a moment.

"Hope. It has always been hope. Someday I am going to be older, an adult and I will have my whole life, free to be true to who I really am. Without having to conform or try to fit in or be who I am expected to be. Even now I know that will never be good enough in my family's eyes. But still, there is a part of me that still tries to please, still tries to fit in. And the more I try to fit in, the more of an outsider I feel, but I can't help it.

So yeah, it's hope. That's what keeps me going. You said that Mary was very psychic, is she really?" Saoirse progressed the conversation.

"Absolutely, but she really doesn't like anyone saying that about her. She honestly believes that everyone has a gift, a knowing and like she said we just need to listen to it, that's all. She has made some whopper predictions though. She told my uncle that he would have a number one single ten years ago. He was working on new material at the time, and the album went to No.1 in the Irish charts." Alvagh was wide eyed, clearly proud of her friends' prediction and her uncle.

"She told May here that she would be back when she was leaving for France. May told me that she laughed at her at the time. She was twenty-two and heading off to make a name for herself in Europe, doing what she loved. Yet, she learned all that France could teach her and missed home. So, late last year she packed up her life in France and returned to open this place, ironically right under Mary's nose." She nodded out the window over to Mary's shop across the courtyard.

"She has said lots of things that have come to pass but what I love about her is her warmth, she is like an angel," said Alvagh.

"Yes, I get that" Saoirse agreed. "In the nature of putting everything out on the table today, I have another confession to make." Saoirse leaned over towards Alvagh; her palms rested flat on the table poised in the announcement. A big brave smile filled her face, she took a deep breath and looked her pal right in the eyes. "When I was younger, I was really psychic too, but I didn't know that's what it was at the time, I thought everyone could see dead people, not just me."

"You are joking me! No way! Tell me, what, who, where, how, when?" Alvagh animated forward in her seat clearly intrigued to hear about Saoirse's gift, that enabled her to see beyond the veil.

"Ah, it's nothing really. I don't ever talk about it, and it seems to be all shut down now anyway. But I could see, I suppose you would call them 'angels' for want of a better word. At the time I just thought that they were these loving 'beings', helping me to figure everything out as a child. I never knew it to be anything different to what anyone else could see.

Neighbours who were passing away used to come and say goodbye. I used to have all sorts of dreams predicting what was going to happen, sometimes good things, sometimes bad things, but stuff always came to pass. It was like as if events were happening on some other dimension during my dream time and it took a few weeks or even days for them to happen in real life.

That's why I really believe in all that stuff; it was a huge part of who I was before I was told it was wrong. Now nothing really happens anymore. I guess either I have shut it down or 'they' are leaving me alone, who knows?" Saoirse explained her extra-sensory world to Alvagh in a way that it all sounded very 'normal.'

Alvagh was leaning across the table with her jaw and eyes wide open.

"I don't believe you. Well, I do believe you, but I can't believe you never told me any of this before! I am mad into all that stuff! Why and when did you shut it down?" she asked.

"Oh here we go again" Saoirse threw her eyes to heaven excusing herself for boring Alvagh.

"I really don't want to play the victim here but...... Do you remember Sr. Agnes told me I was evil the day I arrived at the convent? I had one more 'visitation' that night, by a beautiful lady. She came to my bedside and reassured me that everything would be alright. I was so sad that night I really thought I was going to die. In fact, it was that painful I would have preferred to die at the time. Words can't express the sadness I felt. My mum and dad had rejected and abandoned me, dumped me in this Godforsaken horrible institution. My whole world was ripped from under me, and I could hardly make a sound the pain was so great, and there she was. A beautiful lady, her eyes were so kind and her smile so warm. It wasn't so much what she said; it was her very presence that soothed my pain and brought me comfort. It was like as if she reminded me, with her presence, of who I am and what's important, even though I didn't fully understand at the time, she brought deep comfort, so I guess on some level I did understand. Then she went, and I have rarely experienced anything since, except for recently in fact. This time it was different though. Mam and Dad tore me to shreds one evening when I was trying to do my homework because I shouted at my cousins for making noise in the next bedroom. It was the usual message: 'you're thick, stupid, useless, nothing' etc.

That night I really felt so sad and hopeless. I felt like something was leaving me. It was like as if I was letting go of some kind of knowing deep down inside. I mean that part of me that knew that no matter what they say or how horrible they were, deep down, I do have something to give. But this night it felt like that part of me was leaving, and I was beginning to have nothing left, but the words of my parents.

I know this is going to sound crazy, but the strongest voice came in, right behind my head and said the words:

'Where there's a will there's a way.'

It repeated the same message a couple of times, and in those moments Alvagh, everything changed. It was like some gentle, powerful, unshakable strength came over me. All of the pain lifted and dissolved, and peace and clarity took its place. The harsh words of my parents didn't matter anymore because I knew there was something greater.

I know it sounds crazy, but it was there. I heard it, and I felt it.

That's when I sat up and wrote: 'Losing a friend' cue my first ever A+. I absolutely know that I didn't write that essay on my own." Saoirse smiled through the lump in her throat and tears in her eyes as she recalled that powerful night filled with love.

"Oh Saoirse, it's no wonder you are so strong," Alvagh said with tears in her eyes. "I dunno, it's like as if you have help with you from a Divine Power or something."

"But it's like Mary says, I believe everyone does," Saoirse shrugged her shoulders in the certainty of what she knew, but most forget. "Alvagh, please, don't tell anyone I told you, please!" Saoirse felt a sense of panic at her reveal and begged her friend's trust and confidence to keep her secret.

"Mums the word, my lips are sealed" Alvagh threw her hand over her mouth "Oh for goodness sake there I go again, no pun intended Saoirse".

Saoirse laughed "Even if you tried you couldn't be funnier" then it suddenly dawned on her that she had walked away without paying Mary for the crystal, "Oh the crystal, I still have it! I meant to give it back to Mary." "Oh gosh, Alvagh the woman probably thinks I lifted it! What am I like?" she panicked.

"Sure we can go over now on the way," Alvagh assured, draining the last cold drop of hot chocolate from the mug, reaching for her jacket draped over the back of her chair.

The girls thanked May and left the quaint coffee shop in the direction of Mary's.

"Mary, I am so sorry I walked off with your crystal, talk about first impressions!" Saoirse excused herself.

"What? No, you keep that Saoirse. That's your crystal a gift from me to you, love." Mary was taking the last few display boards of jewellery and trays of crystals inside closing up shop for the weekend.

"Oh gosh no, I couldn't, how much do I owe you?" Saoirse insisted and rummaged through her purse for the price of the amethyst.

"Sweetheart, you don't owe me anything. Honestly, it's a gift from me. Pop it into some salt water when you get home too, love, and leave it there for a few days. Then it really is yours forever." Mary paused in the doorway and advised Saoirse with the same authenticity and warmth she radiated earlier today.

"Thank you, Mary. That's so kind of you. It was lovely meeting you, and I am sure I will see you again," Saoirse smiled and carefully tucked the crystal into a small pocket in the front zipper of her gym bag and threw the bag over her shoulder.

She arrived home to an empty sitting room. Signs of summer were in the air, and Joe was out cutting the grass in the back garden. Lil had gone to mass.

She felt a sense of wholeness in her heart after her afternoon with Alvagh in Stillorgan. Right now, the way she felt earlier that morning when she left for her hockey match seemed like a world away.

She turned on the TV and sat down to watch an old movie. The movie was called Boys Town. It was a true story about an Irish priest who founded a home for underprivileged boys in Omaha, Nebraska. The priests' name was Fr. Flanagan, and his motto was that there is no such thing as a bad boy. A philosophy he applied to all of his work.

Saoirse had watched many movies when she was growing up.

Before she went to the convent, Lil always sat with her and watched The Evening Matinee, which was usually an old black and white movie broadcasted on an Irish TV channel. But there was something about this movie. Scenes made their way deep into her psyche. There was something about the wonderful priest who took all of those boys under his wing and loved them like they were his own. No matter what they did or how wayward they went, he continued to guide them, to love them. Saoirse's face was soaked with tears of love right throughout the whole movie and it quietly took long-term residence in her memory. She knew the story would stay with her for a long time to come, yet she had no idea why.

Chapter 25

Fiona sat at the top of her bed, watching her mammy cycle down the lane towards home. Mammy's thick brown hair hung under her head-scarf which was tied under her chin. Fiona always thought that that brown trench coat aged her Mammy no end.

Like clockwork Maisie arrived home every day from work at noon. She worked three mornings a week cleaning houses just outside Bun-ratty. The extra few pound went towards the endless hand-outs to the school and the bus fares in and out of school for her four children.

Fiona was off sick again today. She had missed more time than usual in school over the past few weeks. She refused to go to the doc-tor insisting it must be food poisoning at first, which then evolved into a bad bug and maybe it was even a virus. Either way, it was something that would sort itself out and the doctor couldn't help.

Fiona was sixteen and the eldest in the family. Followed by her younger brother William, then Padraig and Jennifer was the baby. All Maisie's children arrived one year apart. Maisie's mammy, Ellen used to say that they were like 'steps of the stairs' growing up.

Maisie opened the back-yard door into the kitchen and called Fio-na.

"Yeah I'm here Mammy. I'll be down now" She looked at herself in the dressing table mirror. Her shoulder length dark hair was tied back in a pony tail. She was wearing a baggy sweatshirt again today. She fixed her light blue jeans so as the turn ups were even at the end. She took a deep breath feeling her heart race in her chest. She had to tell her mammy the news before she found out for herself.

"Hiya Love, how are you feeling today, still sick?" Maisie raised her eye brows and looked knowingly at Fiona. She was putting the few bits of shopping away in the kitchen presses. The kettle was al-ready on with the tea pot topped with two tea bags ready and waiting.

Fiona folded her arms, pulled out a kitchen chair with her foot and sat at the table in the centre of the kitchen. She pulled her chair right in as far as it would go and kept her arms folded over her torso. She could feel the blood rush to her face. Her tummy felt like an army of butterflies were doing summer salts in there.

"Mammy, can you sit down?" her voice reflected the tension in her body.

"Just wait for the kettle to boil love, and we'll have a cup of tea, ok?" Fiona knew that Maisie knew. Her heart was beating faster, her whole body felt cold and she could hardly speak.

Maisie placed the tea pot complete with tea cosy on the table, along with the milk and two mugs.

"Go on Love" She sat opposite Fiona and invited her to share her news.

"Mammy I'm sorry, I really am. We only did it the once" Fiona couldn't help it, she broke down in tears. Her head hung into her chest and the tears flowed down her cheeks. She grabbed a tissue to blow her nose between the sobs. "I'm so sorry Mammy, I really am"

"Oh sweat Divine Mother of God" Even though Maisie knew Fiona was expecting a baby she hoped her instinct was wrong this time. She blessed herself and looked up to God not really knowing what she was looking for. "Jesus Love. How long are you gone, do you know?" She looked at her daughter, using deep breaths to keep her cool.

"About four months I think" Fiona swallowed back the tears and took a deep breath. She had been going out with a lad from school since Christmas, his name was Frank. They got together at the Christmas disco and had been inseparable since. Despite Maisie and her friends warning her to make time for her friends even though she had a boyfriend now, she didn't listen. They spent every waking day together, whether her friends or mother liked it or not.

"Have you told Frank? Is he going to stand by you?" Maisie asked.

Fiona shook her head and broke down again "He's gone Mammy, he doesn't want to know"

"The little pup" Maisie muttered. She continued to apply her deep breath technique, restraining herself from laying into her daughter, but couldn't help herself to go on "Fiona, what kind of...I mean I warned you. What were you thinking? For God's sake would you not listen? When are you ever going to start doing as I say? Now look at you?" Maisie's voice was always soft spoken, even now when she was trying to shout, but Fiona could tell she was angry and disappointed. They had always been close. Maisie was only nineteen when

Fiona was born. She met Pat a year after returning from the Mother and Baby Home. It took a long time before she came back from letting her first baby girl go. It was almost a whole year before she felt like making any effort to regain a social life. The devastation that Mary was gone for good and someone else's daughter now hit her hard.

In the end she surrendered to the disempowerment that her only option was to move on and put Mary behind her. The pain never went away, not a day went by that she did not think of her baby girl. For the past eighteen years she wondered how she was getting on and hoped she was happy. Her greatest fear was that she might not be, and every day she silently carried both her secret and her burdening fear.

One full year after St Patrick's Maisie forced herself to pick her life up and move forward. That was when Pat stole her heart. He was kind, funny and lived in the same town. His was a carpenter and worked with his dad. He could turn his hand to anything and was never shy of stepping up to hard work. Maisie and Pat fell for each other immediately and despite Maisie's vows to self that she will never have anything to do with another man ever again, Pat was the light at the end of the long dark tunnel of isolation.

They were only dating a couple of months when history repeated itself and she found herself expecting her second child. This time Pat's response was different to last time.

"Right, as much as I hoped we would have a couple of years together on our own, it looks like I'm due a word with your Da" Pat assured Maisie with a smile. His eyes told her that he had every intention of marrying her someday, but now that day had arrived a little earlier than planned. The following evening, he asked Maisie's daddy for his permission to marry her. On the 21st September 1966 Maisie and Pat became husband and wife.

Maisie's parents told them they could live in the cottage up the lane behind their home if they did it up themselves. It used to be home to Maisie's great grandparents who passed away a long time ago. They bought it when they moved to County Clare in the early 1900's and it had been derelict for many years since their passing. Pat was not shy about getting stuck in making the home their own. They replumbed, rewired and Pat even put in a new stair case for an upstairs bedroom in the loft.

"Mammy, I'm sorry. I really am I don't know what else to say" Fiona sobbed her heart out. "Mammy please, Mammy don't send me away to one of those Mother and Baby Homes with the nuns," Fiona looked up for the first time, a look of terror filled her big brown eyes, "I've heard tell of those places and they are horrible, please Mammy don't send me to one of those."

Maisie looked at her daughter's perfect young face and saw the fear in her eyes.

It was the thing to do if a young girl committed such a sin, that's the way it had always been. To avoid the shame on the family she must go to the nuns, they will sort it. But Maisie knew that no matter how bad her daughter imagined those homes were, they were a million times worse in reality. The fact that Maisie knew that first hand was a secret she had kept from her husband and her children from day one. It had been eighteen years since she left that place and every day since she kept her secret and never told a soul, but the memories of those days were never far from her mind.

She was angry at Fiona. In fact, she was furious. How could she be so blinking irresponsible? Getting herself pregnant at sixteen, her whole life ahead of her. And that good for nothing young fella doing a runner too.

She looked at Fiona sat across the kitchen table, she was pregnant, scared, helpless and so sad.

All Maisie could see was herself.

"Mammy, please will you say something? I can't go into one of those homes" Fiona begged in a whisper.

Maisie took a deep breath and sat up right "There'll be no Mother and Baby Homes," She reached out and picked up the tea pot and poured the tea. She hadn't even discussed it with Pat yet. Even though she had her suspicions that Fiona might be expecting for the last few weeks, she didn't say anything to Pat. But she had already made up her own mind, that no matter what, her daughter will not be entering the doors of one of those places.

"You'll carry on as normal. There's only a few weeks left of school. You might even be able to sit your Leaving Cert" Maisie entered into regimental mode and poured the tea while she delivered the plan of action, "You've always been clever Fiona and even though you're pregnant I expect you can still sit your exams. I will support you and your father will too. I imagine the baby will be due around September or thereabouts. We'll manage. We will make it work. But there will be no Mother and Baby Homes, that's for sure."

Fiona looked up at her Mammy. She felt the terror leaving her body and her mother's support taking its place "Really Mammy? That's it?"

"Don't you think you're getting away with this lightly young lady. What's done is done and it is what it is. But I am still furious at you. You're going to be a mother and you may step up, do you hear me?" She eye-balled Fiona.

"What about Daddy? He is going to go mad." Fiona sought more support.

"Leave your father to me," Maisie maintained her strict tone and reassured Fiona.

"Mammy, what about the neighbours?" The panic was still in Fiona's voice.

Maisie glanced out the kitchen window and a couple of the usual judgemental suspects in the community passed through her minds' eye. She turned to her daughter and said:

"Fiona Love, listen to me and listen good," She looked straight into her daughter's eyes leaning across the table and took a firm hold of her hands. "Those who mind don't matter and those who matter don't mind. Okay? This place is full of busybodies with nothing better to do. Yes, they are going to talk and they're going to judge. I do not care about them. Let them say what they like," Her firm grip of Fiona's hands and solid eye contact convinced Fiona of her mother's unshakable support "You are what's important. I don't care what the priest says or the holy Joe's. Their opinion is no concern of mine and nor should it concern you. You're concern now is that baby you're carrying. Okay? Stuff the lot of them and let them on, hold your head up high and do your best Love. That's all you can do." She always knew exactly what to say when times got tough. Maisie was a strong woman with the kindest heart and was never afraid to show either.

"Oh Mammy" Fiona got up from the table and threw her arms around her mother "thank you Mammy" She was in tears again, but this time it was tears of relief and comfort.

"Ah for the love of God!" Pat took a mouthful from his pint of Guinness. Maisie suggested they go for a quiet drink in the local pub to break the news. She thought it best that he be far enough away from Fiona, just until he calmed down. Tuesday night was always quiet down in the local and Maisie felt it was as good a place as any to break the news to her husband, sooner rather than later. "She's pregnant? She's sixteen Maisie!" He folded his arms and looked around the bar, shaking his head. His tall frame and well-built physique sat tall beside Maisie. Pat was a handsome man in his late thirties, he had big blue eyes and a completely bald head. Fiona had always been his pride and joy. She was every bar of her Mammy, in looks and mannerism.

"Would you keep your voice down Pat." Maisie scolded.

"What the? What do you expect me to say Maisie?" he attempted to keep his cross tone just above a whisper "I suppose that little so and so ran for the hills?" He looked at Maisie, her face said it all. "The little…." He glanced around the pub and shook his head again. "What happens now? Do we call the priest?" He shrugged his shoulders looking at Maisie and his eyes said the complete opposite to his suggestion.

"We most certainly will not Pat. I don't know what happens next yet, that's something we will have to work out together, but I have already told Fiona, there will be no priest and no Mother and Baby Home talk either" Maisie took a sip of her gin and tonic. She expected Pat to react exactly as he was. She directed every ounce of her energy into holding a calm and collected composure.

"God forsaken places them homes anyway" Pat was showing a hint of calming down. He took another mouthful of his pint, then began to think out loud. "What about her studies, sure her exams are only weeks away. She can kiss them goodbye now anyway, as well as her future. She was going to be a nurse Maisie!"

"Ah for God's sake Pat would you calm down, it's a baby she's having not a prison sentence"

"How can you be so calm about this Maisie? She is sixteen" Pat pressed.

"I know how old she is Pat" Maisie paused and sat back in her seat "I suppose I have had more time to get used to it, maybe that's why" she confessed, not daring to look at her husband.

"What? Ah for...How long have you known, I thought you said she only told you today?" he held his pint up to his lips and looked at Maisie.

"Call it maternal instinct Pat. Anyway, I told her that she can still sit the Leaving Cert, the baby is due around September so that leaves plenty of time to sort something out." Maisie paused. She looked at Pat who was scratching his bald head, he only did that when he felt the world was on top of him. He continued to look around the quiet pub, not taking any notice of his surroundings and shake his head. Maisie knew that there was never going to be a good time to suggest her next idea so now was as good a time as any:

"Pat I was thinking" She sat forward "Do you think you could convert that out building into a small one-bedroom house? You know the one at the end of the yard? There's a solid foundation on it already, thanks to you and your hard graft and it's easily big enough for Fiona and the baby" Maisie completely ignored the look of disbelief on Pat's face. "We'll just need planning, insulation, plumbing, wire it up for electricity and a new roof. Sure I can get a credit union loan to cover the cost. And it wouldn't take much at all, a few months would do it and you can stick a little bathroom in for her and the baby too. What do you think? That way she'll be beside us, at home?" Maisie took a sip of her drink after the deliverance of that mouthful. She knew she was asking for something completely off the wall.

She was fully aware that right now most mothers are concerned about the shame, the disgrace and how and when they should contact the parish priest to arrange their daughters moving away to escape the shame on the family and judgement of the neighbours. But she had been there, done that and there was only one way anything was ever going to change and that was if someone began to do things differently. She knew she was being bold, but it was a step she was willing to take. She had suffered through the hell of her experience and if being bold and courageous was what she had to do to avoid seeing Fiona go through the same, well that's what she was going to do

"Are you completely mad in the head woman?" Pat held on to his pint on the table and his look of total disbelief.

"Well what alternative suggestions do you have?" Her tone was one of intolerance "Well?"

"Ah Maisie this is all a bit too much to take in in one night" Pat folded his arms again "Just, look, just let's handle one thing at a time, ok" He felt the pounding in both his head and his heart.

"OK. I know, I understand, but just consider it will you?" Maisie felt the senses of chaos running around in Pat's mind and at least she had put the idea out there. "But I am aware that time is ticking and I'm also aware of the alternatives. It's either we live like sardines in our cottage with four teenagers, ourselves and a new baby. Or, we send Fiona to England, or call the priest. Neither of that latter two are an option"

"One things for sure this will keep the neighbours going on the steps of the church of a Sunday" Pat looked around the pub again, this time he was taking notice of who was who.

"And like you have always worried what anyone else says or thinks Pat Kelly" Maisie raised her eye brow.

Pat scratched his head again "Ah I know but it's different this time you know? This time it's about Fiona. I just hope no one gives her a tough time"

"Pat, as I told her earlier on, she has us, our support. Of course they'll all have a grand chin wag. It'll keep them going for months for sure! But by God they may not cross me, I tell you that much. Anyway, the most important thing is Fiona and that baby she is carrying. At the end of the day that is her grandchild in there, and that is far more important than those busybodies with nothing better to do." Maisie folded her arms this time. She knew, that all she had to do was tell herself the same for the coming months and that would give her the strength to fight the pressure that lies ahead.

"Mammy, what did Daddy say last night? Did you talk to him?" Fiona arrived into the kitchen wearing her school uniform for the first time in two weeks.

"I did Love," Maisie sat at the kitchen table holding a mug of tea. She had laid the table for breakfast and had the lunches ready to go into the kids' school bags "he was shocked, as you can imagine, but your daddy's a good man, give him time. How are you feeling? Glad to see you back in navy and blue" Maisie noted Fiona from head to toe and smiled. She stood up and rinsed her cup.

"I feel better than yesterday morning Mam, put it that way, and most mornings for the last few weeks for that matter" Fiona poured herself a cup of tea and leaned her back on the kitchen counter.

"Have some breakfast Love, you've plenty of time. Now where in the name of God are your brothers?" Maisie went out into the hall and called the boys to wake up. Jennifer was still in primary school and got to enjoy an extra half hour in bed.

Chapter 26

"Ma, it's me I'm home" Fiona closed the hall door behind her. It was a beautiful sunny June day, Maisie had let out the waist band on Fiona's school skirt to accommodate her growing baby bump. Her baggy school shirt hung over her skirt concealing her tummy. Ever since she confessed the news to her mother that she was having a baby she was back to her old self again, happy, positive and looking ahead.

"How did you get on Love? I have your lunch ready." Maisie couldn't wait for Fiona to come home. She had been worried about her all morning. Today was the start of the Leaving Cert. Fiona worked hard leading up to the exams. She found staying in with her head in the books the easier choice than to socialise with a large bunch of teenagers, in case they found out the news. Instead she kept her head down and put all her energy into protecting herself and studying hard.

"Mammy it went really well," She glowed "off to a good start anyway."

"Oh thanks be to God Love" Maisie could not be prouder of Fiona. She beamed a smile from ear to ear, so happy for her girl, she deserved to feel good and she deserved to do well.

"Listen, you are in for paper two in the afternoon. I'll walk up town with you, I need to get the meat in for the tea tonight"

"Right so" Fiona tucked into her toasted ham and cheese sandwich.

Maisie and Fiona walked the short five-minute walk into the village. Anyone would think they were sisters, not mother and daughter. Maisie was in her mid-thirties and she was blessed with the type of skin that just did not age. Her shoulder length dark hair, big brown eyes and sallow features would have anyone convinced she had just stepped off the Spanish Armada, she was a descendant of the ships passengers for sure.

Fiona was the very same as her mammy, she just looked a little younger that's all. The ladies crossed the street onto the main street. A couple of middle aged ladies stood chatting on the corner as they passed by. The women held their loaded shopping bags by their sides and looked at Maisie to greet her.

"Hello Maisie, how are you? How is your mam?" Mrs Lynch asked with a cold smile. Mrs Lynch never stopped Maisie to make small talk. A nod or wave was usually about the extent of it.

"She's fine Mrs Lynch. I'll tell her you were asking for her. How are you keeping?" Maisie thought she best be polite and stopped for a moment to engage in the small talk, which was a first for her with these ladies.

"I am well thanks be to God," Mrs Lynch glanced at Fiona "Fiona" she nodded, her tone was short.

"Hello Mrs Lynch," Fiona responded standing by her mother's side, she folded her arms across her torso and looked to the ground with a nervous glance.

"Fiona started the Leaving Cert this morning, we're just heading back to the school now for the afternoon exam" Maisie explained, still beaming with pride.

"Yes. I hear that's not the only thing she has started" Mrs Lynch revealed her real reason for stopping Maisie and Fiona.

"I beg your pardon" Maisie frowned, not quite sure if she heard Mrs Lynch correctly, but the sudden butterflies in her tummy told her she had.

"All I can say is I hope for her sake that the good Lord takes mercy on her soul. But there again what hope does she have there, imagine you never even contacted Fr Clancy to make arrangements. Have you even sent her to ask for his forgiveness?" Mrs Lynch looked Maisie up and down and stared at Fiona like she was a piece of dirt at the bottom of her shoe. "Don't you think that's a bit unheard of? Like what were you thinking Maisie, your own daughter, how could you not seek God's salvation and at least give the girl a chance?"

Maisie was completely unprepared. Her blood went from neutral to boil in moments. Her heart raced in her chest and her breath was shallow. She couldn't believe her ears.

Fiona put her head down and stood like a lost little child.

Maisie's mind raced. She knew Mrs Lynch's words aired the voice of the community. She quickly searched her own mind and all that she had told herself in recent weeks in preparation for this moment.

"I have no doubt in my mind that the good Lord above has nothing but good grace for my daughter Mrs Lynch. After all, the miracle of life that she's carrying can only come from Him, isn't that right?" She stood tall and spoke loud and clear. "And while we're about asking forgiveness, I believe the Lords son Jesus said judge not, or prepare to be judged. So I hope for your sake the good Lord above has some forgiveness left over for the likes of you. But maybe you can go and ask Fr Clancy yourself about that one Mrs Lynch, it looks like you're due a visit." Maisie looked at Mrs Lynch from head to toe before turning on her heel and walking away. She stood as tall as she could with her head held high, leaving Mrs Lynch and the other two women catching flies.

"If that will be all we're be on our way. Have a good day ladies" Maisie and Fiona walked on.

"Pay no heed to them Fiona" Maisie looked at the road straight ahead and asserted to her daughter. "Silly old bats with nothing better to do. Hold your head high and put that behind you, my beautiful girl." It took everything Maisie had not to grab Fiona and hug the hurt and humiliation right out of her. News was clearly out about her forth coming arrival and no doubt the whole town had been watching what just happened. The last thing she was going to do was hug her sixteen-year-old in the street on full show to the whole town too.

Fiona tried with everything she had to do as her mother said. She fought back the tears in her eyes. Their words and scornful looks continued to cut right though her. Her whole body was shaking, and sadness was right at the surface.

Maisie turned into a coffee shop off the main street.

"Mammy, what are you doing I'm due back in forty minutes" Fiona now had panic thrown into the mix.

"I know what time it is Fiona, sit yourself down there," Maisie nodded to a free table in the busy coffee shop "I'll order us two cream buns and a pot of tea. You need it."

Maisie sat with Fiona and talked about the exam she was now to face. What she was expecting to come up in the paper and how prepared she felt she was when she got up this morning. Then she talked about the baby and asked has she felt the baby kicking yet.

"Mammy is that when you can feel little flutters at first?" Fiona's beautiful smile was beginning to fill her face again.

"That's right" Maisie's nodded, eye wide and smiling from ear to ear.

"I think that happened only the other day" Fiona intuitively put her hand over her tummy.

"There you go Love. They will get stronger now in the next couple of weeks," Maisie rested her chin in her hands, her elbows on the table.

Maisie told Fiona all about when she was carrying her, how the boys were completely different and then how little Jennifer's pregnancy was quite like hers. She asked her about what baby names she had in mind and discussed their preferences.

"Mammy, I am the luckiest sixteen-year old in Ireland, don't you ever think I don't know that," Fiona finished her tea and sat back in the chair, she gave her mum that familiar appreciative look "I best get going, thanks for this, you are the best"

"It's not many a sixteen-year old will say such a thing to their ma Fiona, I'm the lucky one, and I remind myself of that every day. Go on, good luck in your exam sweetheart"

She watched her daughter leave the busy coffee shop and go back to school to sit her next exam. Fiona gave her mother a smile and final little wave as the door closed behind her, Maisie's heart was bursting with all the love in the world for her beautiful girl who made her so proud every single day.

That evening the boys were gone off to the local field to play football with their friends. Maisie and Jennifer were finishing up the dishes after dinner and Fiona was in her room studying for her exams the following day. Pat arrived in the back door into the kitchen.

"Hello Love, you're home late. We went ahead and had dinner without you. The boys were starving and anxious to get back to their soccer game" Maisie opened the gas oven wearing her oven gloves and took Pat's dinner out. "Jennifer love, set a place there for your daddy will you"

"Hiya Daddy!" Jennifer fetched a knife and fork from the

side board drawer and laid a place for her daddy. "Mammy can I go back out and play? Rosie O' Reilly has to be in by seven o clock."

"Yes love of course, don't go far now" Maisie replied. Jennifer skipped out the back-yard door.

Pat stood tall beside the kitchen table in the centre of the room and took a large A4 size brown envelope from the inside pocket of his jacket and tossed it onto the kitchen table. He gave Maisie the kind of look that invited the next question.

"What's that?" Maisie put his dinner on the table and referenced the envelope.

"That's why I was late home today" Pat was giving very little away, at first, but then Maisie threw him one of her intolerant looks.

"That is a planning application form. I stopped by the council offices on the way home. Figured we best get started with building that little house down the back for Fiona." Pat took off his sleeveless Huskey jacket and laid it on the back of the kitchen chair. His stretched his shoulders back and his chest was out. He had not mentioned renovating the old out building since Maisie suggested it that night in the pub. He had a few weeks to get used to the fact that Fiona was expecting, and their family was growing. The day after Maisie told him the news he sat Fiona down and gave her a good scolding but then he backed up Maisie's message, that together they will support her, once she takes full responsibility for herself and the baby.

Over the last two weeks he planned the renovation of the building out in his mind. He took measurements, tested the structure and figured it should be no bother converting it into a little house. He asked the lads on site at work and his dad if they will help with the renovation during the summer evenings and they agreed. Although he never said who it was for or why he was renovating. The lads just assumed he was doing it because he had four growing kids.

"Pat, you're joking!" Maisie dived on the envelope and took out the application.

"Now Maisie, it's a modest house, a living room and kitchen on one side and bedroom and toilet on the other, that's it" He lay down the conditions, his hands outstretched making his point.

Maisie flicked though the paperwork, her mouth was wide open she could barely speak. "Do you know what, they broke the mould when they made you," Maisie heart burst open, her eyes filled with tears "How did I ever get so lucky to marry you Pat Kelly?" she flung her arms around his neck, bursting with love and appreciation for the kindest man on the planet.

"It'll take a few weeks for the planning application to go through, but I reckon it should be ok to make a start on it," He hugged Maisie back "How long does a credit union loan application take?"

"Oh I got the loan approved already" Maisie fixed her hair behind her ear and looked around the kitchen. She stood in front of Pat. He towered over her, she was only up to his chest.

"You're unbelievable. When did you do that?" Pat raised his eye-brows and smiled at Maisie.

"Ah a few weeks ago, you know, whenever. Do you want tea Love?" Maisie was already filling the kettle.

Pat shook his head. "Blessed am I amongst women is right. If this baby is a girl we may forget it, us lads will be completely outnumbered" Pat resigned to his wife's intuition and cheeky initiative again, knowing that once again, she was right.

Chapter 27

Saoirse was dressing a Mannequin in a school uniform for the shops' front window.

"Hello Mrs Prendergast, long time no see," Saoirse gave a warm smile, fixing her long brown hair behind her shoulders and greeted a loyal customer into Corcoran's, "How are all the family keeping?"

Saoirse had gained quite a reputation with the customers in recent years. They loved her. It had even become necessary to set up an appointment diary to see her at weekends. Confirmation, First Holy Communion and Back to School seasons were always extremely busy. During which times Saoirse arranged to open the shop on an appointment only basis on Sundays to deal with demand.

It was a sunny Tuesday morning and the shop was quiet. Saoirse and Ruth were on duty together. Ruth was the Shop Manager and Saoirse was a full-time sales assistant. Joe came into the shop at weekends, he was spending a lot more time off with Lil nowadays.

Saoirse lived at home with her parents. She was an independent twenty-year-old who insisted on cooking her own meals, doing her own food shop and taking care of her own laundry.

Ruth was in love with Barry, a solicitor from Dalkey. They met in college and had just paid a deposit on a house in Killiney, south county Dublin. It was everything Ruth had ever dreamed of, a large home with a sea view in one of the most prestigious areas of the capital. Barry was in line to inherit his father's legal practice. He was a handsome, dapper twenty-five-year-old, who knew his P's and Q's.

"Hi Billy, are you helping your mammy with the shopping today again?" Saoirse leaned over the shop counter and greeted Mrs Prendergast's youngest son. Mrs Prendergast had five boys. Billy was eight and her eldest was sixteen. Saoirse had dressed every one of them for all family occasions since she started five years ago.

"Yeah, Mammy said if I'm good she'll get me a rubix cube on the way home. All my brothers have one and I know how to work them too," Billy exclaimed, "My big brother can even finish it!" His eyes were almost popping out of his head, mighty impressed and full of chat as always.

"Well as I said, if you're good Billy, and Saoirse he is warned not to take the stickers off and swop them around" Mrs Prendergast repeated the rules and nodded at Billy.

"Oh you can't be doing that, sure that's cheating!" Saoirse gasped "Mind you I have been tempted to do so myself on a couple of occasions!" Saoirse admitted to Billy.

"I came in on the Dart this morning Saoirse, it's great, hop on, hop off, no parking nothing. Only took me quarter of an hour to get to Dun Laoghaire too."

"That all sounds good. I haven't gone on it myself yet, but I'm only hearing good things about it" She picked up the half-dressed Mannequin and put it aside to serve Mrs Prendergast.

Back to School time was months away. It was only early June, but Corcoran's were reputed for stocking the crested uniforms for all National and Secondary Schools in the South County Dublin region. Saoirse was way ahead and had organised delivery of stock in advance of the busy season.

"How can I help you today Mrs. Prendergast?" Saoirse smiled giving Mrs Prendergast her full attention.

"I was looking for…."

"Saoirse, can you vacuum the floor please while it's quiet and those windows are manky we shouldn't let them get that dirty," Ruth marched through the shop towards the front cashier desk "Have you seen my coffee cup anywhere? I can't find it at all." Ruth searched under the front desk for her cup. She always wore the clothes from the shop and called it advertising. Today she was impeccably dressed in a black tailored trouser suit, white blouse and black stiletto heels. Her fair hair tumbled in large defined curls around her shoulders and as always, her nails were groomed to perfection and make-up was flawless.

Saoirse glanced at the front windows. The sun was beaming in highlighting every spec of dirt and dust, but she didn't consider them manky.

"I'm just serving Mrs Prendergast Ruth" she eyeballed her sister.

"Hello" Ruth busily walked past Mrs Prendergast back down into her office at the end of the shop.

"I beg your pardon Mrs Prendergast, you were saying" Saoirse's tone was calm and collected. She was well used to maintaining her professional manner.

Mrs Prendergast shook her head and rolled her eyes in Ruth's direction. "I was looking for the school jumpers and slacks for the lads," She nodded over to the large school uniform section, which lined the side wall towards the front of the shop. "I may get them all now at the start of the holidays. Then they're out of the way, one less thing to worry about."

"No problem. So, it's two St Columba's National School and three St Mary's is that right" Saoirse began to take down the appropriate jerseys for Mrs Prendergast's boys.

"That's spot on, God bless your memory Saoirse" Mrs Prendergast smiled with appreciation.

"And it gets better Mrs Prendergast. I was just about to pop a sign in the window before lunch today. All school socks come free with every pair of slacks bought for the month of June!" Saoirse explained while she double checked the tags for sizes making sure she had her order correct.

"That's a very good offer, in that case I may double up on the slacks so. God only knows what happens to the socks in our house. The hot press is constantly a sea of odd socks, no matter what I do" Mrs Prendergast said with a look of bewilderment.

Billy was watching Saoirse put the order together. He couldn't take his eyes off her.

"Ok five school jumpers, ten pairs of slacks and ten pairs of school socks," She quickly totted the sale up in her head while bagging up the clothes "That will be eighty pounds please when you're ready Mrs Prendergast" Saoirse began to ring the order in to the till.

"You're really clever Saoirse. You can really add," Billy looked up at Saoirse wondering how she did all of those sums in her head so fast.

"Oh I get lots of practice Billy," Saoirse laughed "No doubt you will be as clever when you're as big as me!"

"My granny says that you weren't clever and that's why your daddy sent you to a private school, so as you could get good at school. Granny said that your big sister didn't need to go to private school because she had her daddy's brains" Billy blurted.

"Billy!" Mrs Prendergast snapped, grabbing Billy's arm. "I...I'm sorry Saoirse pay no heed" She fumbled in her handbag for her purse. "Eighty is that right?" Mrs Prendergast put the money on the shop counter, her hands were shaking.

"It's no problem" Saoirse gave a nervous laugh and fixed her hair behind her ear. She could feel her face burning and heart racing.

"She did Mammy. Granny said that Saoirse was lucky to get into a family like the Corcoran's. That way she got the best of everything because they have lots of money," Billy went on.

Mrs Prendergast's heart was racing wishing to God Billy would just stop talking.

Saoirse could feel the heat burn her face, her body temperature dropping.

"and otherwise Saoirse wouldn't have private school or a job. Granny said!" Billy nodded and protested. "But I don't understand because I think you're really nice and really clever" Billy complimented Saoirse.

"Saoirse, I, I am so sorry" Mrs Prendergast couldn't even look at Saoirse.

"Honestly Mrs Prendergast, it's fine" She tried with everything she had to put Mrs Prendergast at ease, but a million questions were filling her mind at the same time. She handed her the bags of clothes.

"Erm, Mrs Prendergast would you like to leave the bags here and collect them when you have the car? It's no problem" Saoirse applied every ounce of her energy to maintain her friendly, professional manner.

"No, no it's fine love. I'll be grand" Mrs Prendergast insisted, taking the bags from Saoirse and failing eye contact.

She left the shop as quick as she could.

"Excuse me. We're giving away free clothes now are we?" Ruth appeared from the back of the shop, leaning on the door frame twirling a pen between her fingers.

"What did he mean by that?" Saoirse's stood behind the shop counter. Her voice was slow and controlled, every part of her was shaking.

"Never mind that. Who do you think you are giving away free

stock?" Ruth pressed "I make the rules around here. I manage this shop. I say what special offers are on and when." Ruth raised her voice, punching the air with her finger with every point she made.

"Ruth," Saoirse looked Ruth right in the eye and began to walk towards her "you do nothing around here but swan about the place giving orders like Little Miss Important. Mrs Prendergast bought an extra five pairs of slacks because of that offer. If you knew your stock you would know that the mark up on socks is a mere five percent. The mark up on slacks is eighty percent. You do the maths on that one or do you want me to get you a calculator to do it for you?" Saoirse's voice was controlled but her blood was boiling. She never stood up to Ruth before. She always bit her tongue when Ruth dished out the orders and let her have her moments. At the end of the day Saoirse knew that the customers came in for her service. Saoirse made the sales and she got on well with all the staff.

Ruth's place was in the back of the shop only showing her face to show her importance.

"How dare you speak to me like that. Who in the name of God do you think you are?" Ruth stood up straight. "I do everything around here." She pointed at her chest with her pen and waved her other arm around the shop. "I carry this place. If it wasn't for me this shop would fall apart and you know it. I, I carry this place."

"Oh yeah? Tell me, what do you do Ruth?" Saoirse was right in front of Ruth now, "Make sales? Eh no, that would be me. Look after the loyal customers and insure new business become loyal customers too? Eh no, that would be me too. Ensure a warm friendly, family service? By God hell would freeze over first Ruth," She counted her questions out with her fingers and didn't take her eyes off Ruth's, "Do you make sure the place is clean Ruth? nope I do that. Do you open-up? No, you swan in everyday after 11. Close-up shop? No, I do that too,"

"How, how dare you. Wait till Daddy hears about this, you, you are going to be so sorry, I, I carry this place" Ruth raged, she was almost in tears and Saoirse was beginning to feel bad for being so nasty. But she saw Billy's innocent little face in her mind's eye and the audio of his words played like a movie in her mind and she went on,

"All you do in here Ruth is count the cash to be banked at the end of the day. I even do the blinking lodgement and fetch you a takeaway coffee on my way back from the bank for goodness sake. YOU DO NOTHING!" Saoirse shouted, her fists were clenched by her side and her whole body tensed with more rage with every word she spoke. "I'm the one who does blinking everything around here, everyone knows it, the staff, the customers and even you!

Now tell me, what did Billy Prendergast mean by that?" She shouted, insisting Ruth reveal the story behind the secret that everyone seemed to know.

Ruth paused before explaining all to Saoirse.

"Oh, poor little Saoirse. Don't you know by now Dad is a clever man?" Ruth's spoke slowly and raised her eye-brows "Back then, when we sent you away, remember?" the question breezed out of Ruth's mouth. She folded her arms and began to circle Saoirse, "Well back in those days the shop was in trouble. Dad, being Dad, always had it sussed that appearance and reputation was everything," she twirled her long blond hair and explained history to Saoirse. "Sending you to private school made it look like we had lots of money, which gave the impression that Corcoran's was hopping with business."

Saoirse listened, her stomach was in knots. Her fists were still clenched, and her heart pounded.

"But the plan was two-fold," Ruth continued her slow, clear tone with every word she spoke.

"Not only did Daddy maintain his business status, he also demonstrated what a good, kind gentleman he was. Doing his very best for the unfortunate, adopted daughter who clearly didn't have the same intelligence that came with his DNA.

He gave you the best chance at life, all thanks to his well-meaning nature and very clever mind. Oh, and everybody knew it too." She summed it all up and stood in front of Saoirse, wearing a tailored suit and an empty smile.

Saoirse looked at Ruth smirking back at her. She clenched her teeth and fought back the tears. The walls of the shop, the ground beneath her and ceiling were closing in and she felt like crumbling to the ground.

Instead, without thinking she turned on her heel and stormed towards the door, grabbing her bag on the way.

"Where are you going?" Ruth called. Saoirse didn't answer. "Saoirse, where are you going? What, what am I supposed to do. You can't just walk out midday!" Ruth panicked, begging Saoirse to come back "Saoirse what am I supposed to do here on my own?"

Saoirse stood in the doorway of her father's shop and looked over her shoulder at Ruth,

"Do what you always do Ruth. Carry it!" she threw the words at her sister and slammed the shop door behind her.

Saoirse reefed the lock off her bicycle which was tied to a lamppost outside the drapery shop and slammed the chain into her bag. Still fighting back the tears for fear that anyone she knew was passing by.

With her hands gripping the handlebars she pushed the pedals with her feet as hard as she could. Once she got out onto the main road she released the tears that screamed inside and cried all the way home.

She turned the key in the lock of her family home in Ashlawn and stormed into the kitchen leaving the front door swinging open behind her.

Joe was standing at the kitchen counter making a cup of tea. Nothing had changed between Joe and Saoirse since she was nine years old. They rarely spoke, if at all.

He gave a half glance over his shoulder, enough to catch sight of Saoirse in his peripheral vision. He gave no reaction to the fact that his daughter was clearly like a bull in a china shop.

"All for bloody money and status eh?" Saoirse's heart pounded like never before. She wanted to grab Joe and tear him apart. Instead she hoped she could articulate the words to do so instead.

"Beg your pardon?" Joe took a sip of his tea and leaned on the kitchen counter.

"You're despicable, do you know that? You are disgusting. You are an excuse for a man." Saoirse spat the words at her father.

Joe's face changed completely, from dismissal to anger. He looked her up and down.

"I beg your pardon? Just who do you think you are?" He

stood up tall and raised his voice.

"I just heard a couple of home truths from your darling daughter, DAD!" Saoirse stepped one step closer to her father. She experienced what it was like to size up to anyone for the first time in her life. "Money and reputation? That's why you sent me to the Convent? Oh, Ruth told me all about it" The anger was exploding in her chest and shot through ever part of her,

"You and your stupid little shop not making money. You had to do something to save the shop and save your reputation. That's why I got carted off to The Sister of Charity."

Saoirse's words downloaded in Joe's mind, "Saoirse that's not true, I,"

"Ruth just gave me the full history! Don't try wriggle out of it DAD. How in the name of God could you?" Saoirse could not stop shouting, she could feel the raw in the back of her throat and it was beginning to hurt but the last thing she planned to do right now was save her voice.

"Saoirse, listen to me, that's not true" Joe put his hand up in attempt to stop her and calm her down, but he couldn't get a word in.

"You know I always felt different growing up. I always knew I was different, I was the adopted one, Ruth was yours. But when I was little I always knew that didn't matter. You loved me, and I knew it. Well how wrong was I eh?" She stood back, looking Joe up and down, her voice trembled. "First sign of trouble and alas there's the underdog, sure she's only the adopted one at the end of the day. Not only is blood thicker than water, so is business." She did not take her eyes off Joes, "Let's save the business, let's save our family and use Saoirse to do it. And now for the bonus," Saoirse raised her voice and her sarcasm flowed "not only will everyone know that we're rich, they'll also see what a total hero I am at the same time, saving a poor unfortunate illegitimate child and giving her a chance in life with a good, private, convent education. Well bravo to you. Round of a-bloody-plause Joe. You nailed it" Saoirse shook her head and clapped her hands. The tears flowed down her face.

"Saoirse, will you please let me explain?"

"No. I've heard it all Joe. I've had enough explaining for one day" Saoirse had made her point and tried to shut down.

"Saoirse"

"How? Just how could you live with yourself?" She looked at Joe really trying to understand. "Like, we all know Ireland's view on the 'mortal sin' that brings about little babies being adopted but to take advantage of that to make yourself look good? To take advantage of me? Jesus Christ Joe," Saoirse took a step back, her palm rested on her chest and she shook her head.

"Saoirse stop" Joe pleaded.

"Why? Hearing the truth hurts you, does it Joe?"

"Saoirse, I didn't send you away for those reasons," Joe took advantage of the space her question gave him. He didn't want her believing what Ruth said. It was far from the truth.

"Yes, you did" She stated.

"Saoirse, I did not" Joe desperately tried to stop her.

"Oh, oh so darling Ruth is a liar now, is she?" She raised her eye brows and placed her hands on her hips, "Seriously, Joe where do you stop? It just doesn't end with you"

"SAOIRSE, I SENT YOU AWAY BECAUSE YOU WERE BRINGING BAD LUCK" Joe blurted.

This time Saoirse had no answer.

The silence in the kitchen was deafening.

Every ounce of Joe's consistent authority was gone.

He stood at the kitchen counter with his head bowed to the ground, searching his mind for something to say, he had nothing to give. He knew he had just killed the air with his words and his relationship with Saoirse for good.

"What?" She whispered.

The strength and determination she had moments ago was gone. In its place flowed memories from the past and they flashed through her mind like a movie. She saw Mr Ryan, and their beautiful encounter the night he came to say goodbye, the light that surrounded him, his face filled with love. She remembered Mr Bennett and her dream predicting his passing. She saw Mrs Bennett's face and the love in her eyes when she gave Saoirse her husband's watch on the day of his funeral.

She stood in the kitchen before her father and the little girl who lay in the bed on the first night in the convent rose to the surface and the same guilt and shame returned to every cell in her body, mind and her heart along with the echo of Sr Agnes words:

The reason you are here is because you are evil

"That's what she meant" All was beginning to make sense in her mind.

She had no idea all those years ago why she felt such shame and guilt, until now.

"Jesus Christ Dad," Saoirse joined her hands and placed them over her mouth.

"Saoirse, you have to understand, I was scared. Everyone was dying. The church says…"

She cut Joe short "The church says what? That your innocent child is evil? First she's born of a fallen woman and now she sees dead people. Well that just compounds it altogether doesn't it?" Perhaps it was the shock, but her tone was collected. "Did you ever think to look outside the box Joe?"

"Saoirse stop calling me Joe" Joe closed his eyes and shook his head.

Saoirse laughed "Seriously, Father? Is that what you want me to call you? Do you mean the noun or the verb Father?"

"Saoirse, what was I supposed to think or feel? I didn't know. I was scared, afraid. Everyone was dropping dead like flies. Your ma's mother, my sister, her husband, even my best friend," Joe begged Saoirse's understanding.

"And you never thought to think that maybe, just maybe all this was just happening? You never thought to look at me and see what or who was there, as opposed to some made up psycho crap by the church? I was AN INNOCENT NINE-YEAR-OLD LITTLE GIRL JOE! I WAS NINE YEARS OLD" Saoirse's fury and pain rushed through her anatomy "You were an adult, my father. Jesus, I depended on you to be a man, to see me for what I was, not what the church dictated" She paused for a moment trying desperately to get some grip on the reality that dawned in her mind.

She looked at Joe and quietly asked: "What was your heart telling you Joe?"

Joe looked to the ground, "I was afraid Saoirse"

"Tell me" She spoke through the tears "Was your heart telling you I was evil too?" the lump in her throat throbbed and her voice trembled.

Joe looked up at Saoirse, his eyes welled up with tears.

He shook his head.

"Joe, why is the hall door wide open? You may cut that front grass this evening, everyone's out cutting theirs," Lil returned home from shopping in Blackrock. "Saoirse, why aren't you in the shop helping Ruth?" She looked at the pair in the kitchen.

"What's wrong? Joe why are you upset?" She placed her shopping bags on the kitchen table. "Saoirse what did you say to your father?"

Saoirse closed her eyes and took a deep breath.

"I am going upstairs," She looked at Joe ignoring her mother's question "I am packing my bag and I am cutting all ties." She stated in a quiet, clear tone.

"What?" Lil panicked. "Saoirse, what do you mean?" She followed Saoirse out to the hall. "Joe, Joe what's going on?" Lil walked in and out of the kitchen to the hall and again, "What does she mean she's cutting all ties. What did she do?"

Joe stood in the kitchen unresponsive to Lil's panic and confusion. His tall, filled out frame was numb. The heaviness in his heart right now drowned out all light flowing into the room from the glorious sunshine outside.

Lil looked at her husband "Joe, what's has happened" she calmed herself, she knew that look. It was the same look that Joe had when his best friend, Alan Bennet died.

Joe had no words to give.

"Hello, Murphy's Seafood Restaurant, Maria speaking" Maria's upbeat voice was like the brightest ray of sunshine.

"Hi Maria" Saoirse forced. Her eyes were swollen like balloons. Her face, her throat and even her body hurt with shock and heartbreak. She stood in the tiny payphone box at the end of her road with a large canvas bag containing her life. She knew that all she had to do was hold it together one step at a time and she would figure out the next step as she went along.

"I just rang you in the shop and Ruth said you weren't there!" Maria bounced "I thought you were off yesterday? Anyway listen, I have loads to tell you. How did that date go with your man from Friday night? Saoirse, he was a fine thing! You always have the fine things running around after you" Maria exploded into catch up mode. Her newly permed dark hair tickled her forehead and face as the curls bounced with each animated expression.

She was working in a Sea Food Restaurant in North County Dublin. She was about to enter her final year in college in Hospitality Management and had just begun working full time hours in the restaurant for the summer.

The lunchtime rush was beginning to quieten down, and Maria stood at the front desk, taking in the view of the sun glistening off the Irish sea as it met Dublin's coastline.

She had been trying to catch up with Saoirse all morning "And I need you to break the rules and come out with me on a school night too. I have brilliant news, can't wait to tell you" Her smile beamed from ear to ear.

"Ok. Maria, what time are you off today" Saoirse had no interest in reliving last Saturday night's date with an idiot called Steve who thought he was God's gift to women and the last thing she was in form for was going out tonight too.

"Oh sweetie, what's wrong?" Maria heard her friends upset.

"I can't tell you over the phone. It's too big" Saoirse felt her eyes well up again.

"Listen," Maria put her assertive hat on, "get yourself on the Dart out to Howth. When you get off the train ask anyone to direct you to Murphy's Seafood Restaurant and they will show you," Then she thought of a better idea "No actually, I'll tell you what, get to Howth, go to the Main Street. You'll see Harris' Music Shop. The owners name is Tom. He is Alvagh's third cousin, or something like that. Anyway, tell him who you are, and you are looking for the key to the flat upstairs" Maria picked up that Saoirse could do with being somewhere more private.

"That's your flat isn't it?" Saoirse snuffled.

"Yep. I'll ring him now and tell him you're on your way," Maria checked her watch "I'm finished at three, but I should be able to get out a bit earlier being Tuesday and I'll meet you there when I'm done ok?"

"Ok, I should be there in an hour or so. I'll get a taxi to the Dart station" Saoirse threw her heavy bag over her shoulder and checked the time.

"Oh Sweetheart, no matter what it is, I know everything is going to be ok. As you always say, it'll all work out in the end" Maria knew by Saoirse's tone it was something very serious this time. She also knew that it had to be Saoirse's family. For as long as she had known Saoirse they were the only people who had the ability to upset her.

Chapter 28

"Hello" Saoirse called. She couldn't see any staff in the music shop and she hoped the sound of the bell when she opened the door would alert the man called Tom to the shop floor. The music shop was long and rectangular shaped. It contained every musical instrument one could imagine. They air was filled with the scent of wood from the polished guitars hanging from the walls and others that stood proud on the floor, each one silently vibrating the potential of its sound.

Saoirse strolled towards the counter at the back of the shop, taking in her surroundings. She couldn't resist but to reach out and touch one of the polished oak guitars on the floor. She stroked the smooth timber with her fingertips.

"How are ye" A male voice suddenly filled the silence in the shop causing Saoirse to jump. With that, the guitar slid and fell flat to the floor, taking two more guitars with it. The thud of the instruments and echo of the strings in the hallow did not sound like good news to her very untrained ear.

"Oh sweet Jesus!" fright, panic and mortification shocked through her body all at once. She fumbled with the fallen instruments, trying to stand one back up and balance the other two with the other hand.

"It's alright" A very tall, dark haired, extremely handsome guy in a white T-shirt and blue jeans appeared behind the counter. His large grin smiled from ear to ear and he walked over to save Saoirse from her calamity.

"Happens all the time, I really should hang them all up on the wall" He assured, relieving Saoirse from one of the guitars and then the other two. He effortlessly stood them back on the floor, where they did not budge.

"I, I'm sorry" Saoirse tucked her hair behind her ear. The awkward, mortified sense increased ten-fold when she looked at the guy. She was expecting an older middle-aged man. The last thing she was expecting was this guy. He towered over her, his perfect smile beamed from ear to ear. His wavy dark brown hair sat perfectly brushed back on top. He even smelt uplifting, quite like fresh laundry and wood.

"It's no problem" He laughed sensing Saoirse's awkwardness.

"Ah, you must be the famous Saoirse?" he stood before her observing Saoirse's features.

"Erm, that's right" Saoirse flicked her hair into place so as it sat well around her face.

"Tom" he introduced himself with an outstretched hand.

"Hi Tom, nice to meet you" Saoirse shook Tom's large, soft hand. "I was expecting your dad or something. Not sure why" She tittered, and immediately inwardly scolded herself for choosing those words out of all the words she could have chosen in the English language.

Tom laughed. "No, you're right. It's my dad's shop. I work here too and he's the other Tom."

Tom's smile would not leave his face. The pair stood opposite each other, looking at each other and then realised that they had run out of things to say.

"Oh the key!" Saoirse remembered "Maria said you have the key to upstairs?"

Tom raised his forefinger high in the air. "The key, that's right, I do," he swung round on his heel and went back behind the counter.

"Here you go" he popped the key into Saoirse's hand.

"Thanks Tom, and again, I hope I didn't do any damage" Saoirse nodded to the guitars.

"Not at all, happens all the time. Are you sticking around for the night or?"

"Oh, erm, I'm not sure really. I'll have a chat with Maria later I suppose and see" She found herself smiling.

"In that case I might see you later so" Tom stood tall, shoulders back, still smiling.

Chapter 29

Saoirse sat on the couch in Maria's flat, drinking a mug of tea and over-looking the panoramic view of the Dublin coast line. The bright, peaceful flat was quiet all for the distant sound of light traffic passing through the main street outside.

She relaxed back on the couch, noticing how tired and heavy her body felt. Her mind filled with reflections of her day. Ruth harping lies, Joe's divulgence of the truth and her mother's concern for everyone but her. Her eyes filled up with tears. Anger and disappointment for what never was, caused her heart to break. Today magnified the sense of ever present separation, this time to a point of no return. Right now, she knew she could never go back.

She reflected on Sr Agnes and what she represented. She was supposed to represent God, Jesus, Mother Mary and the way to God. She was supposed to represent love, joy and the peace that comes from God. Religion was supposed to be a path that teaches us about God, who He is and how to be close to Him.

Sr Agnes neither represented or taught any of that. She was the furthest thing from a vessel of love that Saoirse could imagine.

Her mind went back to the first evening at the convent, when she was standing in Sr Agnes' office and the nun was telling her that she was evil. Seeing the reality from the new dimension that today revealed gave clarity to her confusion and guilt through the years. Now she knew the type of conversations that took place that resulted in the decisions to send her away. She imagined Joe going to the convent, turning to the nun for understanding of what he did not. Sr Agnes understood alright. But her stand point was not from the place of unconditional love and acceptance, peace and compassion for all. Instead it was seeped in judgement and hate and so was her ruling. She never represented God, at least not the God Saoirse knew.

Joe's words today echoed through her mind.

Saoirse, I didn't understand. I didn't know what to do. I was afraid.

He turned to Sr Agnes, God's representative seeking understanding and clarity. Instead she took control and killed innocence and he agreed to it.

She recalled all the times Joe ignored her during her teenage years. How he and Ruth humiliated her when she tried to join in conversations, killing her confidence to speak up, have a voice and express her opinions.

She checked the time knowing Maria should be home soon. It was almost four o clock. Maria was late, but Saoirse knew that Maria being Maria was most likely being her loyal self and not leaving the restaurant in the lurch.

Which brought her mind to how she walked out of her father's shop today and left Ruth in the lurch. She reflected on the years of separation between herself and Ruth. They were never the best of friends. As they got older they tolerated each other. She thought of how different herself and Ruth were. Ruth was proper and perfect in every way. People stood to her requests and demands and did what she said. She was mammy and daddy's favourite girl and she knew it, everyone knew it. But outside of that Ruth was stone cold. Everything was about status and how it appeared on the outside was what mattered. This reflected in the highfalutin friends she had. Saoirse always felt they were cold, plastic people and never got on with the any of them. They looked through her anytime they visited the shop or her home, constantly filled with a sense of their own importance.

Saoirse, on the other hand knew she was warm, kind and she knew she was able to connect with people, right from the heart. Ok maybe she wasn't as well -groomed or fashion conscious as Ruth was, but she always turned herself out well. Saoirse was drawn to what worked for her, not what worked to make a statement.

Ruth also had a completely different temperament to hers. Ruth was highly strung, everything had to be perfect, otherwise there was a hissy fit over the most trivial things. Saoirse was easy going, she just got on with it. She never understood how Ruth could run another's efforts down and not care how they feel. She remembered reading in a book one time that those who require our tolerance the most, are usually the most intolerant of all. She never forgot that and always called it to mind when Ruth demanded her tolerance. It brought her comfort in a strange kind of way, like she wasn't alone, whoever wrote that obviously had a similar experience.

Saoirse's mind went back to where it all began and remembered

Ms Cross who lived next door. She remembered the evening she was standing in the scullery kitchen of the old lady's home, overhearing her words.

I'm telling you Ruth have nothing to with her, she is nothing, a nobody.

Saoirse's eyes filled up with tears for the little girl inside who was witness to those words.

"Such bloody pointless devastation, bloody poisonous" she said out loud. She curled up on the couch with her knees to her chest, both hands wrapped around her mug of tea, which had gone cold by now. The tears soaked her face and she sobbed and sobbed as she looked over the Dublin landscape on the most beautiful Summers evening, alone.

"Saoirse" The door of the flat opened and Maria walked in carrying shopping bags filled with groceries.

"Hi" Saoirse pressed her face and dried her tears before standing up off the couch.

"Oh no. Oh no" Maria took one look at Saoirse, dropped the bags and ran towards her friend to give her the biggest heart felt hug, the kind of hugs that are embraced with the wish to take the pain away, even if it was just for now.

She held Saoirse in silence for a few moments before asking "What did they do? I know it's really bad this time."

"It's over Maria. I'm done, I'm really done this time" Saoirse wiped the tears that kept flowing. She had threatened to leave several times before when the tension was too great or the sense of being out numbered was too isolating. The thoughts of knowing that if she did leave, she would not only have to leave home, she would also have to leave her job and her career. Each time, the dust settled, and she got on with tolerating the sense of separation, favouritism and unfairness. But today things had gone to the point of no return.

"He said he sent me to the convent because I was bringing bad luck to the family," Saoirse sat on the couch and held a cushion to her chest.

"It was horrible Maria" Saoirse stared at the coffee table in front of the couch. "Basically, a little fella, he's only a child was in the shop with his mam this morning and the poor little guy divulged that his granny told him I was thick, that's why I was sent to Sisters of Charity. I felt sorry for the mother, she nearly died. Anyway, Ruth and I had a blazing row because I asked her what he meant. I told her what I thought of her, how lazy she is and so full of her own self-importance. And her come-back was to put me in my place, telling me that Dad sent me to private school to make it look like the Corcoran's were loaded. Apparently the shop was in trouble and not doing a whole lot of business back then. She banged on about how well that made dad look, a hero to the poor unfortunate adopted child"

"Jesus Christ Saoirse, this is, this is...How cruel!" Maria sat beside Saoirse trying to get a sense of how awful Saoirse's day was. "Flipping heck Saoirse" she whispered.

"Anyway, I went home and tore into Dad. I was furious from what Ruth said" Saoirse snuffled and pressed her wrist on her eyes "The long and short of it was that he kept saying that it wasn't true and to let him explain and of course I knew it was true because of little Billy. Eventually he blurted the real reason I was sent away. It was more an effort to stop me going on and set me straight." She swallowed and sighed a deep breath before saying the words out loud, "Anyway, he said I was bringing bad luck and that's the reason why he sent me away" She took a deep breath, huddled back in the couch in foetal position, hugging the cushion on to her chest.

"Hang on. I'm confused" Maria frowned. "So how come Billy said what he said though if your dad..." she paused and allowed it to fall into place in her mind "Oh my God!" Her chin almost dropped to the floor "So your dad thought you were bringing bad luck. Didn't want to tell anyone that side of the story and told everyone, including Ruth that you had to go to the convent because you weren't clever like his real daughter" Maria grasped sense of Saoirse's words, "What a disaster, you couldn't make this stuff up"

"Do you remember I told you that when I was little I was quite psychic? I could see people who have passed away, I had dreams of forth coming events and that." Saoirse reminded Maria

"Yeah, yeah, I know, I get you," Maria looked at her friends broken state "and today you found out that that was the reason why, my gosh. I really don't know what to say. I am lost for words. I feel so bad for you sweetheart. So when Aggie told you you were evil, that's what she meant too. What a bitch, the poisonous shrivelled up cow, oh come here sweat heart" Maria tried to hug the pain out of Saoirse.

"I had no idea, and do you know I always felt really guilty back then and I never knew the reason why" Saoirse forced her words through her swollen throat and burning eyes, her head felt like it was about to explode..

"Anyway, it's over, I told him I was cutting all ties and I meant every word. I'm never going back"

Maria looked at Saoirse's broken state and she knew it was the end.

"Anyway, listen, thanks for letting me come here, you're a life saver" Saoirse tried with everything she had to perk up.

"I am delighted you're here. Sure I've been trying to get you out here for years" Maria shone her effortless warm grin, knowing Saoirse wanted to change the subject for now.

"Erm, so you met Tom?" She fixed her eyes on Saoirse's and that warm grin turned into a cheeky smile.

"Oh my God. Where did you get him?" Saoirse's face transformed.

"I knew it! I knew it" Maria slapped her knees "I've been saying it to myself for years, you two would make a lovely couple"

"Maria!" Saoirse felt the energy lift and her cheeks fill with fire. "Maria, I was mortified" She threw the cushion on the couch, sat up and faced her friend. "I thought I was going in to get the key from the other Tom, big Tom or dad Tom whichever. I knocked half the shop over and everything"

"Oh I know" Maria said mischievously.

"What?"

"He told me"

"Tom told you? When?"

"Oh yeah. He called the restaurant after you left to tell me that you were in to pick up the key"

"Oh right"

"Yeah. Tom never rings me in work. In fact, Tom has never rung me before" Maria continued her mischievous tone and stood up to put the groceries away.

"So?" Saoirse was trying to hold back the smile that was bursting through on her face and swung round on the couch, her eyes following Maria.

"Yeah. He just said that he thought he would ring to let me know, that's all. Oh, and then he asked if we were up to anything tonight or if we were around, or anything" She explained putting the bread in the bread bin and ham and cheese in the fridge.

"Don't worry. I knew you wouldn't be in form for much tonight. Oh, I got up a few bottles of Budweiser instead if that's ok?" Maria held up a six pack of Budweiser and popped it in the fridge.

"He's single you know. In fact, he's been single for a long time. He only ever shows interest if he's REALLY interested," her eyes nearly popped out of her head, "like today, when he rang to ask all about you." Maria pursed her lips. Her matter of fact tone was no match for that smile she was trying to hide.

"Well Saoirse? Say something"

But Saoirse sat back on the couch hugging the cushion again, wearing an involuntary smile from ear to ear.

"Ah, we'll see" She bit her lip and played with the gold chain around her neck.

"Maria, you said you had news, brilliant news. What is it?" Saoirse remembered both Maria's news and her manners and jumped up off the couch to help her finish putting the groceries away.

"Oh yes!" Maria bounced. "I can't wait to tell you. Sit down, I'll stick the kettle on"

The girls made the tea and settled on the couch, with chocolate biscuits.

"Well, you know the way I took up full-time hours at the restaurant for the summer?" Maria explained dunking her biscuit into the mug of tea and raced it to her mouth before it broke.

"This morning my boss sat me down and explained that he was looking for a new Restaurant Manager because the hotel group is opening a swanky new hotel in Temple Bar and he is going to run that restaurant." Maria had been working in the restaurant for three years. It was part of the exquisite world-renowned Strand Hotel Group. She started just after she finished the Leaving Cert and worked part time during college, taking up the full-time hours during holidays.

"Anyway, long story short he told me that he would like to give me first refusal on taking over his position. I said, 'No thank you, forget the refusal I'll take the job if that's ok" Her eyes lit up. "So, I have a new job, in Restaurant Management and a three-grand pay rise! He even arranged with HR to support my final year in college and pay my fees too!" Maria glowed, this was her dream come true. A year ago, she faced the fact that the last thing she wanted to do was move her life up to Donegal and work in her parents' restaurant. Her life was in Dublin. The hardest part was telling her parents her plans to stay put. They were not in the least impressed at first, but eventually saw her perspective and agreed to support her decision. Ever since then she felt pressure to show that she had made the right choice and today was a definite breakthrough in doing so. The Strand Hotel Group was recognised on a global scale and Murphy's Sea Food Restaurant attracted visitors worldwide. Maria knew this was a mile stone step in her career and a turning point in her life.

"Maria, that's fantastic! I'm so happy for you. You deserve all the success in the world" Saoirse sat up straight on the edge of the couch and saw a whole new world open up for her friend.

"I know and supporting the final year college fees and everything. I can hardly believe it. I've been pinching myself all day!" Maria giggled, then thought for a moment and looked at Saoirse, "I don't mean to go back to talking about earlier today. I know you want the break and change of subject but," she paused, "you walked out on your life today. So that means you also walked out of your job, right?"

Saoirse slumped into the couch.

"No, no, hear me out," Maria waved her hand, "Part of my new job is to recruit staff and this being the beginning of the Summer season I'll have to be tending to that sooner rather than later" She reached for another chocolate biscuit.

"Maria, I'm not following you"

Maria dunked her chocolate biscuit into her tea and raced it to her mouth again before explaining: "It looks like I am holding my very first interview" She clarified through a mouthful of chocolate digestive "When can you start?"

Saoirse looked at Maria's smiley face, her eyes shining big and bright.

"Me? The Restaurant? But…. Maria, I don't know the first thing about seafood" Saoirse checked.

"Oh for goodness sake, have you heard of cod, mackerel, crab?" Maria dismissed, "You know customers and how to deal with people. You're friendly, professional and trustworthy. Plus, I'll be your boss and I know where you live and who your friends are, you know? Just in case you try and pull a sicky after a night on the tiles" Maria nodded with a teasing smile. "You're the ideal candidate" She concluded and took a sip of her tea.

"You are seriously offering me a job" Saoirse hugged her knees to her chest, observing Maria's eyes. "Hold on, what do you mean: you know where I live?"

"Well you can move in here?" Maria offered "That's if you want to? I for one would love to have you as a room-mate and as you always say, everything happens for a reason and all that"

Saoirse laughed in disbelief at the new chapter in her life was seamlessly falling into place. "Seriously? Maria really?"

"I know, let's get a Chinese takeaway to celebrate!" Marias bounced up off the couch, her eyes sparkling.

The girls ordered their Chinese and settled in to their first night of what was to become many years of moments shared and memories made. The tone was set with laughter, a little reflection and effortless synchronicity, while the pair delighted in the joy of their unique bond.

Part Two

Chapter 30

Saoirse pulled up outside a row of shops in a largely residential area of Rathfarnham.

She checked the time and she was a half an hour early. She was never familiar with that area of Dublin and had allowed plenty of time to drive across the city and find where she was going.

She had only been driving a few months and was still building her confidence. Once she hit her twenty-fifth birthday her car insurance fees dramatically decreased, and she was able to afford both the new car and insurance.

Dusk was approaching, and the lights of the residential houses across the road were beginning to come on. Most of the houses in the area were built in the 1960s. They were mainly five bed-roomed, red brick and semi-detached homes with garages or conversions to the side.

Freda, her work colleague had told her that the meditation group was above the Launderette. Saoirse looked above the Laundrette and could see signs of life as the lights were on up there too. Her mind filled with wonder as to what was going on the other side of the drawn venetian blind.

Freda highly recommended Mary, the group facilitator. Saoirse knew she had to reach out for help in supporting and guiding her 'ability' as she called it. Everyone else called it a gift that enabled her to see beyond the physical dimension.

Saoirse turned off the engine and sat back to rest in the front seat of her little Nissan Micra. It was too early to go in now, she had a whole half hour to kill and didn't want to head off anywhere else for fear of getting lost.

She recalled the Saturday morning two years ago when she went into The House of Astrology in Dublin's City Centre. She called it her 'favourite shop in the world'. The shop was filled with crystals, gems and books on metaphysics, astrology, the laws of the universe and everything in between.

Earlier that week, Saoirse served a large party in the restaurant who were delighted with her attendance to their table. So much so, that they left her a tip equivalent to the size of her weeks pay packet. She made the decision there and then that she could now justify spending her money on a deck of tarot cards. She had eyeballed the Ryder Waite Tarot Deck for months and now she could finally pick them up and bring them up to the shop counter for purchase.

She smiled to herself, remembering walking out of the shop that morning with her Ryder Waite Tarot Card Deck on her person and that feeling inside of being one step closer to complete.

She spent hours and hours sat at the small kitchen table of the flat she shared with Maria, teaching herself the language hidden in the mystical deck. Each time, she felt like she had returned home to some familiar place that she did not know.

After about two years word got out in the restaurant that Saoirse could read the tarot cards. Although Saoirse did not take herself or her predictions too seriously and never felt she was much good.

One by one the waitresses in Murphy's Seafood Restaurant sat down before her for their turn to have a reading. And each time Saoirse explained herself away from the very beginning saying that she 'wasn't that good' and not to expect much.

Yet right from the start she was accurately predicting relationships, pregnancies, house purchases and many more specific upcoming happenings, which at the time were unplanned or unknown to the recipient. She became known for her spot-on timing and accuracy. No-one was more surprised by this than Saoirse herself.

In no time word spread and she was asked to attend group reading sessions in stranger's homes. Accurate information flowed into her mind as she related it to the sitter. She never had any idea if she was going to be right or not but more often than not she was correct. So much so that she asked Maria if she could relieve her from working two nights a week, to keep up with the demand for attending house parties across Dublin's northside.

That's why she was here, sat outside a Launderette waiting on a meditation group upstairs to commence. She needed help, someone to talk to and bounce her experiences off. Her conscious understanding of how spirit works was limited. Yet at the same time, she was already doing what she was seeking to understand. The logical part of her mind yearned to make sense of it all.

The last few months had been crazy. She had read about signs the universe gives us, that lead us along our path to fulfilling our life purpose. She understood that they present themselves as coincidences through events, opportunities and the right people showing up in one's life at the right time. She hoped that the recent demand for her services was one of those signs, guiding her to become a psychic, and work with 'Spirit', as she called them.

She looked out the window of her car. Two ladies walked by wearing jog pants and high viz jackets. Saoirse assumed they were mother and daughter. They didn't notice her in the car as they briskly walked by, engrossed in chat among themselves.

She watched the two complete strangers and felt the ache in her heart of that familiar pain. Its presence ran deep and was never too far away. The loss for what she never had was like an abyss of grief residing in her heart. Sometimes it roared, sometimes it whispered but it was always there.

She had not seen Lil, Joe or Ruth in over five years. After she left Lil tried to reach out to her. She called the restaurant and wrote letters too. But Saoirse declined. She failed to see the point in circling the same cycle of pain over and over again.

The hurt went deep, and she knew she could never go back. Yet it didn't stop the ever-present torment in her mind. It was everywhere. When she was in the restaurant, particularly on Sundays, serving happy united families their Sunday lunch. She often observed each member of the strangers around their dinner table, wondering if or which one of them was the proverbial black sheep of the family. She looked at the mother and tried to assess if she had her favourites. She watched the grown-up children to see if any of them felt out of place, or different.

Her mind was constantly tormented, trying to secure the notion that her family story was normal.

She lay her head back on the head rest and looked out the window of the drivers' door. It was almost dark now and the dusky skies created silhouettes of the trees, cars and redbrick homes. More and more artificial light from the windows and traffic lit the evening landscape.

Thoughts of Lil, Joe and Ruth were replaced with thoughts of her birth mother and how life in the restaurant reminded her of the mystery that was her mother. Especially when she served a lady who was around the same age as her birth mother. Even more so if she had dark hair and dark eyes and her skin was sallow. Saoirse couldn't help wonder if maybe, just maybe that lady could be her.

"You're a tumbleweed Saoirse," she said quietly to herself, gazing out the car window "a little floating tumbleweed."

The pull of the longing for a mother who loved her, and the grief of its loss pained every part of her being once again, just like many times before. With it, came the guilt and the shame and wore heavy in her heart, simply for being different to everyone else.

She reflected on how much life had moved on in the last five years.

She was madly in love with Tom and she knew he would move mountains for her if he could. He was the kindest, most caring guy she had ever met, and he made her laugh right from her belly every single day that dawned.

Once she moved in with Maria, Tom made it his business to stop by the flat, wondering if they needed anything. Maria observed that he suddenly developed a very considerate nature, calling in to say that he was just popping out to the deli across the road, to get a roll for lunch and ask if the girls had lunch too, or if they wanted a takeaway coffee, or anything.

Not before long he was considerate enough to ask Saoirse if she wished to share a taxi into town the following Friday evening, with him, if she fancied a night out, perhaps.

Saoirse was smitten and within one month of leaving Ashlawn, she had a new job, new home and new beginning with the love of her life.

Saoirse and Maria stayed in regular contact with Alvagh, who was now living in New York pursuing her music career. Her success suited her larger than life presence. She had released two successful albums and was working on her third. Regardless of how hectic her schedule was, she always made time to return home every Christmas and the girls still promise to visit New York one of these days.

Saoirse was now balancing her fulltime job and tending to the development of her psychic ability, working with a higher power, knowing that bringing it to its full potential was all she wanted to do.

It was almost eight and the last half hour had seen the sun descend and the night skies take its place.

Feeling apprehensive and quite nervous Saoirse locked her car and approached the door. She had no idea what to expect tonight, but some-how she knew that she was supposed to be there. She hoped her instinct was right.

The white door was ajar at the bottom of the narrow staircase. All Saoirse could see from the bottom of the stairs was a dim light landing. The welcoming smell of incense wafting down the stairs invited her as soon as she stepped inside the door. She could hear soft Native American Music playing upstairs. The wallpaper was old, and very seventies with large mustard coloured flowers over a dull cream background. The carpet was dark blue and looked old but freshly vacuumed.

She began to walk up the stairs, listening for voices but all she could hear was the sound of her own heartbeat thumping away in her chest.

She arrived on the landing, and there was a room to the left and two more rooms to her right. She wasn't sure which way to go so she followed the smell of the incense and the sound of the music to her right.

"Well, you took your time, love."

A soft-spoken voice came from the room behind her. She turned around to see a well-rounded, middle-aged lady, wearing a long, free-flowing skirt and comfort fit white shirt. The lady was short, and her silver-grey hair was softly tied back in a bun at the nape of her neck. She had the most beautiful skin and clearest complexion. Her complexion revealed that she was a lot younger than her dress sense impressed. She stood smiling at Saoirse. She had a cup of tea in one hand, and she was stirring it with a spoon in the other.

Saoirse immediately recognised that soft-spoken voice. It took a moment, but the warmth in the lady's eyes was one that she remembered seeing before. It was unique and one that she had never forgotten.

Her eyes lit up and her heart exploded with love. She ran to throw her arms around Mary.

"Oh my God, it's you! Mary. Oh, it's so good to see you!"

"Hello love, how are you? I knew it was you when Freda rang" Mary embraced her friend and Saoirse hugged her right back, holding her so tight her whole body was bursting with love.

"Mary would you believe I went back looking for you in Stillorgan, about two years ago, just after I bought my tarot cards and you were gone. Everyone was gone in fact. it was really sad, anyway, how are you? How long are you here? How is it going? Oh, it's so good to see you"

"I'm good love, I'm good. They told us we had to leave there about five years ago. Some big builder bought all the premises and developed the land into apartments. That was such a good place to be, back in the day."

"Well, how are you getting on? Freda certainly sings your praises big time. I should have known it was you" Saoirse asked.

"I took over this place when Stillorgan closed up and left the retail end of things behind. Now, we run meditation and spiritual development groups from here. That large room there on your left is the meditation room and straight ahead is where I do my readings. So it's very busy all of the time, people are looking for the help love, you know."

Listening to Mary's soft, husky tone brought her right back to when she was that 16-year-old girl, so unsure of herself and carrying a deep, heavy sadness, trapped inside her heart. She felt the pang of pain from the girl she once was, back when the hope for the future was all she had to hold on to.

Mary's had the very same gentle presence, so strong and motherly. It was as strong today as it was when Saoirse met her all those years ago. She was a modest, humble woman that radiated the depths of wisdom only an old soul can. There was something so nurturing about her presence that Saoirse loved her right now, just as much as she ever did.

"Anyway, how have you been Saoirse love? I'm was glad to hear you have come into your own."

"Oh Mary, I wouldn't go that far. I'm good; I'm great in fact. Oh my gosh where do I start I've so much to tell you, plus I can't believe it's you!" Saoirse's eyes sparkled.

"Come on in here love and sit down," Mary guided Saoirse into the large room at the front of the building "I've made the tea, I'll just get the pot and a mug for yourself"

Mary led the way into her meditation room. It was dimly lit with candles scattered in each corner and upon the large mantlepiece above the open fire. The glow from the flames danced around the room. There was a large couch along the opposite wall, underneath the long window and two large armchairs either side. In between stood wooden chairs arranged in a semi-circle shape around the open fire. The walls were sparsely decorated with pictures of Native American Indian Chiefs, a large picture of Christ and another of Padre Pio. There was another image on the wall that Saoirse did not recognise. She stared at the image, the young woman's long, fiery red hair framed her face and her eyes spoke the deepest wisdom, the kind of wisdom that dwells beyond human understanding and its clarity rests in the soul. Mary saw that it caught her attention:

"That's Sophia, The Divine Feminine" Mary smiled knowingly at Saoirse, "sit down love,"

"This is lovely Mary, I could live here happily ever after" Saoirse poured her tea.

"Speaking of which, where are you living? Are you still at home with your parents?"

"Oh No." Saoirse shook her head, wide eyed. "That's a long story Mary. But no is the short answer.

I'm married, to Tom. We bought our forever home last year in the Wicklow Mountains. It's gorgeous, I love the house. It's nothing fancy mind. It's a little cottage, built over a hundred years ago"

"Sounds lovely" Mary tilted her head to the side and smiled.

"It's mad really because the original plan was to save for a year for a decent deposit. Tom wanted to move to the countryside and I was never going to have it any other way. Anyway, once we decided to save all of this happened." Saoirse explained, nodding at the artyfacts in Mary's meditation room. "People began to look for readings, then the house parties came flooding in. I saved every penny from the readings into a big pot for the deposit and Tom began to give guitar lessons. Within three months we had more than we thought we would save in a year and began looking for a house" Saoirse engaged with sharing her history to Mary, taking her mind back to the flow of synchronicity and how she came to find her forever home.

"Anyway" she took a sip of her tea and topped up her and Mary's mug. "I called an estate agent in Wicklow and told him what I was looking for, a cottage style home, with a bit of land not too far away from the village. He pretty much laughed at me when I told him our budget, especially for the area we were looking in"

"Why Wicklow Saoirse?" Mary asked Saoirse's heart.

Saoirse looked into nowhere "I don't know. There was something about the area. I was just drawn to it really. The area is called Alainn Ri. Are you familiar with it?"

"That's one beautiful part of the country and one of Irelands best kept secrets" Mary's closed her eyes calling Alainn Ri to her mind's eye. "Lots of history there Saoirse. There's tell of folklore and white witches who settled there, hundreds of years ago. I imagine that's why you were drawn to the place. Such a mystical place, it's truly beautiful."

"I'm not surprised. You can feel the history, the power. It's just," Saoirse thought for the right word "Peaceful, it's filled with peace.

"Anyway, there's more," She sat forward and went on "the estate agent called me a couple of days later, related his shock saying that a cottage had come up for sale within my budget, meeting the criteria I had requested. We went to look at it and the rest is history." Saoirse concluded.

"But yeah, the house is quaint. There's even a sun-dial in the garden. Apparently, the man who originally built the house over a hundred years ago made it himself. There's something so special about that. In fact sitting by that sun-dial is by far my favourite spot in the garden, it's just outside the back door" Saoirse's eyes wandered off again into a daze while her mind drifted miles away.

"Magical love, definitely sounds like the house found you" The light sparkled in Mary's eyes, she smiled warmth from her heart for her long-lost friend.

"I told you you were an old soul that first day I met you, now you are coming to realise that yourself, it's wonderful" Mary rested back in her chair, her hands hugged her mug of tea.

"Hence why I am here Mary, even though whatever I am doing is working, I feel like I want to know more about what exactly is happening and how I can understand it, first of all, and then how to nurture it."

"I see, but you know what is happening, you always did love. It's just that analytical mind that doesn't understand, that's all," Mary tapped the side of her forehead. "The gift that flows now is something that has always been within you, it has just woken up that's all"

"Mary," Saoirse sat back in her chair and curled up in comfort. "When I was little I could always see my spirit guides, as clear as day. They were just always, well always there. As I grew older and especially as soon as I went to the convent everything shut down. The first night in the convent a beautiful lady visited me, she was so familiar and so full of love. That was the very last experience I had, until recently, apart from one very pivotal experience."

"Go on," Mary encouraged.

"Well I think it's no secret that I never really got on with my parents?"

"They don't understand love, that's all" Mary gentle tone was full of wisdom and understanding that Saoirse's anger did not want to hear right now.

"Anyway, one evening we had a huge row. It was horrible. My dad screamed insults at me, repeatedly telling me I was thick, 'a nobody' and stupid. He continuously told me to shut up, it was awful," Saoirse's hand was intuitively holding her chest "for the first time ever that night I really felt like something was leaving me, like I was shutting down from something big. Within moments I began to believe their words, that I was worthless.

And then out of nowhere Mary, this voice came. I know it sounds crazy, but I heard it, it was real.

All it said was:

Where there's a will there's a way

The words echoed in my mind and the whole room changed" She looked at Mary's face smiling so calmly back at her. "it was like the whole room filled with this peaceful power, it was infinite, and I was part of it.

"I will never know who or what that voice was, I couldn't see it like I could see my spirit guides or anyone who crossed over, but it was bigger than anything I had ever seen. Greater than anything I had ever seen.

To this day I still believe that moment changed my path."

"Milestones and contracts" Mary closed her eyes and nodded.

"Sorry?" Saoirse needed explaining.

"It was a turning point love. You could have chosen to dismiss the power and fall into your pain. Instead you chose to stay in the power and allow it to take you through your pain. In doing so you saved yourself."

"Who do you think the voice was?" Saoirse asked.

Mary shrugged her shoulders, "You said it yourself love, a power greater than you, in it you found your own power".

The gentlest warmth filled Saoirse heart and flowed to every part of her being. Right now, she felt perfect. Everything was perfect. She was home.

The warm glow of the open fire danced around the room. The two ladies sat together and chatted about all things Spiritual.

The hours passed by, long into the night. They discussed spirit guides, Angels, life purpose, soul groups, sacred contracts and mediumship.

Saoirse seemed to know a lot more than she thought she did. It was quite like when she was teaching herself how to read the tarot cards; she felt as if she was just revising what she already knew.

Mary showed her a couple of meditation exercises on how to connect with your spirit guides and bring her awareness of their presence from a sub-conscious to conscious awareness. She also showed her how to tell the difference between which spirit guide she is working with and gave her a few tips and techniques for fine-tuning her senses, all six of them.

"You're getting tired now love; I think we'll call it a night," Mary suggested.

Saoirse looked at the clock in the centre of the mantelpiece.

"Oh, my good God Mary, how did that happen? Is it 1.25am? Where did that night go?

Hold on. I thought you had a meditation class coming tonight?"

"I did," Mary's smile filled her face.

Saoirse put her coat on and gathered her things.

"Here Hun, I will help you clean up the mugs," gathering the leftovers from the tea and biscuits, Saoirse made her way to the small kitchen at the end of the landing.

"Leave them there Saoirse, get yourself home now, love, it's late.

Here's my number, stay in touch sweet-heart will you?"

Saoirse took the small business card from her friend and tucked it safely into her wallet.

"I certainly will Mary. And thank you for tonight. You have helped me more than you know. Oh...one last thing before I go." Saoirse unzipped an inside pocket of her bag and reached inside to take out a crystal. "Do you remember this?"

She held an amethyst crystal in the palm of her hand.

It was the one Mary had gifted to her on the day they first met. She had kept it on her person every single day since and never went anywhere without it.

In the months that followed Saoirse continued to gain momentum building a clientele. Herself and Mary stayed in regular contact and continued to nurture their very close, effortless bond. Saoirse often described Mary as her 'soul sister'.

Along with the guidance and direction from her 'soul sister' and commitment to building more and more clarity with her spiritual work and psychic development she felt she was anchored on the clear path, one where she felt quietly confident and in the best of hands.

Chapter 31

The road continued to rise to meet Saoirse along her path.

The demand for her psychic readings grew and grew as did the pressure to find balance in life. Between working at the restaurant and tending group readings on her evenings off, there came a point where she felt something had to give.

"Tom…. Tom are you here?" She decided to pop into Tom's music shop before returning from her lunch break and tell him the news,

"Hiya Hun," Tom emerged from his music studio at the back of the shop. He was preparing for a guitar lesson after lunch. "This is a nice surprise," His face lit up.

"Tom, I don't have long, I'm due back in a few minutes" She nodded at the clock on the wall above the counter, "But listen, I have something really important to tell you" she clasped her hands.

"Oh no" Tom groaned, he knew that tone and it always came just before Saoirse was about to reveal a leap of faith decision that came straight from her instincts. He trusted her completely but was also a guy who was driven by a more pragmatic, logical approach when it came to decision making, it was what worked for him. His wife, on the other hand, lived straight from the heart, it was what worked for her, but scared the life out of him at the best of times.

Saoirse's eyes were popping out of her head and she looked like she was about to burst.

"I'm going to leave the restaurant," she sighed a huge sigh of relief "There I said it"

Tom was silent, he stood before her searching for words.

"Tom hun, look, I've thought about this and weighed things up over and over in my head. I can't keep going the way I'm going, I'll be no use to anyone if I do and something's got to give. I love working in the restaurant, but long term the spiritual work is what I want to pursue. I'm already backed up with clients for the next three months and without the shifts at the restaurant in the way I just know it will open up the space for something else to come in within the spiritual field," she searched his face for agreement and even though she didn't see it, she kept going "As for the mortgage and the bills, we can tighten our belts for now and trust that something will come up, I know it will" She paused and looked into his eyes.

"Tom hun, please say something?"

Eventually, Tom took a deep breath and let out a big sigh, "Ok, I hear you and you are right. But Saoirse you know it scares the living daylights out of me knowing there is no steady income coming in, especially with the mortgage and that," Saoirse's heart sank, she hoped he wasn't going to do the 'responsible adult' thing, "But on the other hand, I know you." He towered over her, the love of his life, looking deep into her eyes, "I know that you are one of the hardest working people I know, and I know that you are one of those people who were put on this planet to chase your dreams, helping as many people as you can along the way. And I know if there is anyone that can make this work, it's you," he paused,

"for that reason Saoirse Harris, you've got to do this, and I'm behind you every step of the way"

Her heart was bursting with gratitude for the love of her life "They broke the mould when they made you Tom Harris", her arms flung round this great man's neck, "broke the blinking mould!"

Maybe it was coincidence or maybe it was something else, but one month later, within a week of leaving Murphy's Seafood Restaurant, she received a call from Mary:

"Hello love how are ya?" Mary's motherly gentleness flowed down the phone line.

"Hiya Mary, I'm good, how are you?" Saoirse was just in from a walk in the Wicklow Hills.

"Good love, I'm good. Listen, I bumped into a colleague today who runs a spiritual practice in Newbridge, Co Kildare. Her health has taken bad and she has decided to step back from the practice for a while, and is looking for someone to come in and run it for her" Saoirse's heart skipped a beat. "She doesn't know how long she is taking off, but it will be a considerable amount of time anyway. I thought of you straight away.

She does all the same things you do, and she runs mediation groups and psychic development groups too, very much the same as my own place. It's an established practice, so you will just have to go in and pick up where she left off"

Saoirse could feel the light and the power of spirit surrounding her, guiding her, knowing this was more than just coincidence. Instead, she responded to Mary from her small mind:

"But Mary, I don't know how to run psychic development or meditation groups" Her heart was beating like crazy and one million ideas were birthing in her head with what she could do in the practice, feeling incredibly blessed for such an opportunity, she also felt the heavy darkness of worthlessness take its grip.

"Nor did you know how to do a psychic reading until the very first time you did one Saoirse. Remember all you are doing is passing on what you already know, that's all. Trust me, Spirit will do the rest, they will guide you." The reassurance in Mary's words calmed her mind, she knew she was right, but there was still that part of her that hoped she was right. It was the part of her that enabled fear to take its grip and cripple her potential.

A few days later, she made her decision. In true Saoirse Harris nature, on nothing less than a wing and a prayer, she chose to go with her heart and face the fear along the way.

The following morning she called out to the centre in Newbridge and met with Trudy. They hit it off straight away, Saoirse loved the centre and she made the arrangements to take ownership of her new position and run the Spiritual Practice

Chapter 32

17th February 1992.

To Whom It May Concern,

My name is Saoirse Harris, and I was born in St. Patrick's Mother and Baby home on the 22nd February 1965.

The following Jul,y I was adopted by Elizabeth and Joseph Corcoran, from Dublin.

I would like to begin my search for my birth mother and would appreciate if you could contact me regarding same. I have included my contact telephone numbers should you require any further information. Feel free to contact me at your convenience.

I look forward to hearing from you,

Yours sincerely,

Saoirse Harris.

Catherine Ellis, a middle aged social worker with the Eastern Health Board sat at her desk reading the letter before her.

The office was particularly busy this morning, but Catherine's morning had been freed up by a last-minute cancellation from a son who was going to be re-united with his birth mother today. It was always heart-breaking when either mother or child experiences cold feet at the last minute.

"Good morning, could I speak to Saoirse Harris, please?" A lady's voice asked.

"Yes, this is she."

"Good morning Saoirse. My name is Catherine Ellis. I am a social worker with the Eastern Health Board. I am just giving you a ring to let you know that we received your letter with regards to tracing your birth mother." Saoirse's heart skipped a beat. She was preparing content in the healing centre for a new psychic development group due to commence that evening. Two years had passed since she sent the letter to the adoption agency. Back then, she sent the letter and put it to the back of her mind, expecting to hear news whenever she heard, knowing it could take a very long time.

"I was wondering if you would like to meet with me, at your convenience of course to discuss some non-identifying information about your birth mum?"

"Yes, thank you, Catherine, that would be great," Saoirse's could feel her heart racing now.

At the time she had thought long and hard about sending that letter. Each and every different scenario ran through her mind again and again. She chose not to share the letter with anyone. That way she would be able to avoid questions of follow up information should anyone ask.

The whisper of who her birth mother might be had tormented her mind all her life. Sometimes she fantasised, other times she just wondered, either way the ever-present deep curiosity to find out who this lady was, was never too far from her mind.

"I am free most weekday mornings if it would suit for you? Are you based in Dublin?"

"I am in Dublin Saoirse, but I can travel to you no problem?"

Saoirse thought for a moment. "Actually, that would be great. I am in Newbridge most weekdays?"

"You're only down the road Saoirse. How does next Wednesday morning suit for you?"

Saoirse gave a quick glance in the diary. "Wednesday is perfect, how about 11am in the Queens Hotel Ms Ellis, it's just off the main street beside the Church?"

"Catherine please Saoirse, you're making me sound old" Catherine laughed. "11am Wednesday is perfect. I will meet you there"

The ladies finished up the surreal phone call. Saoirse replaced the receiver on the handset. Her hands were rattling. Moments ago, her morning was as normal as could be, now with one phone call she was one step closer to receiving the answers to a lifetime of haunting questions. Just like that.

The journey had begun.

Wednesday morning came, and Saoirse woke with today's milestone hitting her hard. She lay in the bed feeling the weight of her tired body trying to waken up, but her mind had already rushed ahead to the forthcoming event hours away.

Newbridge was busy, and the cool March air welcomed the sunshine as it filled the town with the warmth and freshness of springtime. She ordered a coffee in the hotel bar and took a seat by the window, looking out onto the courtyard outside.

The hotel was quiet and other than a few mammies enjoying a catch-up over pots of tea, while they intermittently ran around after their wandering toddlers there was only smart dressed hotel staff preparing for the hours ahead.

Saoirse made every effort to settle herself in the chair and despite her nerves and racing heart she hoped she was doing a good job at looking cool, calm and collected. She watched the staff breeze in and out of the lounge area, setting tables and topping up condiments. It brought her mind back to her days in the restaurant with Maria. She loved working with her best friend and although she would never trade her current career to be back there, she missed seeing Maria as often as she used to. The radio came on in the bar and she heard a familiar tune, one that she loved, by a girl she loved. It was Alvagh's new single. Alvagh was rocking the United States now, enjoying her exceptional success in what she was born to do. Saoirse smiled with pride for her forever friend.

"Hello, Saoirse is it?"

Her daydream was awakened by a soft-spoken voice beside her table. It was the same voice she had heard over the phone last week.

"Catherine, yes. I'm very pleased to meet you." Saoirse stood up to shake Catherine's hand and gestured to her to sit down beside her.

Catherine was a middle-aged lady. She was quite tall with very fine, light brown hair. She wore a tailored grey suit and carried a soft leather briefcase, with her handbag thrown over her shoulder.

"Thank you, Saoirse. I'm just going to get some tea; can I get you anything?"

"I'm good thank you."

Catherine returned and placed her briefcase on the table. She explained to Saoirse that she would be able to give some information today but not anything that would identify who her mother might be. She took a brown folder from her briefcase and placed it on the table.

"Now, we'll put this big thing out of the way, and we'll have more room" The large, soft leather briefcase was placed on the floor.

"Saoirse, have you ever wondered where you are from?"

What kind of stupid question is that? Saoirse thought to herself.

"Erm, yes I have."

"Co Clare. Your birth mother lived in Co. Clare. She had just turned 17 years old when she had you. She stayed with you for one month after you were born, in St. Patrick's Mother and Baby Home on the Navan Road and then gave you up for adoption. Oh, I have her first name here too. Where is it gone now...?" Catherine lifted pages and opened and closed the folder.

Saoirse couldn't help noticing how cautious Catherine was to make sure she did not see anything that was written on file, Saoirse's file. Catherine opened the file, checked the information, closed the file and related it to Saoirse.

"Oh, here's her name. Maisie, your mothers' name is Maisie."

Saoirse's eyes filled up with tears. She remembered the doll she had as a young child, the little doll that went everywhere with her. The little doll that she loved. The little doll that she could not bear to be separated from. She remembered that she called the little doll Maisie before she could even speak. Maisie, her mother's name was, of course, Maisie.

Emotion drowned her within moments. The news and information that was related all fell into place. She felt for the very first time that something that had been unplugged had found its place and it fit perfectly. All of these feelings for so many years, thoughts, senses and knowing within her mind with nowhere to anchor it to, now finally had a place.

They talk of a bond between mother and child. Some say that this is the strongest bond there is. It goes far beyond the limits of human comprehension, and no explanation can do it justice to the depths that it deserves.

For some, this bond is severed, ripped and torn apart. To take a child from its mother and assume that the child will not know any otherwise is probably one of the biggest misjudgements one can make in the eyes of the natural law. To think that the child was too young to know any different is a denial of the natural intelligence held within us all.

Logic and reason may compensate by saying that it is for the best. Yet no amount of rationale can possibly deny the sense of abandonment or rejection a child naturally feels when the decision is made to sever the most natural bond in the world.

The severance causes harm, loss, grief and pain, but it will never destroy. For what is given by nature cannot ever be destroyed. It may change, but it can never be undone.

Saoirse's mind raced to understand how that little baby must have felt when she called her little doll Maisie when she was not yet two years old. Her mind and her heart must have been reaching out in search of her mammy. Too young to understand and not knowing any different other than she is gone and the most natural feeling in the world was to have her back. Instead, her great little mind compensated and resolved to call this little doll her mothers' name and give her love and attachment to her.

"Saoirse, are you ok?" Catherine asked, still holding the folder closed with her finger bookmarking the page.

"Yes, I'm ok, please carry on." She fought back the tears and put everything she had into extending a composed demeanour and kept herself together.

"I don't have much information on your birth father other than it says here that he was a musician. He was a lead singer in a band, and Maisie used to go to the bar that he played in.

They began a relationship. They were dating for a few months, and when the Sisters asked her what they used to do on their dates, she replied that they used to go to the cinema. She also said that he was in his early twenties. But that's all the information there is on him."

Saoirse's heart leapt. Of course he was a lead singer in a band. Memories of herself and Alvagh in the music room all those years ago came flooding back. She heard Alvagh's words 'You just have it' echo in her mind along with her friend's confident smiley face. Not to mention the love of her life, Tom, a music teacher who owned a music shop. Her heart raced, everything was falling into place, as far as non-identifying information goes, right now Saoirse completely disagreed. She shuffled in the chair holding in her excitement as to who she is. She could feel her face bursting, clenching her teeth and pursing her lips ensuring a composed demeanour.

She cleared her throat "I wonder how long Maisie was in the mother and baby home?"

"I have that information here. She entered the home in December 1964. She was there for four months."

Saoirse's mind raced. Maisie was a sixteen-year-old girl. She was pregnant and sent far away from home to an institution for girls to have her baby. How hard must that have been? It must have been devastating.

She still had no idea if it was Maisie's choice to give her up for adoption, but she figured that the young girl was only a child and regardless of her decision, how could she possibly know what to do for the best? How could a sixteen or seventeen-year-old teenager know the correct answer to the dilemma? Whether to keep her baby or to let her baby go?

Saoirse took a chance knowing that it was never Maisie's choice. She knew that the judgemental society in which she lived, took that choice away and made it for her.

Then she thought, she was a little baby left in the home for over three months, she wondered why Maisie left when she did.

"Catherine, I was in the home until July. Do you think Maisie had to leave after a month or would it have been her choice?" She felt her voice tremble and lip quiver.

Catherine sighed and looked at Saoirse, her eyes filled with understanding. "I don't know Saoirse. A lot of the time the girls had jobs and had to go back to them. I don't know about Maisie I'm afraid" Catherine's soft tone brought ease to Saoirse's mind. "But I'll tell you what I suggest: The next step, if you wish, if you would like to go ahead with tracing and meeting Maisie?"

Saoirse nodded.

"Ok, I'll back to the office now and this afternoon I will draft up a letter to Maisie explaining that you have been in touch and would like to meet and we take it from there. How does that sound?"

Saoirse felt shivers and goose bumps run through her whole body. "Thanks Catherine" The emotion formed a lump in her throat and her eyes filled with tears.

She fought back the tears watching Catherine pack up her belongings. She knew that this lady had so much resource. She was the bridge between Saoirse and Maisie. This lady, a stranger was the person who held power to unite two women who shared the deepest bond there is, this stranger, wearing a tailored grey suit and white blouse.

For Saoirse, it was a reunification of what was lost, the loss that had torn her apart and left her seeking self all of her life. For almost thirty years she had sought validation, approval and the unconditional love that was so abruptly taken from her. It was taken long before she could make any conscious sense of what, or why she felt the way she did.

She had always felt like a tumbleweed floating around with no root or no home, never quite fitting in. Countless times she observed her family, Lil, Joe, Ruth, her aunts, uncles and cousins and observed the likeness and similarities. She observed same in friends and their families and was never able to see the same for herself. She also observed the natural bond among her relatives and her absence from same. She was different. She never fit in, despite trying it was impossible to make that so.

But now, Catherine would write a letter, to her mother's address, her mother's home, where she lived and 'take it from there'.

Saoirse thanked Catherine. She agreed to keep in touch and meant every word when she said that she looks forward to hearing from her soon. She left the meeting and drove back home to Alainn Ri.

6th April 1994
STRICTLY PRIVATE AND CONFIDENTIAL
Dear Maisie,
My name is Catherine Ellis and I am a social worker with the Eastern Health Board.
We recently had contact from your daughter who wishes to re-connect with you.

I met with your daughter recently and she is a very balanced, kind hearted lady. Please be assured that she has the best intentions to meet with you and wishes no interference or disruption to you or your family. In my opinion she is authentic and warm with an honest, sincere nature.

Should you agree, I would be delighted to assist you both with your re-union.

I understand this is a sensitive matter, please be assured that the strictest confidence applies always.

You can contact our office on the number above at your convenience.

Yours sincerely,
Catherine Ellis

Maisie sat at the kitchen table holding the registered letter from the Eastern Health Board. Her hands were shaking, and her heart raced.

She took a sip from her mug of morning coffee. She had just returned from dropping her granddaughter Eilish to school. Fiona was working the day shift at the hospital, and the house was quiet.

Her eyes filled with tears and she read and re-read the registered letter over and over.

The secret she held close for thirty years was almost sitting on her kitchen table and breathing air. Her baby girl, that tiny bundle she held so close all those years ago, memories of her tiny, beautiful, pure baby girl flooded into her mind. For the briefest moment Maisie could get her smell, she could hear her sounds. The innocence, the perfection.

Then came the memory of the horror the moment the Sister snatched her away, her life, her world, her womb ripped away. She could hear Mary's cries as she watched the Sister disappear down the corridor with her world in her arms.

Although, she's hardly called Mary now. No doubt she has some other name.

The pink outfit. She wondered if she still had the pink outfit. Maisie recalled the day she bought it with her mammy in Dublin town.

She glanced around her kitchen and thought of how long ago that was, a different time. When she was only a child herself.

She thought of the Mother and Baby Home. The hell, the pain.

She remembered the ache in her back from scrubbing those floors for hours at a time. She shook her head to dismiss the memory of the hell. But it continued to flow. She remembered the cruelty and the punishment to the girls. In particular, she remembered the girl in the bed next to her, who was dragged away for soiling her bed and the echo of her pleas of apology deadened her mind. Maisie winced as she recalled Alice's return the following night burned and beaten, her beautiful red hair cut to the scalp.

'bloody bastards, God above forgive me' She said out loud.

Her eyes returned to the letter in her hands,

...she is a very balanced, kind hearted lady.... she is authentic and warm with an honest, sincere nature...

Maisie smiled through the tears. Her baby girl, a grown woman now, honest and kind hearted. She knew then and there she had a good upbringing. The terror she carried in silence for thirty years was somewhat replaced by peace. The torment of worry that Mary went to a family who did not love her was now something she could set aside, and she knew she was loved.

Maisie thought of the others, Pat and the kids. What will they say? How will she tell them? Fear and worry took its grip. She rested her hand over her mouth and she thought for a moment, imagining the conversations in her mind and her families' reactions to her news. She took a deep breath and assured herself that this was too much to think about right now. For now, she decided to concentrate on absorbing the news herself. That the daughter she loved so deeply was now closer than she had ever been, and the prospective new dawn that awaits.

She reached for the phone and dialled the number on the letter, being extra careful to press the right buttons. Her hands were shaking more than ever now, accompanied by the thud of her heart in her chest.

"Good Morning, I would like to speak to Catherine Ellis please...".

Chapter 33

"Hello is that Saoirse, the psychic?"

"Yes, hi, how are you."

"Good thank you, Saoirse my wife told me about you. She was with you in Newbridge a few weeks back and I was wondering if I could come and see you please? But the only thing is I don't live far from you in Wicklow, could I come and see you at your home place, instead of driving to Newbridge please." The friendly male voice politely asked.

"Of course, I don't see why not. Would tomorrow morning at 10am suit for you?"

"Could you make it Friday, Saoirse?"

"I normally could but I'm at a friends' wedding in Cork this weekend and we're on the road early Friday morning."

"Oh don't talk to me. It's at that stage for me too. Every time I turn around there's another one of my mates getting married. Costs a fortune doesn't it? That's a hundred percent Saoirse, I know where you are anyway, and I will see you tomorrow at 10am."

"Tell me about it. Thanks for that, what's the name?"

"It's Sean."

"Cheers Sean, any bother finding me, just give me a ring otherwise see you tomorrow."

Saoirse hung up the phone to the stranger feeling quite pleased. She had never thought about taking appointments at home. After all she had the space, as it was only herself and Tom. She thought that she would put the idea in the back of her mind for now and maybe give it more thought after the wedding.

She was so excited for the weekend. Alvagh, was marrying Colin. After college Alvagh went to live in New York and follow her dreams in the music industry. There she found more than she bargained for when she met Colin. He was an Irish guy from Dublin. They immediately fell in love. He shared her love for music too and together they formed a Rock band. Colin was a music producer and together they accomplished success beyond their wildest dreams, even by Alvagh's standards. They produced three platinum albums and enjoyed the life of celebrity status. They travelled the United States to sell out gigs everywhere they played. When Alvagh discovered she was expecting their baby son Ciaran they decided that the music industry had offered them all it could for now and came home and settled in West Cork.

Saoirse could not have been happier for her friend. She knew Colin was the love of Alvagh's life and although she had never come across as the romantic type, Saoirse knew that Alvagh had soul and being happy was fundamentally the most important thing in the world.

Saoirse woke up with one hundred things on her mental to do list. She knew Sean was coming for his reading at ten and the rest of the day was going to be spent packing for Cork.

She had to collect Tom's suit from the dry cleaners, go shopping to finally find a pair of shoes to go with that dress and clean the house before she went, just in case robbers broke in and thought she kept a dirty home.

There was one other thing she had to do, a pregnancy test.

She held out very little hope that she was actually pregnant, despite being late. She was thirty now and resigned to the fact that maybe she and Tom were one of those couples who just couldn't have children. They had been trying for over a year and month after month she was met with disappointment. But, despite having little hope, she told herself that she was going to the wedding and of course going to be having a glass of wine or more realistically - lots of them. So, in the name of being a responsible adult she had better take the test, just to be on the safe side.

She lay in bed and tried to move, she could not believe how tired she was. Her body felt like it weighed a tonne and all she wanted to do was go back to sleep. She glanced at the clock, it was just after half past nine.

"Holy God in heaven, how in the name of God is it that late?" She said out loud, jumping out of bed, panicking and feeling like she had just been hit by a double decker bus.

Sean was arriving in twenty minutes and she looked like she had just been run over by that double decker bus too.

She fell into the bathroom and grabbed the pregnancy test. She really needed to be giving this test the time of day like a hole in the head right now, but she knew that if she didn't do it now, the errands of the rest of the day would run away with her and she would forget.

'I know it won't be positive anyway, but at least that means I can have a glass of wine tomorrow and not feel guilty,' she told herself.

She took the test, threw it on top of the wash hand basin and continued to rush like a mad woman to be ready on time for Sean's arrival. She wrestled into her clothes, wishing she had more time to prepare for Sean's session. It was the very first reading she had ever done at home and she really wished it was one that she could have remembered as being more prepared and organised, even spiritual. As opposed to throwing herself together in the hope that she will do, slapping on make-up like a demo video on fast forward mode and running a brush through her hair while shoving her feet into her shoes.

Ding Dong.

"Aw, for goodness sake Sean!" she said out loud, but not too loud, glancing at the clock. He was a whole ten minutes early.

It was ok, she thought to herself. She was ready. She went back into the bathroom to check that test just before she went downstairs.

She held the test in her hand thinking that it will say negative and she could toss it in the bin and go on with her day.

+

There it was. The little sign.

Saoirse thought for a moment and then thought that she must be wrong.

'Plus means positive, so that means I'm pregnant. No Saoirse, you're all stressed now, you are not pregnant, and this is telling you that what you thought is positive is right. Yes, I am positive I am not pregnant, or is it yes you are pregnant?' She was very aware of the ridiculous conversation she was having with herself.

In her panic she became more and more confused.

Sean gave another ring on the door bell.

Saoirse had to look at the box and checked which was positive and which negative.

+   = Pregnant

She looked at the very simple explanation.

'It says I am pregnant! I am pregnant!' Saoirse repeated the words to herself.

'I have a little baby in my tummy, our little baby, right now.'

She took a moment to sit on the side of her bed, her eyes searched around her for a sense of knowing, to see and understand what she could only feel within. In her state of awe, she placed her hands over her tummy and greeted the little stranger with unconditional love. In that moment, she knew that the love she felt right now, was the very beginning of a celebration that would never ever die.

Completely centred in a feeling of mesmerisation and wonder, she stood up to make her way down the stairs to answer the door to Sean, trusting that she could ground herself along the way and get back to the work of the moment.

The paces down the stairs from the bedroom to the front door were not many. With each step she took, she prepared to put her news aside and be there for Sean. In an hour or so, she could get back to the news and burst with excitement, if she chose.

But for now, she had to be there for Sean.

The very first reading session Saoirse ever had at home was possibly the most difficult reading she had ever done. The act of being there completely for Sean, a farmer in his early thirties, was a challenge at the very least.

In between what felt like every breath, her mind would go back to the little plus sign on the little white stick that told her she was carrying new life. There was a little person in her womb. That tiny person had been there for that last few weeks and during which time, nobody knew, only him or her. Now, the only two people on the planet who knew was his or her mother, and them.

The last time Saoirse was part of a mother and infant embrace was when she was the baby. Now, she was the mother. She knew that this little baby needed her, depended on her and she also knew that she loved this little baby completely and unconditionally.

And there was not a single thing in the world that could ever have the ability to disturb that love.

Chapter 34

Spring 1995 was full of the joys of celebrating new beginnings.

Trudy approached Saoirse and asked her if she would be interested in purchasing the healing practice in Newbridge. By now, she was running Meditation Groups and Psychic Development Courses five days a week to keep up with demand. The Centre was becoming more established by the day. It was a no brainer decision for Saoirse. She discussed it with Tom and her credit union manager, arranged the loan and bought herself her very own Healing Centre.

Word of mouth had also begun to sound her sweet vibration around Saoirse's home county. More and more people from around Co Wicklow were ringing Saoirse to make appointments to see her. She had earned an unfailing reputation for excellence, accuracy and authenticity.

Saoirse had a natural gift for helping people. She had a unique ability to identify with a persons' pain effortlessly. From there she spoke in a language that the person in front of her would understand, regardless of age, creed, sex or belief system.

One of the reasons her services were sought by so many was because she brought each person back to the remembrance of who they really are: A Spirit Being having a human experience. She guided them back into their Power. When they left her company, they were centred back in their strength, they had clarity, and they were filled with a deep, natural sense of peace within.

She never once claimed ownership of her 'gift' or her ability to help people in the tremendous ways that she did. Nor did she ever think that she was working alone. Anytime someone told her how amazing she was or how gifted she was she always replied with the same response:

"I can't help you if they don't help me to do so. It's a team effort, every time."

By 'them' she meant her spirit guides, the angelic realm and the loved ones who have passed onto higher realms of life that came to help her during her sessions.

One day she received a phone call from the local women's community group. She had no idea that such a thing or who they were and pardoned her ignorance when she had to ask.

"We're a group of ladies in the community here in Alainn Ri Saoirse. We meet up once a week for tea and a chat," the lady on the phone replied. "We heard that you talk to angels and the like. We have a little bit of money in the kitty. It's for guest speakers to come in and talk to us about what they do. Last month we had a girl come in and do flower arranging with us and this month we have a lady coming in to show us how to wear costume jewellery. We were hoping Saoirse that you could come to us next month. Guest speaker night is the first Tuesday of every month in the parish hall, 7pm."

"Wow, that sounds lovely. Thank you for asking. Do you mind if I ask the type of age group I will be speaking to?" Saoirse was thinking of a hundred ideas in her head about what to do.

"Well, now that's the thing Saoirse. I am the youngest in our group. I'm sixty-seven, and we range in age right up to age eighty-two. Most of the ladies are on the older end of the spectrum if you understand me."

The obvious immediately filled Saoirse's mind. These ladies were of a generation who were bred and reared in staunch Catholic Ireland. What in the name of God was she going to say? Somehow, she didn't think it would be suitable, to begin with, an opening line such as:

"Hi, I'm Saoirse, and I see dead people and angels."

She scolded herself for being so judgemental and agreed to give the talk, even though it scared the living daylights out of her. She could only imagine the glares she was going to receive. However, she reminded herself that they contacted her, not the other way around so there must be some interest in what she had to say.

Saoirse had one friend in Alainn Ri. That was Robin, a Scottish gentleman who had trained in Reiki Healing in Scotland and was now retired and living with his wife and mother in law around the corner from Saoirse. He had heard about a girl in the area who reads tarot cards and made it his business to call by one day and introduce himself. The pair hit it off straight away. Robin was a straight up, no nonsense character with the sharpest wit Saoirse had ever seen. A highly spiritual guy too with his feet firmly anchored on planet earth, Saoirse had enjoyed many hours of conversation with the no nonsense Scottish gentleman. He was in his late sixties and turned himself out every day in a three-piece suit, shirt and tie.

He welcomed Saoirse's company as much as she valued his. Robin's elderly mother in law was less than entertaining of his Masters in Reiki and made no bones about her disapproval towards his profession. Her hostility towards him and Reiki was no secret.

Like clockwork he called in for his usual early evening chat and cup of tea. He had heard about the phone call from the ladies group and found it absolutely hilarious.

"Ah, Robin stop. I'm sure they are a lovely bunch of ladies. I'm actually really looking forward to it." Saoirse sat at her kitchen table; her hands wrapped around a mug of tea.

She knew she was trying to convince herself more than Robin when she said she was looking forward to it. She was dreading it. She was terrified. Deep, dark core fears of old were singing a scary, monotone chorus within her core. The chorus was filled with words of cold judgement and rejection because she was who she was and even though things had changed dramatically over the years, her fear of not being accepted and loved for whom she was, had never gone away.

"Put it this way Saoirse, Mother in Law will be there. She will be sitting right in the very front, with her other Catholic friends. She already thinks you're a witch as it is." Robin could not wipe the smirk off his face as he drank his mug of tea.

"Oh for crying out loud. Well, then why are they asking me to give the talk so, if it's all judgement, judgement, judgement? Maybe they are the ones who need to hear it most of all. I just wish God, or whoever, chose someone else to give the talk.

What in the name of God am I going to say? She whined.

"At the end of the day, there is not a whole lot of difference in their beliefs and mine I suppose. They believe that there is a God who watches over us and he is the one in charge. They also believe that there is no power greater than God's power. I believe that too.

The only difference is that they fear God will strike them down to hell if they as much as look beyond the walls of the Roman Catholic Church to seek empowerment. According to them, that's some kind of bad evil power.

I believe God is all there is. In reality, there is no other power. Whether you are looking inside or outside the walls of the church, once you are looking through the eyes of love you are naturally aligned with the only power there is, and that's heaven." Robin listened and allowed Saoirse air sense of it all.

"They believe heaven and hell are places you go to depending on how good or bad you were during your lifetime. I believe they are experiential states, depending on the lens through which we are looking through. Cause and effect and all that. Gosh, Robin the RCC really have them by the short and curlies, don't they?

God, universal power, whatever you want to call the oneness or all that is, at the end of the day, and every moment in between, there is no separation. We are all part of the same Power. Therefore, we are that Power. It flows through us and around us regardless of how aware of it we are." Saoirse's face changed, wisdom relaxed in her eyes as she came back home.

"When you remove the physical dimension part, it's so easy to see that. Our happiness, joy, nirvana is due to feeling connected to that love, of that love, because it is our natural state. That's why we feel so peaceful when we sit in a church and pray or sit in the woods or on a beach and do same; it's because then we are centred back in our awareness to who we really are, and we can feel the peace that resides within that state. We are centred back in love, wisdom, divine intelligence. It is in those moments we can feel it, we know it.

As for hell, well that too is an experiential state, when we are looking away from love, our natural state. It's not a place with eternal fire and a bloke with hooves and horns. It's the pain that we suffer when we forget that we are of true love and peace. It is a very real illusion that is unavoidable to the human being, you know?

But then along comes the RCC and twists it all around and separates the whole thing. God has all the power, and we are the sinners who need to pray for his love, if we do, then he will give it, what nonsense.

Oh dear Lord God in heaven Robin what am I going to say to these women?" she looked to Robin begging divine intervention.

"I have no idea Saoirse, but knowing you, you will figure something out. Just be thankful it's not Halloween, or they would have reserved a parking spot for you and your broomstick." Robin clearly continued to see the funny side.

Saoirse did her best to put the event out of her mind until closer to the time. If she found herself worrying she reminded herself that it was only one hour, that's all, and then it will all be over. She could not help think of Ms Cross and Sr Agnes. The ladies at the talk would be not far behind in age and under the same spell of influence and belief system.

Those two women, neighbour and nun, were convinced Saoirse was evil and doing the devils work. Ms Cross believed it because she was born out of wedlock and Sr Agnes believed so because Saoirse was able to see realms beyond the physical realm. To believe that either was the devil's work was nothing less than an utter load of baloney. She now understood it to be the Catholic Churches way of controlling society, as opposed to encouraging empowerment, the celebration of uniqueness and growth. Even still, their fear-based influence worked, and the people remained in the dark to the source of potential within all.

The evening arrived, and Saoirse was guided into the parish hall and onto the makeshift stage. There was a podium with a microphone. Saoirse looked around the busy room full of old ladies in rows of seats, chatting amongst themselves waiting for her to speak. In the corner was a table with two large teapots and several trays of biscuits, homemade queen cakes, all covered with cling film. A large jug of milk and countless mugs waited to the side.

The hall smelled of damp and cold. Large electric heaters were strategically placed in the corners and half way along the walls of the hall, filling the room with their warm artificial heat.

Saoirse was well used to speaking in front of groups of people. She had given talks to small groups of up to twenty people and spoke on the larger scale of audiences of five hundred. Each time she always felt nervous before her talks. This time she felt unbelievably nervous. Her hands were sweaty, her throat was dry, and anxiety gripped hold of her whole body and mind to the point that she could not shake it or become distracted from its deadening paralysis of empowering emotion.

She glanced around the room to assess the crowd, looking for nice friendly faces, people who had a warmth about them, even forgiveness. Most of the ladies looked just like that. They seemed warm, kind and even quite motherly, or grandmotherly.

"Good evening ladies. Can I have your attention, please? Our guest speaker tonight is Saoirse. Saoirse lives here in Alainn Ri ladies, and she is going to talk to you about.... erm...well about readings and that, angels and things. Anyway, put your hands together please for Saoirse."

Thanks be to God she did not mention the code words like psychic, tarot, mediumship, Saoirse thought to herself observing the chairpersons caution with words. She smiled at the crowd and stepped up to the podium.

"Good evening ladies. I am here this evening to talk you about taking the mystery out of the mysterious and draw a sense of clarity around of what I do."

Where in the name of God did that line come from? She thought to herself, but she immediately surrendered to it and carried on from there.

She spoke for about forty-five minutes about angels, spirit guides, how she works and the help that was available to us all. What's more, she explained how easily and naturally we can access that help. Her words effortlessly flowed.

It was as if she was allowing something else to talk through her.

She had no idea what she was going to say next at any given time throughout the whole talk, but as she spoke she observed the audience.

Most of the ladies sat forward in their seats, glued to every word. From time to time she noticed them nodding in agreement. They were interested in what Saoirse had to say. She could see that they were relating to her words too. There was obvious resonance.

Every now and again she glanced down at the very front row. A very elderly lady sat centre row, looking nothing less than completely disgusted. Her expression was sour, and her body language was dismissive. She sat with her arms folded staring stone-faced at Saoirse. She guessed it was Robin's mother in law. Every-time Saoirse glanced at her she saw Sr Agnes's face. She had no idea if 'mother in law' looked like Sr Agnes and even though Sr Agnes had passed away a long time ago, Saoirse thought that the two ladies were one in the same. Maybe in some strange way they were.

But there was an irony to the situation. She found herself in Sr Agnes's company due to rejection. She found herself in Mother in Law's company due to invitation. Yet, the interesting thing was that the reason she was in the company of both ladies was the very same: Saoirse had the ability to communicate with higher realms of existence.

As a child, she was sent away because of this.

As an adult, she was invited to be heard.

She took a breath during that talk to thank God for the welcome shift.

After the talk, the audience met her with a loud applause. Some ladies even stood up out of their seats and clapped, pressing their lips together in passionate welcome for Saoirse's words.

Mother in Law turned to the ladies beside her, and her apathetic demeanour continued to speak volumes. The ladies in her immediate company tended to her with the great fuss. It was apparent that she demanded respect and the ladies did not fail to give it.

Saoirse was invited to stay for tea. During which time the women gathered around her table, feeding her with biscuits, cake and tea, asking her question after question about the after-life.

Several of the ladies confessed that they too could see spirits and one after the other they related their experiences to Saoirse and the rest of the group.

Saoirse was fascinated with the stories the ladies shared. They sat forward wide-eyed, divulging stories of nights long ago when they saw 'ghosts' and 'spirits' in the local area and had not told a soul. She was equally fascinated by the way one lady was able to finish the others' sentences because she had the very same experience.

For the very first time, the ladies of Alainn Ri shared stories and experiences which they had never dared reveal to anyone. In doing so, they realised that they had not been the only one who saw 'ghosts' on the same street, or in the same field, late at night, many years ago.

There was an excitement in the air that night as secrets were revealed and met with acceptance.

It was a night that Saoirse had dreaded for over a month but turned out to be insightful, revealing and even magical. For sure it was a night that Saoirse knew she would never forget and always hold close in her heart. She wished she could remember all of the stories, but there was not a chance, there was so many.

At the very end of the night, when most had gone home, the handful of ladies remaining revealed the deep, mysterious secrets of Alainn Ri to Saoirse. They were the secrets that only get told, to the worthy ones. The secrets revealed truths about the sacred folk who guarded that land from dimensions beyond and centuries ago.

Saoirse was both fascinated and honoured that the ladies felt drawn to share the secrets of the area with her. She respected them, and she also respected the sacred folk who guarded this land from another plane. After all, she was a stranger to this land but deep in her heart, she loved it from day one.

That night she began to understand why.

Chapter 35

"Tom seriously, would you please come on! The appointment for the scan is at 10am. It's an hour to the hospital, and you're still sipping coffee."

Saoirse ran around the house, grabbing keys and wallets and throwing them into her bag. Her long dark hair was falling loose, each layer framing her face. Her trainers made no sound on the kitchen tiles and snuggled her feet in comfort as did her black legging and sweatshirt, allowing room for her growing baby bump.

She was loving pregnancy, and she embraced every part of it. By now she was over the tired spell of the first trimester, and her energy levels had returned to normal, allowing her to tend to days filled with the life she loved.

She had not felt the baby kicking yet, and every hope and worry filled her mind that everything was ok. But today was the routine twenty-week scan day, and she was not only going to find out if everything was ok, but she was also going to get to see their baby on screen for the very first time.

"Saoirse it's only 8am we have lots of time." Tom relaxed at the kitchen table and took a gulp of his coffee.

"Tom, what if we get stuck in traffic or behind a tractor or something? Seriously they won't wait in the hospital, come on we can get coffee on the way."

Tom reluctantly stood up and threw back the last of his morning drink.

"I'm so excited! I can't wait to see little boo." Saoirse fastened her seat belt and turned to Tom in the driver's seat.

"I know Saoirse, me too." Tom's smile filled his face.

"I'm nervous as heck too, I hope everything's ok" She could feel the butterflies in her tummy and knew it wasn't the baby's first kicks.

The couple arrived at the hospital within the hour, without a tractor or traffic jam in sight. No sooner had they sat down and the nurse called Saoirse's name.

"Hello guys, is this your first baby?"

"Yes," Saoirse beamed.

"Ah lovely, it's an exciting time, isn't it? How is Mam?" The nurse invited Saoirse to lie on the examination bed in the scan room.

"I'm great thanks; not a bother thank God."

"That's what you want. How old is Mum?"

"I'm thirty."

"That's grand, perfect. I am just going to pop this gel on your tummy Mum, sorry if it's a bit cold."

The gel was cold, but Saoirse didn't care. She was twenty weeks pregnant, the halfway mark and today she was going to see her baby for the very first time. Who cared about cold gel?

"There we are now; do you see the baby?" The fair-haired nurse smiled, mapping her finger around the outline of their baby on screen "there's the heartbeat, the head, you see the spine there"

Saoirse and Tom looked at the monitor in the dim lit examination room. A little tiny head extended into a body with two little legs and arms took form on the screen. The baby seemed to be sure they were on camera because they began to jump up and down and wave arms in excitement.

Saoirse squeezed Tom's hand and took a gasp of breath. They watched their little bundle jump about in blissful happiness.

"You have an active one there...Do you want to find out the sex of the baby?"

"No!"

They both replied in unison. Neither had asked the other if they wanted to find out the sex of the baby before now. They both took their eyes away from the monitor for a moment and looked at each other. Toms' eyes were filled with tears of joy and Saoirse's face was soaked with tears of same.

"Ah, are you two ok?"

"I can't believe it, it kind of surreal really," Tom watched his little bundle on the monitor, jumping about happy in their own little world.

"Well everything looks perfect guys, baby seems perfectly healthy. I'll just take their first photo now, and we're done."

Chapter 36

Saoirse stood in the small kitchen upstairs at the back of the Healing Centre. She watched the kettle boil, in a dreamy state, miles away from the moment. Her mind was away with Lil, Joe and Ruth. She was wondering how they were and contemplating her mixed emotions about not being in touch, especially now that she was expecting. A combination of guilt, anger and sadness pained in her heart. The pain was always there, the heavy grief that weighted within. Sometimes she listened to it, most times she ignored it, but the pain of loss persisted.

Her baby bump was growing by the day, and she continued to stay busy as her pregnancy progressed. She was convinced that although things would change once the baby arrived, she was adamant that she was going to continue to work as hard then as she had always done. The only difference was that she would work around her new arrival. She was woken from her daydream by the phone ringing.

"Hello, Saoirse," a vaguely familiar voice greeted her.

She searched her mind trying to remember whose voice it was.

"Saoirse, it's Catherine Ellis here. I am calling you from the Health Board. You might recall we spoke before with regards to your birth mother, Maisie."

"Hi Catherine, how are you? It's been a while," Saoirse felt a strong belt of butterflies. The last time she heard from Catherine was shortly after they met. Catherine rang to profusely apologize to Saoirse saying the Maisie had contacted their offices having received their letter to say that Saoirse had been in touch, but the receptionist made an error when taking down Maisie's phone number. They had not been able to contact Maisie since.

"I am well, Saoirse. I am calling you with some news. It's good news. I decided to give one last try to contact Maisie. I tried writing to her several times over the last few months after that unfortunate mishap with her contact number," Saoirse listened with anticipation and held on to Catherine's words 'It's good news'.

"But each time I never got any response. So I sent her a final letter last week, explaining that this would be the last effort to contact her and that we all understand and support whatever decision she makes. But this time she returned contact with our office.

So, I spoke with her on the phone earlier today, and I have arranged to meet with her later this week in Ennis, Co Clare. I just thought I would give you a quick call to fill you in and I will be in touch after I meet with her. We can take it from there if that's ok?"

"Right, okay. Thank you, Catherine, erm…," Saoirse had to ask, "how did Maisie sound on the phone?" She held her breath and bit her lip.

"Like a lady Saoirse," She could tell Catherine was smiling. "Maisie is a very soft-spoken lady, quite like yourself actually" Saoirse could hear the authenticity in Catherine's observation "she said she was delighted you made contact and is very much looking forward to meeting you".

Saoirse felt the peace and acceptance flow into her heart and shoot right up, to form a big lump in her throat and tears in her eyes.

"Thank you for your persistence Catherine, I really mean that, thank you." She half considered asking if Maisie addressed why she had not responded to earlier correspondence but thought she would leave it on a high.

"No problem at all Saoirse. It's my pleasure. I will keep you updated ok."

Saoirse hung up the phone with her heart beating like crazy. She poured her tea smiling unknowns to herself with her hands shaking like a leaf.

…Like a lady…. soft spoken lady…. quite like yourself. Catherine's words echoed in her mind over and over.

The following Friday Catherine called Saoirse and explained that she met with Maisie in a coffee shop close to her home place.

"Saoirse, Maisie is a lovely lady. She is strong, but gentle. She is very down to earth and easy to get on with. A very warm lady with the sharpest wit." Saoirse listened to Catherine, wishing she could bottle her words somewhere safe to call upon whenever she desired. "She talked a lot about how she desperately wanted to keep you, I will let her tell you all about that herself when you meet. She asked me to tell you that not a day went by that she didn't think about you. Her biggest fear was that you went to a home where you were unhappy"

Saoirse stayed silent, the tears rolled down her cheeks. She held her breath and closed her eyes.

Catherine knew she was still on the line because she heard her sniffling.

"She is a mother to four more children. Two girls and two boys" Saoirse recalled all the times when she was younger wondering what it would be like to have a brother. Now, there were two strangers out there somewhere, that were her brothers and another two sisters. A strange sense of belonging grew and grew in her heart, it was like a secret treasure chest, filled with jewels was opening up, the jewels shining and glistening, filling the whole room with its rays.

"Maisie got quite teary and upset when she recalled giving you up. She explained that she had a terrible time afterwards. I am sure she will talk to you about that herself when you meet.

She is married to a wonderful man by the sound of things! Although she told me that she never told anyone about the baby, not even her husband."

"So nobody knows? Not even her family?" Saoirse tried desperately to hold onto the essence of love and acceptance that waved though her cellular being moments ago.

"It's the way it was I'm afraid Saoirse. She was told not to talk about it and to move on"

Saoirse felt Maisie's shame grip her like a dark entity.

"She met her husband a year later and had a baby the following year. This time, Maisie and the baby's father joined in wedlock prior to her baby being born."

"Did Maisie talk about why she had not returned contact for so long after the mishap with the phone number?"

"She was full of apology about that Saoirse. She explained that she had been extremely busy with family occasions in the last few months. Her son got married, and there was also the arrival of another grandchild too. She is a very motherly lady, her family come first. I don't mean that puts you on the back burner by any means, my sense was that she wanted to be able to be in the head space when she met you, so as she could enjoy it, if that makes sense."

"That's ok, I appreciate that" Saoirse accepted.

"Anyway, Saoirse myself and Maisie agreed to on a date three Saturdays from now, it's the 21st of this month. So we'll go with that date if you could pop it in your diary."

Saoirse agreed immediately. She knew that her diary was full of appointments for psychic readings that day, just like any other Saturday. It didn't take a second thought for her to reschedule all the appointments.

They ended the phone call and Saoirse looked around the room without looking at anything in particular. The words of the conversation echoed in her mind.

She imagined the picture of Maisie's life, her four siblings, Maisie's character. She was delighted to hear that Maisie's husband was a great man and it sounded like she was still in love after all these years. Her mother sounded like a lady who had a happy life. She sounded like someone who was kind, supportive, strong and brave. A new sense of love flowed into her awareness and took resonance deep in her heart.

Saoirse was one step closer to home.

For the following three weeks Saoirse could hardly think of anything else. She tried very hard to put it out of her mind and distract herself, but it was easier said than done. Every emotion, anticipation, thought, fear and hope flowed through her mind.

What surprised Saoirse the most was how incredibly guilty she felt about meeting Maisie behind Lil and Joe's back. Saoirse couldn't help feeling that she was betraying them. After all, her childhood and upbringing were a credit to them.

Okay they were no longer part of her life, and they rejected her when she was nine. But they were the only parents she ever knew. Her mind was tormented with confliction.

One part of her mind told her that they were only human. They were just people who were afraid. She recalled Joe's face standing in the kitchen on the day she said goodbye. His tall presence filled with vulnerability, the humility in his eyes, the silent call for forgiveness for years of what could never be undone.

He was her dad, but he was also just a human being filled with fear of what he did not understand.

The other part of her mind saw Joe behind the steering wheel of his car, driving past her standing in the rain.

She recalled the day they sent her away to the Convent. Joe's eyes fixed on the kitchen table and the guilt on Lil's face. They knew in their hearts their decision was wrong.

She remembered Lil arriving home with the shopping on the day she said goodbye, faffing around blaming her for Joe's upset and her concern for Ruth in the shop on her own.

The countless times they ignored her, underestimated her and most of all told her to shut up. Their words that evening while she tried to write her English essay thundered through her mind like a steam train 'you're a nothing, a nobody' and the look on Joe's face. She saw his hate.

The memories tugged for attention saying that they should have been stronger. They should have stood up to their own guilt, their own frustration and they should have stood up to the system. They should have been unconditionally loving parents. They should have accepted her. But they failed to do so. They gave in to judgement and went with the status quo beliefs, ignoring their hearts and ignoring her.

But still, the guilt remained.

"Hello Saoirse, it's Catherine Ellis here."

Saoirse was finishing up a few things in the Healing Centre before heading home to get a good nights' sleep in preparation for the early start to Dublin the following day. Her practical approach to feeling useful also helped take her mind off the enormity of the day ahead. It felt like D day. Finally, the reunion with her birth mother was only hours away.

"Saoirse, I just came off the phone to Maisie. I am so terribly sorry, but Maisie had bad news I'm afraid. She said that her husband has taken poorly, and she is not going to be able to make tomorrows' meeting."

"Oh...." Saoirse's heart sank.

"I hope it's not too serious?"

"I'm not too sure to be completely honest with you, but I told her I would give her a call next week and we can go from there. That's all I could do at this point I'm afraid."

Saoirse extended her understanding and ended the phone call.

She stood in the centre of the meditation room in her healing centre with the receiver in the palm of her hand and sighed.

Within moments the whole room had changed.

A moment ago, it was the room she was present in the night before she met her mother for the very first time. Now, it was an empty space filled with disappointment and a dissolved plan to meet with her birth mother.

She felt let down and angry. So much energy had gone into the last couple of weeks. She had rearranged all her appointments. She even waved becoming upset at clients who were annoyed at her for cancelling.

When Catherine told her that the meeting to reunite with her birth mother had been decided, she wondered why nobody asked her if the date suited. But she told herself to see the bigger picture here and go along with it.

Tom had cancelled a night out with friends in Dublin. Maria had also arranged to come down and stay with Saoirse while Tom was away, just in case she went into labour, even though she was only seven months pregnant. Most of Saoirse's income was earned on Saturdays too. She couldn't help feeling that she had wasted so much energy on all levels.

But after all Maisie's husband was sick, and it couldn't be helped. Maybe it was Saoirse's intuition or sense of feeling annoyed, but she didn't know if she fully believed that story, it just didn't sit with her.

She turned out the lights of the centre, locked everything up and drove home to Tom.

She took the time during the drive home to get her head around the sharp change in events. She still couldn't believe the phone call just happened, but it did, and it brought up so many feelings for her.

Saoirse could not help feeling that she was suiting everyone else around the arrangements to reunite with Maisie. The last thing she was going to do was confront Catherine like a spoiled child asking something along the lines of:

'What about me and my feelings, did anyone think about that eh? How inconsiderate could everyone be here? You and your big black briefcase can just hang up the phone, walk away and go home with a day off tomorrow now.

And while I'm at it, why didn't anyone ask if the date agreed suited me? It seems to me that no-one is asking for my opinion on what happens here at all. There again what has changed? I wasn't asked 30 years ago how I felt about this. In fact, while I'm at it, not only was I not asked how I felt 30 years ago, I have never been asked since how I feel about this, not once, not ever, in my whole life, and I am still not being asked now! What a joke."

But to confront Catherine like that would just be wrong.

She drove home along the country roads, ranting out loud, rehearsing a conversation that she knew she would never have and the whole time little Boo kicked, bounced and tumbled happily in utero.

Saoirse sub-consciously had her hand over baby Boo's bump rubbing it gently as she ranted, to no-one.

"Like for God's sake, and I mean that literally by the way. I have a job, a life. People depended on me tomorrow, and I let them all down, to accommodate your plan. I am now short the best part of a weeks' wage, my husband doesn't get to see his friends, ok maybe that's minimal, but my point is, no-one gives any tiny iota of consideration for how I feel or how this impacts me. I'm still just the baby, who cares? What does it matter how she feels? She can just fall in with the plan and go along with it. Who cares how it impacts her, again."

Meanwhile, baby continued to dance in her womb. Saoirse's heart was beating fast. She arrived at a T junction at the end of the road, just along the Kildare/Wicklow boarder. The traffic lights in front of her turned red. Her eyes were fixed firmly on the lights, and she let out a huge sigh, in an attempt to let it go.

She enjoyed having her little rant, albeit to no one but her dashboard. It was done now as was the change of plan. She knew that her only choice was to accept it.

She waited in a daydream staring at the red light waiting for it to turn green. She glanced to her left at the road she was about to make headway onto. Her fingertips resting on her womb noticed a little tap and then another against her fingertips. Her awareness was brought to her bump, and even though she had been subconsciously aware of baby bouncing around for the last half an hour, she turned her attention to being present in the moment and feeling the level of movement in her tummy.

Saoirse had read somewhere that the baby does a 180-degree turn to position them self with their head engaged in preparation for birth. Although she knew she was carrying an active baby, she couldn't help feeling he/she was particularly active this evening. Suddenly she found herself smiling, looking down on her tummy watching her belly protrude in all directions.

The lights went green. She put the car in gear and turned left onto the main road. There was a small housing estate just off the road, and Saoirse indicated left and found a spot to pull in where it was safe.

In the darkness of the night, she sat back in the driver's seat and smiled down at her womb. For the next twenty minutes, she watched in awe, her baby making his turn in her tummy in preparation for birth. She felt blessed by God above to be witness to the incredible miracle of divine intelligence happening before her eyes.

After a short while, everything settled, and baby was quiet. Saoirse thought he must be gone asleep after all that hard work.

Right then, all her disappointment and anger had left. It was gone. The only thing she could feel was love.

Just like before, once again, everything changed.

An hour ago, Saoirse was within hours of laying eyes on her own flesh and blood for the very first time, her mother. But now that was not to happen.

She sat in the car, on that September night and made her decision. The first time she met her own flesh and blood was not going to be when she met her mother. It was going to be when she meets her child.

"Saoirse, I know you have been having doubts and second thoughts in the past about this, but take it from me, once the baby comes along in the next few weeks everything else in your life will go on the back burner," Catherine urged Saoirse when she called to rearrange her reunion with her mother. "Maisie's very much looking forward to meeting you now, and I really think it a good idea to meet her before your baby is born."

"Thank you, Catherine, for your advice I do appreciate it. But I have made my decision and as I said I have chosen to wait until after the baby is born to meet with Maisie. It is the decision that feels right for me."

Chapter 37

"Push, push, push, push, push Saoirse. Oh, Daddy, she's not pushing hard enough."

"Eh, I am here you know!" Saoirse scolded the nun who happened to be the midwife on duty when Saoirse progressed into the throes of labour.

Every night for the last five months Saoirse woke just after two in the morning. Not once did she disturb Tom from his sleep. Despite trying, she could never go back to sleep and was always awake until just after dawn. She managed to fall asleep for an hour or so before getting started on her day.

This morning, she woke, and she knew this was it. She had no pain, but she knew the baby was on the way.

She called Tom who jumped up out of bed and fell over himself to get dressed while Saoirse called the hospital, feeling completely relaxed and in control.

The midwife knew from what Saoirse had told her that her waters had broken. But she also knew that there was no panic and asked Saoirse to take her time and come to the hospital when she was ready.

She was sitting at the kitchen table, sipping her coffee. It was pitch dark, and there was not a sign of life outside.

She had also made coffee for Tom, who arrived into the kitchen completely panicked, battling his arms into his T-shirt and grabbing his car keys in one hand and shoes in the other.

"It's half two. We'll be grand. There'll be nothing on the road. Are you right?" Tom looked at Saoirse who sat back on the kitchen chair, obviously in no rush to go anywhere.

"Saoirse, what are you at? Would you come on?"

"Relax love, have your coffee, we've lots of time."

"Did you ring the hospital, what did they say? Saoirse I really think we better make a move."

"Tom would you stop looking at your wrist. You're not wearing a watch. We have lots of time. Baby won't be here for a few hours yet. And yes. I rang the midwife in the hospital, and she said the very same thing"

"What are you laughing at? Saoirse, seriously...."

"Tom Harris you are the most relaxed, laid back person I know. I have never seen you so panicked." Saoirse couldn't help give way to her kinks of laughter.

"Have you got the bag? Where's the hospital bag?" Tom paced the small area of the kitchen floor, searching aimlessly for the hospital bag and walked in and out of the hall every now and then.

"It has been in the boot of my car for the last month, will you sit down and have your coffee. Anyone would think you were having the baby or something."

"It's not funny Saoirse," Tom sat down and tried to relax, seated in front of his coffee at the kitchen table. His foot had a mind of its own tapping like crazy on the tiled floor.

The couple arrived at the hospital just after eight. Saoirse insisted they get breakfast in a 24-hour petrol station on the way. Tom did not relax until they were in the hospital and Saoirse was being examined by a midwife.

The midwives changed shifts a couple of hours later, and that is when Sr. Anne was assigned to Saoirse.

"Now, now Saoirse, you are going to have to push harder. I am going on my lunch break in ten minutes, and I don't want you delaying me." The middle-aged, grey haired nun eye-balled Saoirse.

Saoirse had been rude enough to the nun already and wanted to preserve her energy for the hard labour of birth. She was in the throes of the most tremendous pain she had ever experienced in her life.

"Could you close that window, or do you have an extra blanket, I'm a bit cold."

"Cold? It's not cold in here at all. Are you cold Daddy?"

"Could I just have a blanket please?"

Tom removed his jumper and placed it around Saoirse's shoulders.

Saoirse's contractions were becoming stronger, and Sr Anne was becoming more impatient, Saoirse could not help feeling vulnerable in her care. She was relieved when it turned one o clock, and the nun went off on her lunch break.

"Hello there," a beautiful, young midwife with shoulder length fair hair tied into a pony tail entered the labour ward and checked Saoirse's file, "Saoirse, how are we getting on?" her warm smile melted the pain even just for that moment.

"A lot better now that you're here,"

"You are doing great Saoirse, just relax in between the contractions, baby will come in their own time. I'm Lucy by the way." Lucy's smile beamed, her very presence said that everything was under control.

An hour later, Saoirse was still in labour. Sr Anne returned. The young midwife stayed but was pushed firmly into the background.

"Well, still here I see. I am telling you, Daddy. She's not pushing hard enough. Come on now Saoirse, next contraction, push push push push push, ok?"

Every time she said that Saoirse thought she was calling a little kitten to her side.

The nun had put on a radio station playing music that Saoirse could not bear. She was in the depths of pain, cold and hungry and she had reached her threshold, not sure if she had any more to give. She just wanted to sleep, no longer had the energy to do the work she needed to do.

"Now, now Saoirse, that's why they call it 'labour'. It's hard work, and you have to put your back into it."

"Turn that shite off that radio, close that stupid window and get me a blanket. Now!"

"My oh my! Now that's not very nice carry on, is it? I am shocked. Never in my life have I."

"Oh button it Sister, somehow I find that very hard to believe"

Sr Anne's mouth hung wide open catching flies. Tom and Lucy continued as they were, except Tom's eyes were popping out of his head, his lips pursed to hold in the kinks of laughter, Lucy mirrored his expression.

Eventually, feeling another contraction coming on Saoirse thought to herself,

Just go for it Girl, push so hard your body might break and that means that you will never have to listen to or lay eyes on this horrible woman ever again.

So she did.

"Well done Saoirse!" Lucy encouraged "Just one more push now and you're there, I can see baby's big head of black hair"

Tom, burst into tears when he saw the baby's head.

The excitement in the delivery ward was palpable. Everything began to happen so fast, and there was a slight air of panic in the room. The pain was more than Saoirse could bear but she knew she had to keep going.

With everything she had she released that one last push with a prayer to God to help her survive the unbearable pain. At that moment Saoirse truly felt like she was going to die.

Then, with a smile right from her heart, the young midwife lifted a tiny bundle and handed Saoirse, her own beautiful baby daughter.

Saoirse reached out to take the new life in her arms.

Her tiny baby girl was the most beautiful thing she had ever seen. Her big new born eyes looked up at Saoirse; her eyes searched to find the voice she knew so well. Her perfect face looked as panicked as Saoirse had felt moments before. Saoirse held perfection in her arms right then and there. She greeted her daughter and held her close, and the precious baby girl settled immediately.

Tom was in a heap; he completely broke down in tears of joy.

"Saoirse, look what you did. You did this. She is perfect."

"Oh Tom, we did this, she is beautiful isn't she?" Saoirse took her eyes off their beautiful bundle just for a moment and smiled up at her husband.

The pain, the panic and the fear of moments before had completely dissolved into non-existence.

Only love filled that room as the new family sat immersed in the purity of the joy together, for the very first time.

Nobody rushed the new family back to the maternity ward. They stayed at one in the joy of the moment. It was a couple of hours before Saoirse was wheeled back down to the ward.

It was visiting time. Families gathered around beds to visit new mums and met their new born bundles of joy.

Saoirse noticed a couple of mums had older children also. She looked at the mothers thinking they were off their heads. She thought that they must be mad people. She could not understand why any woman would want to put herself through that pain more than once.

She decided then and there, that was going to be the last time she ever gave birth. Once was enough for her.

"Ah would you look at her," Mary leaned over Bridget's crib by Saoirse's bedside. Her eyes were filled with tears of joy for her beautiful friend, "Saoirse, she is beautiful"

"Thanks Mary, I can't believe we have finally met her" Saoirse sat up in the bed her head resting back on the stack of propped pillows.

"She's an old, old soul, isn't she?"

"It's funny, more than one of the mid-wives have said that she is like a little papoose"

"She is," Mary said knowingly.

"Knock, knock we're here to see Mammy!" Alvagh walked into the ward with her husband Colin. Alvagh's presence was as larger than life as ever. Although she was dressed down in jeans and a sweatshirt and minimum make up, one would have to be blind not to notice she was a big star. She carried that presence when Saoirse met her all those years ago and she radiated the very same confidence today.

"Look at you, you look fantastic, honey" She placed the large bunch of flowers on the locker and hugged her best friend.

"Oh it's so good to see you guys. Did you come up from Cork today? Alvagh you smell gorgeous!" Saoirse absorbed the fresh scent of Alvagh's perfume.

"We were up anyway visiting Colin's parents"

Colin hugged Saoirse and kissed her on the cheek. "Well done Saoirse, congratulations"

Alvagh was drawn to Bridget like a magnet. She picked her up and sat in the armchair beside the bed cradling the new little person in everyone's life.

"Oh I have never seen a more beautiful baby," she paused and looked around the room "apart from my own of course! Ciaran was a beautiful baby too. Maria is on her way, I was talking to her earlier on, she should be here any minute"

"Look who I found wandering the corridors" Tom walked in with Maria. He had popped home earlier to fetch a bag for Saoirse and Bridget.

"Saoirse, I have cried the whole way here!" Maria's eyes were popping out of her head. "I can't say how happy I am for you. Love you to bits honey" Maria hugged Saoirse so tight before turning to take Bridget out of Alvagh's arms, "My turn, up you get" She claimed Alvagh's arm chair and doted on Bridget.

The new family and close friends sat in the ward chatting and doting on how beautiful Bridget was. No-one could take their eyes off her. Saoirse took a moment to glance around at the most important people in her life. Her soul family.

She couldn't help to think of Lil, Joe and Ruth. Amidst the happiness she couldn't help feeling the silent pull of emptiness in her heart. It was a strange feeling among the fulfilment of the moment. A mix between wishing they were here and not wanting them there at all, was testament to the history of their relationship.

"Oh! Saoirse" Tom remembered. "I was packing the bag earlier and rooting for your things" Saoirse rolled her eyes and smiled to herself at that very image, Tom wouldn't have a clue where anything was.

"Anyway, I found this watch" he pulled a little digital watch out of the bag.

"Mr Bennetts watch" Saoirse whispered.

"Yeah, I remember you telling me years ago that his wife gave it to you after he passed away"

"That's right. Gosh, I was only eight or nine. She said that he wanted me to have it because I had impeccable timing" a reminiscent smile filled her face, "It was the day of his funeral in his house".

"Oh, I remember you telling me about that" Alvagh said. "Didn't you have a dream or something, before he died, a premonition?"

Saoirse nodded "Yes, but..."

"Yeah, Hun just let me tell you" Tom interrupted, "it was in the drawer of your bedside locker. I was looking for your hair-dryer or something and there it was" Tom held the digital watch in his hand.

"But Tom I...."

"Just listen for a sec," Tom didn't stop to take a breath, "given the day that's in it I brought it into Clancy's jewellers on the way here," the new dad stood tall, shoulders back, "and asked him if he could fix it. He went off with the watch and after a minute he came back saying that there was nothing wrong with that watch at all. It's working fine" Tom marvelled and glanced around the group and back to Saoirse.

"But Tom, I haven't seen that watch since I gave it to mam.

When Mrs Bennett gave it to me that day I asked mam to mind it. She put it into her bag and I've never seen it since. That was twenty-two years ago"

Saoirse got up to sit at the side of the bed and took Mr Bennett's watch in her hands. She held it, noting the digital number display and the second indicator flashing in synchronicity with time.

She looked up to Maria and Colin, knowing they were open but not so aware of how heaven works "You know, they say that when things happen that we can't explain with logic, that's heavens fingerprints right there," Saoirse explained to her soul family with a gratuitous smile.

"Wow, I'm gonna cry, that's amazing" Alvagh swallowed back the lump in her throat and fanned her face with her hand.

The others stayed silent, together absorbing yet another miracle of this day.

Saoirse smiled with a quiet prayer of gratitude to Mr Bennet. She knew that wherever he was right now, he was not too far away.

"There you go" Mary said with her everlasting wisdom "there is no separation".

Bridget attracted a lot of attention in her first couple of days. This was mainly due to the unusual head of hair she was born with. It was so long and thick that Saoirse could braid it. The mid-wives continued to say that she was just like a little papoose. Saoirse and Tom completely agreed. She had the long dark hair, sallow skin and eye lashes that Saoirse was sure were tickling Bridget's cheeks.

She stayed in the hospital for as long as she could. The other mums and mid-wives were a world of support and she was learning so much about motherhood from them that she decided to stay an extra day at the hospital. The-first-time mum knew that once she went home she was on her own.

Motherhood suited Saoirse. Every morning she woke up feeling like she was going to burst with love for her bundle of perfection. She felt blessed by God and thanked him every-day for his blessings.

During Bridget's first month Saoirse contemplated a lot on what life must have been like for Maisie a generation ago. Catherine Ellis had told her that Maisie stayed with her in the Mother and Baby home until she was one month old before she had to take the life changing step and walk away from her infant, to go back home.

Four weeks into Bridget's infancy thoughts of same haunted her mind all that day. She sat and watched perfection before her. She felt the explosion of love and the bond between herself and Bridget. She thought about Maisie and the unthinkable task she had to do when she was a young mother and Saoirse was one month old.

Jesus, it must have ripped her heart out. She fought back the tears of devastation exploding in her heart, watching Bridget sleep peacefully in her Moses basket, snuggled up in cotton, the soft lamb's wool top blanket brushed softly on her chin, her little chest rising and falling, in peaceful slumber. There's no two ways about it, that would kill me, where did she find the strength to go on?

She also thought of herself as an infant and what she must have went through. Imagining her mother being gone, just not there anymore. She could feel the bond between herself and Bridget and she knew Bridget felt it too, the way she calmed immediately once Saoirse cradled her in her arms. The way she looked around the room recognising Saoirse's voice. It was unthinkable to think that that bond was snatched away so abruptly.

She wondered how she coped as an infant. Did she cry? If so who tended to her? Who came and soothed her tears? The thoughts were breaking her heart and her very presence was the only proof that she had that she obviously got through it.

Chapter 38

"Good Morning Saoirse, congratulations to you, what did you have?"

"Thank you, Catherine. I had a baby girl. Bridget, after the saint. She has her strength." Saoirse knew this call was coming. But she had not encouraged it and eighteen months had passed since she last spoke to Catherine Ellis.

"Right, that's lovely Saoirse....erm I suppose I am just touching base with you. I know you are most likely up to your eyes these days, but would you be open to setting up another meeting with Maisie, now that things have settled down?"

"Yes, absolutely Catherine, I am free most days, once I have enough notice I can be available."

"Oh, that's great Saoirse, great. Well, I have spoken to Maisie, and she said that she would work with you this time. She understands that she let you down that last time and at such short notice too."

"How is Maisie's husband do you know?"

"Oh he is fine, I think, she never mentioned it actually. Saoirse, I am just looking at my diary here. Would next Tuesday be good for you? That's a week from today?"

"I'll say it to Tom, just to ensure he can book the day off work and give you a ring back shortly if that's ok?"

Saoirse wrapped up the phone call. When she hung up, she noticed that her hands had begun to shake.

She phoned Tom and then Mary to ask if she was free to mind Bridget and from there called Catherine back to arrange.

"God, what a seventies building Tom isn't it?" Saoirse's butterflies in her tummy turned up their volume as she looked out the windscreen at the tall, long, grey building.

"I think it's in here anyway." Tom turned the car into the large car park of the multi-storey building belonged to the Easter Health Board, near Dublin city centre.

Bridget was in the back of the car. Mary called this morning to say that she had to let Saoirse down last minute due to a desperate dose of the flu. Mary had never let her down before about anything in her life. Saoirse knew there was a reason beyond human control. She urged her friend to stay in bed and do nothing but stay warm and get better.

Bridget wore a pink cardigan and pretty, pink dress. Saoirse refused to give her food from the time she put the cardigan on her because no doubt it would be covered in same food by the time they arrived. She had her long mane tied up in two high ponytails, and her pretty, pink dress sat over her multicoloured tights, she already kicked her shoes off before the car left the driveway. She was sixteen months now, and Saoirse lovingly nicknamed her Happy because she wore a smile from one end of the day to the other. It was the type of smile that came right from her heart, into her eyes and onto her face.

She was a typical first born, into everything and once she began crawling Saoirse felt like she needed eyes in the back of her head. One day the hall door was open. Saoirse had left Bridget playing on the kitchen floor while she took the shopping in from the car. One moment Bridget was playing happily with her telly tubby and the next minute, she was gone.

Saoirse ran frantically outside looking for her. There was no way she could have crawled out to the drive and onto the road that quick. Saoirse ran around the outside of the house and closed the gate just in case. Every second seemed like forever. She looked everywhere for Bridget. The child just seemed to disappear. The worst thoughts possible ran through Saoirse's mind.

She searched every room in the house, and lastly, she checked the downstairs guest room. She still could not find Bridget. What felt like a ridiculous hunch told her to look under the bed. When she did, Bridget was lying flat on her belly, feeling the carpet with her fingers tips as she lay in a daydream. Her little face filled with the happiest grin when her mother's head appeared before her.

Bridget was a little explorer who clearly did her own thing, her own way. Despite the sporadic moments and episodes of sheer panic, for the most part, Saoirse supported the quality of Bridget's independence.

"How are you feeling Hun?" Tom turned off the engine and put his arm around his wife.

"I'm not too bad Tom. I know it's a big day, but the whole

journey along in the car I have been thinking of Maisie's family, her kids. Gosh it's a huge wrecking ball for them, isn't it? By the way, you have a long-lost sister. Her name is Saoirse." Saoirse's heart pounded.

"Listen, would you let someone else worry about that for now. Today is yours and Maisie's day, worry about everyone else another time." Tom's tall body was like a tower of strength holding her in the biggest supportive embrace.

"Thanks, Tom. You always know what to say exactly, I'm so lucky."

"I keep telling you. I'm the lucky one, sure look at the pair of you." Tom glanced at the back of the car to Bridget and back to Saoirse.

Saoirse knew he meant every word.

"Right, let's do this."

She took a deep breath and looked up at the tall grey building. She looked at the many windows on each floor, and the thought ran through her mind that in there somewhere was her mother.

She took a moment to anticipate the scene that was to unfold over the next half hour or so. She felt incredibly calm, but she also felt very all over the place. She knew she was ungrounded and searched to centre herself in her own power during the short walk into the building's reception area.

Bridget babbled her little head off all the way through the car park, and Saoirse welcomed the distraction of pure love and innocence.

They stepped out of the lift on the 4th floor, following the directions the receptionist had related.

"Saoirse, is that you? My goodness, you have changed so much. You look absolutely fantastic. You have lost so much weight!" Catherine met Saoirse with a warm smile.

Saoirse turned to answer Catherine and couldn't help thinking that she must have looked horrendous the last time they met. She was still struggling to lose the baby weight but tried her best today to make an effort and turn herself out half decent at least.

"Hi Catherine, it's lovely to see you. This is my husband Tom, and this is Bridget."

After exchanging pleasantries, Catherine directed them into one of the rooms off the corridor on the right.

She invited them to sit down on the couch for a moment and explain the procedure. The room was cosy and very 1980s décor. One could see that the effort was made to create a relaxed, comforting atmosphere. Small lamps stood on mahogany tables in the corners, and a brass framed picture of a country landscape hung on the wall above the couch. It was modest but nice, but the dull orange and brown carpet on the floor was worn and did absolutely nothing for the sense of relaxation and calm in the room all the same.

"Right, how are you feeling Saoirse?"

"I'm ok Catherine, I'm ready."

"Ok, well Maisie and her husband arrived about twenty minutes ago. They are in the adjoining room there, that's why I'm whispering you see. In a moment, I am going to go in and tell her that you are here, and I will open the door and bring you in. Is that ok?"

"Oh my God, there go the butterflies kicking up a storm" Saoirse suddenly felt her tummy go on fire with nerves. She looked at the adjoining door. It was about three feet from the couch she was seated on. Behind that partition wall, right now, at this very moment, was her birth mother, Maisie.

Her stomach felt like a washing machine on a full load spin, and her heart was jumping right out of her chest with every beat. She joined her hands over her knees and noticed her fingertips were cold, and her palms were soaked. She took a deep breath to release the tsunami of anxiety rushing through her veins.

"It's ok Saoirse. Maisie is lovely, and so is her husband, Pat. You will be fine. Are you ready?"

Saoirse nodded.

Catherine left the room and went into Maisie's room. Tom sat down beside Saoirse and gave her the biggest, longest hug. One of Catherine's colleagues played with Bridget in the corner, just until after the ladies reunited.

"Ok Saoirse, whenever you're ready" Catherine's stood with her hand on the adjoining door handle, her encouraging smile met Saoirse and she waited patiently for Saoirse to come to the door in her own time.

Saoirse approached the door and glanced inside. A middle-aged

lady and a very tall man with a bald head sat side by side on one of
the two couches.

"Maisie, this is Saoirse, isn't she beautiful?" Catherine opened the
door wide and stood back.

"Oh my God, she's like a model." Maisie stood up and walked the
few paces towards Saoirse with her arms outstretched.

Saoirse looked at the familiar stranger walking towards her.

Immediately she recognised her, and she went with the pull of an
invisible magnetic force that drew her towards this lady pacing towards her, smiling and fighting back the tears that filled her eyes. In
that moment the familiar completeness returned and filled her whole
being.

She was completely familiar. It was her essence, her presence. Of-
course this was what she looked like, and there was no one else in
existence that could take her place.

She also recognised the similarity in her mothers' looks and features immediately. Saoirse had never seen anyone with the same eyes
as hers, but Maisie had the very same eyes, the same face shape, the
same cheeks and chin. It was like looking at an older self, for the very
first time.

The ladies joined in an embrace for the first time in a lifetime.

In those moments all of the years that separated them did not make
a difference to what each of them felt. The bond between them spi-
ralled into live animation once again. They each felt the similarity, the
knowing, the sense that only the two of them could ever know.

They hugged in the middle of that room for as long as the other
would not let go.

Catherine invited them to sit on the couch. They sat side by side,
complete with snuffles, nervous giggles and sobs. The conversation
began to flow like two old friends catching up after many moons apart.

Maisie told Saoirse that she had been so nervous since last night.
Maisie went straight into explaining to Saoirse's her birth fathers
name, where he is and that she can put her in touch with him if she
wished. Saoirse had no interest in finding her birth father right now.
One reunion of its sort was enough for now.

"Do you still have the pink outfit?" Maisie's eyes lit up

"Pink outfit?" Saoirse frowned

"The day before I gave you up, mammy and I went into town to buy you an outfit to wear for when you met your new family. I got you the most gorgeous pink dress and little cardigan" Maisie explained touching her chest, "It was gorgeous, Saoirse. You don't still have it, no?"

"Oh Maisie." Saoirse frowned dismay, "I don't, but Mam and Dad didn't collect me from the home until months after you left" she looked into Maisie's eyes "did you think I had left then, I mean when I was a month old?"

"Saoirse, I saw them driving away with you in the car," Maisie looked straight ahead, recalling the memory "The nun came down the corridor and said I'm taking your baby now. Oh sweet Jesus, I thought I was going to die, I screamed and cried and screamed and cried and she just walked away with you in her arms. Then I watched them out the window, taking you into a big car and drive away"

Saoirse listened, tears flowed down her face for her mother's pain, "Maisie, that wasn't me. I didn't leave St Pat's until the following July, and mam told me that she had to knit me a dress because they had no clothes".

"I'm so sorry you went through so much pain" Saoirse wished she could take the pain of her mother's experience and wipe it completely from her memory.

"Don't you worry about me Saoirse," Maisie placed her hand on Saoirse's knee "My biggest fear through all these years was that you went to a home where you weren't celebrated or loved like you should have been?"

Saoirse took a deep breath, "Well look, I'd be lying if I assured you that that didn't happen. But that's another day's story and for now let's just say I believe everything happens for a reason" Saoirse didn't want to go into the history of Lil and Joe's choices right now, she was too happy.

"I would like to hear all about that sometime Saoirse" she met Saoirse's eyes with a mother's' love "Oh Catherine tells me you are a psychic!" Maisie remembered.

"Yes, that's true, I…."

"You get that from my side" Maisie sat up straight and announced. "My daddy's mother, your great grandmother used to read cards, you know the normal playing cards" she pretended to shuffle an invisible deck of cards in her hands "it was so taboo back then, we're talking late 1950's rural Bunratty now, can you imagine?" Maisie threw her eyes to heaven and shook her head "So no one was told what she did, but everyone knew. People used to come and go and come and go in the evenings, in and out of her little cottage. Anytime any of us kids asked what Granny was doing and why so many people were coming and going from the house, we were told she was teaching them how to play 21's, you know the card game? But she was reading their cards. I'm very psychic too, but it frightens the living day lights out of me to be honest" Maisie leaned into Saoirse and chuckled.

"That's so amazing, wow!" Saoirse tried to get her head around the welcoming fact that her gift did come from somewhere, it was something that she had inherited and not a fabrication of her own imagination.

"In fact, I called you after her. Her name was Mary, Daddy's mammy." Maisie could not wipe the smile from her face. She had the warmest eyes Saoirse had ever seen. She was strong, motherly and gentle. She was kind, soft spoken and so easy to connect with.

"What an incredibly brave lady!" Saoirse observed.

"There's no two ways about it Saoirse, you come from a long lineage of incredibly strong and brave women, and you have that very same strength. I can see it in you"

"You know Maisie, it doesn't end there with names." Saoirse could hardly take everything in, and there was so much she wanted to share with her mother. She was trying to bank everything in her mind and get everything out at the same time.

"When I was a little toddler, I had a favourite doll. Mam won her on the bingo one night and gave her to me around my second birthday," She looked at Maisie, maintaining composure, swallowing back the emotion "I could hardly speak at the time and I called the doll 'Maymie'. It was only after a few months when my speech became more articulate that Maymie became Maisie" She watched her mother's face light up and her eyes once again fill with tears. Saoirse smiled back her own tears, her joy was bursting from her heart, "Maisie religiously came with me everywhere I went, she never left my side" Saoirse forced the words out. "It might be worth saying that I had never heard of the name Maisie at the time, there were no relatives or neighbours called Maisie, but I just knew the name" she shrugged and met her mother's eyes.

"Maisie, my birth father, what was he like?"

Maisie told her all about her birth father. How they met, that he was lead singer in band. She then told Saoirse the story of how her father, Saoirse's grandfather, would not allow her to keep her baby and how she desperately wanted to and how in the end she just had to let go and get on with it.

As they chatted, Saoirse could not help thinking to herself the difficulties Maisie's experience of motherhood had brought. She thought of her secret pregnancy, being sent away to the Mother and Baby home, giving her baby away and experiencing such hell when she was so young. Not to mention giving birth again to her subsequent children and living with the separation from her firstborn all these years.

"Maisie" Pat, her husband, spoke for the very first time "the photos" he gave an encouraging nod towards Maisie's hand bag.

"Oh, that's right. I almost forgot!, thanks Pat love" Maisie reached for her hand bag and began to root inside "Saoirse, Catherine tells me you live in Wicklow"

"We do. It's a two-storey cottage on about an acre of land. It's old and modest but we love it" She glanced at Tom, who was nodding agreement.

There goes that smile on Maisie's face again, "Well I have never been to Wicklow myself, but my great grandfather and great grandmother on my mother's side hale from Co Wicklow. He built a house there in fact many moons ago. I suppose it must have been around the turn of the century. I have a photograph of it here. It's a long shot, but you never know" She flicked through a bunch of photos, some were old black and white photos, some were in colour. "Ah, here it is. They would be your great-great-grand parents."

She handed the old black and white photo to Saoirse.

Saoirse knew it was a long shot because Wicklow is such a huge country, but politely took the photo in her hands.

The picture was of a man and woman dressed in the attire of the time. The lady stood on the right and wore a long black skirt to her ankles, her hair tied up in a bun. The man stood tall, shoulders back, chest out, posing proudly in front of the home he built.

Saoirse examined what was becoming a familiar scene.

She threw her hand to her mouth. She double checked the image making sure she wasn't imagining things.

"Saoirse, what's wrong love?" Maisie asked concerned.

Saoirse shook her head, unable to speak. She handed the photo to Tom.

"Look at the sundial" she forced the words out to her husband.

"Oh yes, that's right!" Maisie said. "He made that sun dial himself. I heard tell that it was his favourite spot in the garden and one of the things he missed most when he moved down to Clare. In fact, he even built another one down home. It's still there in fact. That's my house now and it's in the same spot as it was in his old house in Wicklow, just outside the back door."

Tom was shaking his head, staring at the photo in disbelief before looking up to his wife, wide-eyed and speechless.

"Maisie," every part of Saoirse's body was rattling. "that same sundial is in our garden. Not one like it, the very same one, in the very same place, just outside the back door. That's our house."

The room fell silent.

Saoirse surrendered her failing search for words. She joined her hands in prayer over her mouth and closed her eyes, she could feel her heart pounding in her chest.

"I'm by no means a religious man" Pat's beautiful and strong voice broke the silence and filled the room for the very first time. His tall, well-built frame sat forward on the couch, "But I have heard tell of what God brings together, no man can separate" He smiled knowingly at the two ladies.

"That's amazing," Saoirse eventually said, "you couldn't plan it if you tried"

"My God, I am speechless" Maisie whispered.

"That's a first let me tell ya" Pat joked.

"Saoirse always said that the house found us. I guess you were spot on love" Tom smiled.

"Maisie, I don't mean to change the subject, and it's going to take me a long time to get my head around this one let me tell you. But on an entirely different note, I have to ask you. Life in the mother and baby home? What was it like" Saoirse asked.

"Oh God love it was horrendous. Some of the Sisters were ok, but the one in charge was horrendous" Maisie looked into nowhere recalling the hell she experienced. "Most of my days were spent scrubbing floors 'til my back was breaking." She shook her head grimacing at the memory of the pain. "Each day I kept my head down and just got on with it. But no-one was safe. In fact, I remember one girl in the bed next to me. She only had her son a couple of days before I think, or maybe the day before, I'm not sure. Alice was her name. The Sister went around every morning and examined our beds" the others listened to Maisie recall hell, "This particular morning Alice's bed was slightly soiled. Well that nun went into a rage. She dragged Alice out of the dorm. The poor girl screamed and begged pardon, but the Sister was having none of it. She took her away and she wasn't back until the following night, her beautiful long auburn hair all cut off and she had scald marks all over her hands and bruises on her back. It was awful" Maisie closed her eyes and paused. The room was silent "When she returned, she was told that her baby had died, and she was told to feed another baby.

If you could imagine the worst version of hell that you can think of, that Mother and Baby Home was a hundred times worse."

"Sweet Jesus, that's horrific Maisie" Saoirse whispered.

The lads shook their heads.

"I want to speak my opinion, but I will refrain, too much bad language, the bastards, how they got away with it" Pat said, his body completely tensed up.

"How could you ever get over that?" Saoirse asked the others, knowing that there was no answer to her question.

"I know love, but do you know what, we did," Maisie gave a gentle slap on Saoirse leg, rubbing it with assurance. "the only thing that got me through my days in there was you. You were the most beautiful baby," she tilted her head and smiled "You were placid and a real bundle of joy.

I remember when you were born, thinking I had never seen anything so beautiful in all my life. I couldn't take my eyes off you.

And you hardly cried" she sat up straight, her eyes widened "and always stopped as soon as I walked into the room. Most of the time I didn't even have to get as far as your crib, now I know you must have sensed me when I walked in. Magical, just beautiful."

Even amidst the pain and loss that had been part of the journey to bring about this union, it was a mother and daughter reunion that could not have gone better. Everyone involved felt like it was the most natural thing in the world. There were no awkward moments, no misunderstandings and certainly no disappointments.

Just a family reunited in a space filled with only love.

And even though the painful memories of the years apart were very present and aired, their effect disappeared for those couple of hours.

They chatted and laughed as if they had known each other all of their lives, naturally.

Chapter 39

The following years were to bring more growth. Saoirse broke her vow to herself that she had done her bit for pro-creation and welcomed twin boys, Daniel and Fionn a year after meeting Maisie.

Four years later when all her children were in school she had one more baby, Michaela.

Her reputation and clientele also continued to grow. Family life was increasingly busy and the commute to Newbridge began to take its toll on Saoirse and her young family.

Eventually, she took another leap of faith and bought a large log cabin studio which took pride of place in the back garden of her forever home and developed her practice from there.

Maisie, Tom and her new brothers and sisters became part of her life. When Maisie broke the news to her children that they had a long-lost sister they each welcomed her with open arms and love. Fiona was over the moon to have an older sister to look up to. William and Padraig joked to the girls that they were now blown out and Jennifer made it her business to stay in contact as much as possible. They each embraced their new sibling and her family into their lives and loved her from day one.

Her relationship with her birth family was one that was strange yet perfect. She loved them and felt their love, yet there was always the absence of childhood memories and the natural bonds that childhood creates.

Those bonds were with Lil, Joe and Ruth and Saoirse knew only too well the pull of guilt in her heart the more she loved her birth family. Guilt for the injustice she was doing to the human beings who, despite everything took her in and loved her. They gave her childhood and her memories of same. No-one could take that away from them, no matter what choices they made, or how angry she was towards them.

Despite Maisie's perfection, she could never take the place of Lil and Joe and her new siblings could never take the place of Ruth. Despite the rejection and the anger, there was part of her heart that still loved them and still yearned for a perfect family bond and the pain of its loss ran deep, every day.

Chapter 40

When she was thirty-six years old, Saoirse woke one bright summers morning to the cries of her baby girl, Michaela. She knew that cry, and it said:

'Mummy I'm hungry.'

The darkness had almost disappeared from the skies becoming filled with the light of the rising sun.

Right now, was Saoirse's favourite time of day. It was dawn. She was able to begin the day with just herself and Michaela.

Tom, Bridget and the twins slept soundly in their beds. The house was still and quiet. Saoirse treasured the moments, lost in the peacefulness of feeding her infant.

All the others had been Autumn babies. When they were infants, the morning skies were dark and most of the early morning feeds were done in bed.

Michaela was born early June. The morning skies were bright as the sun began its high rise in the sky.

When Saoirse and Tom discovered they were expecting baby number four, they decided to extend the cottage. Saoirse had dreamt of building a large open plan family room. It was a space where the whole family could be in at once. As the children grew, the intention was that memories could be made and shared in that open space, while life was going on all around them, creating the precious moments that would become treasured memories. It was a two-storey extension at the end of the house, the open plan room was downstairs and two new en-suite bedrooms upstairs, overlooking the spectacular rolling hills and Wicklow landscape.

The extension took six months to complete. It was all hands-on deck, each tradesman working faster than Saoirse's bump could grow.

Three weeks before her due date Saoirse and Tom sat in their newly extended forever home, feeling a combination of massive relief, exhaustion and pride at the same time.

The scaffolding came down, everything was put in place, and they were able to enjoy what felt like a brand-new dimension to their home.

That morning Saoirse sat in the quiet peacefulness of the new day.

Her infant lay in her arms with big blue eyes fixed in wonder on Saoirse's face. She looked at this beautiful bundle of peace and joy, a brand-new life, so innocent, pure and happy. She was the personification of perfection. In those moments with her baby girl, there was only love and peace.

Saoirse sat back on the couch and looked out the large window into her back garden. Tom had landscaped the garden to something to be proud of over the years, and Saoirse loved the space, the trees and the maturing shrubs that bordered the large green lawn, scattered with swings, slides and a tree house' for the kids.

She sighed a peaceful sigh of deep contentment for all she could see, because it was reflective of what she loved so deeply, her life, her husband and her beautiful, perfect children.

The moment of perfection was rudely interrupted by the thought of her parents, and all that was wrong, not unusual for Saoirse. The habit she had developed so well, for thoughts of her parents' behaviour long ago and how much it saddened her to overshadow the perfection that was.

She looked down once again at her beautiful bundle's big blue eyes. Complete love and dependency.

Her thoughts went to Maisie. The words she shared with her on the miraculous day,

You were the most beautiful thing I had ever seen in my whole life.

She thought of her mother's strength. The strength she had to leave her infant and the strength she had to go on and the strength she had to come back. She marvelled at the pure powerhouse that was her birth mother. She now understood what fuels that pure strength, the immeasurable power of a mother's love.

Her thoughts went back to Lil. She had no doubt that Lil thought of her. In the beginning she made several attempts to contact Saoirse, but the pain was too great for Saoirse to go back. Their choices let her down to a point where she failed to see a way forward with them. She looked at purity in her arms and thought of how much Lil failed her. She should have been stronger, she should have spoken up and spoken out. But she failed, its effect created a hole in Saoirse heart, where love could not flow.

She thought of Joe. She wondered if he held guilt in his heart. On some level she knew he did. He was always a man that did everything right, but when it came to her his fear crippled him and suffocated both his courage and his love for his daughter. Memories of long ago flashed through her mind, how he decided to send her away, and rejected her on her return, favouring Ruth and ignoring her very presence. She subconsciously shook her head trying to imagine Tom doing the same to one of their children, which was like trying to imagine the unimaginable.

Last year she bumped into an old school friend of Ruth's who told her that Ruth was also a mother now to twin girls. Saoirse knew the demands of twins and wondered how Ruth coped. When she asked how she was getting on Ruth's friend explained that she has lots of help from her au pair, her mother and her housekeeper was amazing.

She thought of how blessed she was to have the love of such a good man. Tom was a modest, tower of strength and love. His eyes had smiled with joy since that very first day she met him. Their love was testament to the reality of love at first sight. She smiled to herself and silently thanked God for the man she loved so deeply.

Her thoughts went to her forever friends Alvagh, Maria and Mary. Alvagh was now a wonderful mother, living in Cork in a beautiful home over-looking Inchydoney beach. Her music career had been fully realised and she was a full-on mum and wife, home-schooling her two beautiful boys. Saoirse had no idea how she was doing it and admired her friend for doing something so unheard of, but that was Alvagh, a breath of fresh air, that took life by the horns with passion.

She reflected on the memory of that magical day when she was a lost teenager and Alvagh brought her to Stillorgan. Mary's wise eyes saw straight into her soul. She wondered where she would be now, or how she would ever have coped without such good friends. Surely it was another blessing.

She smiled to herself as the image of Maria's smiley, bubbly little face filled her mind's eye. She recalled that first morning in the Convent when Maria slowed up to introduce herself and how unknown to them both, that in those moments a bond that was to last a lifetime was being born. That girl just took life on with one big happy smile every day and did what she had to do. She was married now to a head chef Arthur and together they ran a four-star restaurant in Dublin's City Centre. The team couple afforded more accolades and awards than one could recall, all hung proudly in the entrance to their fine restaurant.

She glanced around her home and her eyes met the sun-dial right outside her window. Once again, she whispered a prayer of gratitude to her ancestors for watching over her and loving her in a world where fear has power and makes the predominant sound.

Thank you for the courage, thank you for the guidance and thank you for being by my side.

She remembered that Robin was calling down this morning. The kids loved Robin and he loved them. Every time he came into their home the house was in chaos within minutes. He turned into an over grown six-year-old and chased the kids all-round the house and the garden. The screeches and screams from the kids could be heard for at least a half a mile down the road.

She laughed to herself, forever thankful for the life that was hers.

She looked down at perfection in her arms and sighed a deep sigh of gratitude. Then, once again, the haunting thoughts of Lil, Joe and Ruth filled that hole in her heart. She was sick of it. Her tolerance for the pain had reached its end. She was happy, her life was happy. Her family was perfect, as was her home and she had created all of this with the love of God, self and the love of the great people in her life. She no longer wanted to feel this pain.

Suddenly, it hit her. That thought came into her mind as if from nowhere.

I have to forgive them. To be truly happy, I have to forgive them.

Suddenly she was lifted into complete clarity. No amount of wishing things had been different was ever going to change what happened, no amount of regret, grief or going over and over the pain again and again, the happier her life became. What's more, they were never going to come back, or change. Even if they did come back she knew there would be far too much self-reflection involved in the healing process. They would never do it. It was easier to remain in the blinkered illusion than to atone.

In those moments Saoirse realised that the only way she could possibly heal the wounds inside that dictated every subconscious thought and chatter within her mind was to heal herself, and to truly heal herself, she knew she had to let go of her pain.

The realisation hit her that although her parents had caused the pain, it was her pain now and she was responsible for feeling it and letting it go or feeling it and staying in the suffering.

She knew she had to discover how, by now, she knew it was her salvation.

Saoirse understood forgiveness to be a process, that began with a choice. That choice that says something along the lines of:

'Do you know what? You hurt me deeply, and I am in a huge amount of pain. I am no longer willing to carry this pain around anymore. For as long as I harbour anger, resentment, bitterness or any other negative emotion towards you, I will be in this pain. But I understand it is my pain, my responsibility. I am going to let it go. I know it's going to be hard work and take a lot of discipline and commitment on my part. But to be free, I am going to do the work, and one day, then, I can let it go.'

What Saoirse wanted was to find a way to love and accept herself completely and unconditionally. She wanted to see what everyone else could see. A pure loving soul that had a part to play in this world and that she mattered, wholly, deeply and completely.

And so began the inner journey that would transform her and align her with the truth of who she was.

The following morning, she woke feeling refreshed for the first time in a very long time. She felt she had a sense of clarity that morning and there was a strong sense that she had work to do. Even though she had no idea what that work was.

She stood by the coffee machine watching the dark brown coffee fill the cup. She had two clients this morning. She felt a sense of excitement for the day ahead. But she also found herself wishing her morning was free, with no clients. She felt like she had something else to do and she knew it wasn't in her log cabin with clients.

She checked her phone, and there were two text messages. Each message was an apology from her clients that they needed to cancel their appointments this morning. She read each text and felt the relief. Those texts meant she had the whole day off and she could get to work.

She went up to her bedroom, closed the door and threw herself on the bed.

'Right God, I have no idea how I am going to do this, so I am going to need your help. I want to get there. Give me understanding. Give me clarity. Help me to see the truth, for what it is. And help me to forgive and let go.

Now here's what I suggest. How about I meditate for about ten minutes every day because I know I can grab ten minutes and we work together. I hope that suits you God, if not I'm sure you'll let me know.

Here goes, and by the way, Thank you, God.'

Saoirse closed her eyes and took a deep breath. She connected with her Spirit Guides and the Arch Angels of healing, strength, wisdom and communication. Most people knew them as Arch Angels Raphael, Michael, Uriel and Gabriel. She called in her Higher Self and of course the greatest power of all: God.

During her meditation, she visualised, where her pain was in her body and in her mind. She spoke to the pain with love and gratitude. In the beginning, the pain was depicted as a big black blob of dark energy, just hanging there, influencing her every thought. She asked it what it was teaching her. The answer was always the same.

'I am your teacher. I am here to show you who you are not. That is why you incarnated. Without me, you can never know yourself as Pure Light while you walk the earth plane.

But do not become me, for you are not me. You are Truth, and You are Love. It is only in your struggle to overcome me; can you realise your strength and your Truth. For I am the illusion, I am reflective of the untrue belief that you are imperfect. Therefore, in Truth, I do not exist.

Work with me Saoirse, for it is only when you see yourself through the eyes of your Truth that you will realise your strength and begin to let me go, for then I will no longer exist in the depths of your subconscious mind, and I can become Love too.'

She accepted everything her pain told her and allowed it to speak. As she listened, her perspective began to change. She experienced a paradigm shift.

Up until now, she had understood her pain to be an obstacle. A debilitating source of destruction that caused chaos in her mind, blinding her to the belief that she was, in fact, perfect and so was everyone else.

Her paradigm shift helped her to understand that Lil, Joe and Ruth were her teachers. They were the three people on this planet whose beliefs tormented her mind and became her own inner voice.

The underlying forever murmur that told her that she was not good enough, worthy enough, clever enough. The crippling suggestion within her psyche that reminded her that she was 'a nothing' had become the shadow before her shining heart and diffused her awareness of her perfection. It was the small deafening voice that thundered through her mind always, telling her that she was not good enough. The beliefs originally came from her family, but now it was her inner voice and the cause of her torture and torment. She was sick of her pain. She had reached a point of intolerance and resignation that regardless of what others thought, did or said: she had to shift how she saw herself within her own mind.

She understood that she was the only person alive who could dissolve the subconscious non-sense that demanded and dictated power over her every thought. In those moments came understanding that the only way to do so was through the deep self-love that silently shone in its majestic radiance within her heart.

'God let's go, take me right into the centre of that Light.'

Immediately she was whole, calm, in the depths of peace and strength. Centred in the true light of who she really is, she recognised her wise, beautiful soul for the very first time. She felt her majesty, her beauty and the radiant Light that she forever was. She was perfection. She felt her kindness, her warmth and her beautiful nature. She felt her Power. For those moments, as she completely embodied herself in her true Light, her pain dissolved, and her perfection was at the fore.

She understood that we come to this planet to create joy. We are the Creators. We co-create with the Universe, with God, with Love.

The understanding began to download in her mind that the Universe was co-creating through her. God was co-creating through her.

Love was co-creating through her, and through everyone else, when we see ourselves through the eyes of the Love that we Are.

She got it! Saoirse's mind was rapidly re-shuffling and re-framing everything that she thought she knew and saw it in a new light. Suddenly, she had effortless clarity and it answered all questions that before she did not understand.

She understood what the scriptures meant when they said:

'In the beginning, there was only Light.'

Light being Love, there is only Love. Before that there was nothing.

The shift in awareness aligned her with Love and the Universal Truth. She understood who she really was and who everyone else is.

She immediately brought her awareness back to her fears and her pain, and she began to see her pain in a completely different light. Just as her pain had told her:

'Do not become me, for you are not me.'

She saw the image of Lil and Joe in her mind, and she saw that they had become trapped in the illusion and the forgetfulness of the Truth, just like she had been. They were in darkness. Immediately the blast of clarity filled her mind. She got what great people meant when they said:

'Darkness is not something in itself. Darkness is merely the absence of light.'

Pain is the absence of Love. When we forget who we truly are and experience pain, we believe the pain to be a reflection of who we are, but that is untrue. It is merely an illusion that does not exist, except in our minds. Saoirse completely understood the difference between statements such as:

"I am angry," and, "I feel anger."

The former statement is a dismissal of who she really is, limiting her in pain. The latter speaks from an awareness of who she really is and sees the emotion (anger) as something that her true self had become aware of, but she was not defined by it. Then she is able to separate from the anger and be centred in her Strength.

"The purpose of pain is not to break us. The purpose of pain is to teach us how strong we are."

She then realised that she needed to do as her pain said. See it as her teacher. Embrace it, be with it and work with it. Allow it to teach her who she was.

Through the process of recognising that she was not her pain, knowing that she was in fact pure love and perfection, she naturally centred in the strength to transcend her pain.

The very process of transcending through her pain in this way caused her to real-is-e how strong she actually was. This is an experience that was impossible without the pain in the first place.

In doing so, the true self could emerge, and she gave life to joy. By the very nature of the process, her pain dissolved, and she grew in happiness, peace and joy.

All a Spirit Being wants to do when they come to this planet is create and experience joy. But on a humanistic level, Saoirse could never know joy in its immensity and magnitude if she did not know pain.

She spoke to herself in her mind and told herself that she had two choices going forward on her journey called life:

To fear the illusion of darkness and allow it to become who I think I am

To embrace it from a place of self-love, with the remembrance of Who I Am, and seek to transcend it.

'Dear God, show me why we forget who we truly are. Why do we forget our power?' She lay on the bed with her eyes closed and continued to work with her Creator.

Immediately a memory flashed up in her mind from when she was a child. It was a clear image of Joe, and it played out like a movie in her mind's eye.

Joe had returned home from work one day when Saoirse was about six years old. He was standing in front of the open fire in the living room. His expression was strained and stressed. He looked sad, not-present and under pressure.

At such an innocent age she looked up at her Daddy. She could see the bright clouded light surrounding Joe's physical body, and it was extending into the room. The light met with Saoirse's light, Lil's light and Ruth's too. Her young mind began to wonder why he was so stressed. She knew the ever-present light to be the magnificent power and infinite intelligence that was her real Daddy, her real family. The answer flowed into her mind effortlessly:

'He forgets who we are; he forgets who he is. He thinks he is just his body and small mind. Therefore, he sees himself and his potential as limited. That is why he feels unable and stressed'.

Joe had fallen into the illusion. He believed himself to be a limited human being trapped and restricted to a body. He believed his body to be the limitation of himself. He thought he was separated from his power.

He had forgotten that we are all within the great infinite magnificent Oneness. We are all aspects of the Oneness. We are all aspects the Creator. We are all part of to the Creator. The Creator is Love. The mass of billions of cells that make up our body is also of that same Love. Our physical body is simply an instrument to serve the purpose in which to navigate through the three-dimensional world that we inhabit. But most have come to believe our body to be all that we are. Most have forgotten that we are of the Divine Source of Intelligence: that is the Universe. We are One Consciousness. There is no separation.

Therefore, each one of us has access to the infinite dimensions of that consciousness.

Saoirse always remembered this, albeit subconsciously and that was how she was able to access the dimensions beyond the physical realm. She accessed the realms of the hereafter, the realms of angels and even the realms of the past and the present that was not visible to our physical eyes.

When the image of Joe flashed in her mind, she understood the distinct difference to what most people believe and what she believed.

The proverbial penny dropped, and everything consciously fell into place within her mind.

From the time we are little, manmade religious beliefs tell us that there is a god who will send us to hell if we do not fear him and abide by him. Even as a child, Saoirse always knew that this was simply nonsense. Why would an all loving God send us to a horrific place just because he could not control us? That is not love.

That morning Saoirse's pain showed her the true meaning of hell.

God is Love. Love is omnipresent. Therefore, it can have no opposite. Effectively, hell only exists in one place: within in our own minds.

Man-made religion teaches us that there is punishment when we do not do as they say, and they pose this to be the word of god. When the true reality is, that hell (fear) can only exist when we are looking away from Love and forgetting who we are. The 'punishment' they speak of, is the hell we experience within our own minds.

That morning, lying on her bed, in deep meditation Saoirse understood that the power and potential for self-realisation were within us all. It was the essence of who we are. It was our nature. Most people just did not believe this to be the reality. The reason why? It was not the predominant belief system that nurtured and fostered throughout society.

Instead, most people sought outside of themselves to define who they were, for a sense of identity. They looked to family, friends, society, religion, even the media, for an unnecessary validation and definition of themselves.

Lying on the bed, she opened her eyes and began to speak out loud, answering the insight to flood in.

"The trouble is that we live in a world where these platforms are distorted and believe in an illusion based on fear. The disabling fabrications of fear take over our minds and our self-belief. Many emotions such as doubt, pain, sadness, guilt, judgement, resentment and hate, take residence in our minds and poison our awareness.

"We forget who we are and effectively step out of our Power. When we are out of our Power these emotions cause us to live in hell, within our minds. We believe them to be real. Therefore they are, and they become the voice that navigates our thoughts into an illusion of pain.

"OK, God. I get what you are showing me and THANK YOU! How much sense is this making?!

"But I have another question." She closed her eyes and frowned.

"How can one possibly continue to believe the still strong voice within, that knows we are perfection when we live in a world that is ruled and governed by fear, every day?"

Immediately she found herself surrounded by the great spirit beings that had always accompanied her as a child. They were as tall and majestic as she remembered them to be, and equally as unconditionally loving, patient and understanding.

Thoughts of clarity flowed from her deep subconscious awareness and became a conscious knowing:

As long as we seek our Power outside of ourselves, we are left without. We need to look within our hearts and our minds from a place of Love, to love. That is where the Power is.

Then we will connect with our Power, centre ourselves into it and extend ourselves out into the world through connecting with people, family, friends and society. From there, our lives begin to change, and the Universe will take care of the rest.

We are channels of peace, hope and love. God can only do for us what he can do through us. Therefore, when we seek outside of ourselves to find our power, we effectively disengage from the God-given Power and potential within us all.

On that beautiful brand-new morning in June, Saoirse knew that the only way her life would begin to change, was when she began to do four things consciously, every single day:

Perceive her pain as an opportunity for growth.

Seek within her own heart to align with her Power

Integrate herself with the awareness that she is the personification of Pure Love, and so is everyone else, even though they have forgotten.

Do the above steps from a place of pure unconditional love, through the channels of an open heart and a wise mind.

Saoirse disciplined herself to commit to at least ten minutes each day connecting with her Higher Mind. She wrote letters of forgiveness to her family. The letters were for her eyes only. She continued to remind herself that her family and in fact anyone who sought to hurt her, were coming from their own place of pain, lost in the illusion of this three-dimensional society.

Even though it took a long time to make the transition, she gradually began to see Lil and Joe as people as well as her parents. In doing so, she recognised that they were also in pain. When she was a child and a teenager they directed their pain towards her. She made a habit of embracing the hurtful behaviour as an opportunity to heal the open wounds in her psyche.

Chapter 41

Over the years she grew in strength. Some days were good, and some were spent thrown into the depths of hallows that cried out for her parents love. Each time she committed and disciplined herself to the process of healing and forgiveness.

The constant upward spiral of perception reminded her that she is a spirit being having a human experience. So sometimes, she allowed herself to be human and experience the pain, understanding she needed her pain to come to self-realisation. Each time she became better at re-aligning with the Great Power that comes with a Higher Perspective. It wasn't always easy, but she committed to her mission none the less.

Eventually, there came a time, when she no longer needed her history to change to feel validated.

Instead a very real and deep sense of true love and self-acceptance emerged.

She grew to deeply love who she was and what she had to bring to this world.

She recognised her uniqueness and her beautiful essence, and she knew that it was her gift to this earth plane.

There was no one else on the planet that could be Saoirse Harris. Eventually, the real Saoirse Harris stood up and took ownership of who she was. She began to celebrate herself.

By now, Saoirse was in her late thirties, and her own children were growing. Their ages and stages reminded her of who she was when she was their age. Equally, their innocence and perfection reminded her of her own, they gave her love and showed her who she was.

There was one last thing she needed to do.

There was another little girl who needed her.

That beautiful little girl needed to hear how perfect she was. She needed to hear it from a voice that Saoirse knew she would trust completely.

And one day, when Saoirse was in her fortieth year, she paid a visit to that little girl.

"Saoirse, I'm just going to town to get paint." Tom popped his head around the kitchen door. He still looked as handsome as ever, even with his paint stained T-shirt and old blue jeans. His thick dark hair had tiny lights of silver peeking through. His huge presence and warm smile continued to lift the air wherever he went.

"Ah you are joking Tom, five litres of paint have gone into that room already?" Saoirse paused from the mission of completing the endless piles of ironing stacked up in the laundry basket by the kitchen window.

"And the rest. I'll stop off in Tesco's on the way home and get pizzas for the dinner ok?"

"Ah sure go on, it's Saturday after all, thanks Tom, saves me going out today." A smile of love and gratitude filled her face.

"I'm coming," Bridget emerged from her bedroom

"We're coming too," The twins raced each other through the living room door, abandoning their DS'

"Where are we going? I'm coming too." Michaela took her head out of her dolls house, leaving an imaginary world of unicorns and Barbie dolls to their own devices.

Saoirse's family left the house. She went up to her bedroom and threw herself into her sacred meditation space: her bed. She closed her eyes, thought about where she needed to go and who she was about to visit. Her heart filled with love and her face filled with an involuntary smile.

'God this is a really special journey today. I have never done this before, so take me there safely ok. Thank you, God, for everything.'

She closed her eyes, relaxed her body and allowed her mind to go blank, surrendering to where she needed to go. Within moments, she was there.

I am a mother standing over your crib.

Beautiful baby girl, you are just one month old, and you already radiate the embodiment of perfection that you are.

I cannot stay long but may the words I am about to share with you whisper in your heart forever and always.

Always know that you are stronger than your pain,

Always know that you are stronger than any depths of sadness and tears you may cry

Some will understand you and many will not. Either way, you have a courageous heart. You are a force of Love

You are perfection; therefore, you are always enough.

Remember my words, my beautiful child. May they take resonance in your heart and always remind you of the Strength that is you.

Before I go, there is one more thing I want you to hold within the precious wisdom of your heart. When you feel you are trapped and lost in your darkest moments, when the confusion and sadness weigh deep in your heart: know that the pain you experience will never leave you blind to your truth.

The love that is You will fill all of your being. It will empower you in your darkest moments and guide you back to who you are. And so it is. I have to go now, but we will meet again. Until then my wish for you is that you may always hear that still strong still voice down deep in your heart, as it whispers the reminder of the strength and love that is you.

My beautiful child, listen to the force within that reminds you, that you are strong, you are loved, and you are always enough.

Saoirse smiled at the baby in the crib. For just a few moments she watched her sleeping. She smiled as she watched her tiny chest rising and falling with every breath that she took.

She found herself wishing the deepest wisdom and peace to her little body, so perfect and strong.

She wished her depths of unconditional love and prepared to leave. She wished she could stay right there and allow the hours to pass, just staring at the perfect infant before her, but she knew she had more to do.

Her physical body lay on the bed at home in the house that she loved so much. She set her intention to go even deeper into her meditative state. She let herself go, releasing all logic and rational. She took another deep breath embracing the Universal Power that she knew she was part of.

One more time she travelled through her mind, beyond the barriers of time and space. Within a few moments, she arrived at her destination.

Her heart broke open with compassion for the little girl lying curled up in the bed. She glanced around the cold room in the institutional building. The high ceilings gave no comfort. The grey sheets on the beds encouraged the shallow depth within the soul of the authority that ruled this awful place.

The little girl in the bed was completely lost in the depths of sadness, confusion and hopelessness. Saoirse's heart broke for her as she watched her cry so hard, that she made no sound. Her hands were holding her face and tensed in pain.

"Saoirse, beautiful girl, don't cry."

She assured the broken child and gently took her hand.

The child looked up through her tears to see Saoirse at her bedside.

"I'm so sad, there is no hope, Why? Why do they hate me? What did I do?" The confused little girl asked, her eyes raw with tears. Her face showed so much pain. Saoirse could feel the heaviness of the child's heartache.

Beautiful child, you didn't do anything wrong.

No matter what they say. or what they do, this is no reflection on you. That's no easy to understand right now, but it is the truth.

They are trapped in the hypnosis of illusion. Their words are not true, and they are not reflective of who you are. However, they are going to keep on saying these words. They are also going to keep on believing these words too.

But Saoirse, that's not what's important.

What is important is that you know who you are. You are a beautiful child with a huge heart. You are caring, loving and clever and you have the most magnificent imagination, own your imagination, own your gifts.

Your body is young, but your soul is old. Therefore, you are wise.

Beautiful child, be in that wisdom now. Know who you are and be true to you.

Know that they are caught in a belief system that traps and enslaves. Many fall into the trap. But my beautiful shining angel of strength, you know that it was never your destiny to do so.

Not now, not ever.

You came here, to this place called life, to help set them free.

You know that deep down in your soul. And that dear child is exactly what you will do.

But for now, you must stay here in this awful place. It's part of your journey.

Saoirse, know that I am with you, every step of the way. You may not always see me but know that I am always there.

You are made of strong stuff dear child. You are courageous and beautiful and strong. You have a heart so pure that no wrong can destroy it. Be strong and know that I am here, always.

The little girl smiled at Saoirse and her heart filled with a sense of belonging. In her smile, Saoirse could see that she had heard her message of deep love and self-recognition.

Little Saoirse's eyes told that she inherently trusted her every word. She knew that Saoirse truly recognised her pain and met that pain with understanding.

In those moments, Saoirse knew that her younger self had felt the message she had come to share, so as she could go on.

She felt a deep quiet confidence that young Saoirse would hear the constant whisper in her heart, reminding her who she was, that she was not alone, and she was loved unconditionally.

Chapter 42

"PIZZA'S UP! Hi Mam, I'm starving."

"Mammy, we got pepperoni."

"Mam, did you set the table?"

"I'm sitting beside Mammy!"

"Hi, we're home."

The hall door opened, and Saoirse's family entered her home one by one. She lay on the bed for just a few moments with her eyes open, bringing her presence fully back into the room.

Her thoughts raced towards the little girl she just visited. She checked in with her consciousness to see how she was doing. Immediately she saw an image of that little girl smiling an expression of gratitude.

The knowing of who she was reflected in her eyes. Deep down the little girl knew where she came from. Her wisdom was something that she was happy to treasure within her own heart, for now, until she could express and explore it further.

But more importantly, she saw that little girl's sense of self-love and knowing that she was who she thought she is.

Right now, she no longer held confusion or guilt for being different. She understood that others might not understand, but for now, that was ok.

"I love you. Now walk on.

Even if it's only as far as the kitchen to get pizza, for now."

At some future point in her journey called life, she would need the love she just had experienced, she would need to give that love and belonging to eight hundred. To millions more with the same story.

March 3rd, 2017

Saoirse was at home. Bridget had just come home from college with her brothers. Saoirse and Tom enjoyed the convenience that came with each of the kids choosing courses in UCD, that way most days allowed them to commute together. Michaela had just completed her mocks and did exceptionally well, a lot better than she thought so would. She was a high achiever and worked hard. Despite the constant attempts from Saoirse and Tom to let up on herself.

The house was in its usual chaotic state of a Friday evening. Everyone was starving, the oven was on and the battle to get a word in edgeways was in full flow.

Saoirse was in the middle of lighting the fire, and the sun was well on her descend for the evening.

"Mum, text message," Bridget handed her mother the phone.

Saoirse opened the text message. It was from Mary.

"Saoirse, check Facebook, sent you a link."

Saoirse opened her Facebook account, and there were several tags and notifications which all began with the same words.

Almost 800 infant bodies discovered in a septic tank in Tuam Mother and Baby home.

She read through the many articles with devastation and disbelief. The horror of the words on the screen jumped out at her, each one pulling her into a swamp of pain for the little children whose lives had been taken.

One million thoughts filled her mind, and she felt thrown through every emotion imaginable. The anger, grief, disbelief, horror, and a guilty sense that it did not happen to her were among the pillars upon the roller coaster she felt herself on.

Tears of sadness for the little lives stolen streamed from her eyes. Her heart was breaking.

Over the coming weeks, Saoirse went deep into an abyss of sadness, disbelief and grief for the cruelty done on such innocent, dependent lives. She searched her mind for what she could do. Something inside told her to digest it for now.

She read articles detailing that the abuse stretched over sixty years. It was in full flow when she was born and didn't end until two decades later, which was around the time she left for her new life. The horror that it could have just as easily been her and the chances that it happened to her crib mates thundered a crippling agony through her mind. There was no doubt that it happened to them too. She recalled Maisie's words:

Her name was Alice. The sister dragged her away. When she came back the following evening she was told her baby had died.

She had no doubt there was more crib mates who had fallen victim to such horrific, unimaginable fate. How many more was a question that may never be answered.

One morning in late March 2017 Saoirse wandered around the house in a daze.

Memories continued to visit her mind of times as a child when she was told to shut up, when she was told she was worthless, and a nobody.

She recalled the many messages from the past, telling her voice did not matter. The times when she was taught to believe that she was nobody with nothing of value to offer.

These little bundles of innocent perfection had been silenced forever. Their voice, their lives taken away, destroyed and hidden.

All the experiences and opportunities they came to create, killed.

The love they had to give, murdered.

The joy and memories they came to share, suffocated.

The friendship, relationships and families they were to bond, thrown away.

Forever disposed of into a pit of silent devastation.

But she was here. She was alive. She had a voice.

Her heart burst wide open with compassion for these little ones, born of magnificence.

She sat once again in her meditation space. She asked God to help her to do her part. She knew she could not change the past but for the sake of these little ones she wanted to give them a voice.

'Saoirse, write the story.'

The words of guidance from God confused her. She had no idea what he meant. What story?

"God, thank you for the guidance, but I have no idea what you mean. Could you clarify?"

"Saoirse, write the story"

Centered in trust, she surrendered. She stood up from her meditation space, with God's words still in her mind.

She walked over to her computer. She sat down and placed her fingers on the keyboard.

She remembered standing in Ms Cross' kitchen, filled with the innocence of six years old and over hearing Ms Cross' message to Ruth

I'm telling you Ruth, have nothing to do with her. She is adopted and adopted people are 'nobodies'. She is a nobody.

She saw her English teacher, Ms Murphy in fourth class. She remembered her encouraging words.

You have a real gift for writing....one that cannot be taught.... I have not come across one as gifted as you

Then she saw Sr Agnes, sitting at her parents' kitchen table. The day hell came to take her away.

Suddenly, she was thrown back to her teenage bedroom watching Joe shout his anger and frustration 'shut up, shut up' over and over and the powerful voice that told her, 'Where there's a will, there's a way'

She had left all writing behind a long time ago, but right now her heart was breaking for these little ones, stolen of life and thrown away. But she was here, she had survived, and she had a voice.

Taking a deep breath, she looked up to heaven and said:

"God, for these little ones, help me to do this."

She looked at the blank screen before her eyes, and she began to write the story.

About the Author

Hilary Connor is a Spiritual Development Coach. She lives in Wexford, Ireland with her husband Brian and three daughters.

Hilary is a natural psychic medium, Consulting Hypnotherapist and Spiritual Practitioner, with qualifications in training and counselling. Hilary runs her Spiritual Practice from her home in Wexford where she helps clients from all over the world overcome self-limiting thoughts systems and align with their true God given power, a power that Hilary believes is universally available to us all. Her greatest passion is to help herself and everyone else discover the natural power within us all and attune our minds to give birth to the very best versions of ourselves that we can, thus enabling us to give forth to the progressive evolution of self and this planet that we share.

Her favourite thing to do is spend family time with her husband Brian and three daughters, especially enjoying meals out together at weekends and walking it all off during the week along with their two dogs, Tara and Annabelle.

Her website is www.hilaryconnor.com

Email: info@hilaryconnor.com

Twitter: @HilaryBauthor